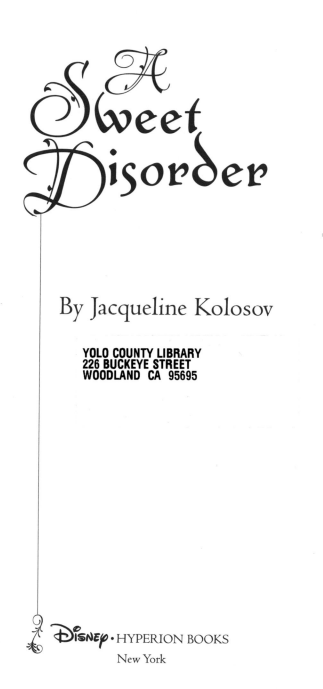

A Sweet Disorder

By Jacqueline Kolosov

DISNEP · HYPERION BOOKS
New York

For Sophie

Text copyright © 2009 by Jacqueline Kolosov

All rights reserved.

Published by Disney • Hyperion Books, an imprint of Disney Book Group.

No part of this book may be reproduced or transmitted in any form
or by any means, electronic or mechanical, including photocopying, recording, or by any
information storage and retrieval system, without written permission from the publisher.

For information address Disney • Hyperion Books, 114 Fifth Avenue,
New York, New York 10011-5690.

Printed in the United States of America

First Edition

10 9 8 7 6 5 4 3 2 1

Library of Congress Cataloging-in-Publication Data on file.

ISBN 978-1-4231-1245-7

Reinforced binding

Visit www.hyperionteens.com

A sweet disorder in the dress
Kindles in clothes a wantonness.
A lawn about the shoulders thrown
Into a fine distractiòn;
An erring lace, which here and there
Enthralls the crimson stomacher;
A cuff neglectful, and thereby
Ribbons to flow confusedly;
A winning wave, deserving note,
In the tempestuous petticoat;
A careless shoe string, in whose tie
I see a wild civility;
Do more bewitch me than when art
Is too precise in every part.

"Delight in Disorder"
—ROBERT HERRICK

PROLOGUE

December 27, 1579

"LORD GREY WAS ON THE SHIP THAT SHOULD have carried Father back to us," Mother said, once we were gathered together in the sitting room with its bay window overlooking the wintering garden, the air tinged with the smoky fragrance of the candles.

"The ship was delayed three days at the Irish port," Lord Grey said, his salt-and-pepper beard concealing his expression. "This is the reason why I am so late in bringing the news—"

A grasping dread rooted itself along my spine as I met the gaze of Father's portrait, the blue of his eyes so intense it felt as if some part of him still presided over the room.

"Father and Uncle Thomas, and two of their manservants, fell ill," Mother continued, the flames from the hearth transforming her auburn hair into a fiery halo.

"Mother—" My sister, Laura, stood, her voice breaking, her sleeping son stirring in her arms.

All of us knew that illness was one of Ireland's

great perils. The country was even wetter than England, its damp seeping through clothes and settling beneath the skin. Yet Father had always dressed in heat-saving layers. Yes, he jested that he liked to wear as many of my mother's and my own joyfully embroidered clothes as possible—in order to feel close to us. But such precautions served the equally if not more essential purpose of keeping him warm and dry.

"Father and Uncle Thomas died just days before the ship's crossing," Mother told us now.

The logs crackled in the hearth, and the dread sank deeper into me. It was as if I'd fallen down a well, nothingness reaching up to swallow me whole.

How was it possible that only last night I'd sat beside the window, the doublet I had been embroidering for my father resting on my lap, the firelight animating the birds and animals I had brought to life with my needle—creatures culled from my father's tales of distant places: strange humpbacked horses and bright pink birds, their looping necks like question marks.

"Where are their bodies now?" my brother-in-law, Christopher, asked, his high freckled forehead furrowed with worry, his lips a tight line.

"It would have been impossible to transport the bodies to England in enough time for a decent burial," Lord Grey said quietly.

"You're telling us that our father is buried there—in Ireland?" Laura asked, the tears falling quickly now.

Lord Grey shifted in his heavy, mud-stained boots. "I assure you they were given a proper English funeral."

"Thank you," Mother said, sinking into her chair.

Lord Grey bowed to Mother, then left the room.

"Tea, m'lady?" Kate said, standing in the doorway and looking at our solemn faces.

"Yes, please, Kate, come in." Mother's voice was hollowed out, empty.

Once Kate had carried in a tray, my mother focused too intently on serving tea and the manchet bread we had baked especially for Christmas. I noticed how the cold December sunlight betrayed the violet shadows beneath her green eyes, the creases marring her brow. I thought I'd heard her crying the night before. How long had she suspected this?

Reminded of the love my parents felt for each other, holding hands as they walked in the garden and often talking quietly beside the fire deep into the night, I longed to comfort her, this strong woman who had once devoted herself to court dances and galloping rides; this woman who now spoke firmly but kindly to the tenant farmers on our lands and met with the lawyers to handle the estate's accounts; this woman who lingered beside my bed whenever I had a fever, and first taught me to keep my saddle on her spirited white mare, Idyll. But if I tried, would she be able to keep her voice from breaking? Would she be able to hold back the tears?

"You know Father borrowed some twenty thousand pounds from the crown over the last ten years," she said, once Kate had gone.

"Is the amount as great as that?" Robert asked, the catch in his voice a reminder of Father's promise to pass the title and property on to his only son unencumbered by the debt he believed he could at last clear on this past journey.

"I'm afraid it is," Mother said.

"Our father lost his life in the queen's service," I said, looking gently at my brother, understanding only now how burdened he'd become at eighteen. "Her Majesty must make allowance for that."

"Many men lose their lives in the queen's service," Mother said, then stood and stepped over to the window. Beyond lay the ornamental garden, its fountain now filled with ice, the desiccated hollyhocks holding tight to their fistfuls of seeds, only the skeletons of the roses visible this late in the year.

"Unfortunately, these debts will influence many of our family's plans," she said, her voice snagging on "family."

"In what way?" Laura asked.

"Your engagement was formally announced when you

were sixteen," Mother said, turning away from the window. "As we all know, throughout this last year, Father wrote to me about the husband he hoped for Miranda."

"The late Sir Raleigh's son, yes?" Laura asked, brushing away a lock of hair as golden as our father's.

"It was Father's greatest hope to see Miranda and Henry Raleigh wed," Mother said gently.

I tried to meet her eye. Was she, too, asking if events might have been different had Henry Raleigh stayed with Father until the end, instead of returning some two months earlier because, Father wrote, the queen had called him back?

"Like our own, Henry Raleigh's is an ancient house," she said, her fingertips tracing the pattern of the lace curtains she had sewn from the fine linen Father had purchased on an early journey to Holland.

Trusting she would tell me that the man Father had intended as my husband had found a way to help us, I looked up at her hopefully.

"And like our house," Mother continued, "that house is a poor one—why such a match would no longer be advantageous."

"Mother?" I pleaded, finding my voice at last.

"Father always swore Henry Raleigh was a man of his word," Robert said.

"Robert is right, Mother. You're not telling us he has

ceased all discussion of the engagement?" Laura said, worry marring the gentleness of her voice.

"It is his uncle, Burton Raleigh, who has ceased the discussion." Mother turned toward me, and as her eyes met my own, I wondered again how long she had been keeping this news. Until now, I had always believed she and I had no secrets. How could we, when all our days were spent together? How, when my auburn hair, though not as lustrous, and my wide green eyes, though not as luminous, were still patterned after her own?

"But why?" Robert asked.

Mother did not answer, just held herself very tall so that she became again the proud woman who had served as lady-in-waiting to the queen during Elizabeth's first year on the throne. Everyone said that was the year Mother became known for her will as well as for her beauty.

"Unfortunately," Mother said at last, "the very qualities your father admired in Henry Raleigh now compel him to heed his uncle's request."

Even I, who had heard countless stories of Henry Raleigh's noblesse, understood that Burton Raleigh had convinced his nephew to end the engagement because of my father's debts, which inevitably meant that despite the beauty that was my mother's legacy, and the good name that was my father's, the very small dowry I would bring to the marriage was no longer enough, especially for an impoverished noble like Henry Raleigh with no lands of his own.

"And then your father made a provision in his will of which I remained not uninformed," she continued, her body still and statuelike, "but at the very least, a provision I am powerless to resist."

"What sort of provision?" I heard myself ask, stupidly parroting her words.

"Although I will stay on at Plowden Hall with Robert's permission, you, Miranda, are to become the ward of your father's cousin, John Hardwood, and his wife."

"Impossible," Laura protested, a fierceness I'd never heard before coming into her voice. "They live at least a week's journey from here."

"Yes," Mother said, her own voice close to breaking. "Had your Uncle Thomas lived," she added, "he would have become Miranda's guardian."

"The earl and his wife are strangers to me," I said, my voice tight and small in my throat.

"Even so, they are family." My mother's hand sought the pearl necklace she had inherited from my grand-mother, a cherished heirloom that would one day belong to my older sister, Laura. Although she was only six years my elder, how very different our histories were becoming.

"What of Uncle Edward?" Laura persisted.

"My younger brother is even more of a nomad than

your father, and he lacks any ties to the queen," Mother said, sounding far older than her forty-two years. "He is therefore a most unfit person to bring Miranda to court."

"But he always cared for her, for all of us—" Laura said.

My eyes pleaded with my mother, but her features were quickly taking on the faraway look I had last seen when my grandmother died.

"Had Miranda's engagement with Henry gone forward, her removal would never have become necessary."

"But, Mother . . ." I recalled all those times she had managed to make the household accounts balance despite the loss of a herd of sheep or the failure of a crop during the drought years.

"I'm sorry, darling," she said, the melancholy in her voice a testament to a woman's powerlessness, especially a woman who was now a widow, left not with adequate dower, but with her husband's legacy of debt.

"If the engagement with Raleigh cannot go forward," Robert said, "I will protect Miranda."

Mother sighed deeply, her hands continuing to worry her pearls. "Must I remind you that you are now the eighteen-year-old earl of an encumbered property? You have not yet finished your studies, and after that you will be expected to pay your knight service to the queen. Furthermore, you will be expected to marry and produce an heir. Otherwise, the title of earl and the property will pass to your father's nephew, George."

"Mother—" Robert said again.

"Quite simply, you have become a man of responsibility, a man who will have a great deal to prove. Protecting your sister"—her words came out clean and cold, cut from some part of her none of us had seen before—"despite the nobility of your intentions, is an act you cannot, at present, fulfill."

PART ONE
Purgatory

CHAPTER ONE
January 1580

ALL THROUGH A JOURNEY LENGTHENED BY rain and by roads made slippery with mud, I looked out at the trees stripped of their leaves, at the stark black birds of winter framed against an opaque white sky. As the horses' hooves kept time with my heart, I clung to the image of my mother standing in the doorway of Plowden Hall, her long-fingered hand—graceful as a departing bird—raised in farewell.

This year, once the flowering plants bore fruit, Mother and I would not make tarts from the fragrant strawberries we had always gathered by the basketful in the early morning sun. Nor would we place the fairest cherries in the cool dark of a hay-lined barrel, preserving sweetness for another year. As for how much time would pass before we would once more sit

3

down to refurbish our gowns with new guards of grosgrain taffeta or velvet, or dust a pattern with charcoal before embroidering a jacket or shawl, I could not say. And if I needed to recover her stories of her growing up and early womanhood, I would have to rely on memory, that fickle organ capable of bringing as much sadness as pleasure.

The coachman had told me more than once that Turbury was a ten days' journey along the old Roman road under the best of conditions, a circumstance that made my hopes of seeing my mother anytime soon extremely slim. Even so, I clung to her promise to come once she had settled the affairs on my father's estate, affairs that could take several months, if not the entire year.

On the eighth day of the journey, the carriage came at last into Yorkshire. Looking out, I sought some spark of beauty or mystery in the country in which I now found myself. But it was early January, a time when the earth is at her solemnest, when such emptiness could only remind me further of all that I had lost.

I reached Turbury three days later.

Unlike the umber stone of my ancestral home, which looked out on the rolling meadowlands, the earl and countess's gray manor house dated back to those more primitive times when families made war on each other.

More than two centuries later, the nearest village remained a half day's ride away. Even if it had been closer, there would have been little reason for us to visit it, as Turbury possessed its own chapel, and its cellars stored sufficient vegetables and grains to last through the winter, a circumstance that rendered even the noisy pleasure of market-going unnecessary. Nor would we need to go elsewhere for the flesh of beast and fowl when the earl and countess were said to be such accurate shots.

As if the moat that surrounded the house were not proof enough of Turbury's fortresslike origins, there was its location on a particularly desolate stretch of ground that the countess's ancestor had chosen, or so I came to believe, precisely because one could spot an enemy from a distance of five furlongs.

For the first few minutes, a light drizzle dampened my hood as I sat within the carriage, unable to move. But then I recalled my last breakfast of porridge and mead taken among strangers at yet another roadside inn, and I allowed the driver to help me step outside.

No sooner had I reached the high wooden door than it swung open, and a sturdy woman in a cotton smock and apron stood before me, her hands chapped by hard work, her ankles swollen beneath her petticoats. "My name's Emily," she said, her full lips softening into what I took to be a genuine smile. "Lady Miranda Molyneux, yes?"

I nodded, then stepped inside as the driver unloaded my belongings.

"You've been traveling for at least a week, haven't you?"

"Eleven days," I said, surprised by the pungent odor of lye that hung about the air.

"And your journey, it passed smoothly?" Emily wiped her hands on her apron, her careful gaze making me thankful I had remembered to put on my best shoes before leaving the inn that morning.

"Thankfully, yes," I said, relieved not to have met with any of the clapperdudgeons who disguised themselves as lepers so as to beg or steal alms from those who tried to pass.

"Well, there's gratitude in that," Emily said, then turned toward the interior of the house, where I heard the sound of light footsteps.

She motioned toward the shadows, and a slim girl stepped forward, a girl with the same walnut-colored hair and wide gray eyes. "My daughter, Eliza," she said, as the girl—who was probably only a year older than myself—curtsied and bowed her head. "She'll see to your things."

"But the trunk is far too heavy," I said, reminded of how difficult it was for me to lift it, and my figure was on a grander or at least a plumper scale than Eliza's.

"The driver will carry the heavier trunk upstairs." Emily nodded to where he still stood on the drive, watering the horses. "Eliza can manage the other one. She has chopped much of the wood this year. And it's she who is responsible for the milking. No," Emily said, when I stood there staring, "my Eliza is as strong as any boy."

The slender Eliza curtsied a second time before she stood again, and our eyes met. I admired the straight way she stood in her sky blue kirtle, which had been laced in the old-fashioned way. I hoped she would stay and talk, but before I could think of how to keep her, she turned and made her way up a precariously steep flight of stairs, the smaller of my two trunks in tow.

"Turbury isn't a place where one finds much company, and tonight it'll be just the countess joining you," Emily explained as I followed her to a sparely furnished dining room, which remained remarkably cold and damp despite the fire that burned in the hearth.

"When will the earl return?" I asked, noting the absence of any adornment on the cupboards and cabinets, the plainness of the buffet, the whitewashed silence of the walls.

"Difficult to say." Emily poked at a log in the fire. "But I wouldn't expect him before February's come and gone." I must have flinched, for she said, "You didn't know, then, that he'd be away?"

"No," I said, trying to coax inside a skinny black cat that stood in the doorway.

"Well, no great matter in that," Emily said as the cat twined itself about her legs. "It'll be the countess who sees to your care anyway. She's raised half a dozen gentlemen's daughters these last ten years."

Tempted as I was to learn more about the fates of these daughters, for whom the countess must have found husbands, I could not ask such a question of my guardian's housekeeper. "And the cat?" I said instead, my fingertips tracing the outline of spine and bone beneath the coarse fur.

Emily's gruff laugh was friendly. "What about her?"

"She's so skinny." I recalled my own Griselda's hearty appetite as well as her habit of lying all day in the sun. "Does she belong to the house?"

"As much as anyone does. I call her Burr. She's not much of a mouser, has yet to learn she has to earn her keep."

I tried to scoop Burr up, but she jumped away and fled the room.

"She'll come around," Emily said. "Like most creatures around here, she can't resist a bit of kindness. For now I've set biscuits and tea on the table for you. The countess will be here soon."

I thanked her, wishing she would stay and talk. But it was clear she had work to do. Alone once more, I found myself standing before a long table upon which two settings of scarred silver plates had been laid on either end.

Politeness demanded I remain on my feet until I met

the countess. Still, I found it odd that she expected me to sit at one end, and she at the other. How would we speak to each other across such a distance?

On all of my previous visits to others' homes, I'd found keys to their characters in the rooms themselves. What was I to make, then, of this high-ceilinged space without a single ancestral portrait on the wall? Here there was not even a grouping of vases or other curios on display in an open cupboard. As for containing anything like the beloved tapestry of the lady with the unicorn that graced our own dining room—a tapestry my grandmother had carried back from France during her service with Anne Boleyn—not one piece of art, howsoever humble, enlivened the room, which, despite its whiteness, possessed a cavernous feel.

"So you are Miranda Molyneux," the countess said, startling me as she strode into the room in a stiff black dress, her handsome face framed by a wide white collar. Her body was uncannily lean, and she must have stood six feet. Though I was tall like my father, she stood at least a head higher than I did, an extraordinary thing in a woman.

"Yes, ma'am," I replied, training my gaze on the floor until she gave me permission to look directly at her. When she did, I beheld the gold-flecked eyes of a real beauty, her sculptural features framed by tightly bound hair dark as a rook's wing. All the same, there was something troubling about the countess's aquiline nose, her high cheekbones, her perfect oval of a face. In her features I could find neither any imperfection—a mole, a scar, a laugh line—nor, I feared, much sign of kindness.

"You have your mother's look about you," she said, her tone more calculating than praising. "Still, I see you stand nearly as high as the door. Unless you marry a man as tall as the earl," she said without a hint of humor, "you will have to learn to stoop a little."

I had no words for this.

"And how was the journey?" the countess continued. "Exceedingly long?" She twitched the gold pomander at her waist, releasing the unexpectedly exotic fragrance of oranges and spices.

"Eleven days," I said, still believing I could hear the horses' hoofbeats keeping pace with my heart.

"And the roads," she continued, scrutinizing my hair, my skin, my clothes, "how did you find them?"

"Fairly good."

"Potholes? Ragged ground?"

"In places."

"So, you fare no better in Cumberland than we do here in Yorkshire," the countess said. "Why our queen does not apportion a part of the country's coffers to mend the roads I will never understand. Instead, she lavishes our monies on court masques and processions. Despite her early show of modesty, she is proving to be Henry VIII's daughter after all."

Unsure of how I might answer, knowing nothing of the countess's politics, and having never expected such outspoken talk about the queen in front of a newcomer, I chose the safest course and thanked her for having Emily and her daughter see to my arrival.

"Emily is a hard worker, and her daughter takes after her in this way," the countess said, then motioned to me to sit down. "I trust Eliza helped see to your belongings."

Reminded of Eliza's straight-backed figure in the sky blue kirtle, but also of what Emily had said about the skinny Burr, I said, "Right away."

"I'm glad to hear it. She and Emily have been dyeing wool these last few weeks."

At the possibility of joining such work, my heart lifted. That explained the smell of lye.

"Such an extravagance of color!" the countess said, my hopes plummeting at once. "Had they kept the choices simpler, they would have been finished days ago.

"Have you brought a great deal with you?" The countess spoke more sharply now as she studied the pattern of honeysuckle and roses threading the bodice of my gown. "I asked your mother to keep your provisions simple."

"Two trunks," I replied, wondering at her words, given the vastness of this house.

"Two?" The countess seemed to weigh this fact as her hand clasped the pomander.

"Clothes mostly, and my books."

"Tell me," the countess said, "what do you read?"

"*The Maiden's Dream* and *The Melancholy Knight* are two of my favorites," I said eagerly. "Though the one I could not be without is a collection of Marie de France's *Lais*."

"Ah, the Frenchwoman who served in Henry II's court?"

"Yes. It was a birthday gift from my father."

"You are fond of reading for pleasure, then?" the countess asked. "And possibly have read the Greeks?"

"Oh yes—Mother and I read *The Odyssey* last summer."

"A scandalous work, I am told," she said, her gaze narrowing, "in which an adulterous husband returns after many years to his wife."

"That is the premise, but the story is so much more than that," I said, hoping she would ask me to explain.

But the countess just frowned, so it was a relief when Emily reentered, carrying with her a steaming wild goose pie, on her face only a glimmer of her former smile.

"I favor simple cookery," the countess continued as Emily sliced the pie.

"Simple" to me suggested "bland," but this pie had been seasoned with thyme and marjoram, herbs that extend a food's longevity and give it a woodsy flavor I particularly liked. I ate the first helping quickly, then made to reach for another slice.

"Miranda," the countess said, "please ask before taking another plate of food."

"I'm sorry. I haven't eaten since late morning."

I expected her to offer me a large portion, but she cut only a narrow slice. "Given the precedent of your parents, you are fuller in figure than I expected. Here at Turbury," she said, her rook-dark hair glinting in the candlelight, "we live a disciplined life, believing a disciplined body to be the key to a disciplined soul."

"Yes, ma'am," I replied, recalling the ease and liveliness at Plowden Hall during mealtimes, my mother's belief that a hearty appetite was an indication of one's zest for life.

The goose pie was followed by roast saltwater eel served with a small loaf of oat bread that must have been several days old, for it crumbled dryly in my mouth. Although I did not like eel and was surprised to find it in this part of Yorkshire, so far from the coast, I was hungry enough to finish my entire portion. Besides, I understood the countess would not approve of my turning away from what I was being offered.

Afterward, there was a carefully apportioned apple and a slice of cheese. Reminded of my mother's practice of serving spiced wine in the evening because she believed it paved the way for good dreams, I found myself hoping the countess would somehow uphold this practice also.

Instead, from a pewter teapot she poured what proved to be steeping water into two cups that each held only a slice of lemon and a few fennel seeds. "For the digestion," the countess said, and handed a cup to me.

"Is the earl away?" I asked, sensing it would not be prudent for me to reveal that Emily had already told me this.

"He is." She cocked an eyebrow, as if considering the significance of my question. And when I said nothing further, she added, "I do not expect him back until sometime in March."

"Does he often travel?" I asked, curious to learn more about my father's cousin, for perhaps they did share this passion for adventure.

"Only when he must. You see, Miranda," she said, her fingertips toying with the pomander, "my husband views travel as a necessity, not a pleasure. He has no need to see other countries, other ways of life. Is it not at home where one's responsibilities lie?"

"I do not know," I said, recalling the sketches of my father's travels that adorned his study walls, but also the sketch I had carried with me—a drawing he had made just before departing, a drawing of his return.

"You're thinking of your father?"

"Yes—"

"You must remember your father lost his life abroad. That reminds me, I should have told you as soon as you arrived. How sorry I was—as was the earl—to learn about his death. So sudden." Her eyes met my own. "And among the heathens of Ireland.

"Of course," she continued, "I met your father only once, and it was a rather brief meeting. Still, most said he was a good, albeit imprudent man."

"My father was a very good man," I said, aware of the edge in my voice. "He lost his life at the service of Her Majesty the Queen."

"Yes," the countess said neutrally. "Unfortunately, the Irish cause is not one in which I place much faith."

We sat in silence as the remaining log crackled in the hearth. I concentrated on the fire, watching the flames lick the wood so that the area surrounding the grate smoked just a little.

"It's time for me to show you where you will sleep," the countess said, indicating with a swift flick of the wrist that I should rise.

We proceeded down the poorly lit hallway, and I followed her up the stairs and down a very long, very damp corridor. Once again, no portraits adorned the dark walls; only a solitary candle to light the way.

At the end of the passage, the countess opened a heavy door.

Inside, I surveyed a small bedroom furnished with a narrow bed, a dresser, and a simple washstand. As for a mirror or a silver basin and ewer, there was no sign of any of these things. Nor did there linger about the room the inviting almond or lavender fragrance of homemade soap. And the hearth, though it burned with a small fire, seemed to create little warmth.

"I trust you will be comfortable enough here," the countess said, then drew closed the heavy curtains that would seal away any possibility of light finding its way through the window come sunrise.

"Yes," I said, breathing the stale smell of the hay rushes strewn along the floor.

"Good night, then." Already the countess was reaching for the latch on the door. "I will send Emily up here at six to wake you."

After she left, I stood for a while, shivering in the chill air and listening to her diminishing steps in the hall. Once more the image of my mother lingering in the doorway of Plowden Hall returned. This time I recalled the sunlight slanting across her face, casting the right half in shadow while illuminating the tears that traced her left cheek.

I undressed and washed in a basin into which I poured cold water from a crackle-glazed pitcher, then slipped on my nightgown, which still smelled of my room at home. The bed, I discovered as I pulled back the thick blankets, was only a pallet of straw. Touching its coarse material, I tried to remind myself of the rough provisions of my father's journeys. But even when he slept out of doors, Father always remembered to look up at the stars, believing they were keeping watch.

Inevitably my thoughts turned to my own room's soft feather mattress, the shimmering branches of the willow tree beyond my window, my beloved cat, Griselda, Mother's temperate step on the stair.

Soon I was beside the heavier of my two trunks, searching for the gown that had once belonged to her. I feared it had been crushed by the journey, but when I lifted it into the candlelight, the wrinkles fell away, and the pale pink satin—still glossy despite the years—shone just as it had when I'd admired it in my mother's room. I touched the flowers she had embroidered along the bodice, admiring the intricacy of her stitches, remembering her touch through the feel of the Cyprus gold thread.

On the morning of my departure, before the coachman had arrived, I stepped into her room, where the wardrobe presided, a great piece of furniture she had brought with her from her father's house. For as long as I could remember, I had been entranced by the clothing secreted there, not by the sturdy gowns of wool and cotton that my mother wore every day—gowns I often helped her sew and later mend.

No, what held me captive were those magical survivors stitched from velvet, damask, and satin—gowns with slashed sleeves and delicate beading that she had worn during her time at court. And for each of these enchanted survivors, my mother had a story: the gown of Genoan silk with its bobbin lace she had worn to Elizabeth's coronation in Westminster Abbey; the ivory satin with the gray-blue skirt she had favored during her year as a lady-in-waiting, its sleeves embroidered with columbine and violets, its bodice discreetly adorned with pearls.

Always I believed these gowns would be my legacy. Like my mother and my sister after her, I, too, would one day walk through the gilded landscape of the court. I, too, would partake of the masques, the tournaments, the concerts, the lavish meals attended by visiting dignitaries, the gay evenings where the handsomest of the courtiers would ask me to dance a spirited galliard. Not for very long—for like my father, my mother was wary of the court's intrigues, and believed too much time there inevitably spoiled one for the simpler pleasures. Yet she loved it also. Her stories had told me as much, as had her occasional sadnesses during those long months when Father had been away.

What compelled me to take the gown without her permission, I could not say. I knew only that I needed its soaring birds and brightly stitched butterflies, its garden of pinks and carnations, its trim of lace. I needed, too, the memory of her enfolded in its fabric: lute music mingling with the murmur of the Thames as she danced in my father's arms, arrayed in a gown the precise shade of a maiden's blush—the shade of innocence. And yet many understood this to be the shade of vanity.

When my mother found me among her things, she did not ask what I was about. Instead, she placed the pink satin in my arms and told me she trusted I would pack it well.

CHAPTER TWO

January 1580

FIRST LIGHT HAD JUST BEGUN TO BREAK through the curtains when a knock at the door startled me away from dreams of Plowden Hall, where I still sat with my mother and listened to her describe a long-ago party held on one of the queen's barges. There, musicians filled the air with love songs and lyrical tales of romance, the beauty of their art enough for my mother to forget the ambitions masked behind too many of the courtiers' and the ladies' smiles—at least for a while.

"Good morning, miss," Emily said as she stepped into the room, bringing with her not just a reassuring smile, but a waft of cold air.

"Is it six o'clock already?" I said, relieved but perhaps also a bit sad when she said nothing about the satin gown still draped across the chair, its butterflies so vivid they seemed to have just flown in from some distant summery garden.

"It is." Emily placed a tray bearing a pot of what I hoped was tea, a plate of eggs, and two slices of bread on a cloth atop the dresser.

"Be grateful for the extra hour," Emily added as I slunk beneath the covers. "The usual rising time at Turbury is five."

"Truly?" I said as Emily opened the curtains onto a view of the solemn browns of the moors, now tinged with softest lavender in the coming light.

"The countess expects all of us at our duties at sunup."

What did the countess expect of me today? I wondered as Emily bent to stoke the fire, the muscles in her forearms lit by flame, her profile outlined against the stone hearth.

"Best to get a foot into the day, miss," Emily said when she noticed me staring. "You're to meet the countess in the chamber room just to the left of the staircase at seven o'clock."

I was about to complain, but then I tipped the pot and was relieved to find not just water, but hot steeping tea.

Wearing the sage green gown I had inherited from Laura, one my mother had helped me to refurbish before my departure, with silver-gray guards at the wrists and hem, I descended the staircase. It was early yet, and so I wandered through the dim hall, listening for sounds and secretly hoping I might encounter Burr or better yet, Eliza. If the countess found me first, I told myself, poking my head into a series of moth-colored rooms, each one as spare as the one before, I knew I could pretend to be lost.

Around the corner, the swish of a black tail. Burr. Careful not to frighten her, I crept up behind, only to see the cat slip through the kitchen door.

I followed.

Eliza turned to face me. "Oh, miss, you gave me such a fright!"

"I am sorry," I said as Burr twined herself around Eliza's legs.

"Did you lose your way?"

When I shrugged, Eliza's wide gray eyes softened, and she smiled.

"What are you making?" I asked, noticing the bowl, the fine muslin cloth, the bottle of red wine vinegar.

"A cure for restless nights," Eliza said as I peered into a bowl fragrant with chamomile blossoms and anise.

"Do you have trouble sleeping?" I said, recalling what her mother had said about her strength and energy.

"Not me, miss." Eliza began pummeling the mixture in the bowl. "It is the earl who is plagued by this trouble. Most nights you can hear him walking up and down the stone floors of the great hall."

"But the earl is away, is he not?"

"He is. I thought I'd best make use of the time and the ingredients." Eliza began stirring several spoonfuls of vinegar into the recipe.

"How did you learn to make this remedy?"

"My father taught me. He said I had his healing touch."

"Was your father a doctor, then, or an apothecary?"

"He was nothing so fine as that," Eliza said, and blushed. "No, he worked with horses."

"My father, too, was fond of horses," I said, hoping to bridge the loneliness of this place. "As is my mother."

"Your mother rides?"

"She does. Some say she is as good a rider as any man for miles around."

"Beg your pardon, miss, but I wouldn't expect that from such a fine lady."

"My mother may be a lady," I said, "but she's not too fine for an energetic ride."

Neither one of us spoke after that. Still, it calmed me to watch as Eliza continued to prepare the remedy.

"Your father was interested in medicine, then?" I said after a while.

"He was. Once," she said proudly, "the priest even sent for him to cure the falling evil."

"That is an honor," I said, reminded of how careful—not to mention suspicious—the clergy could be about the fine line between medicine and witchcraft, but also struck by the spirit of Eliza's response. "And your father taught you what he knew?"

"He did. I can heal a burn, treat jaundice, soothe the nerves. I'm trying now to decipher the cure for dropsy. Trouble is, I cannot read well, and there's still so much to learn."

"Perhaps I can help you," I heard myself say.

"Oh no, miss. It wouldn't be right."

Before we could say more, there came the sound of footsteps, and Emily entered, a broom in her hands, perspiration dappling her forehead and arms. She looked from her daughter to me and said, "You'd do well to seek the chamber room, miss."

"Very well," I said, wishing I could linger in this warm room scented with apples, the hopeful promise of seedlings nesting in tiny pots along the windowsill.

I found the chamber room quickly. Unlike the sparely furnished rooms I had seen thus far, here each corner held a suit of armor, among them a suit very much like the one my grandfather had worn during the reign of Henry VIII.

Beside them someone had mounted the head of a stag.

Where it once had had eyes, there were now only glossy black stones. Looking into the creature's lifeless face brought back my own twilight discoveries of deer that had died in the woods surrounding Plowden Hall, and I turned away.

"This is all that remains of the stag that eluded my father for nearly a dozen years," the countess said, her heavy skirts rustling as she strode into the room. "The year I came of age, Father finally brought the animal down. For nearly two weeks, we supped on venison stew."

I turned toward the countess as a long-forgotten memory stirred within me. It involved a pair of Arabian horses a neighbor had brought with him when he'd returned from the Holy Land. When they'd first arrived on his property, the horses—one as black as onyx, the other the dappled gray of the cliff hawks who soar far out over the sea— resisted the halter by rising up on their hind legs, their nostrils flaring as they kicked up dust. After six months of being penned in a gated ring and whipped whenever they reared up, neither one protested when their master placed the cold steel bit in its mouth; proof enough, he later said, their spirits had at last been broken.

Troubled by the memory, I continued to stand mute before the stag until the countess, dressed this morning in a deep blue gown and the same white collar, called me to a great oak table, around which stood four plain stools. "Sit, please," she said.

When I did, she placed a piece of paper in front of me. "Here you will find the topics of study with which we will concern ourselves."

In a meticulous yet daggered script, she had written out a program that consisted of the study and memorization of Scripture and Other Improving Texts, silent prayer, conduct lessons, and cookery.

"What of singing and the study of music?" I asked. "Am I not to have a romance to translate from the French? My mother always told me I would require my French, as well as a little Spanish, when I went to court."

"Well then, your mother's training in these areas will have to suffice," she said sharply. "Young ladies in my care develop more necessary skills."

I wanted to say something about the necessity of music and drawing, but how could I, given the silence of Turbury? How, given the lack of stories, indeed the absence of anything of beauty within its walls?

"Perhaps," the countess said, a little more kindly, "we should move more slowly. Given your penchant for narrative, I think we should begin with a text I myself return to for strength and courage." Already she began to approach the floor-to-ceiling shelves at the far end of the room.

"Ah, here it is." She ran her fingers along the book's spine.

I hoped she might bring forth *The Heroic Virtues of*

England's Queens, The Ladies' Looking Glass, or *The Excellencies of Good Women.*

"*A Pattern of Piety* by Katherine Spencer," the countess said instead. "An Englishwoman of our own time."

"Is she still living?"

"Mistress Spencer died in childbirth at twenty," the countess said. "In the months before her second lying-in, she wrote the story of her life and a confession of her faith."

"I'm sorry," I said, painfully reminded of my mother's dear friend, Lady Throckmorton, who had died of puerperal fever just two days after giving birth to her ninth child.

"Mistress Spencer was an exemplar to our sex. There is no cause for pity," the countess said, and placed the book on the table before me. "For the next three hours, I will leave you to discover her virtues on your own. When I return we will discuss what you can extract from her example."

Without another word, she left, and I had no choice but to open the little black book. If I must read, I thought, staring out at a landscape dominated by a sky made bleaker by the absence of sun, I would have preferred one of Marie de France's *Lais,* or my mother's guide to needlework, which my father had especially chosen for her because it had been composed in sonnet form. Even *A Chain of Pearl: Lessons on Virtue* would have been preferable to a volume that smelled like old shoes left to sit in the cellar too long.

Sitting there, I envied Eliza her industry, and almost wished I could join her, despite what my mother would say. Though she'd taught me it was God's grace that enabled my privilege, she could never approve of my need to befriend the housekeeper's daughter.

Once the stag's eyes seemed to follow my own, I knew my thoughts were getting the better of me. I had no choice, then, but to open the book. The story may have lacked chivalry and romance. Yet as I turned the pages, Katherine Spencer began to speak to me, in particular her chronicle of the time that followed her thirteenth birthday, when she began to volunteer at a charity school in London.

Five days a week, Katherine wrote, *I walked to school to help care for the little ones in the nursery run by good Lady Carey. In the beginning, I found my way to the school because I wanted to repay God for saving my mother, who narrowly escaped the terrors of life on the streets when she was taken in at Lady Burghley's school for orphans. But as is so often God's way, I soon discovered I loved the work itself. And how could I not when the little ones' faces shone so when I entered the nursery? How, when they clung to my skirts and begged me to carry them in my arms?*

Such work I understood to be a labor of love, so that when my parents betrothed me to Jonathan Phillips, I struggled to understand why God was calling me away from these children I could have cared for as my own, especially when the man He had chosen for me was older than my father.

⚜

I had ceased thinking of the hour by the time Katherine Spencer found herself the sixteen-year-old bride of a man more than twenty years her senior, one who expected her to share his meals and his bed, but did not believe her fit to share her ideas on history or literature.

Within a year of her marriage, she was pregnant.

Though I knew I must and would be grateful to the Lord if the babe was a boy or a girl, Katherine wrote, *I silently hoped for a daughter, a hope that sets my hand to trembling even as I write now, almost three years later. It was not my place to cherish such a wish. And yet I could not help myself. A son's chief duty would be to his father. A little maid would belong to me—at least until the time came for her to marry.*

Once I discovered Katherine had cherished a particular dream—for a daughter—she became all the more real to me, not because I, too, shared this desire. In truth, I had not yet thought of myself as a mother.

But Katherine's dream—her yearning—*this* I understood. How tenderly she spoke of the children in the nursery, demonstrating that it is love that is a maker of beauty, love that invests what one cares for with grace. And then there were her descriptions of sunlight slanting across a newly scrubbed table, the patchwork of colors found in a calico cat, the iridescent light of the stained glass windows in the church where she prayed.

⸻❈⸻

By the time I turned toward the sound of the countess's firm step outside the door, I knew that Katherine had borne and lost that child, a baby girl.

A daughter, with a spun-gold crown of hair and dark eyes, came into the world too early, or so the midwife said when she placed her in my arms. The Lord allowed her to remain just long enough to receive the minister's blessing. Despite the grief which abides within me even now, I know I must trust in the mercies of the Lord for my daughter's salvation. Her death, though it split my heart open, is a part of His plan, one infinitely larger and wiser than I can see. . . .

I had heard such talk before, but until I read Katherine Spencer's story, I had never believed that the person who said such things was truly convinced of them. How could I when my own mother had wept for many weeks after the priest said a final prayer for the soul of my younger brother, William? And then there was my sister, Laura's, loss, having twice delivered a stillborn child. . . .

Here was a woman who could look at the lifeless

child she had borne and say—with what seemed true conviction—*Her death, though it split my heart open, is a part of His plan.*

Did the countess believe such things also? Was it possible that she, too, had borne and lost children?

I recalled a statue of Mary, one of the icons the Church had not destroyed when it wrestled England away from the popish faith. It stood in a shadowy corner of a small church of whitewashed stone not far from Plowden Hall. Each time I visited there, I found myself drawn to the corner that held this statue. It had been carved from the whitest marble, a stone that had turned luminous in the sculptor's skilled hands. Yes, my parents were good Protestants, as our queen required. Still they were glad, they said, she had not allowed something so beautiful and so true to be destroyed.

Neither my mother nor my father explained what they meant by the *truth* of the little statue, nor did I find any explanation necessary, not when my heart opened before the graceful figure bent over her newborn, her downcast eyes and smile the very image of tenderness itself.

⸎

"It has been three hours, Miranda," the countess said, striding into the room and bringing with her the fragrance

31

of cloves and oranges. By the time I looked up, she had seated herself on the stool opposite my own. "Tell me, what have you gained for your own life from Katherine Spencer's life thus far?"

"I am not sure," I answered truthfully, "though I admire how deeply Katherine cared for the children at the charity school."

The countess smiled thinly. "A formative chapter in her life, no doubt."

"I wish——" I said, realizing the countess had not understood.

She curved toward me, her gold-flecked eyes glimmering. "Yes?"

"I wish Katherine had been allowed to stay at the charity school nursery. She had a talent for caring for the children there——"

The countess leaned closer, on her face a look of mild interest. "But, Miranda, does a life not always proceed according to God's wisdom?"

I did not know how to answer.

The countess did not even blink her eyes, so intently did she seem to continue to wait for me to speak.

"But Katherine lost her daughter," I said at last.

Still the countess did not speak.

"My mother and my sister have both lost children," I heard myself say. "Neither one ever spoke of these deaths as part of God's plan. I do not believe they could be convinced of this."

"Then they doubt God's will, and in so doing are committing a sin."

"Is it a sin to lose the desire to rise from bed when one need only look out the window to see the newly dug grave of one's child?" I asked, reminded of the weeks my mother had spent in mourning. Every April and again in August, she continued to plant flowers beside the headstone.

"Yes, Miranda," the countess said, her features still and unmoving. "It is a very serious sin indeed."

CHAPTER THREE

Late January 1580

AT TURBURY, ONE GRAY DAY FOLLOWED THE next, my lessons resuming each morning without fail, so that I understood anew why the many shades of gray were inevitably associated with the more difficult emotions: despair, sadness, and of course, patience. The only exception was Sunday, when the countess allowed an hour-later rising. Although Sunday was not crowded with studies, the countess expected every member of her household to devote a good part of the day to silent prayer and contemplation.

I tried to focus on the passages in the prayer book or in one of the edifying texts the countess had me read. But with the exception of Katherine Spencer's story, such selections rarely held my interest. How could they when there were no intriguing characters, lands, or enchanted creatures around which to spin stories? No ladies giving their favors to the knights who wore the tokens on their sleeves, or pinned over their hearts? No court masques or balcony serenades?

Under circumstances such as these, it was difficult not to think about Henry Raleigh, and even more difficult to reconcile his recent behavior with what I had always believed about him. Though I had met him only once in January, some three years ago, I had always imagined Henry to be a man as adventurous and generous as my father. After all, my father once said he could come to love him as his own son.

I no longer remembered the reason why Henry had accompanied my father back to Plowden Hall. One wintry afternoon they'd stood there, framed in the doorway, their cheeks bright with cold, snow dusting their cloaks and boots.

From the beginning I had been struck by the deep indigo of his eyes and a manner that, although reserved, suggested true gentility, a quality my parents valued as much as a good name. Why? In times of hardship, they said time and again, it is one's character far more than one's wealth that sees a person and his family through. And Henry, my father had told us, had quickly risen to a position of responsibility, thereby providing for his mother after his father's death, when he was only thirteen.

On the evening of their arrival at Plowden Hall, Henry had knelt beside me before the fire in the great hall, where I sat turning the pages of a book of Greek myths my father had carried back for me, Griselda curled at my side.

As the fire warmed us both, Henry's chestnut hair strayed over his brow, and he spoke to me of Ireland, presenting hardships and challenges as a piece of the whole adventure, the way an embroidered leaf or bird is part of the whole design.

I listened eagerly to his tales, and with equal attentiveness heard his recollections of domestic life, especially when he described his favorite haunts—a hollow oak tree more than a century old, a cave where he kept his treasures and sometimes came to read by candlelight, a pond secreting turtles on the edge of his family's remaining plot of land.

And then there were the animals in his family's care: "We've several cats at home, and none of them want for a bit of milk from the bowl. But I'll confess something." A smile crept across his lips. "I prefer horses and dogs."

"Why?" I said, studying his callused hands, their roughness further proof of the adventures he had lived.

"I suppose it's because they are more loyal."

"Cats, too, can be loyal," I told him. "It's just their affection is harder to win."

Henry laughed at this. "Your father did not speak in jest. You are a spirited girl."

What would my father say now of the man he would have loved as his own son? A man who had turned away from his daughter once my father's fortunes—and his life— came to an end? Would Father still find gentility in his behavior? And even if he did, would he have forgiven Henry? Could I?

With so little companionship at Turbury, such thoughts troubled me often, so it was a comfort when Emily stepped into my room and dispelled the silence and fear that seemed to wait beneath the bed or in a shadowy corner. After she refreshed the fire and filled my pitcher with water, I tried and often did convince her to stay for a few minutes.

"Just this once," Emily said when she accepted, mentioning the tasks the countess had laid before her, never once complaining.

The first time I looked at Emily, she seemed a good deal older than my mother. Her fingers were as knobbed and rough as an old tree's branches, and a trellis of lines had etched themselves into the corners of her eyes and along the edges of her mouth. But once she joined me in the hard chairs beside the hearth, and the firelight softened her features, the years fell away and I realized she might be far younger than I originally thought. Hard work, I knew, could age a person as much as time.

On one of these mornings I discovered that although Emily could perform almost any household task, her true passion was cooking; hence the deliciously unexpected meals, no matter how simple.

"One must select only the ripest fruits to be dried, then pare them, take out the cores, and slice them thinly," she said, having brought for my breakfast a bowl of dried apples, pears, and quinces. "This is common knowledge. What is not," her tone turned confiding, "is the importance of laying the fruit to dry in the sun on a very smooth stone, and not within a metal dish. It is stone that best dries a fruit without stealing its sweetness, so that it can be enjoyed throughout the year."

As soon as I bit into one of her dried apples, instantly releasing the golden aromas of the season of turning leaves and honeybees in the high grass, I knew exactly what she meant.

January 12, 1580
Dearest Miranda,

You have been gone only a few days, and already the house feels empty without you. Upon waking I often forget the changes in our lives, and I find myself eager to share a dream or a story. And sometimes after a neighbor has visited

(Lady Shrewsbury has promised to come tomorrow with her granddaughter, Felicity, who is staying with her while Lord Shrewsbury recovers; and good Margaret Laton has visited twice now, always arriving with a cake or a pie), I think, How happy Miranda will be when she learns the Laton's mare has foaled . . . or What will Miranda say when I tell her Lord Shrewsbury plans to import a fountain for his garden? Then I recall the distance that now separates us, and I resolve to put my thoughts into my letters. And so I shall . . .

In addition to the kindness of our neighbors, I find myself beholden to Lord Grey. While he was here, I confided in him my fear about capturing just the right tone in my petition to the queen. He must have remembered my worry, because he now writes to say he will return to Plowden Hall within the week so as to help me. And then there are the accounts of the estate to settle. Here, too, Lord Grey has promised to come to my aid. His many years of managing his own property make him the most fit person in these matters.

I will write again soon. Remember me to the countess. As you adjust to her manner of living, try to bring forth the joy I always wanted you to find in your daily activities. It is the most important gift I could possibly have given you—along with compassion, a sense of humor, and your inquisitive, shining eyes.

I send you all my love,
Mother

Postscript: So distracted have I been since Christmas I failed to notice the remarkable change taking place before me. Late last night, your dear old Griselda gave birth to six kittens. The father I suspect to be the gray tom that can often be found stalking mice in the kitchen garden.

I knew that I should feel at least some gratitude toward Lord Grey for helping my mother write to her cousin, the queen, not only because of the difficulty of her circumstances, but because the queen had distanced herself almost entirely from my mother, saying once that she had become "a bit too provincial" for court life.

"In truth, it is my spirit my cousin protests," Mother had said.

"As well as your beauty," added Father, his face betraying his admiration.

Given that my mother was now dependent on the queen for her dower, few people were as well-equipped as the worldly Lord Grey to help her win her cousin's ear without irking her famous temper.

Why, then, did his return to Plowden Hall vex me so?

⟨─✳─⟩

"The countess has given you leave to go for a walk this morning," Eliza said, surprising me when she and not her mother brought breakfast to my room.

I must have sighed or given some sign of discontent, for Eliza said, "You may find it dreary here now when winter still lingers along the moors. But just wait until springtime."

"It is a different country here then?" I said, my words a soft challenge.

Eliza's gray eyes seemed to catch the light as she rose to meet me. "It is. There will be flowers shaped like stars, and rosy heather, as well as cowslip, foxglove, and buttercup. You'll see."

A current of hope washed through me at the idea of bright skies, less rain, a tapestry of ever-changing flowers. "I will look forward to that."

"Always you must keep a lookout for the Exmoor ponies. If fortune is with you, you'll encounter them on your walks. But remember, they're shy creatures and tend to keep far from this house." The light left her eyes, and Eliza's face seemed to close, and once again that barrier rose between us.

January 20, 1580
Dearest Miranda,

All through the morning, while Griselda nursed her tiny offspring in an old leather trunk that once belonged to your father, I resumed work on the jacket you began in November. Practicality and the feeling of the work bringing you close compel my fingers to follow the path your own set in motion.

As I studied the fineness of your stitches, I thought back to the time—more than eight years ago—when I first taught you how to embroider using a scrap of Holland lawn. I would never have thought that the little girl who fretted so over the braid stitch, and once swore she would never master the ladder, would grow into a skilled embroideress capable of creating caterpillars and swallows and trellises of the most beautiful flowers found in nature.

Surely you will have occasion to put your talents to use at Turbury. Yes, the countess must favor plainer work. Nevertheless, I must believe she will recognize and value your abilities—at least a fraction as much as I do. Lord Grey agrees. He arrived yesterday afternoon and immediately praised the fineness of your embroidery in the guest rooms in the left wing.

And that brings me to the matter of the petition: although instinct told me to ask for a dower of 150 pounds per annum, Lord Grey thought the request too great, especially since I am writing on behalf of Robert also. I have therefore asked for 120 pounds. Lord Grey has promised to deliver the petition himself when he travels to London after he leaves here. If all goes well, I should have an answer within a month's time.

I miss you, my daughter,
Mother

On the day this letter arrived, the countess left to see a distant neighbor about buying a horse, a journey that would prevent her from returning until first light the next morning. Ordinarily I would have relished the reprieve from my studies and our silent dinners, having begun at last to embroider the plain coverlet in my room. In one of my letters I told my mother such work helped me to recover a feeling of home, thinking it safer—were the countess to read my words—not to put down in writing anything akin to the thrill of subversion I felt in creating the leafy Vandyke stitch, the woven web, and the French knot amid such dour surroundings.

And then there was the pleasure of defying not just the countess, but Old Man Winter himself. I therefore chose the pliant garland stitch to create leaves and bouquets of the flowers found in the garden I had always helped my mother to tend, from the time the first crocuses appeared in March until the last of the roses and marigolds finished blooming in October. With great looping stitches, I sewed blousy hollyhocks, using soft pinks and delicate yellows. Amethyst and violet brought the delicate petals of forget-me-nots and star-shaped asters into being. Oranges and saucy yellows I reserved for the spicy nasturtium; deep pinks for sweet peas and bleeding hearts. Rich colors like aubergine, cinnabar, and blue gave dimension to the roses and brought a pleasing liveliness to the breasts and wings of thrushes and other summering birds. Verdure, ivy, moss, and other shades of green became the foliage, and pure white, the graceful eglantine.

But that evening not even the challenge of the interlaced herringbone stitch or the coiled bullion stitch could keep the image of Lord Grey and my mother's new closeness away. To depend upon a man who was not family, even if he held a privileged position with the queen, troubled me, especially when I recalled the way his eyes had lingered on her person when she left a room, the intimacy in his address, the way he lay his hand on her forearm before he took what I thought would be his final leave of Plowden Hall.

I thought of the kitchen redolent with the inviting scents of Emily's cooking, the windowsill lined with bouquets in earthenware jugs, and bundles of herbs. In the kitchen there was always the chance of company. And if not that, I could at least count on a slice of pie or a chunk of bread.

I found Burr asleep at the foot of the stairs. Often I tried to coax her into being stroked or held, only to have the cat flee from me. But tonight she looked up, her wide yellow eyes two full moons.

"Looks like we would both like some company tonight," I said, and knelt to stroke her fur. When she began to purr, I scooped her up, struck again by how much lighter she was than Griselda. "Perhaps we can find a bit of milk for you in the kitchen."

I expected to find the kitchen deserted at this hour.

Instead, Eliza stood at the table, a pitcher of cream, a loaf of bread, half a dozen eggs, and a bowl of dried currants before her.

"What are you making?" I asked as Burr leaped from my arms.

"Hasty pudding for Sunday's supper." Eliza brushed away a long dark curl that had escaped from her cap. "It's Mum's recipe, but she was so tired tonight."

"I saw her scouring the floors earlier," I said.

"Yes." Eliza looked up at me; in her eyes was that habitual distance, but this time there was something else as well.

I moved closer to the table, and Burr twined around my legs, her silky tail tickling my ankles.

"She likes you," Eliza said, her voice a bit friendlier.

"Tonight is the first time she let me hold her." I bent to stroke the cat's fur as she arched her back and nuzzled the back of my hand with her whiskers.

"Well, it won't be long before she becomes your friend for life. Or at least," Eliza said more cautiously as she broke the eggs into the bowl, "for as long as you are here."

"When you're finished with the pudding," I said, "would you like me to help you with your reading?"

"There's still the mutton pie to be made." Eliza wiped the perspiration from her forehead.

"Perhaps I could help you with the mutton pie?"

Eliza's eyes widened. "You couldn't possibly do that, miss."

"Do not worry. I won't say anything to the countess."

Eliza scrutinized me more closely. "Pardon my saying, but you're not like the other girls who've come under the countess's care."

Although I was curious about them—these others—I thought it best not to ask. Besides, I was so lonely at Turbury, so desperate for a friend. "Tell me how I can help," I said instead.

"You truly wish to help, miss?" she said, still wary.

"Yes. So silent is my room, I feared the furniture would begin talking to me if I lingered there much longer."

"Very well." A smile crept across her lips. "But you mustn't say a word, not even to Mum."

"I won't. Now, may I ask you something?"

Once again, Eliza's gaze became wary, and her shoulders stiffened. "Yes?"

"Please don't call me miss."

Eliza's smile became a wide grin that revealed a prominent gap between her two front teeth. "What then?"

"Miranda," I said warmly.

"I've already made the coffin." Eliza pointed to the pie crust. "The next thing to be done is to gather the ingredients."

I followed her into the pantry, where we selected pepper, salt, nutmeg, mace, dried apples, vinegar, and sugar from the high shelves.

"Aren't we forgetting something?" I asked, once we had all the ingredients on the table.

Eliza surveyed the loaf of bread, the eggs, several apples, and the bunch of parsley. "I do not think so."

"What about the mutton?"

Eliza laughed, a reckless sort of schoolboy laugh that buoyed me on the inside. "The bread and the apples take the place of the mutton."

"Then why is it called mutton pie?"

Eliza's gray eyes turned serious once more. "You're not used to making do, are you?"

I recalled my mother's care in saving for the Christmas dinner of roast quail, venison with chestnuts, and rich brandied pudding; the ways we'd made an old gown look new by altering the sleeves or by trimming a hem with reticella lace, and I was about to say yes; but how could I ignore the many carefully matched patches on Eliza's skirt, the absence of adornment, the fabric worn thin at the bodice and along the elbows of the sleeves. "There are degrees of making do," I said finally; "though I cannot say I know of a mutton pie made without mutton."

"Well then," Eliza said, her tone lightening once more, "now is your chance to learn."

After we placed the pie in the oven, and the kitchen grew warm and fragrant with the smells of spices and eggs and the flaky pastry, Eliza divided the remaining bread between us, and we ate it with a sweet jam containing chunks of summer strawberries, a jam very like the one my mother and I made.

"It's grown late," Eliza said, pushing the empty plate toward Burr, who gobbled up the crumbs and purred.

"Do you still want me to read to you?"

Eliza studied me for a moment. But then both of us smiled at once, and before I knew it, she was stepping over to a high shelf. There she fetched a worn black book she handled with a mixture of familiarity and care.

Burr followed us down the hall. I hoped she would come all the way to my room. But at the foot of the staircase, the cat escaped into the darkness once more.

Inside my room Eliza's gaze was immediately drawn to the coverlet. "Your work?" she said, her eyes growing luminous as they traced the stitches.

"Yes."

"And the thread—the colors are like jewels. Surely you could not have dyed the silk yourself?"

"No," I said. "My father brought it back for me. Much of the thread comes from Italy, and some from the Far East."

"As far away as that? Why, I've never traveled beyond Yorkshire."

"My father was a great traveler," I said, traces of his stories lingering within me, especially that of Innisfree, a little Irish village he loved, where the purple glow of evening was further enchanted by the linnet's song.

"Is it true, miss—Miranda, I mean—your father lost his life abroad?"

"In Ireland," I said, wondering what the countess had told her of my history.

As if she sensed the painfulness of this subject, Eliza said, "Well, you're fortunate to have materials as beautiful as these with which to work. Where does the yellow come from? I'd wear it every day if I could, for it's my favorite color."

"From Persia," I said. "Its source the stamen of a magnificent flower called an orchid."

Eliza's eyes widened. "And the red?"

"Beetles."

She wrinkled her nose. "Good to know such creatures do more than eat the roses."

I tried to place the coverlet in her hands so she could examine it more closely, but she shook her head. "I couldn't."

"Well then," I said, "what would you like to study?"

"Lesser ailments," Eliza replied, though her gaze still lingered on the coverlet.

I reached for the book. "The lesser ailments include toothache, cough, bad breath, bed-wetting"—here I stuttered and tried to hide my blush—"constipation, hemorrhoids, tetters, indigestion. . . ."

"It would be grand to learn all of these," Eliza said. "Tonight I'll settle for learning how to cure toothache and indigestion, if "—she hesitated—"that's not too much to ask. It is late, and you've already helped me. . . ."

"Not at all." And then in a clear voice I read, "'To take away pain in the teeth, wash the mouth two or three times together in a morning with white wine wherein the root of spurge has been sodden . . .'"

<hr />

Eliza's responsibilities and my own prevented our meeting every day, especially given the countess's watchful gaze. Still, we managed to come together at least once a week to further study cures.

"What shall we look at tonight?" I asked, once the rest of the house had gone to bed and we sat down before the hearth in my room.

"A recipe for lustrous hair."

When I looked at her quizzically, she said, "May, the

daughter of one of Mum's friends, has just sold her hair. She is going to marry, and they need the money if they are to make a proper start."

"But her hair—"

"It will grow back, but *yes*—if you must know, she's cried herself to sleep many nights, and so her mother asked Mum if she knew of any cure."

"Well then," I said, "we must help her."

I opened the book. "'Take three good spoonfuls of honey and a good handful of parsley sprigs and beat them well. Afterward, strain their juice and heat it with dried tansy flowers.'"

"Tansy flowers?" Eliza said, frowning.

"Here," I said, fetching paper and pen, then sketching the round cluster of flowers with its fernlike leaves. "The tansy is yellow."

"How is it you know this flower so well?" Eliza asked, realizing she had seen it before growing wild after the heavy spring rains.

"Embroidery requires careful observation, just as healing does."

"Ah," Eliza said, "and I thought it just made life prettier."

"Beauty can have a curative effect," I told her, recalling the lightness I felt when I sat and sewed, my fears and sorrows forgotten for the time I practiced my art.

January 30, 1580

Dearest Miranda,

Caroline Willoughby and her parents came to see me this afternoon. They brought with them the Oxfordshire cake we all love. Unfortunately, the expressions on their faces, and the sorrow in Caroline's eyes, told me they had not come only to bring their condolences and talk before the firelight of the great hall.

With Caroline seated between them, her parents asked many questions about our circumstances, cautiously at first but then more boldly as they grew warm from the cake and spiced cider, until it became clear that it is only if a substantial portion of Father's debt is forgiven by the queen that the marriage between your brother, Robert, and Caroline will go forward.

I told the Willoughbys I awaited word from my cousin—feeling rather deceptive in bringing up my kinship with the queen when it has come to so little. At least I could be truthful in explaining the care Lord Grey took with my petition. The Willoughbys, too, are aware of the privileged position he occupies at court.

After today I fear Caroline's parents will marry her to one of the well-established widowers in the area. Already, Lord Standish has paid the family two visits. Yes, he is nearly fifty, with three grown children beside. But he has always admired Caroline. And then there is the solitary Colin Eyre. I always believed Mr. Eyre to be the romantic sort, who still mourned his young wife's death, but his growing interest in Caroline—which her parents mentioned, though discreetly—suggests otherwise. In other circumstances I would not speak thus, Miranda. But necessity is my mistress now.

Keep Robert in your thoughts, my darling, as you remain always in my own.

Mother

CHAPTER FOUR

February 1580

Though the wet winter wind nipped at my cheeks, and I often returned with soiled shoes, the hem of my skirts caked with mud, on those days the countess granted me permission, I continued to explore the moors. She may have believed I was disciplining my body, but I was simply reveling in the freedom of the open air. Often I retraced the steps of badger and roe deer and hare, while keeping a lookout for the wild ponies, of which Eliza had spoken. So as not to lose my way, I searched for markers in the landscape—the hornbeam, its twisting black branches reaching for the sky; or the more plentiful rowan, upon which the migratory thrushes fed, scattering seeds as they traveled. With the tall grass tickling my ankles, and the wind tousling my hair, Turbury's gray stone soon dwindled to a point on the horizon, and I found myself moving more freely.

Unfortunately, walking remained the exception in my days—most mornings found me fidgeting at the table in the classroom. Through the window I would watch Eliza or Emily go about their chores.

One morning, as the silver gray sky spread out above the muted earth, I sat waiting for the countess, finding in the shape-shifting clouds a soaring bird, a grouping of sheep, a rowboat, and several pies. Idling there, I began to wonder if I might find a way to bring this skyscape into being through embroidery. The next thing I knew, I was sketching possible designs. When footsteps sounded in the hall, I hid my drawings and assumed a look of attention.

Instead of the countess, another girl stepped into the armor-lined hall. She was thin and small-boned with coppery hair light as a chick's, which framed a pale, freckled face. In this high-ceilinged room, surrounded by the polished armor and the stag's head, she seemed especially small, creating the initial impression she must be little more than a child.

Only when she came closer did I realize there was nothing childlike about her sharp expression, her high brow softened only by startlingly blue eyes, which put me in mind of the plentiful Cumberland cornflowers that bloomed until midsummer.

"You're new here, then?" she asked.

"Yes, I'm Miranda Molyneux." I noted the fine weave of her gray gown with its plain white collar, her only adornment a silver cross worn around her waist. "And you?"

"Anne," she said, and curtsied. "Anne Goodacre."

"Have you been away?" I asked, noting that in addition to the cross, she carried what looked like a book of prayers in her hands.

"My health required the countess to send me to stay at the doctor's residence. It's a half day's journey from here. I'm of a very delicate constitution, you see."

The sapphire blue veins that floated just beneath her fair skin, and the sharp protrusion of the bones at her wrist were proof enough of this.

"But the countess said nothing—"

A seam appeared in the center of Anne's forehead. "I was gravely ill. Had I not recovered, what good would news of me have been to you then?"

"What ailed you?" I asked, marveling at the dramatic nature of her reply.

"Dizziness." Anne looked down at the floor. "And a very high fever."

"Ague?" I asked, unable to hide my fear.

"No, thankfully I have been spared that. Still, the doctor bled me the first ten days. How relieved I was when he allowed me Eliza's care."

I wondered why neither Eliza nor her mother had

mentioned Anne. Had the countess told them not to? "What did Eliza prescribe?"

"Claret wine for the fever, and a warm poultice containing frankincense and nutmeg to help with the chills. Though I lay in a bed far from my own"—she closed her eyes—"I felt as if I were being cradled in Jesus's arms."

"What are you reading?" I asked, gesturing toward her gold-leafed book.

"The Monument of Matrons," Anne said eagerly. "Do you know it?"

I shook my head.

"Well, you must. It's a book of prayers for any stage in a woman's life. Without its guidance . . . I fear I might be lost."

"Are there others?" I asked Anne now.

Anne looked at me as if she did not understand.

"Other girls?"

"Oh," she said. "There was Priscilla, but she left to be married in late November."

"I stayed back a few minutes so that you could meet each other." The countess entered so silently, both Anne and I startled as the orange clove fragrance filled the air.

"Good morning," we said together.

"Yes, it is a fine morning."

The countess's gold-flecked eyes scanned my features before she turned to Anne. "I trust you have given thanks to God for your return to health, my dear."

"I have," Anne replied, lowering her gaze.

The countess laid a hand on Anne's shoulder. "It may profit you, Miranda, to have Anne as your companion. Although she has been with me for only seven months, with diligent study and absolute faith, she has made remarkable progress. Is this not true, Anne?"

"I am grateful to hear you say so, Countess," Anne said, and began to twist the fabric of her gown.

"I speak only the truth, my dear." The countess began to stroke Anne's hair, and as her long fingers combed her locks, Anne seemed not to move.

From the deep pockets of her gown, the countess retrieved a filmy sheet of paper worn with time and handling. "Before her illness, Anne and I were discussing a letter of counsel my own mother wrote to me just before I married the earl. Anne is well versed in its contents. I thought it fit for you to hear, too, Miranda.

" 'My good daughter,' " the countess read, " 'thou art now going into the world and must leave being a child. As you learn to be a wife and mother, I pray you find the strength and the wisdom to put into practice all I have taught you during the last eighteen years. . . .' "

I tried to listen, but my attention kept straying back to Anne, who was muttering something I could not quite make out; though it was clear, from her furrowed brow, she was concentrating very hard.

"'In all things,'" the countess continued, "'remember you must obey your husband's wishes and serve him. As Saint Paul says, the husband is always head to the woman's body. . . .'"

Recalling the way my mother had taken Laura aside on the eve of her marriage, wrapping her arms around my sister and speaking to her gently of the wedding night and the courage she would need to build her life so far from the home she had always known, I waited for the countess's mother to give her own daughter some advice, or at least some story to hold on to.

What did it mean to find no such tenderness in a letter centered on the eve of a daughter's life-changing event of marriage, I wondered, drawn once more to the window, through which a weak sun now shone.

After the countess had us copy out her mother's letter, believing it would profit both our penmanship and our constitutions, she dismissed us. How much will it took for me not to run out of the chamber room and seek the quiet of the parlor.

Anne followed at a slower pace.

"Good to see you've met." Emily placed the tea and savory pottage on a small trestle table beside the hearth while Anne and I settled into our chairs, which, although not exactly comfortable, offered a break from the chamber room's hard jointed stools.

"At last." I tried to catch Emily's eyes. "And all this time, I thought I was the only one."

Emily just clucked her tongue.

"Do you not find it strange the countess said nothing to me of your presence here?" I asked Anne, once Emily had gone.

"Not terribly. You have been at Turbury just long enough to notice the countess does not devote much time to thinking about people. She always considers her responsibilities and takes them very seriously. But people—"

"Come after their duties," I finished, and Annie nodded. "What brought you here?" I found the courage to ask.

For a moment she seemed to hesitate, but then from one of the pockets of her gown she drew forth a small purse of black velvet onto which a silver cross and the initials GG had been embroidered. "My mother's death," she told me.

"I'm sorry." I touched her hand. "You must miss her a great deal."

"Every day. Inside"—she opened the purse and held out a necklace of polished gold—"I keep my mother's cross so I can have her with me always."

"Perhaps we might work at something together," I said hopefully. "I must show you the coverlet I'm embroidering in my room—"

Anne frowned, and her pale face seemed to close. "Embroidery should be reserved for the glory of God, or the sacred remembrance of a person," she said. "While I worked at my mother's cross, I prayed for her."

February 19, 1580
Dearest Miranda,

The queen has seen fit to grant me only seventy-five pounds per annum, a sum I will have to struggle to survive upon. At least she has forgiven half your father's debt. Poor Robert must still shoulder a heavy burden. But to forgive this much—as Lord Grey assures me—is significant. And then he has convinced the queen to allow us to continue to profit from the sale of our harvest until Robert comes of age. This will enable your brother to complete his education without incurring further debts. Remind Robert of this when you write to him. I fear he will not take the news well, especially now that Caroline's parents have ended the engagement.

Truly, Miranda, I do not know what I would do were it not for Lord Grey. He is as true a friend as your father could have wished for, and we are all in his debt.

With love,
Mother

How could my mother be so certain we were in Lord Grey's debt? What did it matter he was so intimate with the queen and her chief councilors when his actions did nothing to restore me to Plowden Hall, nothing to enable Robert to marry Caroline?

CHAPTER FIVE

March and early April 1580

"W E HAVE NOW ENTERED THE SEASON OF Lent," the countess explained, joining Anne and me in one of the drafty sitting rooms where we sat sipping an infusion of rue. The fabled herb of repentance possessed cheery yellow flowers but also an unfortunate smell I could liken only to that of tomcats.

And before us, instead of Emily's delicious scones or one of her comforting pottages, a plain pewter plate held only bread and a saucer of bitter jelly made from the rowan berries upon which the migratory thrushes fed.

"It is the custom of my family to make simple clothes for the poor living near Turbury," the countess told us once we had finished this penitent reprieve of bread and jelly, one that we would have to endure until Easter. "A custom the young women in my care have always carried out."

"We're to use this fabric?" I asked, scrutinizing a bolt of coarse hemp lockram, its ashy color a symbol of patience in adversity, and a fabric so rough it required patience when one worked with it.

The countess's sharp gaze fixed me with disapproval. "Remember, Miranda, these clothes are not intended for a fancy ball. The people for whom we will sew are used to sturdy wear meant for hard work and changeable weather."

What would the recipients do, and how would they handle their labors were we to gift them with gaily colored shirts of Holland linen and hose of Kendall wool? The question took shape in my mind, though I dared not ask it.

<hr />

Not until Emily stepped into the room to stoke a waning fire did the countess look up from her needle. "That won't be necessary," she said, her gaze lingering on Emily's kirtle, which I had trimmed with rosebuds, the merry pink stitches glinting in the firelight.

"But it's so cold," Emily said, noting the blanket Anne, who always chose the seat farthest from the fire, had wrapped about her legs.

"We are almost finished. Best conserve the wood for the morrow."

Anne and I folded up our sewing and placed fabric, needle, and thread into the wicker baskets at our sides.

I was about to leave when the countess placed a cool but firm hand on my shoulder. "Stay a moment, please."

Anne looked back at me just once before closing the door noiselessly behind her.

"Have I done something wrong?" I asked.

"As I said on the night you arrived, life here is governed by self-discipline and simplicity." The countess paused to tamp the last embers in the grate. "That philosophy extends to everyone. While you are in my care, I require you to honor this. In my view, simple clothing is a reflection of a godly disposition."

"Emily's kirtle—"

"Among other things," the countess said. "Your mother was both a beauty and a court lady during Elizabeth's rather indulgent first year as queen. Such a precedent inevitably requires me to make some allowance for your upbringing."

I knew then the countess had heard something about the coverlet—perhaps she had even come into my room when I was not there. I almost shuddered at the idea of her long-fingered hands ranging among my things.

I longed to ask her what harm could possibly come from the touch of brightness my stitches brought to Emily's life. It was not a great thing, but I believed it made her work lighter.

"Do we understand each other?" the countess said.

"We do," I said, eager to return to my room, where the promise of a letter from my mother waited.

⋅⟞✳⟝⋅

Inside I lit a fire in the hearth, illuminating the stitches of my coverlet so that my garden glowed. Though my eyes strayed to the dove gray envelope addressed in my mother's hand, tonight I prolonged my anticipation, pouring cold water into the basin and washing my face and throat, my hands and arms.

Afterward, traces of dirt seemed to cling to my skin, the residue of the close rooms. I would have to ask Emily to bring me the wooden bathtub soon. How I hated that tub, for despite the cotton cloth with which I lined it, the tub's splinters pricked the skin. The last time I'd bathed, I'd spent more than an hour trying to get them out.

I retrieved the pink satin gown and stood for a few moments holding it up to myself, practicing the dance steps I recalled, as the words of my mother's stories—like a stream of golden butterflies alighting from blossom to blossom—fluttered through my mind. I pictured myself partaking of supper at court, the other lords and ladies pausing to praise the pillows I had embroidered for one of the palace rooms, or asking me to join them for a turn about the garden or a walk along the Thames. How I needed these stories and these images tonight, I realized, my fingertips tracing the embroidery as I sat down on my straw mattress.

March 5, 1580
Dearest Miranda,

On Sunday, the Willoughbys publicly announced their daughter's engagement to Colin Eyre. Although Caroline managed to accept the many congratulations with a measure of grace, her family's housekeeper told Kate the poor girl has been crying herself to sleep each night. Her tears will do her no good. I have seen enough of the ways of the world to be certain of this.

Your brother is, as you can imagine, in extremely poor spirits. The two of you have always been so close that I ask you to write to him.

I continue to think of you every day and love you deeply,
Mother

⟽⟐⟾

March 21, 1580
Dear Robert,

How fortune has changed for all of us since

Christmastime. Of my life here, let me say only that Turbury is nothing like Plowden Hall, where education always proved vibrant, and visitors were as many as they were unexpected. What makes the place bearable is the companionship of two others. Anne is possessed of a few unusual habits—at mealtimes, for example, she eats very little and seems to have an aversion to meat. And then there is her incessant devotion to prayer. Piety is, of course, admirable. But as Father said of his friend who kept such an exact record of his finances, any behavior—when taken to an extreme—can prove dangerous. I pity as well as empathize with Anne, who remains deeply aggrieved by the loss of her mother, and her father's hasty remarriage.

My other friend, someone without whom I could not imagine my life here, is the housekeeper's daughter, Eliza, who hopes to practice medicine. When time allows, I help her to study cures, for despite her natural intelligence, she has little skill at reading. I know you would remind me of the inappropriateness of such a relation, but I have come to see that Eliza is an exceptional person.

A knock at the door interrupted my writing, and Emily entered with my breakfast tray, the golden flowers I had sewn on her skirts no longer visible.

"What's this now, miss?" she said, noticing my letter. "Pardon my saying, but it's no time for writing.

The countess expects you in the kitchen. Do make haste."

⟶※⟵

"You are late, Miranda," the countess said when I found her and Anne already standing at the table, where a dozen skinned peahens had been laid.

"I was writing to my brother. I seemed to forget the time—"

"I wish you would learn to be more considerate of others. The daylight hours are precious, and as you know, I have a great deal to do."

"I'm sorry," I said.

"Very well, let us waste no more time." The countess pointed to the plucked bodies of the hens. "As mistresses of your future husbands' households, you will need to learn how to keep poultry and other game fresh and sweet a long time. To make the flesh go farther, a skill all good husbands will admire, cover it with a mixture of flour and bran."

Each time the countess dipped the meat in the bowl of meal, Anne began to fidget, and beneath her breath I once more heard her murmur the by now familiar words of prayer.

"*Thy mercies Lord I crave. Of Thy strength I feel bereft . . .*"

"Afterward," the countess continued, "add coriander seed and vinegar for freshness."

When the countess sprinkled the hen with the pungent mixture, Anne brought her hand to her mouth.

"Bring me the salve of Your Son, Jesus Christ, for it is only Christ who is to me life . . ."

"How pale you are, Anne," the countess said. "Are you in danger of fainting? We wouldn't want a repeat of that last shameful incident."

"No." Anne's fingers tugged at the edges of her apron.

"What is the matter, then?" Impatience flickered in the countess's voice.

"The hens," she stammered. "I feel unwell."

"My dear Anne," the countess said, and smiled, "I am beginning to think I have done wrong in indulging you. What would your husband say if he asked you to prepare peahens for supper, and you would not do it?"

"Perhaps," I volunteered, remembering how little if any meat Anne took at meals, as well as how intimately her tendency to collapse was linked to eating, "Anne would do better preparing a vegetable pie."

The countess considered this for a moment. "Is meat not one of God's gifts?"

"Yes, ma'am," Anne replied.

"Should we not be grateful for it rather than turning away as if we would place ourselves above God's gifts?"

"That was not my intention."

"No?" The countess looked as if she didn't believe her.

"Many of the great mystics did not take meat," Anne said, her voice a bit stronger now.

"True," the countess said. "But were the mystics married?"

Anne shook her head.

"You see, then,"—the countess smiled thinly—"your father sent me to prepare you for marriage and not for the cloister. I needn't remind you that no good husband will be obliged to humor and indulge you as I have."

Although Anne could not bring herself to handle the hens, she did help seal up the deep crockery pot with herbs, flour, and a small allowance of butter.

Soon Emily entered from outdoors, a basket of apples in her arms. "Are the hens ready for the stove, then?"

"Yes, Emily, thank you," the countess said, her expression taking on a luster I had not seen before. "The earl will return tomorrow," she told us. "Peahen is among the dishes he likes best."

<hr>

Although custom required me to dress with the respect due the earl both as my father's relative and as a nobleman, I could not bring myself to wear the dress I had made for

Christmas, not when the silver-gilt threads I had so lovingly used to create a cascade of snowflakes were likely to bring only frowns. As for the pale pink satin with its whimsical embroidery, it belonged to a different world.

In the end I chose my second-best dress of lightweight wool, its color just a shade lighter than summer's blackberries. It was the newest of my gowns, my mother and I having sewn it only once the decision to come to Turbury had been made. Despite its good fit, its somber color brought me no happiness, and I could not resist winding my grandmother's amethyst pendant around my neck.

Minutes later, I approached the great hall.

After so long a parting, I would have expected husband and wife to sit close together, as my parents had been wont to do even after a short time apart. But the countess stood near the window, and the earl sat facing the hearth. It was their distance from each other that enabled me to catch hold of the following words: ". . . the rich young Seagrave . . . make haste . . . the bustle of the court . . ."

I could not say why, not having a sense of what they were speaking of, but their conversation troubled me more than a little.

"Ah, here at last is Miranda," the countess said, spying me just before I stepped into the room.

The earl stood and faced me. Like his wife, he was tall; his narrow features even and without flaw; his reddish

71

beard neatly trimmed. But some quality about his wide, full-lipped mouth disturbed me, as if it did not belong on such a lean face. Like the countess, he favored black, though his riding hose, sewn from wine-colored leather, were adorned with his initials. Had the countess placed them there?

"I feared you'd be a reedy creature like Anne. Good to see a young woman with meat on her bones. And then"— he bowed—"you do have your mother's look."

I curtsied, unsure of how to respond.

The earl had drunk two glasses of wine before Anne entered dressed in a high-necked gown of black frieze, her silver cross shining at her waist.

"You are looking better, Anne," he said. "Still, I see I must continue to wait for the heather to bloom in your cheeks."

We gathered around a table that, though simply laid, was set with a finer set of china than I had seen previously.

"You will be sixteen in a matter of days," the earl said to me. "Has the countess spoken to you of our plans?"

I looked from the earl to the countess, though hers was a closed face. "No, sir."

"Prudence," he said, "you should have told Miranda of our intention to take her to court after her birthday, weather permitting such a journey."

"You forget, husband," the countess said, coloring, "the invitation from court was not extended until very recently."

"Is Anne not to go to court also?" I asked, aware that Anne had not looked up throughout the meal.

"Not yet," the earl said.

Anne said nothing, although her gaze briefly met my own, her look that of someone used to saying many good-byes.

"Lord Grey's path and my own crossed while I was in London," the earl said as Emily carried in the peahens. "He told me of his recent visit to Plowden Hall, the assistance he was providing to your mother."

I started. "You know him?"

"It would be impossible not to when he is such a highly respected figure at court. Cecil says he might even be appointed to the Star Chamber."

"Lord Grey is among the queen's favorites," the countess added with grim reserve. "I wonder if Her Majesty will look well on the solicitude he has shown to your cousin's widow."

"As usual, you are right, my dear," the earl said, and raised his goblet as if to toast her. "In middle age, our good queen is known for her jealousy as much as for her virtue."

⸺❊⸺

It rained briefly after dawn, but by midmorning the sun was out, and the sky a vivid shade of blue. Because the earl's return had enabled a rare reprieve from studies, I lingered in bed, tracing the embroidery along my coverlet as I thought over the news of the previous day.

I pictured myself entering a grand room at Whitehall. Here at last was the chance to go to court. The opportunity sent shivers of excitement coursing through me, even though I would lose the company of Eliza.

And then there would inevitably be a suitor. What influence would the countess have? And how would I fit into the life at court?

"Not only are the ladies at court, from the very young to the very old, cliquish, but they *talk*," Mother often said.

Inevitably, they would *talk* about me. The question was: would they eventually accept me, as well?

Downstairs, Anne sat before the sitting room fire, but not even the fine, crisp air could tempt her away from her books. "I'm sorry, Miranda, but the earl brought me *The Prayers of Katherine Parr.*"

"Very well," I said, unable to imagine keeping still on such a morning.

❖

How long I walked before I came upon a pair of ponies grazing on a rocky hillside, I do not know, so lost in the rhythm did I become as my feet carried me farther away from Turbury.

Just as Eliza said, the ponies were hardy creatures with thick, shaggy coats meant to withstand the roughest sort of weather. These two were honey-colored, and in the sun their manes had taken on a quiet sheen akin to beaten gold. They stood close together in the treeless landscape, occasionally raising their heads to look my way, regarding me with what seemed neither interest nor fear.

Once I would have found their presence further proof of Yorkshire's desolation, where the only sounds were that of the wind rustling the grass, and my own hurried breathing.

Now, as they continued to graze, occasionally nuzzling their faces against each other, their loneliness in this place became a kind of intimate solitude. Watching them, I found myself feeling almost hopeful, believing—in spite of all that had happened and the uncertainty that lay ahead—I, too, might one day find someone with whom I could feel so at peace.

But was that person likely to be the man the earl and countess had in mind for me? With this question, my trepidation returned, and I no longer saw the ponies' sturdiness, but rather a stubborn endurance—the kind I would need to emulate the wifely obedience and humility the countess encouraged.

⋯⋰❉⋱⋯

By the time I returned to Turbury, it was after supper, and my stomach was rumbling. I expected the countess to scold me. Instead, all was still. Not even Burr slunk along a shadowed wall or watched from beneath the looming armoire. Determined not to draw attention to myself, after fixing myself a meal of bread and cheese in the kitchen, I climbed the staircase to my room.

There on the bed I found a package and a letter in my mother's hand.

March 19, 1580

Dearest Miranda,

> *By the time my words reach you, you will be preparing for your sixteenth birthday. How I wish we could celebrate your coming-of-age together. Please know I shall at least be with you in spirit. In addition to these birthday wishes, I send a package.*

> *So too, dearest, I write to tell you Lord Grey has asked me to be his wife. After careful deliberation and prayer, I have accepted him. I had hoped to visit you and talk all of these matters over in person, but the necessary haste of my marriage coupled with the difficulties of travel—well, my*

daughter, both of these make a visit impossible right now.

At the month's end I will begin making preparations for my departure for Wingfield Park. Kate and her husband will stay on at Plowden Hall, the estate remaining under Lord Grey's discretion and my own until Robert is of age.

I think of you every day and love you deeply,
Your Mother

"Is there some trouble?" Eliza said, gesturing to the letter when she stepped into the room with a tray that held the makings for tea.

"It's my mother," I said, wiping my tears. "She is marrying again."

"But you told us of your mother's circumstances." Her gaze strayed to the untouched package. "Perhaps her difficulties are greater than you believed. Necessity—"

"Can be a hard master." I swallowed hard. "Yes, I know. Still, custom requires a mourning period of six months at least."

Eliza tried to say something more, but I did not hear her, the image of Lord Grey taking shape, with his salt-and-pepper beard and clear eyes, the morning he gave us the news. Was it possible he'd thought of marrying my mother even then?

"Your birthday present," Eliza said, and nudged the package toward me.

"How did you know—?"

"The earl told me to bring it to you. He carried it back with him from court."

I pictured Lord Grey handling the package—and the letter—and shook my head.

"Please," Eliza said, her voice suddenly small.

I faced her, her gray eyes full of anticipation, and wondered if anyone had ever sent her a package. "Very well."

Beneath the brown paper I found the jacket I'd begun embroidering in November. My mother had finished it; her work, as always, was exceptional. In her nimble hands, the satin stitch had been made to create a variety of shapes, including the damson plums and spanish oranges of which we were both so fond. The bullion stitch brought forth star-shaped flowers with yellow hearts, and her clever use of the crewel stitch and coral knot had fashioned a wicker basket overflowing with the most delicate of violets.

"It's beautiful," Eliza said. "I believe I recognize the leafy vervain, yes?"

I nodded, too dispirited to tell her that my mother also used this plant in a tisane for nervousness.

"And these tiny yellow flowers. Are they the same buttercups we have in Yorkshire?"

I nodded. "Since you are familiar with so many of these

plants," I said, the breath catching in my throat, "you may have the jacket."

Eliza stared as I tried to place it in her arms.

"Go on, then," I said. "Remember, you once told me yellow was your favorite color."

"But this is your mother's work," Eliza said.

"I do not want it," I said, looking down at my hands.

"You will not always feel so."

"Won't I?" I said, a little ashamed at the sharpness in my voice.

"No. Besides," she said, touching the fabric, "I'm not pretty enough to wear this."

"You seem to forget what we talked about once."

Eliza frowned. "Hmm?"

"A thing of beauty—whether plant or dress—can have a curative effect."

❦

Having accepted the jacket at last, Eliza had gone. I lay down on my bed, still wearing the clothes in which I had ranged across the moors, the scents of heather and thyme lingering in the fabric. Again my thoughts strayed to the ponies on the moors. Did they sleep out in the open, or had they found shelter beneath one of the rare groupings of trees?

A surprisingly gentle breeze entered through the open window, and as the moon rose in the sky, the stars glimmered as if they were within my reach, something my father had encouraged me to believe on those nights when I was afraid, a belief I had clung to while still a child—and after.

Soon, my mother would be Lord Grey's wife. She would leave Plowden Hall for her husband's house. Wingfield Park, it was called, said to be one of the grandest estates in all of England. I could not picture her in another landscape, much less another house. Always, when I thought of Cumberland and home, my mother's image came to mind—the last time she stood in the doorway and waved me off—how could I have imagined then she would not always be there?

Stung by her betrayal, I knew I would not write to her of my journey to court. I would share with her neither my hopes nor my fears. Why should I when the woman who was marrying Lord Grey, so soon after my father's death, was not the same woman who had told me of the evening she and my father lingered beside the Thames, the pink satin of her gown softening the blush with which she must have accepted his promise of enduring faithfulness and love.

Even so, before I climbed beneath the blankets, I retrieved that same gown and placed it on the chair near my bed, as if its presence—and the stories secreted in its satiny folds—could somehow sweeten my dreams.

PART TWO

Court

CHAPTER SIX

April 8–20, 1580

For the journey to London, the countess hired a coach, which, at the cost of ten shillings a day, proved the cheapest way to travel—at least this was the conclusion I came to, given the way we were jolted and jarred throughout the journey, a sudden turn or bump sending me colliding into the countess.

We spoke little. The daylight hours, the countess passed knitting: gloves, a shawl, a pair of stockings. Or she wrote in a small black journal, which she perched on her sharp knees. "A diary?" I asked, wondering what dreams and hopes it contained (beyond religious salvation), what griefs (the death of her brother?), as well as what disappointments (the difficulties of raising other people's daughters, with whom she had so little in common).

83

"A record," the countess said, thereby ending the conversation.

With the countess as my sole companion, I had little reprieve from my growing nervousness about Whitehall. Yes, I would at last have the opportunity to dance a galliard, stroll the fantastically landscaped grounds, and possibly even partake of one of the queen's famous tournaments. But I would also have my prospective suitor to face, not to mention the daunting task of deciphering and following a code of behavior as intricate as one of the queen's most fantastic gowns. At court, my father told me once, a man could be sent to the Tower for praising the former queen, a fervent Catholic as well as Elizabeth's half sister.

The elaborate code of behavior was one thing. More unpredictable were the queen's caprices. According to my mother, Elizabeth actually dismissed one of her ladies after she failed to remember the queen's favorite dish at supper two days in a row. Another had been made to cover up not just her shoulders, but even her neck after she attracted the attention of one of Elizabeth's favorite courtiers. "And this was during the height of summer, Miranda," my mother stressed. "The temperature so fierce, one could have poached an egg in the golden fountain."

For the first time I consoled myself with the fact that my mother's beauty had been passed down to me in diminished form.

But what about the news of my mother's marriage?

Pursued by such thoughts, I tried to place my faith in my father's belief that one's anticipation is almost always greater than one's reality in good situations as well as bad. It therefore came as a relief when at last the coachman took a sharp turn, and we found ourselves bumped over a noisy road and into London.

Nervousness aside, that morning the Thames sparkled so in the sunlight, I understood why the poets spoke of its waters as liquid crystal. And on the far side of the river there emerged gardens bearing fruit trees and shrubberies, as well as flowers. All was a welcome feast of color along the sloping shore, my pleasure trebled by the difference from Turbury.

"I never enjoy my visits here, London being the most overcrowded and unsanitary place in England," the countess said as we crossed London Bridge, an enormous structure built on twenty arches.

"But the houses are so handsome and well built," I said, admiring the brightly painted shutters and cleanly swept walkways.

"London Bridge is the home of the city's wealthier merchants and haberdashers. Wait until we reach the narrow roads. There you will scarce be able to see, so darkened are the passageways by the overhanging house-fronts. You will understand what I mean then." Already, the countess's hand was at the pomander, whose fragrance had grown stronger in the coach's close quarters.

I, too, covered my mouth and nose as we entered the city's dense network of poorly paved roads, the garbage piled high outside many a door.

After Turbury, I could not deny my interest in the barrage of sights and sounds, even if not all of them were pleasant. Because it was early morning when we arrived, all along the streets, merchants and their apprentices were taking down shutters and opening storefronts. Their gaily painted signs bore exotic names like The Angel, The Parrot, The Mermaid, The Blazing Star.

And everywhere, a mélange of voices announced their wares. "Fine Seville oranges, fine lemons," one woman called, her dress almost as bright as the fruits piled high in the baskets surrounding her.

"Sweep, chimney sweep, mistress, from the bottom to the top. Then shall no soot fall in your porridge pot," a dusty young man cried, his song soon drowned out by the unexpectedly loud voice of a girl shouting, "Hot apple pies, hot oatcakes, fresh herrings!"

From one of the houses pealed the notes of a viola da gamba.

From another, a deep baritone asked, "What do you lack, m'lady?"

A gaily laughing voice answered, "What do I not— pins, points, garters, gloves, ribbons."

We reached St. Paul's, and I recalled my father telling me there had once been a steeple, lost to lightning some twenty years before. Confronted by the cathedral's grandeur, my own hopes and fears seemed suddenly very small, and the realization that I was just one person in a city with centuries of history became a comfort to me.

I reached out to ask the countess if we might stop and look inside. But she was frowning at a pair of lovers strolling past a row of booksellers, hands entwined, heads close together.

The ruined towers of Westminster Palace came into view, and then Westminster Abbey, and I remembered the story my mother once told me about Elizabeth's coronation ceremony: "Hundreds of torches and candles illumined the abbey walls. The tapestries modeled after Raphael glowed as if they'd come to life. I may not share your father's passion for drawing, Miranda, but I understood then what it meant to pour one's soul into one's creation. . . ."

The coach turned sharply into a narrow lane, sending a group of men on foot scurrying into the doorway of a house, from where they stood and cursed us.

"Filthy band of ruffians," the countess said.

Although their language was foul, I could not entirely blame them, not when our driver was at best reckless and at worst mean-spirited in the way he took the London streets, splashing those in his path with mud, and almost never yielding to another coach or cart.

The city had become so great that the twisting old roads could not accommodate the traffic. "The great families travel only by the Thames," the countess explained. So it was not until noon that the carriage careened up the drive leading to Whitehall, leaving a cloud of dust in its path.

I had heard a great deal about the curiosities housed at Elizabeth's favorite London residence: a unicorn's horn, a bathroom reserved for her that actually piped water in from out-of-doors, a secret room tiled entirely from lapis lazuli. I wanted especially to see the surviving thirteenth-century murals, as well as Holbein's renowned painting of the Tudor monarchs, which Henry VIII had commissioned after the much-awaited birth of his only son, Edward; a painting in which neither one of his daughters was depicted, though both Mary and Elizabeth succeeded their half brother.

And then there was the queen's legendary wardrobe, one my mother told me contained more than three thousand gowns of the finest silk, velvet, satin, taffeta, as well as the exceedingly dear cloths of silver and gold. While serving as one of the queen's ladies-in-waiting, my mother had, on more than one occasion, been entrusted with the care of many of these gowns. Years later she could still recall the sumptuous fabrics encrusted with gems and pearls and further lavished with embroidery or intricate steam-patterning. And then there were the new shoes presented to the queen each week, a luxury I could not possibly imagine.

"Two thousand rooms," the countess said as we stepped down from the coach unaided by our driver, who busied himself with tossing our belongings from the coach's roof to the dusty ground.

Confronted with an almost endless network of buildings, the stone so white it shone in the sun, I understood why my mother spoke of Whitehall as the greatest palace in all England.

"Come, Miranda," the countess said as a handsome servant in green-and-white livery bowed dramatically before escorting us inside. Here, trompe l'oeil visions of exotic birds and flowers covered walls gilded with gold, and silver-topped tables bore vases filled with hundreds of narcissus, their sweet fragrance filling the April air, the windows behind them hung with draperies of Indian painted silk.

Although the countess considered my russet gown too showy, telling me I should have worn the blackberry wool instead, I felt as drab as a winter sparrow. Yet another liveried servant led us through a series of rooms hung with tapestries of the four seasons, each of which was represented by a maiden. How I would have liked to study each one, but the servant's pace—and the countess's—told me there was no time.

"The young lady will sleep in the Maidens' Chamber," the servant said, once we paused outside a door that opened onto a light-filled dormitory lined with rows of white beds that, from this distance at least, looked to be as soft as my bed at home, and not filled with Turbury's scratchy straw.

"Where is the Mother of the Maids?" the countess asked, speaking to an imposing man with hawklike features in a more polite tone than I'd ever heard her use at Turbury.

From a sunny corner, a voice called out, "My dear Prudence, here you are at last."

A short, plump woman came toward us, her features obscured by the midday sun, the farthingale beneath her billowing skirts giving her the impression of a very sturdy ship sailing toward us across tranquil seas.

"I am Lady Periwinkle," she continued, catching my smile. "How tall you are. Just like your father. And yet, with such a crown of glossy auburn hair, you could only be Miranda Molyneux, the Countess of Plowden's younger daughter. Why, were we to set back the date some twenty-five years, I would easily believe it was your mother standing before me."

I bowed my head and curtsied.

"How vivid a green your eyes are," Lady Periwinkle

gushed. "And such skin. Like a nymph in a painting by one of the Florentine masters!"

"Really, Lucy," the countess said, "is such a comparison fitting?"

Lady Periwinkle just giggled, and her eyes—the very color of the flower that shared her name—turned up at the corners. "Still so stern, I see! Ah well, I suppose I should be chastened for my romantic heart. But then this is Dorothy Molyneux's daughter."

The countess gave her pomander a furious little twitch, but Lady Periwinkle seemed to take no notice. "Much as I love and admire our good queen," she continued, sneezing at the scent, "I can never understand why she doesn't invite your mother back to court. Ah well, who am I to question the ways of royalty?

"Besides, I always appreciate the chance to see you, Prudence. At times"—her face turned wistful—"our own youth seems as close as yesterday, does it not?"

"To me," the countess said in a more controlled voice, "that time seems long passed."

"You always were a realist." Lady Periwinkle began smoothing out her skirts with her plump little hands. "Perhaps that is why you captured the earl's heart. Such a man might have run to ruin had he kept his word and married a creature like me."

I was eager to hear more, but then another servant

carried in my trunk, and the countess said, "For the duration of your stay, although you and I will meet regularly, I entrust you to Lady Periwinkle's care. Should you require anything, you're to ask for her assistance. Is that understood?"

"It is," I replied, curtsying more deeply than I was wont to do, as Lady Periwinkle looked on approvingly.

After the countess left, her orange-spice fragrance the only sign she had been there, I stood gaping for a few moments, almost unable to believe my good fortune.

"Come along, dear," Lady Periwinkle said, enfolding my hand in her own. "I know you'll miss Prudence, but not to worry—I will take very good care of you."

She sailed down the aisle of the dormitory, her farthingale swaying from side to side, and spoke to me of the other girls in her care, while pointing out their respective places. "Shy Jane Radcliffe has the bed beside the window, though she's caught cold so many times I'll have to move her.

"Boisterous Bridget Seaton sleeps here. Had anyone told me her serious mother would give birth to such an adventurous girl, I would never have believed it. I find myself forever having to remind the dear girl to ride sidesaddle, and then she is always trying to engage some courtier to take her out to shoot. The groundskeepers often complain of the stray arrows they find in the shrubberies.

"And yet"—Lady Periwinkle paused and fixed me with her small blue eyes—"my intuition tells me you will best get along with Arbella Merriweather or Agnes Somerset. You strike me as a country girl—no airs, no urbanity, no artifice whatsoever. Am I correct?"

"You are," I said. "This is my first visit to London."

"The countess wrote to me of your skill at sewing and embroidery," she continued after pointing out some empty drawers in the wardrobe, as well as a nook where I could keep my toiletries. "With your mother as your teacher, your fingers must be nimble. The other young women in my care are already at work on the gowns to be worn in next month's tournament. Such a grand event—I do believe it will cheer you."

"Would you tell me more about the gowns?" I asked eagerly. After all, if Lady Periwinkle recognized my gifts, she might just ask me to try my hand at repairing one of the queen's gowns, the care of which her ladies supervised.

"What about them, dear?" Lady Periwinkle said, clearing out a bit more space for my books.

"Are they in the contemporary style?"

"No, no, we decided on gowns reflective of Edward IV's reign, so many of the maidens being partial to the tight-fitting bodices and high waists. And," she added, patting her own expansive belly, "the fuller skirts are so forgiving."

"Will the headdresses also be in this style?" I asked, recollecting my great-great-grandmother's miniature of

Edward IV's beautiful queen consort, Elizabeth Woodville. "They were so dramatic."

"Yes, ours will be heart-shaped with the gauziest of veils. You do know your fashion.

"Oh dear, how thoughtless of me." She laid a warm hand on my arm. "Here I have been rambling on about clothing without a thought to your grief. Your dear father—how sorry I am. Such a courageous man, and such an adventurous spirit. Even after his youth, he remained one of the very few who still carried about him an air of romance."

"Thank you, Lady Periwinkle," I said, assured of her sincerity.

⤙※⤚

I unpacked my things, then sat down on a deliciously soft feather bed close beside a floor-length window overlooking a bustling courtyard thoroughfare below. From there I surveyed the dormitory's neat rows of some twenty beds, almost all of which seemed to have an occupant, given the profusion of toiletries and other homely possessions scattered throughout the space.

Would the other maidens accept me? I recalled Laura's story of Amelia Goodheart, whose name camouflaged a wicked temper. Toward the beginning of my sister's stay at court, this Amelia, who had taken an instant dislike to Laura for no apparent reason, had tried to sabotage her singing at an intimate performance presented to the queen's circle. "Fortunately for me," Laura said, "Amelia was caught stealing in the royal apothecary."

Before my fears could get the better of me, I left the dormitory by a far door that led to an interior garden, as Lady Periwinkle instructed. Beyond lay a miniature waterfall surrounded by a pool of golden fish. The courtyard was filled not just with various plants, including one that bore heart-shaped leaves, but with cherry trees, their white blossoms already in full bloom.

This floral emblem for virginity possessed a fragile beauty. As I breathed in their fragrance, I recollected my mother's warnings against the travails that befell too many members of our sex at court. Away from home for the first time, more than a few succumbed to the charms of one or another of the courtiers, a few even daring to go out dressed as men to meet their lovers.

One of my mother's friends, Alice Russell, had become pregnant during Elizabeth's first year on the throne. The young queen, eager to establish the legitimacy of her rule, was so angry, the loss of Alice's virtue inevitably reflecting on her own, that she confined the unhappy lady to Fleet Prison for a fortnight, then forbade her from coming to court for life. "Discretion, Miranda," my mother always advised, "as well as foresight and reason, are a woman's best friends, especially at court."

Lady Periwinkle's instructions floated back.

Unsure of how long I'd lingered, I forsook the garden with its soothing sounds and scent of flowers, and proceeded to the Maidens' Hall, a high-ceilinged room, its windows lined with pale yellow-and-green stained glass, its four tables filled with girls around my own age. Something about the way they sat, perhaps it was the arrangement of so many heads bowed over great pieces of emerald green velvet, struck me the way a work of art might. I sensed pattern here, symmetry.

A dozen pair of eyes looked up at me at once when someone said, "A new face at last."

The voice belonged to a very beautiful girl whose violet eyes and raven hair were set off by the whitest skin I had ever seen. "I am Beatrice Cunnington," the girl said, appraising my hair, my face, the amethyst necklace at my throat. When she reached my dress, her gaze lingered, and I could have sworn the edges of her mouth turned up in a smirk. "And you are?"

"Miranda Molyneux."

A flurry of whispers followed, and I stood nervously scanning the room.

From her place at a far table, Lady Periwinkle looked over at me and smiled. With the raven-haired Beatrice's eyes fixed upon me, I wished there were an open seat near our matron; but every bench was filled, the nine girls at her table all pressed very close together.

I had no choice but to join Beatrice Cunnington's table.

"Good." Beatrice placed a needle and thread before me. "We need another pair of hands."

Here, as at every other table, everyone was sewing the long, tight sleeves, which thankfully were not so extreme as to trail the ground. Instead, they tapered into points along the back of the hand.

Despite the way I smiled and tried to catch more than one girl's eye, they all seemed to look anywhere but at me. When one at last glanced in my direction, she quickly proceeded to look away and whisper something in Beatrice's ear.

My stomach succumbed to knots until a voice beside me said, "What a fortunate time to arrive."

I turned toward a girl dressed all in black, her hair the color of spun flax, her eyes bright as a doe's. "Is it?"

"Yes. We are about to have the most spectacular tournament Whitehall has seen since the queen came to the throne."

I smiled at her, hoping I did not seem too eager. "Why now?" I said, trying my utmost to sound nonchalant.

"It has been an exceptionally good year. And, of course, the French ambassadors are still trying to win her hand on behalf of yet another French duke." She squeezed my hand confidingly. "A spectacular tournament is just the sort of event to distract them from their purpose.

"Oh dear," she said, pricking her finger with the needle. "I'm afraid I have no talent for such work."

"It's easy enough to fix," I said, removing her stitches and beginning again.

"Agnes Somerset," she said, introducing herself. And then in a softer voice, "You mustn't worry. Most of us aren't like Beatrice. Just because she is the grandniece of the Duchess of Suffolk, she believes she's entitled to put on airs.

"Still—" She touched the fabric of my dress.

"Is something wrong?" I asked. "Is it torn?"

"It's nothing like that," Agnes said. "Russet is among the most genteel of colors. The queen is particularly fond of it."

"Oh." I felt the blush rise from my throat to my face. Every other girl, with the exception of the two or three who wore dark blue and seemed to be older than the rest, was dressed in some variation of white or black or gray, the colors of purity, constancy, and patience when worn by the young. How could I have been ignorant of this? "Do most girls make such a mistake?"

"Not too often. Usually, a new girl is well-versed in these things beforehand."

No wonder the countess had urged me to wear the

blackberry wool, though I could not bear to arrive at court in the gown sewn for Turbury.

"Should I go back and change?" I asked as Beatrice and a long-nosed girl stared at us. The girl was dark-haired with olive skin and long-lashed hazel eyes, like Beatrice, but not nearly as beautiful. Where Beatrice was all womanly curves, the other was thin as a jousting lance.

"Not now. Lady Periwinkle will never enforce this rule. She's color-blind, you see," said Agnes.

"How very strange," I replied. How could she have been expected to enforce a rule she could not even see? And what would it feel like to look—especially at the sumptuous world of the court—without being able to discern colors?

"Lady Periwinkle can see greens and blues, but many others—red and yellow, for example—she cannot make out. Every once in a while, one of us"—Agnes's eyes strayed toward Beatrice—"will make a nasty jest of it."

Certain this rule had not been in place during Laura's stay here some eight years ago, I could only conclude the queen had created it so youth could not eclipse her beauty, which, like my mother's own, could not last forever.

❀

Having discovered how apt I proved with the needle, not only Agnes but several others soon asked me to correct their faulty stitches or straighten a crooked hem. To my surprise, very few understood that the fitted sleeve required an allowance of extra fabric of just the right proportion so that the sleeve almost covered the hand.

As I rebasted seam allowances or resnipped a shaggy seam head, many of the faces that had been closed to me began to open. Even Beatrice managed to look at me with a shade more approval, a consequence that loosened the tongues of the other maidens, while troubling her skinny companion, who watched me through narrowed eyes.

Once we were nearly finished, a slight girl with a wealth of curly ginger hair, eyes like amber, and skin so pale it would have been translucent were it not for the freckles, approached me with an armful of cabbage. "Jane Radcliffe," she said quietly, then sneezed some half a dozen times before managing to add: "I'd like to use these remnants in mending my best kirtle. Do you think I have enough?"

"We can try." Although the remnants would not have been enough to refurbish a petticoat for a larger girl, Jane was of so fine a build that the pieces—once they were assembled carefully—actually worked.

"I should have known Prudence would not exaggerate when she said you were clever with the needle," Lady Periwinkle said, once I had chalked out a pattern Jane could follow.

"Thank you." I hoped my smile was enough to convey

to her how satisfying it was to be making real use of my abilities at last.

"You do seem eager to display your talents," the skinny maiden said with sneering civility.

"Don't mind Eleanor," Agnes said. "She suffers from the delusion that only those of us from town are entitled to have any accomplishments, and she does cling to Beatrice so. Jane, on the other hand, is one of the most wellborn maidens here." She touched my arm. "You did right to help her."

"Oh, I had no idea." Though I was obliged to Agnes for softening the powers of this Eleanor, I did not add that, wellborn or no, I would have helped Jane anyway.

Sewing was followed by a simple meal of manchet bread and salad, with a particularly rich and most delicious pudding for dessert, of which I took two servings. Afterward, there were evening prayers in the smaller of the Chapels Royal. As I expected, the queen had removed all icons from the chapel, and the prayer service proceeded according to the reformed plan her father had initiated and her half brother had carried out.

Seated beside me in the pew, Agnes pointed out the Tudor coat of arms above the main door, as well as a carved lion and a dragon. "Symbols that once belonged to Prince Cadwaladr. The lion looks a bit like a big kitty," she said, imitating the lion's grimace so perfectly, I began to laugh. "But the dragon," she went on, "that creature is positively grotesque. Were it not for the link to Uther Pendragon, I could not imagine the queen's grandfather choosing it for his own."

"You seem very comfortable here," I said as we made our way back to the Maidens' Chamber, impressed by Agnes's knowledge as well as grateful for her company, especially since all the other girls walked in pairs or in close-knit groups of three and four, my help with the sewing already forgotten.

"I am fortunate to have a grandmother well-versed in life at court. It is my grandmother who brought me here."

"Who is she?"

"Lady Sherringham, though most everyone who is anyone calls her Sherry."

"A relative of the queen's?"

"Her late governess Kat Ashley's godmother," Agnes said, her tone even friendlier than before.

"Ah." I recalled what my mother had said about that governess's unquestionable loyalty but also her occasional lack of judgment. "So your grandmother knew the queen as a little girl."

"She did." Agnes's voice turned wistful. "During those long ago days at Hatfield when no one expected Elizabeth to become queen, my grandmother paid her many visits; she always brought a present."

"Books?" I asked, missing the library at Plowden Hall.

"Of course," Agnes said. "My grandmother was fortunate enough to have been educated almost as well as her brothers. Still, she did not win Princess Elizabeth's heart through books alone."

"What, then?"

"Sweets." She gave my hand a companionable squeeze. "Once the tournament feasts begin, you'll discover how fond our queen is of tarts, fruit pies, and cakes."

My step lightened a little, so pleased was I to learn the queen and I had this susceptibility in common.

Behind us came the sound of footsteps, and soon a hand snagged me by the skirt.

Beatrice. "I shouldn't have been so standoffish earlier," she said, her gaze not a shade less haughty, though her voice at least seemed less forbidding.

"Apology accepted," I said.

"I wasn't apologizing exactly. Having misheard your family name, I didn't realize our brothers are at university together. Edward Cunnington, one of the expert archers at Trinity. Perhaps your brother—Robert, isn't it?— mentioned him?"

"No," I said, "not insofar as I recall."

For just a moment, the corners of her mouth sank. "Well, it is but a trifle," she said, recomposing herself. "I visited last September, and your brother was gracious enough to show me the grounds. But then so many of my brother's friends competed for my attention, and I was there such a short while, he must have understood he never stood a—"

"Be quick now, ladies!" Lady Periwinkle called, holding open the dormitory door, as, two by two, the other maidens hurried inside.

Agnes seized my hand and tried to urge me on. "I wouldn't trust her," she whispered.

"It's not nice to tell secrets, Agnes," Beatrice said, after stepping on her skirt.

"Who's telling secrets?" Agnes matched Beatrice's cutting tone. "I simply don't want Miranda to squander her time, especially not over such a trifle."

Agnes tried to free her dress, but Beatrice kept her foot firmly planted on the hem.

"Ladies!" Lady Periwinkle clapped her chubby hands.

"Really," I said, afraid one of us would get in trouble, and more than a little afraid someone might get hurt, "shouldn't we join the others?"

Beatrice just laughed. "Old Periwinkle is not fit for her post as jailer. She can barely bring herself to ban even the worst among us from the dessert table, and not once has she assigned anyone the chore of darning stockings when we let a curse word slip, or—"

"If she were," Agnes interrupted, "you'd need spectacles

from squinting over your stitches from afternoon until nightfall."

"You're simply jealous," Beatrice said, regarding Agnes as if she were a troublesome hedgehog.

"Ridiculous," Agnes said, though her cheeks turned the color of a lady apple's blush.

"I think not," Beatrice quipped, "when we both know I am the one Henry Raleigh favors."

Grateful for the waning light, I stooped to fidget with my slipper. *Henry Raleigh here at court?*

But of course—the queen had commanded him to return to England. Was this not the reason why he'd left my father's side in Ireland? How could I have been so naive as to overlook this?

"You look unwell. Are you all right?" Agnes asked, once Beatrice linked arms with Jane, the only one still lingering in the courtyard.

"Miranda?" Agnes asked again.

"I'm just not used to so much activity, that's all."

"Your life with the countess was very quiet, then?"

"Quiet as the grave," I said, forcing a laugh as we stepped inside the dormitory.

CHAPTER SEVEN
April 29 & 30, 1580

"If you're wise," agnes told me as we breakfasted on raisin cake, smoked ham, and ale, the queen's preferred beverage, "you'll use your time at court to forge as many of your own relationships as possible."

Ever since coming to my rescue in the Maidens' Hall, Agnes had quickly taken her place as my confidante, not to mention my authority on life at Whitehall, her expertise proving a valuable complement to my mother's teachings, especially since Agnes had managed to thrive at court for nearly two months without incurring, as far as I knew, any incident.

"I haven't quizzed you on all matters spiritual and material. Nevertheless," Agnes considered, returning Beatrice's sneer from across the table, "from all I have observed, I cannot believe you and the countess are very much alike."

"No," I said, relieved that someone had at last commented on the mismatched nature of my wardship.

"I've always been a shrewd judge of character," Agnes continued, drinking heartily. "You can trust me to help you find your way. Besides, my grandmother is all eyes and ears. Very little news escapes her."

"Oh," I said, struck by how perfectly that statement fit Agnes as well. "What did she tell you about the countess?"

Agnes leaned forward confidingly. "Let me just say my grandmother was here when the countess brought another ward to court."

"Priscilla——?" I reached for yet another raisin cake despite the increasing tightness of my bodice.

Agnes hesitated a moment. "No, that wasn't her name. Molly, she was called, or perhaps Maggie or Meg."

"What about her?" I asked, my heartbeat quickening.

"The countess married this girl off to the wealthiest man who looked her way." Agnes spoke in a hushed voice, as several others, including Beatrice and Eleanor, were eavesdropping.

I lay down the cake, unable to eat another bite. Had the countess arranged a profitable marriage for this Molly or Maggie or Meg, she and the earl—as the girl's guardians—would have had some share of the profits, provided the groom made some marriage settlement.

"Were there any other suitors before coming to court?" Agnes asked as she nibbled at her cake.

Once again the admiration in Henry Raleigh's voice as we'd sat beside the fire three years ago echoed in my ear. *"You are a spirited girl."*

"Miranda?" Agnes regarded me closely. "Are you all right? You seem far away."

"I'm sorry," I said, banishing the image. "Your words simply reminded me of someone."

"So there was a suitor—" Agnes leaned over confidingly.

"No—"

Agnes seemed on the verge of another question when Lady Periwinkle's chirruping voice called out, "Agnes, Miranda, follow the others into the library!"

"With all there is to do at court, how is it Lady Periwinkle expects us to while away the hours penning letters home?" Eleanor asked, once Agnes and I sat down at the only two unoccupied places.

"Quite right, El." Beatrice continued to thumb through a volume entitled *The Woman's Haven of Pleasure*, a guide to lovemaking that she had carefully concealed inside the innocuous binding of *The Needleworker's Art*. "I wouldn't dare put all of my doings into a letter to my dear mother."

"You could at least pretend to have a heart," Agnes said. "Or wit enough not to announce your unchaste nature. Then again, perhaps your behavior does not shock your mother. Who has she taken up with this time now your father is once again abroad?"

"At least my mother does not take to her sick bed every time another daughter comes of age," Beatrice said, twin fists of crimson darkening her cheeks as she slapped her book closed.

Even Eleanor seemed to wait for Agnes's reply, but she only bowed her head and took up her pen.

"Your mother is unwell, then?" I said to Agnes as Beatrice grinned.

The others looked on eagerly, while Jane alone shook her head and mouthed the word "Don't."

"My mother is not of a hardy constitution, I'm afraid," Agnes managed.

The silence that followed Agnes's reply told me I had made the mistake of mentioning something everyone else—with the exception of Beatrice—knew, or proved at least kind enough to withhold.

⋯⋇⋯

Once everyone but me was scribbling diligently, Lady

Periwinkle came up so close behind me her farthingale knocked against my back. "Miranda, your letter remains unwritten. What, my dear, is troubling you?"

I stood and beckoned Lady Periwinkle well out of earshot of any of the others. "Honestly," I said, meeting her kindly gaze, "I do not particularly want to write to my mother."

"What can you possibly mean when your good mother must be longing for news of your time here? And the two of you so alike—?"

I looked down at the rush-strewn floor. "I have not written to my mother for many weeks now, not since—"

Lady Periwinkle wrapped an ample arm around my shoulder. "Not since when, child?"

"Not since my mother married Lord Grey," I said, astonished to have said the words aloud.

"Your mother? Remarried? And to Thaddeus Grey— I always believed he'd stay a bachelor." A cloud of worry obscured her cheery gaze. "How your father's death must have preyed upon her. I wonder if the queen knows."

I expected her to say more. Instead she retrieved a golden brooch containing a miniature portrait from deep within the bodice of her gown. "My husband, Walter. He was summoned to heaven twelve years ago. I've since had seven suitors, all of them good men, but somehow I do not have the heart to remarry." She stroked the glass-enclosed painting with her fingertip. "I always believed your parents' marriage to be of the same pattern."

"The portrait is lovely," I said, reminded of the miniature of my father my mother had always worn, but would wear no longer.

"Now then," Lady Pewinkle said, recollecting herself. "I am no monarch and therefore lack the power to force you to write. Still, were you my Jillian or my Amelia, I would take it very hard indeed to have no word. Promise me at least that you will think about writing."

"I will," I said, grateful only that none of the others had overheard what had just passed between us.

✻

"How will such a dithery old bird like Periwinkle ever be able to choose six of us to join the knights in the tourneyers' parade on the opening day of the jousts?" Eleanor directed the question to all of us gathered around the table where, having at last finished the puffed and paned sleeves, we now sat reinforcing the stitches that held the sleeves to the bodice of each gown.

"We can trust Lady Periwinkle to be absolutely fair in her selection," Jane managed, just before a fit of sneezing compelled her to draw forth a handkerchief.

III

"Dear Jane, you are too good," Beatrice said, but not unkindly. "If you ask me, it matters not how our matron chooses, so long as I'm among them."

Beside me Agnes assumed a pained expression. "And if you're not, you'll find a way to try to disgrace those who are."

"Now look! Your constant chatter has caused me to make another mistake." Beatrice lay down her work in frustration.

"Ladies!" Lady Periwinkle said, bustling over, her blue eyes oscillating between the warring pair. "Such quarreling is most unacceptable for the queen's maidens. Whatever is the matter?"

"Beatrice seems unable to complete her sewing," Agnes said innocently.

"Oh my." Lady Periwinkle laid a hand on Beatrice's shoulder. "The way you have pinned the sleeve to the armhole does seem a bit crooked. Surely"—her blue eyes alighted on me—"Miranda can help."

"Of course." Immediately I began repinning the sleeve.

"Miranda does covet center stage," Eleanor whispered, once our matron had gone.

"You're just jealous," Agnes said.

I was about to thank her, but something in my friend's face suggested I had sparked this feeling in her also.

Over the next few days I helped attach skirts to bodices, hemmed edges, and even managed to protect the fabric at the skirt's hem with a braid.

"A brilliant suggestion, Miranda," Lady Periwinkle said, giving my shoulder a little squeeze. "One that will prevent the gowns from being torn when the wearers must join their knights on horseback."

"Brilliant," Eleanor echoed with about as much sincerity as a parrot reciting a sonnet.

At long last the gowns were finished, and it came time for Lady Periwinkle to choose the maidens for the tournament. "All of you are to try on the gowns," she instructed. "Whosoever fits into the gowns will walk alongside the knights during opening day festivities."

With too much eagerness, all thirty-six of us took turns trying them on. After Beatrice, I was the second tallest girl in the room. Even so, the biggest of the gowns, I felt certain, would fit me better than anyone else, especially given my penchant for sweets coupled with the sumptuousness of life at Whitehall, where meals regularly included spice cakes crowned with clove gillyflowers, candied roses, all sorts of fruit tarts, and endless sponge cakes soaked in syrup. Thankfully, the full skirts and high waists of each of these gowns, as Lady Periwinkle said, were marvelously forgiving.

"Each of you has now had a turn," Lady Periwinkle announced, "so it is time for me to name the six of you who will be matched with the six younger knights."

A hush fell over the room as every one of us gazed up hopefully, our hands clasped in agitated anticipation.

"If it were up to me," Lady Periwinkle continued, navigating the room, "all thirty-six of you would participate, for there is not one among you who would not make a fine member of Her Majesty's tourneyers' parade. . . ."

"I do believe she missed her calling," Beatrice said. "If only women were allowed to be preachers, or professors of rhetoric . . ."

Beside her, Eleanor alone giggled.

"When I call your name, step forward to claim your gown. And please, do not cheer or clap if your name is called. Instead"—Lady Periwinkle stood a little taller—"remember how you would feel if you were not chosen. . . ."

"Gracious," Eleanor added, "I do wish she would get on with it. Otherwise the tournament will be over before we even leave this room."

"Jane Radcliffe," Lady Periwinkle began, then placed

the smallest of the dresses in the blushing Jane's arms, the sleeves so narrow only hands as fine as Jane's could manage to squeeze through.

"Eleanor Devereux."

As she seized the dress, Eleanor glanced back and gave Beatrice a victorious smile.

"Agnes Somerset."

Agnes moved forward, her firm step and flushed cheeks a testament to how much she wanted this.

"Bridget Seton."

"Well, at least I won't be required to wear a farthingale," the boyish Bridget said philosophically. As she approached Lady Periwinkle, her ruddy red cheeks turned even ruddier, proof of her embarrassment at such finery.

Beatrice's name was called next, and unlike Bridget, she strode toward Lady Periwinkle, her head held high, and retrieved the gown as if she had been born to wear it.

"And last"—Lady Periwinkle's cheeks were now two bright peonies—"Miranda Molyneux."

"How marvelous," Agnes said, and seized my hand. "Now we will walk together across the grounds of Whitehall. If only I'm to be paired with Henry Raleigh, the day shall be perfect!"

"Come, girls!" Lady Periwinkle saved me from a reply.

"Mustn't dwell on disappointment when there is still the song to rehearse, and then all of you will need to rest, if you are to be at your best for the queen's visit tonight."

⤙※⤚

By eight o'clock, the excitement of every one of us, even those few who took their absence from the tournament especially hard, was at a fever pitch.

"Remember your posture," Lady Periwinkle said, fanning herself as she surveyed our immaculate complexions, our perfectly pressed gowns, our snowy gloves. "And bow your heads—Her Majesty is approaching!"

Immediately all thirty-six of us knelt on the hall's green-and-gold cushions, the tables having been moved to the periphery. We heard footsteps, the rustle of luxurious fabrics, and then a soprano voice said, "You may look up, ladies."

There before our kneeling figures, illuminated by candlelight, stood the queen. She was flanked by two of her ladies, both of whom wore ivory velvet and necklaces bearing a silver falcon—the symbol the queen had salvaged from her mother—a most noteworthy choice since the female falcon was, in this singular case, the larger bird of prey.

That night the queen wore a cloak of emerald satin

trimmed with the snowy ermine's fur, and underneath, a gown of silver cloth encrusted with thousands of pearls, and embroidered with yellow and blue pansies, that symbol of thought, and her favorite flower. Pearls had been threaded through the queen's hair, auburn still, though she had reached her forty-fifth year. And framing her features, a veil of cobweb silk had been pinched into pleats over the top of her head and then wired to stand out over her shoulders.

Beholding Elizabeth now, I understood it was not just an aging woman's vanity that compelled her to have the women at court dress in gowns of white, black, and gray. We were like the night, and she, aglitter with so many jewels they dazzled like stars, was the cosmos, or Diana, virgin huntress and goddess of the moon.

"I have come here on the eve of the tournament accompanied by two of my most devoted ladies, Margaret Stanley, Duchess of Dewberry, and Lettice Bornwell, Lady Denby, to formally welcome all of you to Whitehall," the queen said, her veil, delicate as a butterfly's wing, fluttering as she spoke.

"Her Majesty must attend so many events before the opening ceremonies," the Duchess of Dewberry said, her voice so soothing it recollected a dulcimer air, a quality that must have assured her this coveted place beside our famously nervous queen. "She will therefore not stay and meet each one of you tonight, though in due time she trusts she will."

"Indeed, it is Her Majesty's primary wish tonight that all of you do your very best to prove to the world the English court remains the finest and the most virtuous in all the world," Lady Denby continued, her own voice, although elegant, not nearly as soothing. "She therefore asks you to behave as maidens aware of your responsibilities to the sovereign Virgin Queen. Remember, each of you is like a smaller planet revolving around her sun. The glory and honor you bring to yourselves is ultimately her own."

Only after her two ladies curtsied deeply before her, did the queen place her hand to her breast.

When she did, we bowed our heads and replied as one body: "To do so would be our greatest honor."

"And now, Lady Periwinkle," the queen spoke with a mixture of grandeur and real affection, "I ask you to introduce the young women chosen to represent the maidens tomorrow."

I expected Lady Periwinkle's voice to tremble, but she kept her chin up and spoke clearly as, one by one, the maidens stood, until at last I heard my own name called.

I hoped news of my work on the gowns had reached her, but the queen remained silent, as she had done during the introduction of the others. Only after I dropped into a deep curtsy and looked up did I manage to convince myself that she was smiling.

Perhaps, I thought, seeing me now returned the queen to the few halcyon days of her youth: to that brief span of time when her father had not been displeased with her, a time long before her half sister Mary imprisoned her for suspected treason and that half sister's Spanish husband tried to marry her off to one foreign ally after another. During that time, despite the many treacheries of her childhood, the queen—Princess Elizabeth then—and my mother had rambled together through the gardens at Hatfield.

Before the fire or in one of the palace's shaded court-yards, they staged dramatic readings of Marie de France's *Lais* or improvised scenes of Eleanor of Aquitaine's courtly love. And when it was too hot to wander out of doors and too stifling to stay inside, they went for pleasure outings along the Thames, or rode through the mead-ows on spirited horses. On the strength of that history, the queen had chosen my mother as one of her ladies during those scintillating days that preceded her accession.

As I recollected my mother's stories from those long-gone years, stories that did not forsake entirely the kinship with her cousin, I could not help but hope Elizabeth was gazing at me with real happiness, momentarily forgetting or at least suspending the tensions that had ultimately flared up between my mother and herself.

119

CHAPTER EIGHT
May 1, 1580

OPENING DAY OF THE TOURNAMENT DAWNED bright and sunny, and so mild every window in the Maidens' Chamber had been opened to admit the morning breeze. From these high windows I watched Whitehall's kitchen staff carry trays of food and barrels of ale over to the carts waiting to transport the provisions to the tournament grounds. The hopeful bustle was an inspiration to greet the day.

By seven o'clock all thirty-six of us hurried to bathe and dress for the event for which the court had spent months preparing. This morning not even Jane (whose only flaws seemed to be a tendency toward colds and a habit of oversleeping) woke late.

"I have it on my grandaunt, the Duchess of Suffolk's authority, the Earl of Leicester himself will put in an appearance at the masters tournament," Beatrice said, snatching the last bar of the royal apothecary's milk-and-verbena soap from its silver dish.

"Who?" a younger girl asked as she ran a brush through Beatrice's hair.

"Lord Robert Dudley," Eleanor spoke through a cloud of powder.

Though I said nothing, my curiosity was sparked at the possibility of seeing the man believed to be the queen's only love. No, Elizabeth had not married the son of the man her half sister had justly executed for treason. Yet little by little the queen had elevated him, until the shamed Robert Dudley had become one of the grandest, not to mention wealthiest men in all of England.

"Say, Bea," Eleanor asked, "do you think the earl's godson will also be there?"

"Highly doubtful, given his wife's recent lying-in. The Duchess of Suffolk—"

"On the contrary," Jane said, trying to find a place before the mirror. "I spoke to him just yesterday. He plans to attend."

"Bravo," said Beatrice. "You are learning something from me at last. Now, if you will only muster the courage to speak to his younger brother. George, isn't it?"

"Yes." Quickly, Jane covered her mouth with her hand to hide her smile.

After a special breakfast of cherry cakes, of which I ate only two, accompanied by the choicest cuts of meat, a deliciously mild cheese I managed to simply taste, and refreshing mugs of ale, the six of us chosen for the parade donned our green-and-gold gowns and the high heart-shaped headdresses with their streaming veils.

Meanwhile, Lady Periwinkle bustled around us, a mother hen amid a nest of eager swans. "Careful not to let your hems trail the ground, my dears," she called, then paused to pin Jane's sleeves, which kept slipping from her narrow shoulders. "Jane, dear," Lady Periwinkle urged, tucking one of her curls back in place, "I do think you might bring a shawl so as not to catch another cold."

"Too late," someone whispered as Jane sneezed.

"Oh my, that simply will not do," Lady Periwinkle said when she came to Beatrice, who had arranged her bodice so as to display her breasts to their best, or at least to their fullest, advantage. "My dear, I insist you allow your chemise to show. After all, you must remember what Her Majesty said last night about appearing chaste."

"The *appearance* of chastity is all Beatrice will ever be able to aspire to," Agnes whispered, once Lady Periwinkle turned her attention to Bridget, who somehow managed to look horsy and boyish despite the close-fitting bodice and tapered waist of her gown.

"You are wearing *both* linen chemises, yes?" Lady Periwinkle asked Bridget, this extra precaution having been taken so that the athletic maiden's perspiration would not damage the gown.

As the morning air kissed my cheeks, I held my head high, luxuriating in the caress of velvet. The scratchy lockram cloth of Turbury, despite the calluses embedded in my fingertips, was at long last a distant memory.

"You do look lovely!" Lady Periwinkle pronounced as we stepped outside. At this early hour, the air still held the fragrance of dew on the freshly strewn meadow rushes now covering the grounds.

We progressed toward the tiltyard, and the eyes of many a servant, several courtiers and their ladies, and a clutch of court officials all watched our progress with approving glances and encouraging words. More than a few wished us good luck, including the ancient Lady Woodworth, dressed in the dated Spanish fashions of Catherine of Aragon's time; Thomasina, the queen's dwarf; and beside her, Malvolio, the aging fool, both of them outfitted so richly in carnation mockado, one would have thought them a highborn, albeit diminutive, lady and her lord.

Near the Royal Theater loitered the Duke of Anjou's

ambassadors, arrayed from head to toe in the French fleur de lis, smoking jeweled pipes and speaking in their native tongue.

"The Duke is spoken of as both genteel and handsome," Eleanor said. "His ambassadors brought the queen the latest fashions from France. Perhaps she will be persuaded to marry him after all."

"Nonsense," Beatrice said. "She may love clothing, but my grandaunt swears the queen will never become a Frenchman's wife. . . ."

For me, all talk of yet another of the queen's suitors was instantly eclipsed by the time we reached the royal herb garden, where, amid the fragrances of lavender and thyme, Agnes clasped my hand and began to speak to me of Henry Raleigh. "The best-looking man I have seen in my life, with chestnut hair kissed with copper, elegant hands—and so tall, he stands as high as the palace doors."

"You've met him before, then?" I said, pretending to be absorbed in contemplating a bed of chamomile.

"Oh yes, Grandmother introduced us at Christmastime." Agnes spoke in a slow, measured voice I had not heard before. "He accompanied his older half sister, Charlotte, the poetess, to one of Grandmother's musical evenings." Agnes paused, then carefully stepped around a puddle so as not to wet her skirts. "Charlotte was made one of the Ladies of the Bedchamber just last year."

"A great honor," I said, pretending I had heard nothing of Henry Raleigh's older half sister, who my mother had once described as "haughty."

"He behaved with such gentility and with such perfect courtesy, no one would think he was anything but the happiest of men. Even so, Henry recently suffered a grave disappointment. But then"—Agnes began to study me closely—"you must know about this."

I told myself no one outside our immediate families could have learned about the possible engagement, which, now that it had been abandoned, would certainly not be spoken of again, and especially not in a public place like the court. When Agnes continued to stare, I began to say something about Henry Raleigh having been with my father in Ireland, where they forged a strong friendship.

"Had your father returned home," Agnes interrupted, the emerald gown bringing out a green tinge in her complexion that seemed to echo this emerging jealousy, "Henry would still have reason to hope."

"Hope?" I said, stunned that Agnes, *my friend*, lacked the courtesy to mention the possibility—indeed the *probability*—of Henry Raleigh's grief for my father, given their relationship.

"Because of your mother's remarriage, Henry's own claim to Lord Grey's estates is imperiled. If your mother bears an heir, land and title will pass to her son, and

Lord Grey's cousin, Henry, will be forgotten—"

"Do you mean to say that before we met, you knew about my mother's marriage to Lord Grey?" I said, the politics of inheritance paling beside my discovery of her dishonesty. "You encouraged my confidences when you already knew?"

Agnes's flaxen hair seemed to hold the sun itself. But her eyes regarded me coldly. Still, she said nothing.

Had I been so desperate for a friend as to be tricked so easily? Was Agnes's friendship just a ploy? Even if she was determined to marry Henry Raleigh, I, an impoverished earl's daughter, could no longer pose a threat, especially not when Henry had turned his back on the engagement.

Nevertheless, of all the places in the Maidens' Hall, the one beside Agnes had been the only one available. And how readily she—and no one else—had been willing, almost eager, to accept me, when everything my mother and sister had told me about court had prepared me for a more universally cool reception.

"Like the courtiers, ladies, too, must prove themselves worthy as well as savvy enough to survive at court," my mother had always said.

"Agnes, Miranda!"

Startled away from thoughts of my mother's warnings, I turned to see Lady Periwinkle motioning to the immense tiltyard surrounded by a ten-foot-high wooden palisade, above which rose the royal gallery as well as viewing stands large enough to house an audience of at least one thousand persons. And at the very center, an assembly of ladies and their knights, as well as gentlemen ushers, grooms of the wardrobe, and several porters, all of them engrossed in conversation.

"Please, my dears," she said kindly, "though it pleases me immensely to see what great friends you are becoming, on this day in particular you must be sure to listen to my instructions. Remember, it is not just your own virtue, but our queen's you represent."

"Yes, certainly," Agnes and I stammered, each of us dipping into a low curtsy.

Beside Lady Periwinkle stood a handsome man of fifty, the tips of his black beard threaded with white, his dark brown eyes as friendly as a spaniel's. "Lord Bradstreet," he said, with a flourish of his velvet cape. "I have been appointed to assist Her Majesty's Master of the Revels in the tournament. Along with your dear matron, we will pair each of you with one of the young knights."

There followed soft laughter and the rustle of skirts as we stole glances at the group of men, their armor decked with chosen or inherited emblems. I did not know which one was Henry Raleigh, for just as we wore veils, all of the knights' helms masked their faces from our view.

"Surely, Algernon," Lady Periwinkle suggested, drawing

from the deep pocket of her gown an ivory-paneled fan she began waving before her face, "it would be best to aim for symmetry in the pairing and therefore use height as our measure in matching up each maiden with her knight."

"I beg to differ with you, Lucy," he said with consummate politeness. "Such an arrangement would be visually pleasing. Still, it is my idea Henry Raleigh, who will compete only after one of the other six has emerged the victor, a high honor, as you know, and one requiring he walk at the end of the group, should be paired up with the young woman who has been at court the longest."

"My word," Beatrice said, "excepting his leanness and height, this Bradstreet is exactly like old Periwinkle. No wonder they use each other's Christian names."

In the end, although Lady Periwinkle agreed Lord Bradstreet's was the more logical strategy, she insisted on using height as the measure. "We cannot have a little thing like Jane Radcliffe paired with the largest of your men," she insisted. "Nor would it be kind to place a taller girl beside a knight of slighter build. . . ."

"Very well," Lord Bradstreet conceded, "you have a point there."

"The youngest of Lady Radcliffe's granddaughters, Jane, will be accompanied by George Mountjoy," they began together.

An ebullient Jane stepped forward to meet a

small-boned knight of almost exactly her height who wore blue and white beneath his armor, a pairing that epitomized courtesy.

"Good for her!" Beatrice said with a sincerity I would never have expected. "She got her wish after all!"

Despite the fierce lion treading on a snake on his shield—"the Mountjoy family emblem," Beatrice said with a certain amount of respect—I feared he wouldn't last a single round with any of the others, all of whom were at least two hands taller and broader than he.

". . . Bridget Seton will be accompanied by Thomas Darcy—" Before the sentence was completed, Bridget plunged into an athletic curtsy in front of a knight whose color was fiercest red, his shield embellished by a storm cloud and the inscription: *Obstantia nubila soluent*—They dissolve obstructing clouds. The knight fittingly recollected a character from *Beowulf*, and so gave Bridget's jaunty mannerisms the aura of the most delicate femininity.

". . . Eleanor Devereux by Philip Scudamore," they said, as she stepped forward to greet a knight dressed all in black, his shield bearing the impresio *Ell mon ceur a nauera*—She hath wounded my heart.

". . . Agnes Somerset by John Gainsborough."

Only I guessed the disappointment Agnes must have concealed behind her veil as a lean youth, his shield adorned with the sign of fidelity, a yellow rose, his inscriptio *Semper*, the Latin for Always, bowed before taking his place beside her.

". . . Beatrice Cunnington by Chidiock Kyd . . ."

Beatrice may have tried to dress like a courtesan, but she curtsied as demurely as the highest born of ladies before a knight whose shield bore the sign of a black horse and a most intriguing accompanying inscriptio, *Conantia frangere frangunt*—They break those who are trying to break them.

". . . And Miranda Molyneux by Henry Raleigh."

Never having anticipated our pairing, I felt myself crimson, trebly grateful for my veil. Made of the most gossamer of silks, I could see without being clearly seen. When I lifted my eyes to Henry Raleigh's face hidden behind his helm, he, too, seemed frozen in place. If thoughts were transparent, what would his yield?

Of the two of us, he seemed to recover more quickly. Stepping forward, with consummate courtesy, he bowed deeply. To calm myself, I tried to focus on his armor, studying the shield upon which was painted the firmament, the azure helm—that most contemplative of colors—adorned with stars. The inscription read *Spiritus durissima coquit*—A noble mind digests even the most painful injuries.

The proof of Henry Raleigh's strength lay in the broadness of his shoulders and his height, as well as my father's lavishly narrated stories. His nobleness, however, I now found misleading.

But then our eyes met, and the soulfulness I once believed I'd found there seemed to flicker forth once more. How many years had I spent dreaming about what our reunion would be like? Not once had I imagined it would be like this.

Henry was about to speak when Lord Bradstreet called out, "No, no, my dear Lucy, it is all wrong. The maiden standing beside young Kyd is taller than the one who has been paired with Raleigh."

"Gracious, Algernon, you do have an eagle's eye," Lady Periwinkle said. "Thank goodness you noticed my error."

Something in Henry Raleigh's manner suggested reluctance, and despite my anger, I wished again I knew what he was thinking—how he might explain.

Our eyes met once more, and then he turned away to take his place beside Beatrice, whose blush would have been entirely hidden had it not been for the seam of rose that appeared along her throat and bosom.

"It is time to take your places for the parade," the Master of the Revels, young Joshua Campion, called as someone behind me—Agnes, no doubt—cursed Beatrice's good luck.

Thankful for this reprieve, I joined my peers at the very

front of the progress, determined to banish Henry Raleigh from my thoughts.

So it came to be that, excepting the Master of the Revels gallantly riding a fine Neopolitan charger, its coat a gleaming silver, Jane Radcliffe and George Mountjoy found themselves the first tourneyers glimpsed by a motley assembly of courtiers, ladies, officials, more than a view curious townspeople, as well as invited guests, including those same exquisitely dressed representatives from the French court.

George spurred his great white horse to the front, his courtly impresio, *Te stante virebo*—With you standing, I shall flourish—written in gold. Shy Jane looked back at us and waved, a faux pas dear Lady Periwinkle watched without forsaking her rosy expression.

"May I?" Chidiock Kyd offered his hand, then lifted me onto the horse, where I perched sidesaddle, newly unsteady in the narrowly cut gown, and quite relieved I had not proven too heavy for him.

Decorum, as Lady Periwinkle more than once informed us, required us to be silent throughout our progress around the palace grounds.

For the most part we heeded this rule, though I occasionally heard sneezing (Jane's?) and once a great fit of coughing from somewhere up front when one of the horses startled before a great tomcat, in the process raising a quantity of dust, as well as another knight's temper.

Just once we rode close enough to Beatrice and Henry Raleigh for me to see how tightly she'd curled her arms around his body. Though I had never been so close to a man before, I knew enough about armor to understand that she had managed to find that place between the armor plates where she could touch body linen, the closest thing to skin. And more than once I swore she brought her face menacingly close to his exposed ear. I did not want to begin to imagine what she might be saying.

If I had anything to be thankful for, it was Chidiock Kyd's respectful silence and the ample room he allowed me in the saddle, both of which afforded me the chance to compose myself while I took in the view of the queen's court glimpsed from this height. What would my mother say were she to see me riding so close to the man Father would have had me marry? One who had ultimately proven unworthy of his high regard?

CHAPTER NINE

May 1, 1580

Perhaps an hour later, we returned to the tiltyard and took our places on the viewing stand's lower level, which offered an unobstructed view of the arena and the royal gallery.

"How many people do you think are in attendance?" I asked, surveying a crowd of the grandest, as well as the most notorious, of the queen's subjects, the air thick with a queer mixture of odors: among these perfume, sweat, and stable.

"At least a thousand," Chidiock Kyd said.

My veil was an essential part of my headdress. Beautiful though this covering was, my scalp sweated underneath. Decorum permitted my partner to remove his own helm, which revealed almost elfin features and curly hair, its color a mercurial red. As we sat together and waited for the queen to arrive, he pointed out several noteworthy and unusual people, including the poet-playwright George Montgomery theatrically outfitted in a pink tunic and purple breeches, the latter color traditionally reserved for those of royal blood.

"What do you know about him?" I asked, irritated at myself for being distracted by Henry Raleigh, who sat beside Beatrice in the row before us, and to whom he behaved gallantly. One minute he relieved her of her fan, and in another offered her a drink from his flask.

"When the Earl of Leicester entertained the queen at Kenilworth, he commissioned Montgomery to write the speeches and other entertainments. Montgomery told me of the absurd thrill he took in disguising himself as a wild man covered with real moss and ivy leaves. While the queen was out riding, he suddenly burst forth from the shrubbery."

"What happened?"

"Montgomery, whose humor is his best quality, intended it as a jest. He'd had an entire rhyming poem planned, but he was almost killed when the queen's horse rose up on its hind legs and prepared to charge. Fortunately," he continued, laughing so hard tears sprang to his amber eyes, "the queen is an expert horsewoman and controlled the beast. And of course, she, too, is blessed with a sense of humor."

"Who else do you know here?" I asked, assuming he

must be among the most privileged in the land to have access to so many names and stories.

"To the left of us, in one of the upper seats, you will find Walter Raleigh."

"The man in the yellow waistcoat?" I asked, startled by the name.

"No, the man with the neatly trimmed beard, the one dressed all in sea green."

"What do you know about him?" I asked in a careful voice.

"Only that he came to the queen's notice after his return from Ireland, and is now the most ambitious man at court."

"Oh," I said, relieved to have my veil. "How did he manage that?"

"He plants himself anywhere the queen's likely to be. In fact"—Chidiock leaned closer—"Montgomery told me Raleigh spread his cloak over a puddle so the queen would not wet her skirts. For a time after that, the two were inseparable."

"Ah," I said, realizing how much my mother would relish this story, until I remembered my vow not to write to her.

"And over there." He pointed to a slender boy in a silk suit patterned with yellow and orange diamonds. "Inez, the Spanish fool."

"Tell me more," I said, intrigued by the bizarreness of

his costume, not to mention the color scheme emblematic only of deception.

"*He* is in reality a *she*. Inez came to court disguised as a boy."

"To meet a man?" I said, recalling those foolish women who went out, so-disguised, to meet their lovers.

"No, though that possibility scintillates. Inez was sent by the late queen to spy on her half sister. They say our good queen found her so entertaining she kept Inez on at court."

"She did not worry that Inez would still be loyal to the Spanish?" I said, recalling my mother's stories of King Phillip's spies coupled with his failed attempts to marry Elizabeth off to a Spaniard.

"If she did, Her Majesty's fears did not compare to her need to be amused. Of course," he considered, "they say the queen has become a bit more careful now that she keeps her Scottish cousin under lock and key."

"Have you been here long?" I finally asked, impressed not only by all the people he recognized, but by his interest in singling out characters other than the most nobly born or the most powerful.

"Not very," he said, hesitating before addressing me.

"Miranda," I said, "Miranda Molyneux."

"You've a brother at Trinity College, then?" His voice turned almost cautious.

"Yes, my brother, Robert. Do you know him?"

"We've met."

From the reserve in his voice, I sensed he either did not like my brother, which seemed unlikely, for although self-absorbed, Robert had many friends; or else he didn't know him well. "Where do you hail from, Chidiock?"

"London, though I'd prefer you call me Kyd."

"Why not Chidiock?" I asked as Henry Raleigh removed his helm to reveal a face even finer than I remembered: high cheekbones, a strong jaw, and his eyes—that uncanny indigo I'd seen only once before on a tapestry—all framed by coppery chestnut hair.

"Need I explain?" My partner blushed as red as his hair.

"And the dark horse?" I asked as Henry turned in our direction. Surely he could not be listening at such a distance. "A family emblem?"

"My family has no emblems, unless you include the sign outside my grandfather's shop."

I wanted to ask Kyd how he'd secured an invitation at court, where wealth or a title seemed the key to entry.

"My grandfather was haberdasher to many members of the court. But his son, my father—" He coughed and his voice dropped an octave. "Let's just say my father liked his drink a little more than his customers."

"The dark horse is a personal symbol, then?" I said,

sensing the reason for Kyd's tension with my title-conscious brother.

"It is."

"For one who is not the favorite," I said, "you could not have set your mark higher."

Kyd grinned, and the merriness in his face returned. "If one is to aim high, why not aspire to the best?"

"Do you always set the bar so high," I asked Kyd, realizing how much I was enjoying his company, "or only on the tourneying field?"

"In all things," he said, his red hair shining in the sun.

I was about to say something further about his confidence, but the queen's ladies were now entering on horseback—among them Lady Denby—and behind them, Queen Elizabeth, who rode a pure white palfry, its gleaming leather saddle adorned with gold and pearls. Although the queen was as skilled a rider as any man or woman in the land, one capable of guiding—without breaking—destrier stallion and spirited Arabian alike, the slender shining palfry with the snowy mane and whisper-white hooves trimmed with gold lent a particularly majestic air to her person and to her dress.

To this first day of the tournament, Elizabeth wore a white-and-gold gown with peaked epaulets like wings. The fabric of the gown had been sewn through with diamonds and embroidered with what, from this great distance at least, looked like an array of enchanted beasts including unicorns and sea monsters. In the late morning sunlight the queen's figure so dazzled, it was difficult to look at her directly; and once again I found myself struck by the artistry of which she was so consummate a master.

The queen took her place beneath a golden canopy in the royal gallery, still surrounded by her ladies, all of whom also wore white, though their gowns were not ornamented with jewels.

Afterward, a good one hundred men outfitted in forest green, their caps adorned with broom and furze, hauled in the scenic backdrop to the opening pageant. Had I not seen for myself the mobile forest that now rose before me, I would not have believed this fantasy of hawthorns, oaks, maples, and birches could be re-created. And that wasn't all: perhaps two thousand roses, each one white, adorned the Tudor-green carpet. And whether astride a branch or half hidden behind a shrub, there were beasts and birds of a dazzling variety. These included two peacocks, an antelope, perhaps a dozen blackbirds, a baby elephant, and a lion.

All one thousand of us drew closer to the railings as Lady Dewberry, arrayed in a gown of deep blue velvet, stepped out from behind one of the trees and, in the soothing tones of the night before, lamented the decay of chivalry since Arthur's time.

While she stood weeping, a knight, his armor so highly polished it blinded when the sunlight struck, walked onto the stage, then knelt before her. "Weep not, fair lady," he said. "One day a knight will appear, one who by the might and magic of his arm will begin to restore the ruined seats of virtue."

The greatest of the oak trees opened, and out stepped a white-bearded figure in a robe the color of midnight, its hem bedecked with stars.

"Yet another restaging of the prophecy." Kyd spoke with so little enthusiasm, I thought he might actually yawn.

"You are a hard one to please," I said, not daring to look away as Merlin waved a pearl-encrusted scepter that quickly transformed a bouquet of roses into a golden cage containing a pair of doves.

"Am I? Surely, the queen's artists could be more original. Why not a retelling of Persephone's descent into the underworld, where she is rescued by a goddess of the seasons who is also a queen and mother?

"Or better yet," he said as the Lady of the Lake released the doves, "the birth of a woman of divine beauty costumed as the virgin huntress Diana, her bow and arrow decorated with moonbeams, her companions a half dozen maidens only half as beautiful as she, and"—he paused as the doves soared heavenward—"a snow white hart."

"You do aspire high," I said.

"Being a dark horse," Kyd replied, "I must."

⋯⫘⋯

The staging of the prophecy and the removal of the backdrop was followed by a blaze of trumpets, as twelve courtiers, their armor bedecked with various emblems of desire, rode through the Holbein Gate. "We, the Foster Children of Desire, have come into this land to capture the Palace of Perfect Beauty," they called out together.

Immediately, the same one hundred men, now outfitted all in white, hauled in a roped model adorned with the symbols of our Virgin Queen. Once the fortress had been secured in the center of the tiltyard, four knights rode in and surrounded it. All four of their badges carried the Latin impresa *Sic Nos Non Nobis*—Ours But Not For Us.

"You asked me to point out the Earl of Leicester." Kyd motioned to a defending knight who carried a banner depicting a white bear. "There he is."

The way this knight maneuvered his sleek black warhorse around the tourneying field, expertly avoiding the oncoming lances of his opponents with all the grace of one dancing a galliard, confirmed him to be the Earl of Leicester, a man known to be as agile in the tiltyard as he was on the dance floor.

After the fortress's four defenders vanquished the twelve knights, a towheaded little boy of some eight or nine years of age, outfitted in the Tudor green and white, walked onto the tiltyard and handed the Earl of Leicester a scroll.

"'O divine Beauty,'" the earl cried, reading from the text. "'Although all may desire you, you are the only one never to be conquered by Desire.'"

"Do you think the knights are sending a message to the ambassadors from the French court?" I asked after the queen accepted a bouquet of six dozen white roses from the earl, then allowed him to kiss her hand not once but twice, with a dramatic flourish my mother would have attributed to her cousin's vanity, as well as to her insatiable need for adoration.

"Undoubtedly," Kyd replied, "though I do not know if they are smart enough—or sufficiently conversant in our tongue—to understand the message."

❦

"I'm famished," Kyd said after the last of the knights galloped out of the tiltyard, and everyone in the viewing stands began to stream out of the crowded rows, stretching their limbs and talking excitedly about the awaiting feast.

"A meal would be nice," I said, my stomach's growls mercifully drowned out by the voices of the others as we joined the procession already weaving its way toward the banquet hall beyond the Holbein Gate.

Inside we converged upon a buffet, the lavishness of which I had never seen. On one table alone stood half a dozen silver platters of baked venison, roasted quail, and wild pigeon. There was even a platter decorated with the signature blue-and-green feathers of the peacock, a bird so beautiful I could never bring myself to eat it, especially after having viewed the two astride the pageant stage.

At the next table, silver bowls held salads of tender lettuces, red and green sage sweetened with figs, and honey-glazed currants and almonds. There were also trays of oranges, pears, and other fruit that had been cut or arranged into a fantasy of shapes including the moon and stars, and dozens of intricately cut lady apple fairies. I would have liked to sample them all, but my dress, which was already beginning to feel tight, told me to abstain.

"Shall we?" I asked Kyd, then pointed to the open-air balcony, thinking we could escape being corralled by Eleanor, who was awkwardly holding forth before a small circle of captive listeners.

Too late. No sooner had we turned than she spotted us and called out, her big-toothed smile giving her the unfortunate look of a horse.

"That was quite a spectacle, was it not?" Eleanor asked us once introductions were made. "Yet I must say I'm rather disappointed to learn it was staged."

Several of the listeners toed the ground with their shoes or looked away at the inappropriateness of this remark, but Eleanor was too excited to notice, and soon went on to say the queen rode like a woman of twenty and not of forty-five.

Beside me, Kyd burst into laughter, as if he hoped Eleanor would go on, even though her words were careening toward the unspeakable fact that the queen was no longer a young woman, despite her artists and dressmakers' attempts to prove otherwise.

"If there is a difference in the way a woman of forty-five and a woman of twenty-five rides, then what of someone your own age?" Kyd said, taunting Eleanor, but merrily rather than with malice, as so many others would have done.

"Might I have a word, Miranda?" A voice called from behind.

I turned to find myself face-to-face with Henry Raleigh. Up close his cheekbones were sharper than I remembered, the planes of his face more defined, the indigo of his eyes even more dramatic in the sheltered light.

His only physical imperfection seemed to be a crescent-shaped scar, as long as my ring finger, along his left cheek.

Surely he hadn't had the scar the last time we'd met, or I would have remembered it. How had it come to be there? I found myself asking, ashamed of my curiosity.

He spoke to me, but at first I did not hear his words, so preoccupied was I in finding something to say that was both polite and cutting, something only he would understand.

Instead I could only stand there as if struck dumb, while Beatrice and the others gathered around us, their expressions and bright eyes indicative of their curiosity.

"I may not have had the good fortune of being your father's son," he continued, "but I grieve for your father as only a good son would grieve."

Still I said nothing, this mention of my father pulling the breath from my body.

"Were I master of my own fate," Henry said, as he knelt with what seemed sincere humility—at least for those unfamiliar with our history—"I would have ensured my presence in Ireland at the time of your father's death."

The presence of the others compelled me to say something, if only to put an end to this meeting. But the words would not come. Against my will, I traveled back to the time he'd lingered beside me before the fire at Plowden Hall some three years ago, when I'd found myself studying his lips and breathed in a forest scent redolent with the mystery of Ireland, all the while wondering what it would feel like were he to kiss me. . . .

Until that other scene returned, the one in my mother's sitting room when she told me the engagement was not to be—and I, sent away.

When he continued to kneel, the publicity of the situation forced me to yield my gloved hand for him to kiss. "Thank you for this sympathy," I said, despite the tight knot in my belly.

"How pleased your father would be to see you here," he said, the moon-shaped scar along his cheek lengthening as he smiled.

Such words he no longer had any right to say.

Before I could react, he bowed a second time to me, but also to Chidiock Kyd and to the others gathered around us, before extending his arm to Beatrice, who bid me a courteous enough good-bye.

"Your father was in Ireland?" Kyd asked, as the others resumed their conversation, with Eleanor once again presiding.

"Yes, on expedition for the queen." I fidgeted with my glove, forced myself to look up. "He died there shortly before Christmas."

"I'm sorry." Kyd's eyes were solemn for the first time. "I wondered why you started when I mentioned Walter Raleigh's time there."

"You noticed that?" I said, my clenched hands concealed behind my back.

"A man must study life if he is to master even a fraction of its complexity," he said. This statement unsettled me just a little, especially once I recognized Agnes in the distance, understanding she had viewed all, though her veil, iridescent in the sun, hid all reaction from my view.

CHAPTER TEN

May 1, 1580

NIGHTFALL BROUGHT THE FEAST OF DESSERTS
I had heard so much about: ornately decorated pastries
including a dozen layer cakes with a variety of fillings
and spices, each one requiring three pounds
of butter; marchpane candies shaped like knights and
ladies; even a miniature palace made out of fragile
meringue—all laid out on crystal platters beneath a
canopy in one of Whitehall's most exquisite court-
yards, the whole place illuminated by torches that
flickered over the ivy-covered walls, as liveried
servants in whisper-soft velvet moved among the
guests.

Spying the Spanish fool, Inez, an enormous plate
of airy meringue in her orange-and-gold gloved hands,
deep in conversation with the poet-playwright George

Montgomery, I instantly recalled the story Kyd had told me about Montgomery's near-fatal encounter with the queen's rearing horse, and found myself wishing Kyd were here, if only to dispel my nervousness with his changeling grin and wry assessments.

But Kyd told me he needed to rest before tomorrow's tournament. "Otherwise I fear I won't be able to keep my seat in the saddle. You see"—his face turned momentarily sheepish—"I learned to wield a lance on the stage, not in the tiltyard."

"You did not grow up running at the ring?" I asked, recalling my brother's own exercises.

"Hardly. Though I trained for a month at a school friend's estate, I did not set foot in Greenwich's tiltyard until a fortnight ago."

I almost expected Kyd's merry eyes to erupt into laughter, and hear him tell me it was all a great jest.

Instead he took my gloved hand in his and shook it like a gentleman, though courtesy would have suggested that he kiss it. "I will be expecting your token tomorrow."

"And on the morrow you will have it," I said, looking up from my curtsy just in time to meet his eyes before he turned toward the courtyard gate.

⊷✳⊶

How long I stood there, I do not know before I realized I had begun to follow Inez's hand as she raised the meringue to her lips.

Eager to sample the spun-sugar palace before it disappeared, I was just about to join the others gathered beneath the canopy when Eleanor planted herself just to the right of the meringue, and beside her, Philip Scudamore, whose dour expression and drooping shoulders recollected his shield's impresio, *Ell mon ceur a nauera*—She hath wounded my heart.

I may have been curious to make the connection, but nothing could convince me to join Eleanor, who would inevitably review every aspect of the day's events as if I had not been there also. She might even pester me about Kyd. Earlier, in the Maidens' Chamber, I had heard her talking about him to Beatrice, asking to borrow *The Woman's Haven of Pleasure* after convincing herself his teasing was proof he was in love with her.

Now, while Eleanor examined a life-size sculpture of the queen made entirely from thousands of white rosebuds, I decided to steal away. Before I could, the scent of oranges and spices filled the air.

Beside the countess stood a tall man of at least thirty-five years, his dark hair and manicured beard threaded with russet. Dressed in somber but costly black velvet, the watchwork sleeves of his doublet patterned with staves, he might have been handsome, had his high-bridged nose and heavy-lidded eyes not given him the impression of a skua or other predatory seabird.

"My dear Miranda," the countess said, not with warmth, though with greater civility than I'd previously heard. "I hoped you would wait for me in the Maidens' Chamber, but when I arrived you were nowhere to be found. Did you not receive the message I left with Lady Periwinkle?"

"I'm sorry, no," I said, reminded of my eagerness to avoid Agnes, who was returning to the dormitory just as Lady Periwinkle began calling after me.

"I knew there must be some explanation, Lord Seagrave. Miranda is usually so obedient," the countess said, keeping to this newly civil tone.

Seagrave. Where had I heard this name before?

"I should hope so," he said, stroking his beard and surveying me with what I considered an impertinent blend of criticism and familiarity. "Nothing bespeaks a young lady so well as a malleable disposition."

To hear myself spoken of as if I were a lump of bread dough brought on a fierce wish for Kyd's wit. Yet the words would not come, and I could only manage to direct myself to the countess. "How did you enjoy opening day?" I asked.

"It pleases me to see how the queen has already

honored you. Nevertheless, I did find the pageants a bit too extravagant, especially all of the animals in the opening event. Where in London does the queen keep an elephant?" she asked, her solemnity fractured by the barest smile.

"So true," Lord Seagrave said. "You see, Miranda, your guardian and I are of the same mind when it comes to public entertainments."

"What is your view, then, sir?" I said, wishing all the while that he would go away.

"Necessary but not necessarily presented at such great cost." Then, when I looked at him as if I did not understand, "I suppose you could say I consider it essential to attend such galas, if only to display one's patriotism."

"Lord Seagrave's family has been associated with the Office of the Armory since its founding," the countess told me.

I recalled the armory's troubling location within the Tower of London, where the queen had been imprisoned, and before her, her mother, Anne Boleyn, the scaffold upon which she would kneel before the chopping block visible from her window. "You are employed there, sir?"

"I myself, no," he said stiffly. "My grandfather helped the late king bring the first master armorists to England from Germany and Milan."

"Thanks to Lord Seagrave's grandfather"—the countess

flicked her pomander—"England is no longer dependent upon the costly foreign expertise of armories abroad."

"Given such an association," I said politely, "you are undoubtedly an accomplished jouster. Will you be competing in the tournament?"

"I'm afraid I cannot." He pointed to his leg. "Injury has left me partly lame."

"A riding accident, sir?" I asked.

"No." He flushed and looked away. Then, recovering himself he said, "Besides, I share the melancholy Burton's humor. In my view, the riding of great horses at tournaments has caused far too many gentlemen to gallop right out of their fortunes."

"Ah." Such words put me in mind of the short-lived friendship of my brother and another boy who always criticized the sports in which he himself never participated.

"Miranda is a skilled seamstress, my lord," the countess said. "She saves a great deal by making her own clothes. Is that not true, Miranda?"

I tried to come up with some innocuous reply—until her motivation for introducing him crept over me like a dank fog at dusk. *Seagrave.* This was the name the earl had mentioned that first day of his return. This Lord Seagrave was the suitor the earl and countess had in mind for me.

It was then Henry Raleigh entered, his handsomely embroidered doublet of blue-gray velvet and finely made shoes a defiance of his family's poverty—or proof of the queen's favor; and beside him, her raven hair threaded with jewels, a circlet tracing her brow, walked Beatrice, the ermine edging along her shawl attesting to her family's wealth as well as to her high opinion of herself, her revealing décolletage proof of her want of modesty.

It would have shamed me to have Henry Raleigh a witness to my humiliating conversation. It seemed a fortunate thing, then, that no sooner had they reached the canopy, strolling together in what seemed perfect amity, than they were beckoned by Sir Joshua Campion and his wife, one of the queen's goddaughters, whose loose umber gown and glowing complexion suggested she would soon bear a child.

"Miranda is appropriately modest when it comes to her sewing, Lord Seagrave," the countess continued, the flames from the torches illuminating the perspiration along her nose and brow.

"Very good," he replied, making a crooked steeple of his spidery hands. "And what of the other domestic arts? My estates are so large."

"I have schooled her very well," the countess said, "and in all things, she has proven a swift learner."

His grin recollected the dragon in the chapel. "There is one more thing. Is she able to prepare a mutton pie? In my view, it is essential for all young women to fix a proper mutton pie."

"No," I said. "Mutton is a meat for which I have little taste."

"With which you have little experience." The countess laid a cold hand on my arm.

"Ah." Once again Lord Seagrave caressed his beard. "A crucial distinction."

I longed to flee, but the countess held me fast.

"What a shame it was to hear your mother would not be attending the tournament," she said to Lord Seagrave. "Is it not a great shame, Miranda?"

Determined not to answer, I raised my hand to Jane Radcliffe, who, in the company of George Mountjoy, was wandering the periphery, her cheeks flush as ripe peaches, her eyes bright as the summering bluebirds embroidered along her gown.

"Miranda!" She waved back as she and George approached us.

Given how well they looked together, two slim figures, both of them ginger-haired and of exactly the same height, I expected George to be as quiet as Jane; but within moments he was chatting with both the countess and the unpleasant lord with such ease, I felt forever in his debt.

"Your family are landowners in Essex, are they not?" George asked Lord Seagrave, who assumed a more conciliatory tone once he learned George belonged to a family that could trace its ancestry all the way back to William the Conqueror.

"The Seagraves reside at the former priory, though the first lord modernized it considerably," the countess told George. "My late brother visited there once and spoke of it as among Essex's most magnificent dwellings."

When Lord Seagrave began to say something about his grandfather's loyal service to Henry VIII—"the reason he carried out the king's orders for the dissolution of the religious houses"—George's amiable expression momentarily vanished, and I sensed that, despite his small build, he might prove worthy of the lion emblazoned on his shield.

"I could not imagine stabling a horse in a consecrated place," Jane said simply, "much less feasting there at Easter or Yuletide."

"If you will excuse me," I said, then raised my hand to my forehead with a gesture worthy of the stage, "I need to step away for a moment."

Lord Seagrave offered me a stiff bow, and the countess said something about finding me on the morrow, but I was already hurrying away and simultaneously trying to flee all that Agnes had said—and before Agnes, Anne—about the countess's profitable role in a former ward's marriage.

"Are you quite well, Miranda?" Jane asked, once she and George had caught up with me.

"Perhaps I should bring you something cool to drink." George spoke with real concern. "Cider, perhaps?"

"I'll be fine in a moment, but thank you. I am indebted to you for coming to my rescue."

Jane drew forth her handkerchief and blew her nose. "You see, George. I knew Miranda could not possibly be on intimate terms with such a person."

"So you did. If his grandfather is the man I'm thinking of," George said, "the first Lord Seagrave was one of those to give false evidence at the trial of Sir Thomas More."

"I must go," I said. No longer yearning for a moonlit turn in any of the elaborate gardens, I now wanted only to find the kitchen garden, where I could hide among the parsnips and potatoes.

I hurried into the sheltering darkness beyond the courtyard, until a high soprano voice called out, "Lady Sherringham!"

Agnes's grandmother.

Beholden to the camouflage of night, I crept behind a tree and stood absolutely still, as a formidable woman, her high white forehead remarkably free of age, her sumptuous oxblood gown ornamented by a French hood and necklace, both adorned with garnets, raised her gloved hand in greeting.

"My dear Mariah," she said to the other woman, who, though not as well preserved, was as richly dressed in a gingerline gown trimmed with biche embroidery.

"How long it has been since we last met."

"Half a year at least, if my memory is as good as I suppose," the other woman answered. "I should have known you would look as well as ever, and how much your granddaughter resembles you at that age."

"Ah yes, my Agnes——"

"It must please you enormously to see how she has already been honored. I trust it is you who brought her to court—her mother, I fear, still being unwell."

"Nothing escapes you, Mariah."

"It is why we are such great friends," the other woman added, laughing a little, though not gaily. "What is it this time?"

"A low-grade fever. A titled husband, a grand estate, and she views her life as a prison from which she is forever begging asylum."

"I suppose not all of our sex are able to rise to their destinies."

"A most philosophical way of looking at the situation," Lady Sherringham considered. "It does not change the fact that because my daughter is once again incapable of looking after her daughter's interests, it is up to me to see yet another granddaughter suitably married. Though I far prefer the company of women, I do believe my daughter should have had at least one son."

The Lady Mariah laughed. "I know it has been a hardship. Yet you have done very well with the elder girls. Emily is a perfectly exquisite Lady Stafford. And Gwendolyn—yes, her husband is thrice a widower with almost as many chins as the late king—but such properties! Now, pray tell me, who have you selected for lovely Agnes?"

"Surely, Mariah, you must have your suspicions."

The other woman preened, and her gingerline skirts rustled a little. "Am I right in supposing the man to be George Mountjoy?"

"In this case," she said, sounding pleased, "you are mistaken."

"But, Sherry, of all the knights here, Mountjoy is certainly the best."

"Although the Mountjoy name is impeccable, George is a younger son who will never succeed to his father's title and properties, not when his older brother's health is so good. Besides"—she toed the earth with her satin shoe—"he is not of the mettle the queen is likely to favor."

"He is slight," the Lady Mariah considered.

"He is, and although charming and so well-mannered, he is far too sincere, and will therefore never succeed here."

"Really, Sherry, are you not too hard?"

"Only honest. The younger Mountjoy will certainly

occupy a fine place at court, becoming one of the queen's ministers of finance or foreign policy, especially given his skill at languages, but he will never become a favorite. Who knows? He may even marry that mousy little Radcliffe girl for love. I never saw such a pink nose. Surely her health is not good!"

"But she comes from a fine family."

"What does that matter when, with so many sisters, she cannot possibly have any dowry to speak of?"

"You forget young Mountjoy's late grandmother was an intimate friend of Lady Radcliffe."

"Ah, yes, a relationship that must count for something, so sentimental are these Mountjoys." Lady Sherringham's teeth, remarkably white in any woman beyond forty, glinted in the moonlight.

Lady Mariah laid a gloved hand on Lady Sherringham's arm. "Now, no more suspense. You must tell me. Who will it be for your Agnes?"

"He is one Her Majesty has already shone upon, and his consummate mastery of the courtier's arts coupled with his looks ensures he will go as far as the Earl of Leicester."

"Really, you do think well of him."

"I do. Perhaps"—she paused, clearly reveling in her friend's curiosity—"he will go even further, especially with the proper woman's influence."

"You are not speaking of Henry Raleigh?"

"Ah," Lady Sherringham said, "I knew you would arrive at him at last."

"But, Sherry, the young man may have a distinguished ancestry, but a name is no good without the accompanying riches. And the Raleighs are an impoverished, though exceedingly proud clan. Remember, the late Sir Raleigh was of too adventurous a heart. Besides, the Cunnington girl seems quite taken with him."

"Yes, of course she bears about her all the traces of her mother—the hussy. Even after twenty years I can still remember the woman's brazen attempts to marry the French duke right under poor, dowdy Queen Mary's nose. They say she has invited her master of the house into her household—"

"And into her bed. No wonder her chit of a daughter is running about in a plunging dress."

"Were this the queen's father's day," Lady Sherringham added, "he'd have her as his next bride."

"And shortly thereafter," the Lady Mariah said as merrily, "he'd have her head."

"Ah, well." Lady Sherringham dabbed at her eyes. "Fortune is not fair in blessing the Cunningtons with both title and wealth."

"And such influence as only both of these allow."

"You *are* a kindred spirit, Mariah. As for Henry

Raleigh's lack of fortune, we must trust to time. Mark how the queen already singles him out. The place of honor in the tournament, one traditionally reserved for the previous year's winner. Instead of subjecting Henry Raleigh to the wearing effects of so many jousts, she has allowed him to compete opposite the victor of the first half."

"Unlike George Mountjoy, he will be less fatigued."

"Precisely. And so," Lady Sherringham cooed, "Henry Raleigh will be most likely to win, for his reputation in the tiltyard speaks very well of him. Surely he will receive the prize, one destined to be as grand as this year's tournament itself."

"Nevertheless," the Lady Mariah said, her voice taking on a teasing quality, "I heard some talk of a possible engagement between the Molyneux girl and Henry Raleigh."

"But of course you would have, being so closely related to Burton Raleigh—that darling ogre." Lady Sherringham flashed her white teeth. "I am forever indebted to him for ending that union. If there was ever any thought of a marriage between Miranda Molyneux and Henry Raleigh," she said with unabashed glee, "it is impossible now the girl's father has died abroad. And in such debt, the family will never recover.

"Pity." Lady Sherringham toyed with her garnets. "The late earl was so gallant and good-looking in his youth, but also hopelessly romantic, deluding himself into believing he could restore the Molyneuxs' former glory in Ireland."

"True, true," the Lady Mariah considered. "And what good is romance now the girl has been entrusted to the Countess of Turbury? I never knew there could be so many mournful shades of black."

"Someone should tell her gloom went out of style with Mary. With piety such as hers, it's nearly impossible to believe her father was one of the late king's friends."

"Quite right," added the Lady Mariah. "How many illegitimate brothers and sisters the dour countess must have. Perhaps there are even some among us tonight. Sherry, think you her father's promiscuity is the reason for her own severity? Such was the case with the late Queen Mary, you know, and as the eldest of Henry VIII's children—"

"My dear Mariah, haven't we said enough about the countess?" Lady Sherringham's garnets splintered the moonlight. "She tires me with her doctrines and treatises. Besides, I have something truly dangerous to tell you."

"Please do." The Lady Mariah's voice turned syrupy.

"The late earl's widow has married Thaddeus Grey."

"How terrible," the Lady Mariah purred.

"How sudden."

"He always was one of the queen's gallant favorites. Think you she knows?"

"Given Dorothy Molyneux's daughter's presence in the tournament, I would stake a great deal on her ignorance. When the queen learns of her favorite's marriage—to a lovely, younger cousin, no less, a cousin she could barely abide before she became queen, so jealous are these Tudors—she will betray herself to be a woman whose feet, though adorned with cloth-of-gold slippers, are still made of clay."

I must have made a noise—snapped a twig or rustled some leaves—for the two women squinted into the darkness.

"Who's there?" both women called out at once.

I ordered every part of myself to stand as still as a statue as Agnes's grandmother said, "Announce yourself."

"Perhaps we should continue our conversation within the privacy of the crowd. These days I find the palace gardens increasingly plagued by spies."

"A very good idea, Mariah," Lady Sherringham said, taking the woman's arm.

Not until I was absolutely certain they had gone did I find my way to the nearest of the kitchen gardens, determined to comfort myself among the rows of root vegetables until I could sneak back to the dormitory unobserved.

It was now perfectly clear that Agnes's grandmother and her friend belonged to that conniving breed of court women my mother had warned me of. And Agnes I now knew to be a younger version of such women. I pulled a carrot from the earth and twisted it in my hands.

Hadn't the queen smiled at me just last night? Hadn't the queen once been a small girl who had watched her own mother plead with her father, only to see that mother dragged from her bed to the Tower, never to return? How could such a queen—one who prided herself on the progress she had made for women—punish me for an act my mother had committed?

CHAPTER ELEVEN

May 2, 1580

ALL NIGHT, I FOUND MYSELF STARTLED OUT of nightmares in which the bodiless voices of Lady Sherringham and her companion whispered throughout a ceremony in which I was Lord Seagrave's sacrificial bride, the countess my matron of honor, and Agnes and Beatrice my attendants. I spent the troubled hours that followed beside the window, a single candle to guide my hands as I interwove my hair with golden thread to make Kyd's token, relieved to have this task, as the other maidens slept around me.

Not until that gray hour before dawn did I set down my work, falling at last into a heavy, dreamless sleep.

"Oh good, I thought everyone else had gone. I'm not the last one," Jane said after she joined me before the mirror-lined row of basins where I had just finished bathing my neck and face with rose water. "Where did you go last night? You never returned to the party."

Sure that Jane noticed the shadows tracing my eyes, I almost considered taking her into my confidence, but how could I, given what she'd said last night—her disgust camouflaged only by her good breeding? Besides, even speaking the name of Lord Seagrave seemed a bad omen on this new day.

"I stayed up late working on my token," I said finally, then drew forth the shining rope I had woven into a braid with golden thread and two locks of my own hair.

"A bridle," she said. "You are clever."

"And what will you give to George?"

"One of my gloves," she said shyly.

"A most proper token," I said.

She sneezed. "I confess I'm a little nervous."

"If anyone is meant to play the May Queen, it's you, Jane," I said, easily able to picture her beneath the haw-thorn tree awarding George his prize.

She bit her lip. "You think I am up to it?"

"I cannot imagine any one of us could play the role with more grace or sincerity," I said, wishing this was my greatest worry.

Jane clasped my hands in both of her own. "Really, Miranda, you are a friend."

❖

The tournament opened against the phenomenal scenic backdrop of the day before. The only difference was that the fortress originally used as the Palace of Beauty now stood before a forest peopled not only by beasts of the land and birds of the air, but by a disturbingly real-looking dragon.

Seated beside Kyd and surrounded by the other maidens and their partners, I watched a knight step onto the stage and introduce himself as Callophisus.

"Lover of Beauty," Kyd translated as I admired the intricately detailed dragon adorning his shield, a symbol which unmistakably identified him as the Master of Revels himself, Sir Joshua Campion, whose family seat had supposedly been built upon the very ground that had once held Pendragon Castle.

". . . And before me stands the home of the illustrious Uther Pendragon," the knight continued, then knelt in prayer and paid homage to the father of King Arthur, as a harmonious sextet of the queen's ladies, their hair adorned with laurels of ivy, their costumes a gauzy Grecian white, circled the castle, surrounding it with hundreds of white roses.

After they, too, knelt before the castle, a door no more than four foot high opened, and Uther Pendragon himself stepped forth.

"Surely," I said to Kyd, "you cannot be disappointed in pageantry like this."

"You are right," Kyd said, with real eagerness. "Such pageantry steals my breath away."

It did seem we were holding our breath as Arthur's legendary father removed a stone from the castle, and from deep within retrieved a scroll he displayed to all of us:

*When a Vine on ye Walls in one
night shall grow,
When Roses whiter than the mighty
Crane's wings shall appear,
And the Red Dragon shall seem
like Snow,
Then shall our Land be redeemed
by a Virgin's might.*

The queen herself stood, and before an audience of one thousand, she stepped forward to reveal a face of such porcelain whiteness as only makeup creates, an artificial whiteness that brought back the jagged words Lady Sherringham and her equally artificial friend had spoken about my mother's marriage the night before.

I shuddered as the tiltyard seemed to sway.

"Miranda—" Kyd touched my arm. "Are you quite all right?"

"Just a little tired," I said, grateful for my veil.

Thankfully, any further talk was delayed by a dramatic equestrian display by Reginald Bornwell, the Master of the Horse, who expertly guided six horses through a series of feats including the leaping of six gates, one as tall as a man. Only after the last stallion kicked up a flurry of dust as Reginald Bornwell galloped him through the Holbein Gate, did the herald announce the tournament of the younger knights.

"Your token," I said to Kyd just before he left to mount his horse, which had already been saddled by one of the pages, and now waited for him behind the Holbein Gate.

"A braid of golden thread and two locks of your hair." He held out his arm so that I could fasten it to his armored sleeve.

"Ah, but it is more than that," I said. "We live in the land of enchantment today, do we not? In the land of enchantment, this braid has become a golden bridle, one which will enable you to steer your horse to victory."

"I should thank Fortune as well as Lord Bradstreet and your matron for being creatures of such inaccurate sight," he said, and this time I could find no changeling grin at play about his mouth.

171

"What do you mean?"

"Only that you were rightly matched according to the original plan," he said in a chivalrous voice, "as you must know."

I did not answer, just held out my hand to him, and instead of shaking it as on the previous day, Kyd raised it gently to his lips.

Minutes later he galloped into the tiltyard on a borrowed destrier, legs outstretched, stirrups extended, a position that enabled him to wield the most control over both lance and horse.

And from the opposite end Thomas Darcy rode in, a lance in one hand and a shield bearing a storm cloud in the other.

Kyd managed to keep his saddle as he and Darcy ran at each other twice, both times at speeds so dangerously high they raised a great deal of dust, the horses' shuddering breath echoing through the tiltyard.

Amazed my partner had not trained in Greenwich Tiltyard along with his peers, I found myself cheering him on as their lances clashed on the third run.

Perhaps, I told myself, he will even win.

But on the fourth approach, Darcy rode so hard the perspiration on the flanks of his horse shone like wet velvet. Darcy's helm may have hid his face from view, but in my imagination's eye I saw a look of determination so fierce I did not even startle when Darcy aimed his lance with such accuracy and force at Kyd's helm, his hand struck the horse's shaffron, so that the animal reared up, nearly throwing Kyd in the process.

When Darcy aimed his lance at Kyd's left shoulder, my partner turned to brace his body with the shield in his right hand, only to drop his lance.

Seconds later, Sir Joshua Campion stepped onto the field to pronounce Darcy the victor.

Darcy went on to beat Philip Scudamore, who had competed so well the previous year—an outcome I hoped would raise Kyd's spirits.

But Darcy's third opponent, Agnes's knight, John Gainsborough, proved a more indomitable challenger. Unlike his predecessors, John did not flinch, not even when Darcy galloped toward him at a speed made all the more menacing by his armor-plated size.

John proved himself so good that for a little while I found myself fighting the fear he would defeat Henry Raleigh and emerge as the tournament's ultimate victor, a win that would ensure Agnes the publicity of becoming May Queen. With her formidable grandmother's help, who knew what troubling advantage this role would give her?

But on the seventh run, when Darcy aimed his lance directly at John's helm, as he'd done throughout several of the earlier competitions, Gainsborough ducked, and his distressed horse swerved, enabling Darcy to hit him in the shoulder with such force that he dropped both lance and shield, and was nearly thrown from the saddle.

Once again, Thomas Darcy was pronounced the victor.

—※—

Late afternoon's blue sky gave way to the pinks and lavenders of evening, and it came time for Thomas Darcy to face George Mountjoy, the last of the day's competitors. With Jane's ivory glove clearly visible on his sleeve, he rode into the tiltyard on a freckled gray horse whose mane had been braided with silver.

Although George was never the aggressor, a quality I could not help but find emblematic of his truly courteous nature, he proved such an agile competitor that each time Darcy approached and was about to strike him, George wheeled his horse in a tight circle and made a great show with his bridle, as the animal—though not bred for trotting—almost danced around the tiltyard.

Throughout the competition, Jane sat so still I could not discern any movement from her veil. Not once, I felt sure, did she so much as sneeze.

On Darcy's sixth approach, George again wheeled his horse away at the very last second, causing everyone in the viewing stands to cheer as his opponent fell backward in the saddle, only to break his lance against the wooden palisade as he righted himself; a blunder that brought both his locking gauntlet and his shield to the ground, and caused at least five hundred of us to gasp.

Only then did Sir Joshua Campion step into the tiltyard and stride up to George's horse with a particularly jaunty step. As he pronounced George this portion of the tournament's victor, and invited all of us to wait—with bated breath—for the final competition with Henry Raleigh on the morrow, I could not help but believe Sir Joshua, though his position required he remain impartial, had secretly been cheering for George.

Jane turned to me. Her veil shielded her face, yet I had no doubt of the magnitude of her smile. Following such a demonstration, George Mountjoy, a second son, had surely proven Lady Sherringham wrong in her certainty he lacked the mettle to rise to one of the positions of highest honor in Queen Elizabeth's court.

⟡

"Do you see them?" Jane asked after we climbed the precariously steep staircase that led to the banquet hall, a staircase so winding I could not imagine Henry VIII climbing it, even though the youthful king was said to have reveled in letting his courtiers see him take its steps at a run. "He was quite an impressive figure then, Miranda," my grandmother had often said. Given all that had happened later, I could not imagine it.

Both of us scanned the hall for George Mountjoy and Kyd but found our view—and our path—blocked by two pixilated old ladies so deep in conversation they did not see to let us pass.

"I would never have believed such an elfin boy would grow up to be such a wiry, deft competitor," said the one dressed all in popinjay blue, her hair dyed the color of marigolds.

"The younger Mountjoy's performance should give my grandnephew something to aspire to," added her less colorful companion.

"Yes," said the lady in popinjay blue, "but he will face a master opponent in Sir Raleigh's son."

"So true, my dear. Such ability. So much like his father."

"I only hope Fortune is kinder to him."

"Whatever do you mean? The queen has already singled him out."

"So she has—for the moment." The lady in blue drew forth an azure fan and began to wave it dramatically. "Need I remind you what befell the towheaded Tayleboys?"

Her companion shuddered. "I dare not speak of it."

"Neither would I. Of course, the more immediate

threat lies in the marriage of his bachelor cousin, Lord Grey," the lady in blue said, lowering her voice a little.

"So it's true, then," added her companion, so quietly I had to strain to overhear.

"It is, my dear." The lady in blue sighed heavily. "Should the bride bring forth an heir, poor Henry Raleigh will inherit neither Lord Grey's land nor his title. Such a pity, given the young man's talents."

"Really, my dear, don't you think Dorothy too old to bear a child?"

The lady in blue lay a confiding hand on her friend's arm. "Remember, Henrietta, she comes from a line of long-lived women. I would not be surprised if she does not give birth within the year."

"Are you cold, Miranda?" Jane touched my arm.

"No," I said, wishing I could tell her the real reason I had trembled.

After the two ladies moved on, a silver-haired woman in buttery velvet approached us. "My grandaunt, Lady Cloudberry," Jane said, after I introduced myself.

"George sent me to find her. You do understand?"

"Of course," I said as she guided Jane toward George, whose proud face brightened as she approached where he stood surrounded by a thick group of admirers and wishers-well.

I scanned the hall for Kyd but did not find him—or

Henry Raleigh—among the others. When I turned toward the buffet, I spied the countess near the platters of meat—and beside her, Lord Seagrave.

Trusting she had not yet seen me, I hurried toward the glass doors leading to a balcony that, from this distance at least, seemed unoccupied.

Outside, I closed my eyes and tried to catch my breath.

When I opened them, Agnes and her grandmother obstructed my view of the park. As on the previous night, Lady Sherringham wore the garnet necklace, though her present gown was not oxblood but costly saffron, a color she must have intended to convey not only her high standing at court, but to highlight the lingering hints of gold in her snowy hair. Watching her now, I understood at last why yellow—the color of joy and fruitfulness—could also be associated with deception and jealousy.

Hoping against the impossible that they would not signal me, I tried to leave, when Agnes called out, "Miranda!"

I had no choice but to join them.

"My grandmother, Lady Sherringham," Agnes said, once the older woman acknowledged my curtsy.

"Ah, you look so much like your mother did at your age." Lady Sherringham's silky voice betrayed no trace of last night's venom. "But where is your mother? She would certainly want to be here to witness your triumph at court.

"But of course I seem to have forgotten that Cumberland is such a great distance from London." She fanned herself dramatically. "I understand the country to be very beautiful, though I myself practically live at court. I continually tell myself, 'Sherry, it's time to retreat to the rural beauty of Devonshire.'" She laughed. "I never seem to be able to get away."

"Untrue, Grandmother," Agnes said. "You were in Devonshire at Christmas."

"Ah, yes, how can I forget when we spent such a gay afternoon with Charlotte Raleigh and her brother? Such a well-bred woman. Even when she first came to court, Charlotte understood the most minute tenets of decorum, her mother having taught her well.

"That reminds me, Agnes," Lady Sherringham continued, "when it comes time for our meeting with the queen, I no longer consider the bisque gown with bobbin lace fitting."

"But it's my favorite!"

"That may be, darling, but the queen will not look kindly on all that gold lace. Besides, these days a darker color is so much more fitting—" With a wave of her fan, she acknowledged the bow of a gentleman whose ash-colored complexion mirrored the color of his exquisitely tailored doublet and hose. "Ah, Lord Bristol."

"Charmed to see you again, Sherry," he said, his gaze

oscillating between Agnes and me. "Are these lovely creatures your granddaughters?"

"Only Agnes," Lady Sherringham said. "The other is the daughter of—"

"If you will excuse me," I said. Certain they could see the perspiration along my face and throat, I hurried away, though I knew the report of my rudeness would travel swiftly.

No sooner had I reached the beverage table within the banquet hall then someone laid a hand on my arm.

Beatrice.

"Had old Bradstreet not found reason for us to change partners, you would be one joust away from playing the May Queen," she said. "Honestly, I never thought I'd be indebted to such an old fool."

"Really, Beatrice, not just the knights but the ladies, too, are supposed to embody the codes of chivalry," I said. "At least for the duration of the tournament."

"You are in a foul temper," she said, before handing me a glass of punch and guiding me away from a very stout woman made stouter by the breadth of her farthingale.

"Amid such company I cannot believe you singled me out to provoke me."

"True." Beatrice's violet eyes momentarily took on a dreamy luster. "With so many handsome men dashing about, I'm not inclined to squander a minute."

"Well then?" I said, impatient to be gone.

"I heard some talk about a possible engagement between you and Henry Raleigh."

The breath seemed to leave my lungs.

"At one time," she watched me closely, "your fathers were great friends, were they not?"

"At one time, yes." My father had spoken to me of their meeting at Cambridge, two impoverished young men with only their family names and boundless energy to recommend them.

"Well then?" Beatrice asked with cutting brevity.

"Given your aunt's connections, you must know Sir Raleigh died more than ten years ago," I replied, determined to give nothing away.

"Yes, of course. Even so," Beatrice said, her eyes never leaving my own, "I wanted to be sure you did not have feelings for him."

"And you're quite sure I don't?" I said, sensing some new note in her voice—was it uncertainty?

Beatrice came so close I could smell the spicy sweet punch on her breath. "You haven't my family's connections—or our resources."

"But Agnes does—" My throat seemed to close.

"Yes. Did I tell you I made the countess's acquaintance last night?" A menacing smile played about her lips. "How kind of her to introduce me to the charming Lord Seagrave."

Not just the room, but the people within it seemed to wobble.

"So I have struck a vulnerable place," Beatrice said.

"What do you want?"

"Speak to Henry Raleigh of me, and I will do everything in my power to help you evade your guardian's plans—"

"Why would I have any influence over Raleigh?"

Beatrice pulled me closer, and her voice dropped an octave. "He respects you."

"Respects?" The word, once spoken, tried to unseal something that lay deeper within me. Once more I recalled the deep indigo of his eyes when we met on the tourneying field.

"Yes." The admission seemed to give her pain. "The way Henry spoke about your father last night, I knew he viewed him as a sort of surrogate. A man like Henry Raleigh would naturally extend such feelings to you."

"And you care for him?" I said, the fist in my stomach tightening.

"Let's just say, with me he would be able to rise at court as he should. Make no mistake, Miranda," Beatrice continued, regaining her composure, "I am loyal to my country and to my queen. Henry Raleigh is precisely the sort of statesman Her Majesty needs in the latter years of her reign."

"And you believe the queen needs you for him to become such a person?"

"The queen needs my resources—my family's."

I thought of Elizabeth's mindfulness of England's coffers: her half sister's lovesick debts to Spain, the naive losses of her forlorn brother, the costs of keeping her Scottish cousin in a stylish prison, the necessary brilliance of her court.

"Miranda!" Even before I caught the scent of oranges and spices, I knew whose voice it was now filling the air.

"Give me your word," Beatrice said, toasting me with her glass, "and I will make sure you have time to get away."

Picturing the hawkish Lord Seagrave, the countess's inevitable companion, and the trap she had laid for me, I said, "Very well. You have my word."

Beatrice breathed deeply, her smile one of both victory and relief. "Splendid. And you have mine. Now—go!"

I fled through the double doors and took the stairs two at a time, then continued running. Despite the pebbles scraping the hem of my dress, I ran across the park, not daring to stop until I reached the tennis courts that lay far beyond the Holbein Gate. Had I been able, I would have kept running, away from Whitehall and the countess and the entangling network in which I now found myself, until I reached Plowden Hall—not as it was now, a vacant house brooding over the silence—but as it used to be.

CHAPTER TWELVE
May 3, 1580

"I LOOKED FOR YOU FOLLOWING THE BANQUET," Kyd said as I took my place beside him in the viewing stands the next morning.

"I felt unwell," I said, relieved he at least had not witnessed my flight from the countess and Lord Seagrave. "It must have been something I ate—or the heat."

"I'm sorry to learn you were unwell," Kyd said. "And here I thought you might have been avoiding me."

"Why would I ever do that?"

He raked his fingers through his hair. "Because I proved myself unequal to the competition."

"On the contrary. For one who did not train from early youth or have a run in Greenwich's tiltyard

184

until a few weeks ago, you performed admirably."

"You are a friend." Kyd laid a companionable hand on my own. "If you weren't wearing a skirt and petticoats, I'd invite you to the tavern later."

So intent was Kyd's look just then, it came as a relief when Sir Joshua Campion stepped into the tiltyard to announce the final tournament between Henry Raleigh and George Mountjoy.

Although my head told me to disregard Henry's movements, as the two knights rode in through opposing gates, the stars on his helm did seem the accurate emblem for one who moved as if he had trained not on solid ground, but amid lapis lazuli skies and dreaming clouds.

To steady myself I pictured my father drawing the match, approaching it with a precise balance of light and shadow, taking especial care to render the bearing of each man in the high-backed saddle, the armor on his body polished to a sheen worthy of the queen's jewels. For George, my father would have used a soft pencil, blurring further the line to underscore the elusive nature of George's style—he seemed to be there one moment, and somewhere else the next.

My father would have understood how only a fine, dark line could have portrayed the fearless way Henry Raleigh brought his horse to a gallop. One false move, even a twitch of the hand, could have caused the animal to rear up, then throw him against the palisade, where he risked being trampled. Watching, I found it hard to believe he was not the noble-spirited individual my father had praised in his letters, one who had given another man his sword on an Irish battlefield.

How many times their lances crossed, I do not know, so lost in the rhythm of the joust did I—and the thousand others—become before Henry Raleigh's horse galloped once more toward George's gleaming figure, and with a daring thrust at George's more vulnerable left side, the two lances collided, an action that seemed to bring both horses to a terrifyingly swift standstill, though in reality the animals' legs and heaving flanks kept moving all the time.

What happened next remains a mystery, so swiftly did Henry's horse trot backward, graze the palisade with its rear legs and startle, bucking him as it rose on its hind legs and clawed the air. Henry swiftly regained control of his mount, but in the process he accidentally unnerved his rival's horse. George's horse bucked and tried to throw him.

At that moment, Henry could have easily struck George. Instead he reined his horse in and retreated slightly, giving George a chance to calm his steed. Why Henry looked away then, I do not know; but when he did, he created an opportunity for George to raise his lance and achieve the safest, though not the most dramatic victory as he knocked Henry's lance out of his hand.

For a fraction of a second, all of us remained mute, as if none among us could believe that such a slight figure—George Mountjoy looked like a boy compared to Henry Raleigh—had managed to defeat the favorite.

Once the audience understood what had happened, the applause was ear-shattering. Yes, we were celebrating George's victory. And yet, into the roar of two thousand clapping hands I could not deny some acknowledgment of Henry's chivalry; for despite his behavior outside the tilt-yard, a less noble knight would never have jeopardized his own success to preserve another's safety.

⊰※⊱

It was midafternoon before Jane and George stepped into one of Whitehall's grandest rose gardens following the ceremony at which Jane awarded George a silver sword, its handle ornamented by sapphires and a single square-cut diamond. Diamonds may lose their perfection and strength once cut. Yet Lady Periwinkle told us that this diamond had the revered history of having been taken from a larger diamond that had once adorned the crown of Henry VIII himself.

"The young Lady Jane bears her place of honor remarkably well," Lady Cloudberry said to her companion.

It was true. Not only did Jane manage to keep from sneezing, she held her head high beneath the crown of white roses she wore in place of her heart-shaped headdress and veil. Still, I knew she must be relieved the luncheon at which the queen herself would make a brief appearance (for there was also the master knights' reception requiring her attendance) consisted of perhaps a hundred instead of a thousand intrigued guests.

Fortunately, neither the countess nor Lord Seagrave was among them.

"After such a morning, I thought the refreshments would please, not shock you," Kyd said when he found me on a bench surrounded by a riotous blooms of roses, a place I had chosen for its relative distance from the banquet tables.

"I don't want to pry," Kyd said after handing me a glass of ale, "but you seem quite different from the spirited companion of yesterday. Not feeling unwell again, are you?"

"No," I said as Henry Raleigh circled the rose garden with Beatrice, who continually brought her lips close to his ear, whispering words of reassurance, no doubt; though she seemed by far the more dejected of the two.

"Were I to trust my instincts," Kyd continued, "I'd say your attention was focused on a knight who is not your partner."

"Do you always speak so boldly?" I said, dropping my gaze.

"When necessary, yes."

"No wonder you learned to joust so quickly," I said, meeting his eyes once more, determined to keep to a measured tone.

"Honored as I am by your compliment, I'd wager you are in some sort of trouble."

I shook my head, though I knew the countess and Lord Seagrave would inevitably find me at the ball tonight.

"I can see it in your eyes. They're pretty, by the way, a most unusual shade of green—like a hummingbird's cape, or the sea at dawn."

I smiled in spite of myself.

"That's better. Now"—he took my hand companionably—"why don't you tell old Kyd what's bothering you? Who knows?" His grin made him look more like a creature of enchantment than ever. "I might even help you arrive at a solution."

I increasingly feared that Kyd longed to play the part of suitor. Yet I needed to unburden myself to someone, so I soon found myself telling him about my father's death and his affection for Henry Raleigh, whose own father had died when he was thirteen. But mostly I told Kyd about my wardship with the countess, the rigor of Turbury, and especially of her plans for Lord Seagrave and me. The two things I left out: my promise to Beatrice, and the fact that Henry Raleigh and I had once come very close to being engaged.

"I've always known the fairer sex has the more difficult situation," Kyd said, reaching out a comforting hand. Soon, tears began to press against my eyes. "Mustn't do that now."

"Why not?" I sniffed.

"In such a circumstance, the queen would hold me—a person of low birth—responsible."

I began to laugh, aware I was taking advantage of his kindness.

"Listen," he said more gently, "you haven't blundered in confiding in me. I may not have met this countess yet, or a man who proves our Lord is not always selective enough in assigning our fortunes. Yet I cannot believe either one to be a match for our combined intellects."

"You really believe so?" I said, still drawn to Henry and Beatrice, who had settled themselves in an almost equally secluded spot nearby, where Beatrice sat weaving herself a crown of incarnadine roses.

"I do," he said, aware of whom I was looking at.

⊰※⊱

The queen did not set foot in the rose garden until the reception honoring George Mountjoy and, by extension, Jane Radcliffe, was nearly at an end. As Elizabeth approached, I found myself dazzled by the way the jewels on her gown formed a garden of emerald leaves, the blossoms of the pansy, the rose, and the eglantine shaped from rubies, amethysts, and hundreds of diamonds.

Accompanying her was the serene Lady Dewberry on her left; and on her right, arrayed in flesh-colored satin, a billowing transparent sheath of fabric adorning each of her sleeves, walked an elegant woman with a hooked nose and arctic blue eyes, her skin and hair so fair she reminded me of a wintry ermine, that sleek master of camouflage.

At the coming of the queen, all of us knelt and bowed our heads, remaining prostrate until she gave the command for us to rise.

"My dear George, I congratulate you," the queen said. "To triumph over an opponent like Henry Raleigh, whose father once defeated the Earl of Leicestershire in this very tiltyard, well, such a victory recommends you very well."

"I am honored, Your Grace," George said, then knelt once more as she gave him a much bejeweled hand to kiss.

Jane, too, knelt, trembling a little as the queen lay a hand on her crown, then raised her chin and smiled. "I was deeply pleased to learn Lettice Radcliffe had sent her youngest and most beloved granddaughter to court at last," Elizabeth said with uncommon gentleness. "Your grandmother—though never employed in my service—was very kind to my brother when he was a child. As my brother's sister, I could never forget such kindness. Looking at you, my dear girl, I mark a subtle but noteworthy affinity."

"Thank you, Your Grace," Jane said in a quiet voice.

Though his own head remained bowed, I saw the proud smile playing about George's lips. And for this moment alone I found myself relieved to find Lady Sherringham among the invited guests. Although Agnes's grandmother was at least fifty, I trusted her hearing was still keen enough to understand the significance of Elizabeth's praise.

CHAPTER THIRTEEN

May 3, 1580

Our preparations for the party on the river required several hours. With the exception of Bridget, who actually hinted at the possibility of dressing in gentlemen's clothes for the occasion, a practice that was becoming a bit more permissible during our queen's time (especially given Elizabeth's fondness for breeches), every other one of us was eager to appear as feminine as possible.

Not only was this the first grand gala for most of us, but the event itself was spoken of by courtier and lady alike, by fool and scribe—with a certain measure of exaggeration—to be on a lavishness equaled only by the one held at the queen's accession.

While the less fortunate among us ministered to red or pimpled skin with a wash of salt and lemon juice, scrubbed at our elbows with a paste of butter and apricot seeds, or dusted the shoulders of our gowns with combing cloths to remove dandruff, the vainer among us anointed our faces with a paste of honey and bayberry with all the solemnity of penitents at their ablutions.

"Will you help me fasten my stays?" Jane asked, after I placed the wire frame in her hair, thereby securing her cascade of curls.

"Of course," I said, admiring her milk white gown's intricate embroidery, in particular the square, French-style bodice bedecked with forget-me-nots and seed pearls.

"A gift from my grandmother," Jane said. "I've never had anything so fine.

"These are both beautiful," she said, once I finished helping her, and we stepped over to the wardrobe where I'd hung the pink satin gown and a second one of blue and violet silk. "The style of the pink one reminds me of one my mother wore during her own debut."

"Which would you suggest I wear?" I asked, the wistfulness in Jane's voice telling me that she, too, had spent many years dreaming over her mother's gowns—and the history they embodied.

"The pink satin," Jane said without hesitation. "The other, though certainly beautiful, seems more suitable for a married woman."

"It was passed down to me—after being much altered—through my sister's mother-in-law."

"And no wonder, given the value of such silk. Still"—Jane smiled—"the pink gown seems to have been made for you."

⌐≈≺≻≈¬

Jane wanted to wait for me, but I believed it necessary to remain until Agnes left, suspecting she might sift through my things or worse, were she to leave after me. As if she understood my motive, Agnes lingered at the mirror long after Beatrice finished twining half a dozen ropes of pearls around her neck, long after Eleanor finished padding the bodice of her gown.

So long did Agnes stand there, applying bayberry powder to her shoulders and keeping sly watch over my movements in the glass, that with the exception of Bridget, who seemed determined to keep up her fencing exercises tonight of all nights, I was the very last to leave.

By the time I reached the fantastically decorated barge anchored where Whitehall's grounds met the Thames, Beatrice stood before the railing, feigning nonchalance, the furious beating of her cinnamon-plumed fan alone betraying her impatience.

"A delightful evening, is it not?" she said with calculated brightness as I stepped on board.

195

"It is," I replied, the breeze off the river cooling us both as we passed beneath a gossamer canopy adorned with silver stars and lavender rose petals.

Beyond lay a fragrant array of lilies, the hundreds of star-shaped blossoms inflorescent in their crystal vases. And all along the floor, feathery baskets of ferns impressed us with their green serenity.

"They say Whitehall's greenhouses and gardens did not have enough flowers to accommodate tonight's event, so the Master of the Revels had a barge come up the Thames from Hampton Court; on board, the palace garden's entire supply of flowers," Beatrice said as we passed a pair of women who examined us critically from behind their fans.

Though I heard one of these women whisper something about Beatrice, my companion showered her with a most bewitching smile.

"Vivienne Dormer," she muttered after we passed. "A spiteful creature, nevertheless one entrusted with distributing the queen's cast-off gowns to the maidens, and therefore someone with whom to stay on good terms."

"Ah." I recalled the unattractive black silk gown, the queen's sole gift to my mother—"the pearls of some value"—then smiled back at the woman as lightheartedly as I could manage.

In slippered feet and rustling gowns, we navigated this obstacle course of courtiers and ladies, including one enormously fat man with a saffron-tipped beard who had just been appointed to the Close Care of the Queen's Wardrobe, a position that required him to watch over the transport of her gowns while the court was on progress.

"And over there, Lady Claribel Wynard, with whom the queen's last Master of the Horse fell in love," Beatrice said, nodding to an elegant though not beautiful woman in a green satin gown heavily slashed to show the ivory silk lining, the lace of her ruff and cuffs of exquisite design. "Lady Wynard has learned not to hide her double chin beneath her ruff. Otherwise, the queen would never permit her attendance here at court, so puzzlingly attractive is she to the other sex."

With enviable skill, Beatrice continued to provide clues about our companions' characters while pointing to the songbirds in their gilded cages, their colors ranging throughout the rainbow's spectrum.

Among the members of this floating aviary there was even a pair of popinjays preening on a pedestal. The birds spoke with a mimicked eloquence, besting some of the people assembled here.

A pair of aging courtiers drew so near, the hems of their doublets actually brushed up against our skirts. I feared Lady Sherringham's spies, until their covetous glances made it clear they were primarily interested in

Beatrice's raven beauty set off by her low-necked cinnamon gown hemmed with seed pearls.

"You'll be sure to speak to Henry Raleigh about me?" Beatrice said, smiling at the men.

"I gave you my word. Now how will you keep yours?"

"Without naming any names," she said, the cinnamon fan once again fluttering before us, "I can tell you on very good authority—"

"Your grandaunt's?"

Beatrice brandished her fan. "I cannot say."

"Go on."

"It's that bad leg Lord Seagrave is always dragging about. Had he come by it honorably—were it a war wound, for example, or the result of a riding accident—he wouldn't be so secretive about it."

"What is the source of his injury?" I asked, recalling his flush when I asked about it.

"He seems to have mistreated the well-born but poor son of one of his father's friends, one Lord Gilroy. According to my source"—Beatrice drew closer—"this Gilroy was returning from some skirmish abroad—in Spain, I think it was, or perhaps France. He was decorated by the queen, but there was no money to accompany the honor."

"How am I to have confidence in a story for which you cannot even remember the facts?" I said, doubting anew

Beatrice's ability to save me from a lifetime of dinners opposite Lord Seagrave.

"The important *fact* is that instead of giving Lord Gilroy an honorable post worthy of his title, Seagrave forced him to play shepherd on his property. Imagine a nobleman watching over the sheep and cattle!"

"And the bad leg?" I asked, aware of how humiliating my brother would have found such treatment. And what of my father, who had always lost more than he gained on his ventures abroad?

Beatrice laid a confiding hand on my arm. "It seems Lord Gilroy wanted to marry one of the queen's more expendable ladies-in-waiting—and he asked Seagrave for a loan. When he refused, the desperate Gilroy lost his temper and fired."

"Gilroy shot Lord Seagrave in the leg?" I bit my lip, unsure if I wanted to laugh or cry out.

"He did, and his lady married someone else."

"Where is Lord Gilroy now?"

"After being released from prison—Seagrave is a magistrate, as you know—Lord Gilroy seems to have disappeared."

"Then we have no proof," I said. "And a search might take years."

"I hadn't considered that," Beatrice said, her attention straying to a lanky courtier in cinnabar velvet who smiled her way.

My shoulders sagged, and the beloved pink satin gown seemed to mock all I'd hoped for. "Really, Beatrice, you'll have to do better than this."

"Pity," she said, her gaze growing more flirtatious as the courtier bowed, "I thought I'd done rather well."

"Oh, Beatrice, my dear!" an older woman called out, her moonlight-colored gown precisely the shade of her hair, which only a very nimble-fingered maid could have arranged in its complicated tower of curls accented further with star-shaped gems.

Instantly, Beatrice was all rose petals and smiles. "My grandaunt—"

"But you cannot possibly leave just yet," I said.

Her violet eyes regarded me coolly. "Sorry," she replied before gliding off to a candlelit corner where her grandaunt held court among a group of handsome men half her age, all of whom were attending to her every word. So this was the Duchess of Suffolk. With beauty and magnetism like hers, it was age alone that had saved her from the queen's censure.

While Beatrice flirted with her grandaunt's circle of admirers, carrying on so gaily one would never think she was pining, or at least scheming, for Henry Raleigh, I sought a quiet place at the far end of the barge, then looked out at the water and wondered if I had made a mistake in entering into an alliance with her.

And yet, what choice did I have?

"For once I am indebted to the court's self-absorption for creating this opportunity to speak to you," a voice called from behind, its shadowy depths as inviting as a light touch to the back of the neck.

I turned to face Henry Raleigh. Reminded of what Beatrice had said, heat like the kind that comes with eating too many strawberries flushed my face, and I longed at once for the camouflaging cool of a fan.

"I'm sorry. I seem to have startled you. This was hardly my intention," he said, and bowed.

"Where are your admirers?" I said, aware he was looking at me in a way I could not quite define, only that it unsettled me. "Surely, after today—"

"For the moment they seem to have forgotten me." He stepped closer, and the starlight caressed the crescent-moon scar along his cheek. "As yours have you."

"I have not so many," I said, wondering if in spite of his courteousness he, too, felt all the awkwardness of our circumstance.

"I doubt that"—he smiled, his indigo gaze not once straying from my face—"especially when you keep company with Miss Cunnington."

"Is such a compliment meant for me or for her?" I said, startled to discover he had been watching us—but for how long?

"Both of you, of course." He held out his arm.

"You are courteous," I said, recovering my composure.

He bowed, knowing me too little to detect the edge in my voice.

"Your partner, Chidiock Kyd, seems a likable sort, but isn't he a bit out of his league here at court?" he said as we strolled around the deck, keeping to what at first seemed the safe subject of the tournament.

Several courtiers and ladies turned to stare, more than a few speaking in hushed tones I did not want to decipher.

"Darcy did take him out of the running so early," he said.

"He is new to the tiltyard and lacks the privilege of his peers," I said, the unease within me in marked contrast to the water peacefully lapping at the barge. "Considering that, he did very well."

"I did not expect you to be such a passionate advocate of one you met so recently," Henry said, his tone suggesting jealousy. "One who is not a tourneyer by right of birth."

"I speak only the truth." I met his eyes, determined to reveal nothing more about my feelings for Kyd. "And what of your partner? As Beatrice's close friend, I am curious to know how you are enjoying her company."

"She is one of the court's beauties," he said diplomatically. "And, then, her grandaunt is among the most prominent women here. I am therefore honored to be her partner—for the duration of the tournament."

"Lifelong relationships are often forged in a very brief span of time," I said, longing to unsettle him.

"You do not mince your words," he said, his gaze lingering on my own. "In this way, you are your father's daughter."

"I am," I said, wondering what he would say were I to tell him he was not the man my father believed in—one he would have loved as his own son.

"I am relieved to find it so," he whispered, his breath, or perhaps only the breeze, touching my cheeks.

"Are you?" I said, chastising myself for the way his words affected me.

"Yes. Too many people here at court exist solely on the surface. Try to plumb their depths, and one finds more exquisite behavior—but little substance."

I must have made some sign—a twitch or a frown—for he touched my arm and said, "It may be impertinent, but I ask your leave to speak frankly."

I looked out at the water shining beneath the moon. How could it be the same moon my father and Henry had looked up at in Ireland? The same moon I had glimpsed through my beloved turret window at Plowden Hall?

"Miranda?" Again, that tug when he spoke my name.

Something in my face must have betrayed me. Soon,

Henry was not only very close, but he was speaking too intimately, his voice as soft as the finest velvet.

"What I said to you yesterday—I spoke only the truth when I told you I cherished your father."

Afraid to look at him just then, I kept my gaze on the water.

"Did you?"

"Yes. Had circumstances permitted, I would have honored the understanding between us."

"But circumstances proved less than favorable—for you, at least," I said, resolving to disavow any conciliatory words from a man who, despite his own facility with language, no longer behaved in a way I could understand.

"I ask you to consider what choice I had."

"More choice than I—"

He reached for my arm, but I pulled away.

"Please," he said. "If only I could make you understand that despite my admiration for your father and for you, an alliance of marriage was no longer—"

"Desirable on your part," I said, reminded again of my separation from home, the agony of the countess, the misery of a suitor like Lord Seagrave. "I understand this too well."

"I had no idea you would be entrusted to such guardians. Are your circumstances—?"

"My circumstances are no longer your concern."

"Please," he said, the edge in his voice proof I had kindled in him some reaction.

Once again I faced him, fighting the urge to touch his scar.

"I want only to tell you that the man who will ultimately claim you as his wife will be fortunate indeed," he said.

Standing there, my heart pounding in my ears, I only hoped the darkness hid my expression from his eyes.

"There you are, Henry!"

It was the ermine woman from the reception, the one with the hooked nose and seawater eyes, sumptuously arrayed in a sarcenet gown that could only be of the Italian fashion, given its short-waisted bodice; the very woman who, along with Lady Dewberry, had accompanied the queen earlier that day.

"My sister, Charlotte Raleigh," he said, stepping back from me a little. "And this, Charlotte, is Miranda Molyneux."

"How do you do," I said, curtsying as I tried to recover my calm.

"So good to meet you," she said, though there was no gladness in her voice, and her smile, a veneer of the highest polish with little real feeling underneath.

"Your gown is lovely," I said in spite of myself, finding it impossible not to admire the silver lace at the bodice.

"A gift from an Italian poet," Charlotte said.

"My sister has quite an extensive circle of literary friends," Henry said, the softness of a few moments ago vanishing so quickly I almost doubted I'd heard it.

"Such a pity she never met your father," he continued. "Not only was he an accomplished artist, but he knew so much about the world of ideas. What a great deal I learned from him. And always, when we traveled, he seemed to be reading some marvelous new book! Remember, Charlotte, Father said the late earl's love of reading was one of the things he admired most about him."

"I'm afraid I have forgotten, Henry," she said, allowing her fingertips to idle along the railing. "After all, it was all so long ago—their friendship."

"Was it your father's wish—" Henry asked.

"Come, Henry." She took hold of his arm. "I *am* sorry I have to interrupt, but there are so many people at court whom my brother has yet to meet, not to mention so many by whom he is beloved."

"I give thanks for this opportunity." Henry raised my hand to his lips, his sister looking on with barely veiled disapproval.

"Charlotte is the daughter of the late Sir Raleigh's first wife, Rebecca Mooreland." The voice, although soft, further unsettled me. "A descendent of John of Gaunt."

Agnes. How long had she been standing there?

"Although Henry's mother was much admired for her

grace and beauty," Agnes continued, "my grandmother says the original Lady Raleigh was perfection itself. Quite naturally, Charlotte takes after her mother in this way."

"That may be, and yet you must believe Henry's father to have chosen well, since he is the result of this second union."

"A most diplomatic way of viewing things," Agnes observed.

"I try to view a situation from as many perspectives as possible," I said.

"Do you now?" Her appraising eyes raked my expression.

"Is this not the only means of finding the truth?" I replied, determined to withhold all emotion.

"So it would seem. At least this is the only honorable explanation I can assume for the amount of time you have spent in Beatrice's company since the tournament began."

"And how am I to find an honorable explanation for your behavior to me?"

"My behavior?" Agnes regarded me innocently.

"When I arrived at Whitehall, you pretended to know nothing about me and so lured me into your confidence on false grounds. You pretended—"

"Yes?" Agnes said.

"You pretended to be my friend."

"My, you do take a word—and a person—so literally.

A sign of your naiveté, I suppose. As my grandmother said at the banquet, it is always refreshing to meet someone new to court life, your mother having abandoned it for the country—or was it the court who abandoned her?" Agnes's eyes brandished tiny flames as the doe was transformed into the fox.

"Is the air of a country lass what Henry Raleigh admires in you, I wonder?" She plucked a hair from my dress. "Pity, the impossiblity of you two coming to know each other more closely. Pity, too, you cannot spend more time with Charlotte Raleigh. As my grandmother said, she has always possessed the most exquisite manners. She, more than almost anyone, could teach you that actions, as well as words, have subtle nuances. Without a range of lights and shadows, where would lie the interest? Surely, being the daughter of a painter, you ought to know this."

I did not answer as Agnes raised her glass to Lady Sherringham, who I now recognized among the popinjays, her signature garnets glinting at her throat.

"It is clear you are expected," I said, renewing my vow to help Beatrice in her quest.

"One more thing. Your guardian, the Countess of Turbury, asked me to say she is looking for you." Agnes's mouth twisted into a smirk that betrayed how much she was enjoying this.

"Thank you ever so much." I smiled, fully aware that

she and I stood within a very different sort of tiltyard—
one with its own set of dangers.

Once Agnes left me, I stood there struggling to dismiss
her threat as I puzzled over what seemed to be the contra-
dictions in Henry Raleigh's behavior.

What he said about Kyd suggested an elitism I had
never expected—one I felt sure my father and mother
would have criticized, believing privilege was an act of
grace, not a right. But there had been a note of jealousy
there, too. And what of the kindness in his voice? Was it
possible Henry considered my future? What would he
have asked me about my father had his half sister not
interrupted us?

※

"I searched the barge for you everywhere," Kyd said after he
found me brooding over the water. "That frustrating
young woman, the doleful Scudamore's partner, has been
trailing me for the last half hour. Had I not met him
before, I would have credited her with his woeful
demeanor."

"Eleanor—"

"In the future I will remember never to jest with such a
provoking person—

"What is the matter?" he said when I failed to laugh.

"Here we are on the queen's barge, and you look as if this river led to Hades."

"If only you understood the truth of those words," I said, aware I could not tell him of all that had passed.

"Come now," Kyd said, raking his fingers through his hair, "you may not be as gay as many of the guests, but misery is simply not permissable on the queen's barge."

"How can you be so sure?"

"I've tasted of her fruits firsthand."

"*Her* fruits?"

"Forgive me the slip." His grin was only a bit sheepish. "Real misery is slinking up and down the alleys of London in search of a crust to eat. It is sleeping in an unheated barn to escape the December rain. It is trying to evade a young woman—"

"You have made your point," I said, the trace of a smile tugging at my lips.

"Besides," he said less playfully, "I cannot believe you are all that unhappy, especially when I saw you talking rather heatedly to Henry Raleigh a short while ago."

The jealousy that pierced his tone was impossible to ignore.

"We were speaking of my father. I told you, he was very fond of Henry Raleigh."

"Ah." Newly awkward, he shifted in his boots, then

offered his arm. "Come now, a little food is what we both need to lift our spirits."

"You?" I said, grateful to be pulled away from my thoughts, though I feared I was encouraging him. "Whatever is the matter?"

"On the morrow I shall bid farewell to Whitehall and its luxuries," he sighed. "Given my poor show in the tournament, I assume it will be a very long time before I am invited to taste such delicacies again."

"So soon as that?" I stammered. "But you said you would help me."

Kyd grinned, the corners of his eyes crooking up at the edges. "Chin up, now. There is still tonight."

"One night?" My legs seemed to lose their strength. "What can I possibly accomplish in one night?"

"You can conduct yourself before this abominable lord so he has no desire to make you his wife. It will not put him off forever, but it will give you the advantage of time."

I could not deny the idea's appeal. Besides, it reminded me of our master strategist, the procrastinating queen who flirted with the French ambassadors at supper while assuring her courtiers during dessert that she would not marry a foreign prince.

But how could I make her example my own?

As if to spite my hopes, no sooner had Kyd and I filled our plates with sugared strawberries and other delights, but the countess and Lord Seagrave found us.

"Miranda," the countess said, "why did you not come and find us as we—as I—expected?"

"She would have, dear lady." Kyd spoke with a charm I had not expected from him. "You see, Miranda has been greatly sought out by so many important members of the court. I myself have been waiting all night to speak with her."

For a moment the countess looked unsure if she should believe him or not.

"You should be very proud," Kyd told her. "Miranda is one of the most admired young women at court. The Earl of Leicester—"

"Miranda is with us now," Lord Seagrave said, looking at Kyd as if he'd like to grind him beneath his shoe. "That is what signifies."

"How right you are, Lord Seagrave, and how generous of you. Miranda," the countess said, "Lord Seagrave wishes to speak to you. Surely, your friend—"

"Kyd," he said, with a theatrical bow.

"Surely, Mr. Kyd understands and will excuse you."

I turned to Kyd for help, but already Lord Seagrave was offering his arm.

"Go on, then," the countess urged, her politeness buttressed by a steely will.

I found myself unable to move, so that it was Lord

Seagrave himself who had to steer me away from my guardian and my friend.

"There is a matter of great significance to both of us I wish to speak to you about," he said, once he had me cornered in a dim spot precariously close to the water.

"To both of us, sir?" I said, picturing a forsaken Lord Gilroy among the sheep and cattle, the lady he loved married to someone else. "How can that be when we have only just met?"

"You are very young, Miranda," he said, standing too close for comfort; so close I breathed in his troubling scent—like garlic hung out to dry in damp weather. "Other men might find such naiveté a liability—"

"I am young," I interrupted. "Far too young to undertake any serious responsibilities; far too young to be of interest to you."

"I doubt that very much." Lord Seagrave laughed, though it sounded more like a choking man's cough. "You see, the countess has been speaking to me of you for several weeks now—first in writing, and here again at court."

Like a rabbit trapped by a pack of hunting dogs, or, in this case, by one very unpleasant mastiff who had recently dined on garlic, I trusted silence and immobility to be the moment's only allies.

"Besides, youth is always on a woman's side insofar as it

concerns marriage. You will have many more years to breed, and then look after me." He laid his hand on my arm, and his clammy touch prickled so much, I cried out.

Instantly, the countess joined us. "Is something the matter?"

"It seems Miranda is not prepared to hear me speak to her of my intentions." Lord Seagrave spoke with such glassy hauteur, I realized a sneer suited him far better than a smile.

"Surely Miranda is only overtired from the tournament," the countess said. "So much excitement is foreign to her. Remember, my lord, she has lived so quietly in the country. Unused to the worldliness of the court, she is out of her element."

"A good point," Lord Seagrave said, his disconcerting smile once more restored. "I must make allowances for Miranda's innocence. It is one of the qualities that recommends her."

"It is indeed," the countess said, silvering her words. "If you would excuse Miranda and myself for just a moment," she told Lord Seagrave.

"But of course." He bowed stiffly to her, and then to me.

"You are a very clever girl, Miranda," the countess said. We no longer stood in a secluded place beside the river but were now lit up by candlelight and encircled by many of the guests. "I therefore find it nearly impossible to believe you can be so ignorant when it comes to Lord Seagrave's intentions."

"His intentions?" I said, dizzy at such injustice.

"Yes." Her tone became a challenge. "Not only do you insult Lord Seagrave's honor, and my own, by pretending you do not understand my purpose in bringing the two of you together, but you have behaved in a most unmannerly fashion since the tournament began."

"Untrue," I said softly.

"Explain then how it is you managed to escape the message I left not just with Lady Periwinkle, but with Agnes Somerset?"

"I did not try to escape either message," I said truthfully. It was the countess, not her relayed words, I needed to avoid.

"I find this impossible to believe. I am prepared to let it go—this time—but in the future, I expect you to find me immediately when I request your attendance."

"Yes," I said, hoping politeness would put an end to this meeting, having just noticed Jane Radcliffe and George Mountjoy, both of whom were looking at me sympathetically.

"You are becoming a little too free in your choice of companions," the countess continued. "I warned you of this on our journey to London—"

"You cannot mean——" I said, indicating Jane.

"Certainly not. That young woman's modesty, as well as her ancestry, do much to recommend her."

"Agnes Somerset?"

"That one may come from a family a little too good at spending their money, and anyone else's, but the Somerset name is impeccable, and their coffers are deep." The countess's eyes glittered. "Besides, her grandmother, Lady Sherringham, is a powerful figure in London and here at court. A woman it would not do to have as an enemy.

"No," she said, her gaze so sharp I began to feel faint, "I am speaking of the Cunnington girl."

"Beatrice?" I said dumbly, wondering how much the countess had observed.

"Precisely," the countess hissed. "Despite her family's connections, her reputation—like her mother's before her—is not a good one. Why she was chosen for one of the tournament's maidens, I cannot imagine. Such a person would have shamed all of you as the May Queen.

"Mark my words, Miranda," the countess said. "Those who associate with a Cunnington will come to no good. When her mother was a girl, she managed to have another blamed for her recklessness. Some shocking incident with a courtier behind a tree. Most indecent. On the strength of her mother's lie, that girl went to the Tower. I will not have you meet the same fate. Should you shame yourself, you will damage my own reputation as well, and that," she said grimly, "I cannot possibly allow."

I looked down at my best slippers, irrationally troubled by the new scuff marks along each toe.

"You are far too young to realize that were it not for the Duchess of Suffolk, whose wealth and influence only occasionally rival the queen's, Miss Cunnington would not be welcome here.

"Now," she said, her face an angry moon above her black dress, "you may not know it, but I have exerted a great deal of effort on your behalf."

"Unwanted effort," I said.

"Miranda." She spoke in a low tone no one else could hear. "You are young. As I was. Once."

"I am sixteen," I said. "Old enough to understand my own heart."

For the first time, she laughed, a caricature of real merriness. "Here, of all places, you dare to speak to me of your heart, foolish and most unreliable organ that it is. Very well, then, I will put my intentions in those terms. Your heart may not flutter before Lord Seagrave as it does with Henry Raleigh—yes, I observed you speaking to him tonight, as well. The close way you stood together was most inappropriate under the circumstances. It could have caused talk, but fortunately very few others understood the significance of such a conversation.

"Besides," she continued with calculation, "Raleigh's sister is very influential, both with her brother and with the queen. She never supported the match between the two of you. Now that your circumstances are changed, she is even more against it. To Charlotte Raleigh, your heart is about as valuable as a mouse nest in a wardrobe. Others will see the situation as she does. The sooner you realize that, the better off you will be.

"And then, Henry Raleigh, despite his honorable birth, did not behave so honorably to you or to your family, did he now? Having observed him at Whitehall, you must realize that he has been groomed for one of the central positions here at court. His Irish adventures are most certainly over. You realize the queen will never send him so far away again?

"No, such a man must marry a woman whose resources can further his ambitions. Perhaps the queen herself will choose his bride," the countess said, clearly delighting in this speculation. "Or perhaps the queen will decide to keep him unmarried and absolutely devoted to her, as she has kept Christopher Hatton."

Her words pressed on me, and as her orange-spice fragrance overwhelmed the grassy smell of the river and the many scents of the flowers, I just stood there staring, a creature struck dumb by a hunter's arrow.

"Remember, my dear," the countess said. "Your father sent you to Turbury. All along, his objective was that the earl and I see you suitably settled. Now be prudent. The queen is not indulgent when it comes to her prettier relatives."

"I will turn to my brother."

The cold dazzle of her gold-flecked eyes brought a dozen icy fingers to my spine.

"Perhaps it will make a difference if I tell you that Lord Seagrave recently made your brother's acquaintance, and believe me when I say the young Earl of Plowden was most pleased by his generosity. In time"—she smiled—"it will behoove you to show Lord Seagrave your appreciation."

"Generosity?" I said, noticing with more than a little agony that not only Beatrice but Henry Raleigh, too, had joined Kyd and Lord Seagrave.

"Yes. It seems Robert has become reckless of late, believing gambling to be the way to restore what your father lost. If you are wise, Miranda, you will realize your brother's recklessness will only inhibit your own future further, unless you act on my advice now."

The countess paused, measuring the reaction I was trying so desperately to hide. "There is also the matter of your brother's broken heart—further proof of the uselessness of this organ, as it has caused him to behave impetuously."

"How could you possibly know about Robert's heart unless—?"

"Unless I have been in contact with him. As I said, thanks to Lord Seagrave, I have; and believe me, your brother was grateful. Not only did the good lord help Robert settle his debts, an act of generosity meant to help you, my dear, but he showed your brother quite a time in town. You need only write to Robert to discover the affection that has sprung up between them."

"I don't believe you," I said, a terror sharp as a falcon's talons taking hold within me.

"My dear girl, I wish you would see I am only doing what is best for your future—and the future of your family." Her very words seemed to taint the satin of my gown. "Marrying you well has become my duty.

"Now," she said, feeling herself the victor, "it is time for us to rejoin the others."

Unable to foresee an immediate escape, I followed her back to where Kyd stood, along with Beatrice and Henry and, of course, Lord Seagrave.

"You look pale, Miranda," Kyd observed.

"Not seasick, are you?" Beatrice said a little too playfully.

"We're on a river," I reminded her.

"Miranda's complaint is of a gentler nature," the countess said.

"Then we must excuse her," Henry insisted, a new protectiveness entering his voice, though I dared not meet his eyes.

"I agree with you," Lord Seagrave said, speaking far too intimately. "A good night's rest is what Miranda needs."

"Thank you for your indulgence," the countess told him. "Come morning, Miranda will feel a great deal better, and then her perspective will be restored. She is ultimately a practical young woman as well as a clever one."

Not caring what reason she gave, so long as I was able to get away, I curtsied hastily to the others, then fled the barge, unable to stop for anyone, even though I was to sing in the Maidens' Chorus that followed the meal; even though I heard both Kyd and Beatrice calling after me.

CHAPTER FOURTEEN
May 4, 1580

"My dear Miranda, whatever is the matter?" Lady Periwinkle said after she found me buried beneath two quilts, the lilac-scented breeze drifting through the open windows no match for the shagged ice of the night before. "Is it the courses? Do you have cramps? Are you in need of padding?"

"No, ma'am," I said, coloring at this reference to my monthly visitor.

She lay a hand on my forehead. "No sign of fever. You know what I think, my dear?" She helped me to sit up, then propped me against some pillows, looking at me so intently I almost allowed myself to believe she had guessed my predicament and would somehow come to my rescue. "I think you have had too much excitement. Yes, a tournament is a splendid event. Yet it does tax a person so, especially a young person like you, who has already experienced so much this year."

"You are undoubtedly correct, Lady Periwinkle," I said, grateful for any reason to stay by myself for a while.

"Having raised two daughters, of course I am. Jillian was always one for adventure, but my Amelia could not go out for a week after a party of any sort, so sensitive was she to pleasure. Evenings, I would often fix her hot milk with honey and just a little whiskey for the nerves."

I almost hoped she planned to offer me this concoction, but she held out an envelope instead. "Perhaps this news will cheer you."

My mother?

It was from Turbury, though the handwriting was unfamiliar.

"Now then"—she nudged the food toward me— "drink up the tea, and do not neglect the bread and jellies. You will need to rest today so as to recover your strength as quickly as possible."

"I'm sure I'll be much better in a few days," I said, reminded of the queen's strategy: procrastination.

"No, my dear, you do not understand." Lady Periwinkle's face crinkled with either amusement or concern. "Barring a high fever, you will have to be more expedient than that. The queen would like to see you on the morrow."

"But I never expected a private summons," I said, no

longer able to dream that the queen was singling me out to praise my sewing.

"Why, Miranda, you mustn't be so modest. The queen takes care to acquaint herself with as many of the maidens as possible, and then, of course, there is the precedent of your dear mother."

"But, Lady Periwinkle," I stammered, feeling as if I might just become feverish, "there must be many girls hoping to gain an interview with Her Majesty. It would not be fair of me, and of course I wouldn't want to incur any unwonted jealousy—"

"My dear, if only everyone could be as generous and conscientious as you, my own position would be so much easier," she said, patting my arm. "But in this case, fairness is not the point. When the queen makes up her mind, there is nobody in the world who can persuade her otherwise, except perhaps Lord Burghley or Inez, her fool, though the charming dwarf Thomasina—she is fluent in several languages—can often charm the queen by speaking French while modeling her diminutive gowns. No, Miranda," she said in a tone intended to end all debate, "you will need to be ready and dressed by nine o'clock sharp."

"Will the countess accompany me?"

Her blue eyes seemed almost sympathetic. "You must truly be ill. You speak as if you were about to be gobbled up."

I longed to take Lady Periwinkle into my confidence,

but how could I possibly, given her apparent fondness for the countess.

"Now then"—she patted my hand once more and searched my face for some sign of illness—"drink up your tea. It'll do your body no good once it's cold."

"Yes, ma'am."

"And do be sure to lay out your very best gown. The queen will expect nothing less."

Only once I'd heard the dormitory door close behind her did I open the envelope.

The hand may not have been Eliza's. Still, it was her wobbly signature I recognized at the bottom.

April 23, 1580

Dear Miranda,

As long as my letter does not go awry—I know so little about the world of Whitehall Palace and all you must be experiencing—by the time you read this I will be well away from Turbury. I leave tonight, entrusting Charlie to post my words in the village in the morning.

In case we do not meet again, I want you to know the truth, as I believe the earl and the countess will turn the reasons for my leaving to their own advantage. Some five days ago, Anne fell ill again, having eaten nothing but broth and a few bites of fruit for several days. Once the doctor came and found there was nothing to be done, the earl asked me to look after her.

Understanding Anne was terrified——she confided in both Mama and me of the earl's determination to find her a suitor——I knew the only remedy would not come from tisanes or tinctures, but from assisting her to a monastery in the far north, with which Anne had already established a small correspondence. After some rather hasty planning, I helped her escape. No time to tell you how. If Fortune is so kind as to bring us together again, I will tell you the story in person.

When Mama learned what I had done, she did not scold me. But she did say there would be consequences. Meaning: I would lose my place at Turbury, and so could she, especially once the countess (who is far less tolerant toward women) discovered what had happened. I never dreamed Mama and I would live away from each other, not even for a little while. All the same, I knew I could not stay at Turbury.

I told Charlie of my plans, and he promised to assist me. (It is he who copied out my letter.) Once I reach Casterbridge, where he has family, I will establish myself as a healer and send for Mama. Charlie has promised to look after her until then.

I want you to know you inspired my confidence in my abilities. And in a funny way, Miranda, Anne's own courage——her willingness to take a great risk for happiness—— inspired me too. If Anne can do it, how can I stand by and continue to cook and clean when my dream is to restore others to health and peace of mind?

Hoping to see you again, I remain your friend,

Eliza

Had it not been for the signature, I would never have believed Anne had run off to devote herself to prayer, while Eliza was en route to Casterbridge to live up to her calling. I alone would be trapped if the countess had her way.

"I knew you weren't truly ill," Beatrice said, entering so quietly I did not even hear her.

"Oh, no?" I slunk deeper into the bedding. "You saw me with Lord Seagrave last night."

"I did," Beatrice said, a little too preoccupied with her reflection in the window. "That man could disturb the most phlegmatic creature's humor."

"You speak as if discussing your own experience," I said, catching the ragged edges of her voice.

"Remember, Miranda, I am one in whom the sanguine humor is dominant," Beatrice said.

"I would have pronounced your humor to be amorous, even if I didn't know of your devotion to *A Woman's Haven of Pleasure*," I said, withholding even the trace of a smile.

"Very funny." Beatrice gave me a cheeky grin. "If you must know, more than one of these influential dowagers shunned me last night, their rudeness equal only to the inferior quality of Eleanor's singing—though I'd never tell her as much."

"But why did they shun you?" I said, not realizing the stupidity of my question until it was out.

Beatrice's gaze left the window, her violet eyes settling on my own. "You honestly don't know the story, do you?"

"Story?" I would be shooting myself in the leg were I to bring up what the countess and Lady Sherringham had said about Beatrice's mother.

"Excepting Jane," Beatrice said, grinning, "you must be the only girl at court who hasn't heard of my mother's situation. She's a wicked disgrace, you know."

My cheeks, flushed as October's apples, proved I knew more than I let on.

"So you have heard." Beatrice began to laugh.

"Such a thing is not fit for humor," I managed.

"Oh, no?" Beatrice unfastened her hair and let it cascade around her shoulders, an ebony waterfall. "Really, Miranda, it would disappoint me immeasurably were you to prove yourself to be one of those women who would see me dressed in black and forever at my prayers. As if a dozen Our Fathers could restore my mother's soul and her reputation." Despite the sober subject, she spoke almost luxuriantly. "How dreary and how unfair, especially when a courtier is praised for his conquests. Besides, what good did so much piety do for the late Queen Mary?"

"But laughter—" I said, unable to even consider what Beatrice was suggesting.

"Is a tonic for the spirit. You mustn't walk around Whitehall as if you bear the weight of your family on your shoulders—even if you do. So experience has taught me.

"Now," she said, dangling a slipper from her big toe and watching it with the kind of interest one usually reserves for living things, "is there no one in your family who could step in? Your brother, perhaps? I cannot believe he would relish Lord Seagrave as a brother-in-law. Why, once you share with him the fate of poor Lord Gilroy—"

"I'm afraid my brother isn't in any position of authority right now," I said.

"He has inherited your father's title—"

"And my father's debts," I said, the covers beckoning. "Not to mention his own."

"Your brother is fond of gambling?" Beatrice cocked an eyebrow, obviously intrigued.

"Of late he has become so," I said, thinking the less said here the better.

"Perhaps the queen will come to your rescue, then." A look that could only be described as devilish came into her eyes. "Perhaps that is why she sent for you."

"You know about my meeting?"

"Why, certainly. Our chatty Lady Periwinkle was positively bursting with this news during breakfast—a grand event, by the way. Such an array of delicacies. Had it not been for Agnes's expression"—she ran her fingertips through her hair—"I would have resented you!"

"The breakfast," I said, remembering that today was my last chance to see Kyd.

"Yes, you should have been there. The stuffing in Eleanor's bodice began to slip." Beatrice bit her lip. "It was really quite hilarious, though dear El—how seriously she takes every little thing—did not think so. She does seem smitten by your tournament partner, by the way, and sat up late reading my book on amorous trysts. Why," she said, "you're looking peaked. Whatever is the matter?"

"Kyd told me he had to leave court today."

"But the tournament's only just ended." Beatrice returned to admiring her shoe. "Well, he did seem a funny sort of person, though I'll let you in on a little secret. A few of the queen's ladies told my grandaunt that the queen herself wanted him to sell her his locks for a wig, so great is her admiration of its color. Of course"—Beatrice grew bolder—"my grandaunt swears the queen's own hair—even in her youth—was never so brilliant."

By the time Beatrice left, promising to explain my situation to Kyd and ask for his address, she had pledged me anew to our compact, though I reminded her there was little I could do, especially as I was determined to keep to my bed until the morrow.

But Beatrice being Beatrice, refused to be discouraged.

⇠⊰✳⊱⇢

Determined to use the little time I had to my advantage, I fetched my stationery and sat down beside the window to write to my brother and learn, firsthand, where he stood.

May 4, 1580
Dear Robert,

 I believed my life with the countess had improved now that we had come to court.

 Until last night when the countess told me she planned to marry me to one Lord Seagrave, a man I could not possibly bear as a husband. Once you familiarize yourself with his history, you will undoubtedly agree.

 The countess tells me this lord has been to see you at university, where he seems to have won your trust—and settled your debts. I'm sorry to hear you have been gambling. When will you realize you are risking far more than your own future in playing with our fortunes?

 Please, write to me as soon as you receive this letter and tell me the countess is not speaking the truth. Feeling rather desperate, I await your reply.

Your sister,
Miranda

231

CHAPTER FIFTEEN
May 5, 1580

WHILE THE OTHER GIRLS CONTINUED TO snore around me, I awoke with a headache and a dry mouth, the residue of yet another bad dream lingering. This time I found myself marched down one of the gloomy halls at Turbury, the earl and countess on either side of me, and at the altar, waiting, Lord Seagrave; and beside him, my brother.

The strangest part was that in the midst of the dream, I continually found myself trying to draft a letter to my mother, believing if I discovered the right words, she would somehow be able to rescue me.

As soon as the sun pinked the sky, I climbed out of bed and hurried to the toilette, where I bathed myself with rosewater, taking special care to sweeten my underarms with powder. Afterward, I chewed a sprig of peppermint, then rinsed my mouth out several times, all the while examining myself in the mirror. Though I'd always wished for fuller waves in my hair, now, for the first time, my auburn hair seemed to curl a little too naturally. Even my complexion seemed too fine for the aging queen's liking, despite the reprehensible freckles.

I bound my braids so that none of my curls would be visible, especially now that Beatrice implied the queen's own hair was turning gray. And although it pained me to tamper with my skin, I actually dusted my cheeks—very lightly—with a bit of dun powder to diminish my glow.

Satisfied with my dulled appearance, I stepped over to the wardrobe, the beating of my heart a constant reminder of my nervousness at coming before the queen—especially under circumstances such as these. How I would have liked to dress in the pale pink silk, for its very touch gave me confidence. But hadn't Lady Sherringham told Agnes to be sure to dress in a dark color when she met with the queen?

I searched the rack to make sure my best gown of charcoal velvet was clean and in no need of pressing.

But the gown was not there.

I searched again. Nothing.

What Beatrice had said about Agnes's expression when she'd learned of my appointment with the queen returned. Agnes alone knew I had only one truly fine dark gown. Agnes alone would have the desire to sabotage me.

My only other black dress of worn calico was far from appropriate for a meeting with anyone of rank, and infinitely inappropriate if I was to make a good impression on the queen.

I hurried over to Beatrice's bed, careful not to wake anyone else. "Beatrice," I whispered.

She stirred, groaned, then rolled over onto her side.

"Beatrice," I said, louder this time.

She opened her eyes and squinted in the wan light. "Gracious, Miranda. What on earth do you want at this hour?"

"I need to talk to you."

"Now? Your complexion is absolutely ghastly. Do go back to bed. Whatever it is must wait."

"It cannot."

"Really, you're a perfect fright. And even if you do not value your beauty sleep, I do."

"I need your help," I said, then went on to explain, in hushed tones, what I suspected to have happened.

"The crafty little minx," Beatrice said, with a little too much admiration.

"Please." I pictured myself appearing before the queen in worn calico. "May I borrow one of your black gowns?"

Her fingers caressed her locks, but her eyes regarded me critically. "Black? We may dress in chimney colors around the dormitory, but are you sure you want to appear before the queen in a widow's weeds?"

"It's the most appropriate color," I said.

"I'll have to trust you there," Beatrice said, yawning. "Neither my mother nor I will ever be privileged with a private audience with the queen."

"Please, Beatrice—"

"I do not think one of my gowns will fit you," she said, scrutinizing my ample waist, which had only grown ampler during my time at Whitehall.

"But no one else is as tall as you. Besides," I said, "need I remind you if my future here is jeopardized, so is yours?"

"Very well," Beatrice said, a little more alert now. "I will loan it to you for the duration of the appointment only, but you must swear to be terribly careful."

Once she retrieved the gown from the wardrobe, the door creaking a bit too loudly so that Eleanor and several others stirred but thankfully did not wake, I slipped out of my nightdress and into her gown, tugging a little too firmly so as to fit it over my hips. The scalloped bodice was far too low cut, not to mention far too generous for me, so that the stays stood out absurdly. And the waist was so tight I could barely breathe.

"All I require is a bit of breathing room at the waist and a little less at the breast," I said, examining myself in the mirror.

"Absolutely not," she said as I pulled at the fabric. "I've worn the gown only four times, and Mother ordered it especially from my grandaunt's dressmaker on Wimpole Street. Her work is very fine and never comes cheap. Were you to ruin it—"

"When my meeting with the queen is over, I promise to restore it to its original lines. Please, Beatrice, I cannot possibly stand before the queen wearing a dress in which I cannot carry on a conversation—or draw breath." I spoke as quietly as possible, since the sleepy Eleanor was now watching us from her bed.

"You do have a point," she said, considering my figure. "You really should take only one dessert at mealtimes. I suppose the answer must be yes, then."

"Thank you," I said, torn between the desire to embrace her and the fear I would come to regret my words.

Fortunately, the generous lacings at the bodice's back enabled me to approximate rather than exactly match the size, though the seamstress's work, as Beatrice said, was so fine near the scalloped edges it made removing them more time-consuming and tricky.

Altering the waist proved even more difficult, for once I opened up the seam, I discovered there was not enough fabric for me to enlarge the size.

"Under no circumstances. I have only one such pair, an heirloom from my grandaunt," Beatrice said, when I asked if I could open up her gloves to match the fabric. "I am most sentimental about this pair."

I bit my lip to prevent crying. "What am I to do, then?"

"Why not sew in pieces from your own gown."

"The calico?" I said, only too painfully aware such fabric would never do.

"The pink silk."

"But the color," I said, "it's all wrong."

"For a gown, perhaps, but all you need are two inserts for the waist. Who knows?" Her too-beautiful smile became a challenge. "The queen might even approve. It's possible you will start a new fashion."

Minutes later, my scissors sliced through the satin, and I felt as if I'd begun to fall, but instead of trying—futilely—to right my balance, I embraced my descent, and so made it seem as if the fall were a leap. Rather like the feeling one has when flying over a fence on a swift horse.

"My dear Miranda, don't tell me you've forgotten our appointment," Lady Periwinkle said, after discovering me in the final stages of this task.

"No," I said without looking up.

"Well then, why have you chosen this hour to begin sewing?"

"Because I need to let out the waist of this gown," I said, using a whip stitch to save time.

"Dear, dear, have you overindulged as much as that?" she said, taking absolutely no notice of the pink additions. "No wonder you were ill. Well, be quick about it, then. After all, we mustn't keep the queen waiting."

Lady Periwinkle's diminishing footsteps were soon replaced with someone else's approaching.

"You will look stunning, Miranda," Agnes said, her skin dewy with a good night's sleep and the probable news of my situation. "So good of you to remember to dress in a somber color. Really, where would you be now without my good example? And the delicate pink inserts—such a lovely touch."

"I think so," I replied as frostily as possible, my heart drumming in my ears.

⚜

Although most of us had never been admitted to the queen's apartments, we all knew their arrangement intimately. As at her other palaces, at Whitehall the queen's apartments were arranged like a series of Chinese boxes, with the more public rooms giving way to the more private. One therefore entered the Great Hall first, and then the Presence Chamber. The Privy Chamber, secreted at the very heart, consisted of her private quarters, including her bed and dressing rooms, and were spoken of at Whitehall as her Majesty's *sanctum sanctorum.*

"Good morning, Lady Periwinkle. Good morning, miss," a very solemn, very handsome pair of ushers of the Black Rod said, once we reached the Great Hall.

"It is," Lady Periwinkle said in her cheerful way, and then they unbolted the doors.

The Great Hall proved such a magnificent room, I almost wished that I, too, wore a farthingale of such remarkable breadth, so small did I feel in the grand, high-ceilinged space, the walls adorned with tapestries and paintings. The columns were painted in the Tudor green and white, the tops bedecked with heraldic beasts of the most curious species.

Here, any open space had been filled with portraits of the queen. The painting I felt sure must have been my father's favorite depicted Elizabeth standing on a map of England and the surrounding waters, thereby underscoring her resolve to commit her country to exploration, and so extend England's boundaries beyond the sea.

Nearby, an earlier portrait showed her being carried in a litter by her equally youthful and very good-looking courtiers. I could not say for certain, but the expression of one of the courtiers put me in mind of Lord Grey. Lady Sherringham's words and the countess's bubbled inside me, and I looked away.

There, just to the left, Elizabeth's accession portrait confronted the viewer. Despite the way she now honored Anne Boleyn, here the new queen's red-gold hair and sharp hazel eyes allied her only with her father.

While we waited, I studied an allegorical work that showed the queen triumphing over Hera, Minerva, and Venus, goddesses of Marriage, Wisdom, and Love respectively. I particularly liked the queen's secretive smile, as it seemed the key to understanding this woman who knew a great deal about the goings on of the world—the masculine world, that is—one she had entered and ruled over by right of birth, yes, but more so by tenacious will and cunning.

"To what room are they taking us?" I asked when the ushers returned to direct us to yet another room, where I glimpsed what I thought might be the fabled unicorn's horn presiding on an ornate table of gold.

"To the Presence Chamber," Lady Periwinkle said. "A very promising sign."

We proceeded down a polished hallway where the gilded paneling, in which I saw myself reflected dozens of times, made me dizzy. How relieved I was to reach a room paneled with woods of hues ranging from mahogany to gold, the windows looking out on one of the rose gardens, and beyond that the Thames.

Here, we sat down on a pair of silver chairs padded

with cushions of Indian painted silk; between us, a silver-topped table held a high porcelain vase of perhaps two dozen pink roses. The roses accentuated the panels of my gown. As I ran my fingers along the satin, I felt encouraged rather than afraid.

Above us hung an extraordinary portrait of the queen dressed in a high-necked gown with padded, as well as elaborately bejeweled, black-and-white sleeves.

"The Pelican Portrait," Lady Periwinkle said when I stood to examine the detail more closely.

"Pelican?" I said, entranced by the jeweled armlet on her right sleeve as well as the partlet bordered with black lace.

"The name of the jewel." Lady Periwinkle gestured at an exquisite gem, square in shape and set so that the surrounding gold suggested the sun's rays. "Surely you've heard the legend of the pelican who pierced her own breast in order to feed her young."

"No." I was unsure if this affiliation assured or troubled me, especially as I sensed it was my breast the queen might pierce.

"Remember to keep your head down until the queen gives you permission to rise," Lady Periwinkle said before I could consider the portrait further.

The next thing I knew, the doors opened, and another pair of ushers stepped forward, these two the most handsome and the most youthful thus far.

They were followed by two elegantly dressed women. First came the gentle-voiced Duchess of Dewberry, arrayed in pewter silk and a shawl of filigree lace; and behind her, the ermine-complexioned Charlotte Raleigh dressed in a contemplative gray gown and a tight-fitting jacket of the same shade.

Unlike the duchess, whose smile seemed as genuine as her voice melodic, Charlotte betrayed no emotion, only unfurled a fan of peacock feathers she wore at her waist.

"I was not sure I heard correctly when the queen told me we were to greet you and this young lady in this room," she said to Lady Periwinkle, not even bothering to say "good morning" to me.

"It is an honor," Lady Periwinkle said, so politely I understood that I alone heard the malice in Charlotte's voice.

"A well-deserved one, I'm sure," the Duchess of Dewberry said with sincerity.

Footsteps sounded, Lady Periwinkle clutched my hand, and I dropped to my knees and bowed my head just in time to see the swish of the queen's apricot gown, its many pleats lined with cloth of gold, its ample hem rimmed with a trellis of diamonds and pearls.

And at the very center of the gown's skirt, the triangular opening revealed a forepart of silks of diverse colors ranging from bisque to sea-foam green. I could have marveled at the panel for hours had it not been for the frighteningly real-looking spider and its web embroidered into the very center.

"You may rise," the queen said, her voice surprisingly hoarse and deep, suggesting she was either overtired or had caught a cold.

Intuiting I should be the last to look up, when I did, I was struck by how lined the queen's face appeared in the morning light, the layer of white powder accentuating rather than camouflaging the traces of age she so wanted to hide.

Even so, with her hair adorned with diamonds that made the ribbons of silver in her red-gold hair look intentional, she remained a majestic being. "A quarter hour of my time is more precious than the ordinary man's day," the queen said. "I have therefore made a great exception in meeting with you so early in your stay at Whitehall, Miranda."

"Miranda is quite aware of the honor you are granting her, Your Grace," Lady Periwinkle said.

"Honor?" The queen let the word hang there, a question.

Beside her I felt certain I caught Charlotte Raleigh smirking behind her peacock fan.

"Yes, there is the unfortunate matter of her mother's

marriage, Your Grace," Lady Periwinkle said, offering the bait a bit too quickly, especially since the word "mother" and "marriage" caused the queen to furrow her brow— and so brought forth a troubling likeness to her saturnine father.

"What light, pray tell, can Miranda shed on her mother's marriage?" Charlotte asked.

"I did not invite Miranda here to chastise her for what her mother has done," the queen said. "The news did, of course, keep me up most of the night; a most unfortunate thing, as I have the French ambassadors here at present, as well as most of England's titled class. Too many of our countrymen seem to forget that when a gala ends, it is time to journey home.

"Nevertheless," the queen said, fixing her hazel eyes on me so keenly her gaze seemed to reinforce the threat of the spider on her skirt, "as my subjects, it would have behooved both your mother and her suitor to seek my approval. Their marriage, as you well know, has ramifications for your own future, and that of another person. I do hope your mother has trained you better than she herself has behaved."

Charlotte laughed a little, then flushed a deep scarlet when the queen turned to her and frowned. "If you find something humorous here, Charlotte, I do wish you'd be courteous enough to share it with us. After such a trying few weeks, I find that I am in need of some good cheer—poor Inez being, as you know, unwell."

"I did not mean to make a joke, Your Grace," Charlotte said. "I was simply thinking that in modeling her behavior, Miranda would do well to pattern herself after Agnes Somerset."

The queen's frown only deepened. "I have not observed that this young lady is such an exemplar, Charlotte, never having met with Lady Sherringham's granddaughter in private, though you continue to press her suit with me often enough."

The severe edges in the queen's voice suggested there had been perhaps too much talk of the virtues of one Agnes Somerset on the lips of Charlotte Raleigh.

"It is unfortunately true that my cousin's marriage to Lord Grey is being spoken of a little too freely at Whitehall," the queen continued, her fingers now busy with one of several ropes of black pearls. "But as I said, I have not summoned my cousin's daughter here to discuss that topic.

"Lady Periwinkle," the queen said, after surveying my person, "is it possible Miranda is unaware of the rules regarding the maidens' dress while they are here at Whitehall?"

"Certainly she understands the rules, Your Grace." Lady Periwinkle scrutinized my gown with such obvious innocence it was clear to everyone she did not see a problem.

"Well then, Miranda, why is it you have sewn this rosy color into a gown of black velvet?"

"Rosy?" Lady Periwinkle said, coloring.

"Go on, then." Charlotte stared at the pink panels as if they were coated with poison or some other traitorous substance. "Explain yourself."

"Honestly, Your Grace, I awoke this morning to the discovery my one suitable gown was missing."

Beside me, Lady Periwinkle cleared her throat, and her hands began to flutter like a pair of nervous sparrows.

"Yes," I said. "The other seems to have disappeared, and there was no time—"

"Enough!" The queen held up a much-bejeweled hand, and her skirts swayed so that, for a moment, the spider seemed ready to pounce. "Clearly, your mother has not trained you well, for you seem to have given no thought to the fact that pink is the color not only of youth, but of one who believes she is worthy of envy."

"That was never my intention, Your Grace," I said, prostrating myself before her.

"Your Grace," Lady Periwinkle added, her voice cracking, "I can assure you of Miranda's sincerity."

The queen continued to frown. "Knowing nothing of her character, I have only her mother's precedent by which to judge her."

Nearby, the Duchess of Dewberry cleared her throat.

"Have you something to add, Margaret?" the queen asked as I looked up just long enough to gaze hopefully at the duchess.

"I think it only fitting, Your Grace," the duchess said carefully, "that we allow Miranda to explain the circumstances under which she committed such a faux pas. Being a monarch of such supreme patience and mercy, I trust Your Grace agrees."

At first the queen said nothing. Recollecting my mother's stories, as well as a recent rumor that one of the queen's ladies of the bedchamber had been banished for failing to clean the queen's perfuming pan, and another dismissed for wearing a ruff far too elaborate for her station, I feared all sorts of punishments.

But at last the queen said, "Very well, then, Miranda, I give you leave to explain."

"Thank you, Your Grace," I dropped my eyes to the ground. "As I said, my only suitable gown—one of charcoal velvet—seems to have disappeared. Were it not for Beatrice Cunnington, I would have been forced to appear before you in a workaday gown that would have shamed me—and my family.

"Given the respect due my sovereign queen—respect everyone in my family was determined to uphold," I continued, bowing my head even lower, "I could not do such a thing. Beatrice is slimmer than I am, so I needed to—"

"You mean to tell us you altered another's gown to your own dimensions in so little time?" A new note seemed to enter the queen's voice; one I hoped might be admiration as well as approval.

"Yes, Your Grace," I said, not daring to look up.

"Such ingenuity." The duchess stepped forward to more closely examine my stitches. "And such fine work."

"I did not have the opportunity to tell Your Grace what a superb seamstress Miranda proved during the sewing of the tournament gowns," Lady Periwinkle said, then described the many ways in which I'd saved both fabric and therefore money by being so good at making use of the cabbage. "And, of course, it was Miranda's ingenious suggestion to trim the gowns with braids that preserved them from accident during the tournament."

"This may be true. Yet it does not explain why Miranda would choose the impertinent, yes, impertinent," the queen said when someone—I knew not who, as I kept my eyes on the ground—tried to interrupt, "use of pink. Such an act could be viewed as a ploy to draw attention to herself. Far better to have chosen dark green or even blue or white."

"Exactly so," Charlotte said.

"I would have you explain, Miranda," the queen said. "And do look me in the eye this time. It unnerves me to continually hear someone rehearse a story to the parquet floor. Besides"—she coughed—"my hearing is not so good today."

What choice did I have but to meet her gaze and speak the truth, beginning with the pink gown's place in my mother's wardrobe, a gown that had always symbolized not just her happiness during her time at court, but the possibility of my own as well.

"A most moving story; one that returns me to my own early days at court." Lady Periwinkle touched the miniature of her husband pinned at her breast with one hand, and with the other wiped a tear from her eye.

"Most dramatic," Charlotte observed, "as if such words had been rehearsed."

"I am sure you are wrong," the duchess said kindly. "There is something about the story that rings of absolute authenticity."

"Perhaps." The queen's famously long fingers tightened their hold around the rope of pearls. "At present, what concerns me most are Miranda's abilities. A good seamstress, especially a frugal one, is not so easy to find today."

The queen turned on her heel and paused to breathe the roses, as something akin to joy leaped through my heart. Would I be given a chance as a seamstress here at court? A chance that would mean freedom from an unbearable union with Lord Seagrave?

"Your mother's judgment cannot be trusted," the queen

continued. "But I have always been exceedingly fond of your dear late father. How astonished I was, then, to learn that such a spirited man—a true credit to the realm—had assigned you to be the ward of the Earl and Countess of Turbury."

"As was I, Your Grace," I said quietly. "It is a life very unlike the one I have always known."

"That said, change is a necessary part of this life," the queen continued, plucking a rose—its stem now free of thorns—and placing it within the bodice of her gown.

I dropped to my knees, intuiting humility, or the attitude of it at least, to be my only ally.

"My dear." Lady Periwinkle clutched my arm and tried to raise me.

"What perversity is this?" Charlotte asked when I would not budge.

"Are you ill, Miranda?" asked the duchess.

"Oh dear," Charlotte said. "Is she trying to influence you?"

"Surely not," the dutchess said.

"Miranda may be my cousin's daughter," the queen said. "Yet from all I've now heard of her stay at Whitehall, she seems to be a sensible young woman, one who understands that a young woman's wishes—her desires—are not the essential point in arranging the marriage of a person of her station."

"Miranda is most sensible, Your Grace," Lady Periwinkle said.

"Well then, Miranda?" the queen asked.

I shook my head, my knees trembling so fiercely I did not trust myself to rise.

"It is my dearest wish not to marry Lord Seagrave, Your Grace," I said, taking care to continue to speak as humbly as possible, and not once daring to look up.

The queen tapped her slippered foot. "Perhaps you are not as sensible as I thought. Marriage is, after all, an alliance and not a matter of the heart."

Her words brought those of the countess before me once more, and the sickness within me increased.

"Yours is the better name," the queen continued, as if she stood before a scale: on one side, me; on the other, Lord Seagrave. "But Lord Seagrave brings wealth, not only to you but to your family. You are no doubt mindful of the fact that wealth such as Lord Seagrave's will make a great difference to your life, and your brother's. In these uncertain times, I did what I could in forgiving half your father's debt. Still"—the queen paused and fixed me with her hazel eyes—"your brother has inherited a much-encumbered earldom."

"Is it Your Grace's wish that the marriage suit go forward?" Lady Periwinkle asked, fidgeting with her skirt.

"Certainly it is." Charlotte spoke as if Lady Periwinkle were a simpleton.

"I do not believe you are queen, Charlotte," the queen said in a more severe tone than I'd heard her use before. "Indeed, your current outspokenness prompts me to reconsider the prudence of allowing you to continue your independence. Let me remind you it is not too late to reignite the Italian count's suit. He continues to speak of you in his letters." She handed Charlotte the rose. "In the Genovese Court I believe the servants are even more careful to remove a rose's thorns, howsoever beautiful."

"I am sorry, Your Grace." For the first time, Charlotte Raleigh's voice quivered, and I felt sure she was trembling.

"Concerning the question of Miranda's marriage, Lady Periwinkle, the morning's events now cause me to reconsider." The queen herself stepped a little closer to me so as to see the stitches anchoring the pink panels in place, the fragrance of roses accompanying her. "For now," she said, "let me say only that I would like to see further examples of Miranda's work."

"Anything, Your Grace," I said, unable to hide the desperation in my voice.

"*Anything* is a dangerous word, my dear," the queen said. "I therefore leave it up to my ladies to decide how to best make manifest your talent."

PART THREE
The Test

CHAPTER SIXTEEN
May 9, 1580

D*earest Miranda,*

May is here at last, and still I have had no word from you. Please, my daughter, I ask you to write to me. I remain your mother.

It has not been an easy undertaking, this coming to a new home after so many years. Unlike our beloved Plowden Hall with its rambling rooms, its endless curiosities culled from your father's travels, and always the rolling Cumberland landscape beyond, Wingfield Park is a vast, elegant place built on level ground. The manor may be drafty, but the newer buildings have been made from heat-retaining wood and thankfully possess a more welcoming feel. Given your love of the tower room, it is my belief you would be happiest in the sloping attic room of the gatehouse, or in the old keep with its windows from the famous glass manufactory of Jean Carré—as if one were looking out at the world through pure air.

Now that the weather is fine, I have begun to restore the gardens that Lord Grey's mother once tended. Though still lovely, without a woman's nurturing eye and hand, the gardens, which overlook a small lake surrounded by scented trees, have become overgrown. Beyond the gardens lie parterres with wild strawberries and other fruits. The gardens are further enchanted by the several species of exotic birds that Lord Grey's father brought back from lands as distant as Africa and the Canary Islands. At dawn and once again at dusk, their music fills the air—as if a small piece of heaven has been tethered, for a little while, to earth. How I would like to walk with you around the lake or sit among the sculptures and obelisks in the rose garden, the birds chirruping around us. . . .

I dwell on the details of my new home because I am determined to build a rewarding life here, a decision I believe your father would have approved. Remember, Miranda, he never wanted us to dwell on misfortune or grief.

Lord Grey tells me there is to be a great tournament at Whitehall next month. Of the vibrant impression you will make, I am absolutely confident. Of the goodness of Lady Periwinkle—amazing to think she is now the Mother of the Maids—you must have no doubt. I pray only the queen treats you fairly.

Do write to me as you are able, my daughter. When you
have children of your own, you will understand your silence
is a thorn in my breast.

With love,
Mother

I was not yet able to lay pen to paper, but I could not deny
my mother's words gave me comfort. I missed her. What
she had written about my father was undeniable. His love
of adventure stemmed from an unquenchable love of life,
a creed he lived and died by. "No good can come of
brooding over what has passed," he often said when disappointment or hardship struck. My father's spirit—his
refusal to be defeated—was one of the qualities that not
just my mother, but all of us had loved about him.

"Why, Miranda, you look positively gloomy," Beatrice
said, approaching me in the dormitory garden, her hair
windblown, her lips stained a deep purple.

"Have you been drinking wine?" I asked, trying to slip
my mother's letter out of sight.

"Hardly." She reached into the pockets of her gown.
"Cherries," she said, and tossed me one. "Cook plans
to make pie, but there are so many, she passed around
great heaping bowlfuls after breakfast. Given your love
of sweets, I knew you would not like to be left out."

She pointed to my letter. "Bad news?"

"I do not know if you would call it that."

Beatrice frowned. "How odd you are. Either news is bad, or it is not."

"If you must know, the letter is from my mother. It's the first I've had since her marriage."

"Ah. The new Lady Grey." Beatrice continued to nibble from her hoard. "I must say, the name does have charm. What does she tell you?"

"Mostly she speaks of Wingfield Park—her new home."

"Oh." Instantly, Beatrice's voice became more vibrant, and she claimed the seat beside me. "How I long to see it. You do know Wingfield Park is among the greatest houses in the country. The banqueting house alone is said to be on the scale of one of the queen's own properties. Even the Earl of Leicester covets it, and then there are the grounds—"

"Unlike Agnes," I said, searching her violet eyes for something to mistrust, "it does not seem to trouble you that my mother's marriage—at least for now—stands in the way of Henry Raleigh's inheritance."

"Untrue. Nothing would satisfy me more than to reside at Wingfield Park. Both the art collection and the tapestries from the East are spoken of with high praise. Really"—she smoothed out her skirts—"it doesn't take Lord Burghley or some other shrewd mind to see how well

I'd do as mistress of a great estate.

"And yet," she continued, "Henry Raleigh is so handsome and well-mannered, I could accustom myself to making do with less."

"How very charitable of you," I said, recalling her scarlet gown, her revealing décolletage, but also what Lady Sherringham and the countess had said about her unruly mother. "And what if he is sent to Ireland again?"

"After his success in France, the queen would never dream of banishing him to such a backwater—" She turned the color of the cherries. "Oh, Miranda, I am sorry. I did not mean—"

"I know," I said, understanding hers to be the world's refrain, as I myself tried to banish all thought of him. "Even so, how can you be so certain?"

"Common sense." She brought her hand to her belly then, her features taking on a look of discomfort.

"Perhaps you should refrain from eating so many cherries."

"But they are so sweet and juicy," Beatrice said with a sly grin.

"Don't tell me you came out here just to share your plunder," I said more warily.

"Well, if you must know, it seems that wicked Lady Sherringham is pressing for an interview with the queen."

"From whom did you learn this?"

"Agnes, who else? She speaks of this meeting as if it's to happen at any moment."

"You mean Eleanor speaks of it—"

"Yes. They do seem to have become intimate friends. Odd." Beatrice studied her fingertips, which were also stained with juice. "I thought El was devoted to me."

I did not see any point in reminding Beatrice of the incident at the tournament, the relentless way she had teased Eleanor for stuffing the bodice of her gown, the embarrassing references to Kyd. . . .

"You know what she and her grandmother plan to do, don't you?"

"Yes." I pictured Lady Sherringham, her necklace of garnets as sharp as the words with which she would try to persuade the queen of the rightness of a match between Henry Raleigh and her Agnes.

"Well then," said Beatrice, scooting closer, "the next question is: how are we to stop them?"

<hr />

As it turned out, we didn't have to, though the circumstances that prevented the meeting were not at all what Beatrice had in mind. By the following evening, eight maidens, including Beatrice, had taken to their beds, groaning and sweating with a high temperature that brought with it a terrible headache and chills.

Within an hour of the fever's outbreak, Lady Periwinkle declared the Maidens' Chamber under quarantine.

"But Lady Periwinkle," Agnes protested, "I must see my grandmother. She and I have an engagement."

"I am sorry, Agnes dear. Your devotion to her must be a comfort, but that does not change the facts: no one in the dormitory will be allowed to leave until the fever has broken."

"But the queen——" Agnes's doe eyes became even more doleful.

"Darling girl, the queen cannot possibly risk exposure."

Agnes's plight was interrupted by the arrival of the bald-headed, bespectacled Dr. Snead, a man rumored to be older than almost anyone else at court (excepting Lady Woodhouse, the dowager who still dressed in the Spanish style and seemed to forget that Elizabeth and not Mary was now queen). The doctor had risen to prominence under Henry VIII after discovering a remedy that eased the pain of gout, a malady from which the late king suffered.

"To help with the headache I prescribe an ointment of honey and the gall of a hare," he told Lady Periwinkle with all the authority of a man used to ministering to the court. "You are to apply the ointment to each young woman's forehead in the morning and once again at night."

"Yes, of course," Lady Periwinkle said, taking copious

notes on all of his instructions, an activity that at least temporarily prevented her from fretting over her sick charges.

So too, it distracted her from the ravishing Duchess of Suffolk, who stepped into the dormitory in the midst of Dr. Snead's visit, arrayed in a luxurious gown of deep purple silk, her silvery hair fluffed into an irresistibly airy pouf that glittered with amethysts and pearls, a silk-eared spaniel named Buttercup cradled in her arms.

With the duchess came a good deal of luggage borne by two very well-dressed attendants, and a quiet maid named Lilabet, clothed in palest lavender, her white hands and distant air bearing the stamp of an impoverished woman of high birth.

"Your reason for coming?" Lady Periwinkle asked the duchess, once the doctor disappeared down the dormitory steps, promising to return again in the evening.

"To nurse my niece."

After laying Buttercup on a golden cushion, the duchess proceeded to straighten the pictures while Lilabet pulled down the heavier curtains. Clearly, she planned to replace them with the gauzy set one of the attendants now produced from deep within a very large packing case. "After all," the duchess said to Lady Periwinkle, "we must do something to bring in more light. No wonder poor Bea has fallen ill."

"How long do you plan to stay?" Lady Periwinkle asked.

"Until Beatrice is fully recovered, of course. Really, Lucy," she said, her eyes—an even more velvety shade of violet than her grandniece's—darkening, "you cannot possibly believe I will ramble about this palace while my favorite niece lies feverish."

"Well, when you put it this way." Lady Periwinkle stepped out of the way just in time to avoid colliding with the other attendant, who now proceeded to remove a battered chair, while Cook, who had somehow been recruited, as had the reed-thin Eleanor, carried in a sumptuous chaise lounge done up in an intricate pattern of velvets.

Within two hours of her arrival, not only had the Duchess of Suffolk transformed a section of the dormitory into her own apartment, but she had revised our menu according to her own rather peculiar likes and dislikes. ("Chicken liver for breakfast, fish and only fish that has been broiled for supper, and plenty of ale—it keeps away colds, you know—and plenty of cakes with cherries and golden raisins—but absolutely no nuts. As for butter, it may be rich, yet it keeps the complexion dewy.")

⋯⟡⋯

"Do remind me of Dr. Snead's directions for bringing down the fever," the duchess said later, the silver streaks in her hair shimmering in the moonlight by which I and several others watched her—the younger ones particularly entranced, as if they could not believe such a glamorous, albeit despotic creature had settled among us.

"She is to have a constant supply of springwater sweetened with a julep of violets," Lady Periwinkle said, straining to make sense of her notes, "and a distillation made of tarragon—no, turmeric—and garlic."

"Did the doctor not specify the amount?" the duchess asked, her fine eyebrows arching with disapproval.

Lady Periwinkle shook her head.

"Need I remind you, Lucy dear, my Beatrice is a bigger girl than many of the others? She therefore requires a larger portion of the tonic if she is to get well."

The duchess may have set our matron's nerves on edge, so great was her need to reorder everything in the dormitory, but she did bring a welcome change to our lives.

And then, thanks to the quarantine, not only was Agnes and Lady Sherringham's meeting with the queen (if there actually was a meeting) postponed, there was no chance for me to see either Lord Seagrave or the countess until all signs of illness were gone. The purifying fire and general airing to follow would take at least half a day. I could therefore count on a reprieve of almost a week.

Still, preoccupied with the knowledge that the queen would soon require me to display my talents, I continued to practice the herringbone stitch, the daisy, and others by candlelight, experimenting with various needles and threads, long past the time when even the most gossipy, as well as the most gregarious of the maidens had gone to bed.

"I know you are anxious to begin, Miranda," Lady Periwinkle said when she found me bent over my sewing. "Nevertheless, I wouldn't expect a summons until all danger has passed. Think of the queen's recent bout of dyspepsia, and the strain of late. No," she said, as if she and I had been arguing, "the queen's constitution cannot be strong at the moment. She would not risk one of the maidens among her ladies at this time.

"Now then," she said more kindly, and blew out the candle, "do get to bed. You wouldn't want to spoil your eyes, or your posture."

⁓꙰⁓

"A letter has come for Miranda from Cambridge," Bridget announced on the morning it came her turn to fetch the mail from the edge of the dormitory garden, a duty coveted both for its temporary publicity as well as its promise of fresh air.

"My brother—" I said, then hurried into the garden, determined to read it beside the calming waters of the fountain, away from any prying eyes.

May 4, 1580

Miranda,

You more than anyone must understand how difficult the days have been for me of late. Having believed Caroline would be my wife for as long as I can remember, I must now wake each morning to the knowledge she has married another. The pain is exquisite, and yet I dread its disappearance, the pain being my only remaining link to one I could have loved to my grave.

I know I am not the only one to suffer since Father's death. I think continually of your separation from Mother and Plowden Hall, the sting of the Raleigh family's betrayal. But time and my own disappointments have prompted me to revise my picture of your circumstances, especially now that you have journeyed to Whitehall in the countess's company. Surely, sister, this dramatic improvement more than makes up for the loneliness of your first months in her care.

And then, at the end of last month, I had an unexpected visitor: Lord Reginald Seagrave. By now you must be acquainted with him, as it was his intention to attend the tournament at Whitehall with the sole purpose of meeting you; an honor I hope you have taken to heart.

He told me some thirty tenant farmers reside on his property, and he is the local magistrate in his region, a position that gives him a great deal of authority. Not only is the

266

family land rich, but they have great financial resources,
having long been affiliated with the royal armory.

If I am honest, I must confess he does not seem the
likeliest choice of a husband for you. Yet he clearly understands
the respect due our family, as well as the honor he would gain
in connecting himself with us. And once you are wed, you can
instruct him on the writings of Castiglione, Marie de France,
and those other authors of courtesy and culture you hold so
dear.

I will await your reply and am in no doubt that once
you have time to weigh the matter in your mind, you will
come to see the situation as I do. And please, if you would be
so kind as to remember me to my classmate's sister, Beatrice
Cunnington, I would be so grateful. She visited here last
autumn, and although a dark beauty in her own right, I could
not think about her then, loving Caroline as I did. As I still
do. But time and circumstance now require actions other than
those we planned.

Carpe diem! As father used to say. He would not wish
his only son to continue our family's legacy as the poorest earl
in all of England. . . .

Your Brother,
Robert

Were it not for the handwriting, and this cultivation of
melancholy, I would have pronounced the letter a forgery.

How could this brother who preceded my arrival into this world by less than three years, this brother with whom I once picked wildflowers and dried herbs by the handful, now condemn me to be the wife of a man he knew, in his heart of hearts, was not fit to wipe the boots of our father?

Perhaps, I told myself, like the late queen Katherine Parr's husband, my brother, too, had lost his faculties when he lost the woman he loved. In his right mind, Robert would not have urged such a person upon me, not when our father had brought us up to value dignity and courage along with lineage and wealth.

Or was the real reason for Robert's change of heart— "foolish organ," the countess called it—that he had always been rather weak when it came to money? And now there seemed to be even less than the small amount he expected. Not to mention the debts.

Perhaps this was the reason for his sudden interest in Beatrice, whose dowry as well as her privileged relation to the Duchess of Suffolk outweighed her mother's scandalous reputation.

For a man, there is always another wife. Anne's words spoken once over tea when she confided her father's early second marriage—words which I so fiercely protested as the norm—came flooding back.

"A letter from your brother—tell me, what does he say?"

I did not need to turn around to know who it was stood behind me.

"I didn't open it, if that's what you're thinking," Agnes said, her doe eyes taking on a look I could only describe as predatory. "I simply asked Bridget to see the address."

"How dare you?"

"Simple. I intend to become Lady Raleigh." Agnes began plucking at the fingers of her glove, little by little revealing the white hand beneath, the knuckles unusually knobbed, something I hadn't noticed before. "I must therefore make the most of every piece of information, never knowing—in advance—what might prove most useful."

"I think you overestimate your influence—and your grandmother's," I said. Before Agnes had a chance to reply, I stood, turned sharply on my heel, and walked slowly away, grateful she could not hear the pounding of my heart.

CHAPTER SEVENTEEN
May 16, 1580

A WEEK AFTER THE FEVER'S ONSLAUGHT, seven of the maidens, though still not strong enough to resume their daily activities (especially when convalescence allowed them extra portions of sweet cake with meals, and exempted them from tasks such as letter writing, flower arranging, and silver polishing), were well on the way to being cured.

The only exception was Beatrice.

"Have a look at these patches on my niece's neck and shoulders, Dr. Snead," the Duchess of Suffolk said, once the doctor arrived for his evening visit, the immediate un-frowning of his brow proof of his relief at finding his one remaining patient asleep.

"It looks like a rash."

"I know what it looks like," the duchess said as

Buttercup growled his support. "What is the cause?"

"Please, dear lady. You must give me a minute to think." He removed his cap and rubbed his shiny brow. "Perhaps it's the ointment. She may be sensitive to it."

"Well then," the duchess said, "the ointment must be discontinued and something else applied. Neither my grandniece's health nor her beauty must be compromised in any way. Should this prove to be the pox—"

At the mention of this word, Lady Periwinkle was beside them in an instant, her hands aflutter, her cheeks the shade of an apothecary's rose. "The pox? Is there really talk of the pox?"

"I assure you, Lady Periwinkle, it is nothing so grave as the pox," the doctor said, and drew a finger to his lips.

"Not the pox?" Eleanor said, joining us, her own voice less alarmed than excited, as she flashed a horsy grin.

"For the third time, I assure you all, no," the doctor said.

"If the queen learns of the pox," Eleanor went on with a little too much luster, "Her Majesty is sure to send Beatrice away."

"The queen wouldn't do anything so drastic," Jane said, now that she, too, had joined the group.

"I beg to differ with you," Eleanor said smartly. "The queen endured a particularly severe bout when she was just a little older than all of us. In fact, she almost died—"

"Young ladies," Dr. Snead said a little wearily, "I ask you not to jump to such alarming conclusions."

"You may have risen to prominence under the late king, Dr. Snead," the duchess said, her tone as grand as any queen's, a tone that impressed further the younger girls who hovered around her, "but you must remember we are in a different era now. I have known *Elizabeth* ever since she was a little girl. She has always heeded my wishes and my advice.

"If these spots are not gone by the morrow," the duchess continued, "or at the very least if they are not greatly diminished, I will ask the queen to replace you." She began to pace the aisle between the beds, her long train trailing behind her, the moonlight itself curving around her, a dramatic effect of which she was undoubtedly aware.

"In this same conversation, I will recommend that you be sent to a remote northern village beside the sea," the duchess said. "A very quaint place, doctor, where the villagers are in desperate need of a physician, no one having agreed to settle there for many a year now, given the constant rain."

"Very well, madam," the doctor said as Buttercup nipped at his heels, his continued reserve proof of how much he must have endured during the reign of Henry VIII. "I will see what I can do."

"It seems a bit unfair that Miranda has had both a letter and a package in the same week," Eleanor complained the next morning, once it came my turn to fetch and distribute the mail, taking special care—or so I thought—to draw as little attention to my own bounty as possible.

"It does, doesn't it?" Agnes said, and linked her arm through Eleanor's, then whispered something in her ear.

"A package?" one of the younger girls asked, approaching my bed once Eleanor had stirred up a little too much interest throughout the dormitory. "Perhaps it's sweets."

"Don't be silly," someone else said. "Look at the size of the box. It's as big as you are tall."

"What if it's kittens?" asked another.

"Kittens couldn't possibly travel in a sealed-up box—"

"Oh dear, do you think the poor creatures can breathe?"

Before I untied the string, at least half a dozen maidens had gathered around me, a testament to how restless we were growing under the quarantine.

"What is all the commotion?" Beatrice called from the far end of the dormitory.

"A package," several of the girls shouted, their raised voices drawing forth Lady Periwinkle, whose nervous

273

shushing only garnered the attention of nearly everyone else in the dormitory—including the duchess.

"We're worried about the kittens!"

"Do be a dear, Miranda, and share your bounty with Beatrice," the duchess said, a single beatific look from her instantly stunning the other maidens into worshipful silence.

We found Beatrice leaning against a fortress of her grandaunt's special goose-down pillows. Nearby, Buttercup kept watch from his cushion. And on the table beside Beatrice, a lavender-infused candle radiated a calming aroma that seemed to have put one of the attendants to sleep on a nearby chair, though Beatrice's violet eyes were bright and impatient.

"Open it," she said, her tone having grown more imperious since her grandaunt's arrival.

"Yes, do!" the younger girls chorused.

"Very well," I said, opening the package with particular care, given my audience.

Inside I beheld a cut of exceptionally fine gray wool.

"Why, it's just a bolt of fabric," Bridget said, once I held up the contents.

"Who is it from, Miranda?" Jane asked, examining the satin finish of the Russells wool.

"Yes, Miranda, do tell us," Agnes said, affecting her most insincere smile. "Perhaps you have an admirer."

"Perhaps, Miss Somerset, Miranda had better read her

letter instead of letting her imagination run astray," the Duchess of Suffolk said.

Dear Miranda,

Charlotte and I continue to puzzle over the best way for you to prove your abilities as a seamstress. As was the case with Charlotte, as well as that of the miniaturist, Sabine Eggilsfield, before her, it is our greatest hope that your design will prove fine enough for you to win your independence.

So do be patient, my dear, as we cannot send for you until the quarantine is lifted. In the meantime, I thought you would appreciate this gift of cloth to replace your damaged dress. Though I cannot possibly imagine how the other gown disappeared, or why, I look forward to seeing what you make of the Russells wool. I ordered it especially from my dressmaker, Phoebe Buckingham, who recommends the lightweight material for the mild spring weather.

Do wear your new gown once Charlotte and I are at last able to request your presence. As you are all under quarantine, I am sure you will be very glad to have a project with which to fill this time.

Yours sincerely,
Margaret Stanley, The Duchess of Dewberry

"How fortunate you are," Lady Periwinkle said, caressing the fabric. "I always wanted to go into Phoebe

Buckingham's shop for a fitting, but she is always so busy. What a generous spirit the Duchess of Dewberry is."

"Margaret is that," the Duchess of Suffolk agreed. "Why is it, then, I can never cease thinking about her as a child of six or seven running about her father's estate in Shropshire wearing only her petticoat? Such a wild, untamed little thing she was."

"Truly?" Bridget drew her knees to her chest—revealing her kirtle—and for the first time gave her complete attention to the duchess.

"Yes." The duchess sank more deeply into the velvet lounge. "The way she scatted about with the wolfhounds was scandalous, and then there was her father's pack of scurrilous little terriers that seemed always to be increasing. Margaret would have followed them down the fox holes had she only been small enough."

Bridget grinned. "I attempted that myself—at three."

"Did you, now?" The duchess peered at Bridget with dubious interest, as if seeing her for the first time. "When I think of Margaret then, I would never have thought she would become civilized enough for marriage."

"And now here she is one of the most favored ladies at court," Lady Periwinkle added dreamily, as Bridget yawned.

"As well as one of the most naive."

I did not need to look up to identify Agnes as the

speaker of these words delivered with a quiet clarity destined for me alone.

"Of course, Miranda will face quite a challenge if she is to be measured against Charlotte Raleigh or Miss Eggilsworth," the duchess continued. "Some of her late miniatures are as good as Hilliard's—if not superior. Such a facility she had for painting lace, and that doesn't begin to address the luminosity of her skin tones!"

"You are certainly right," Lady Periwinkle conceded. "Even so, although I am the first to remark upon the benevolence of our queen's reign—what an exemplar she is to all Englishwomen—I cannot believe it a good idea to encourage young women to win their own independence through their talents instead of marrying—"

"Is it true, then, that Charlotte Raleigh did not want to get married?" I asked, aware such an opportunity might not present itself again.

"It is." The duchess motioned to one of the attendants, who immediately produced a box of marchpane candies, fruits, and other sweets. "A reluctance I can well understand, given the fate of her dear friend Isabel."

"What became of her?" Jane asked, accepting a marchpane rabbit.

"She married, of course," Lady Periwinkle said.

"Oh." Disappointed, Bridget seized a handful of candies, then stood and left us.

"And within five years of her marriage, she'd given birth to as many children," added the duchess. "By that time she had ceased writing altogether, a serious loss, given her fluency in Latin and Greek as well as Italian. If I recall, her translations of Tasso were never finished."

"That may be true," Lady Periwinkle said, "but when I consider the joy my daughters brought me, I find it difficult to believe any woman would find more satisfaction in a painting or a pamphlet of poems."

"Difficult to believe or not, Lucy," the duchess said, feeding Buttercup a gingersnap, "the proof of this lies in the person of Charlotte Raleigh."

<hr/>

While the other maidens mended their gloves and stockings, told ghost stories, or gossiped over one too many games of cards, I absorbed myself in the design for my gown. Preoccupied with matters including the dimensions of the sleeves—the forearm needed to be close-fitting while the shoulders wanted just enough lift to create the feeling of wings—I once more knew the challenge of creating clothing that was as pleasing to the eye as it was wearable.

I would have liked to pad the place where sleeve met bodice, as in the Pelican Portrait of the queen, but doing so might prompt the queen's ladies to believe I was overstepping my rank. I therefore settled on sewing a strip of white lawn striped with dark green into each sleeve, matching this effect with a simple pattern of leafy embroidery at the square-necked bodice. But what if the colors, innocuous in themselves, proved dangerous when brought together?

"You needn't fret about that," Jane said, once she joined me at the table where I sat among my pincushions, needles, and spools of thread. "Green and gray are earth tones, as is white. There is no harm in bringing together these colors of nature." And then, looking more closely, "What sort of fastening will you use? Hooks or ties?"

"I prefer ties, though they are more time-consuming. I suppose it will depend upon how quickly the project proceeds."

Sighing, Jane rested her chin in her hands. "I do envy you this work."

"Poor Jane," I said, struck again by the progress she'd made in overcoming her shyness since the tournament, or more precisely, since being reunited with George. Not only did she speak more clearly now, but even her sneezing seemed to have diminished.

"Did I tell you he sent the bouquet of yellow roses?"

"You did not have to," I said as I began to mark up the

cloth with chalk. "I suspected him to be the sender as soon as the bouquet arrived. And yes," I said, as Jane's color deepened, "I have noted the carefully sealed letters that keep arriving daily. How many has he sent by now? A dozen?"

"Fourteen. Do you think the queen will ever agree to an engagement?" Jane said, helping to hold the cloth flat so I could mark it accurately.

"Given the queen's obvious fondness for you and for your grandmother, I can only believe she must."

"I hoped you would say that. When—if—it happens," Jane said almost shyly, "would you consider designing my wedding gown?"

"You have as much faith in me as that?"

Jane laid a hand on my arm. "I do."

"I would be immensely honored," I said sincerely.

Not only did Jane prove remarkably dexterous, but unlike so many of the other maidens, she had little problem sitting still for any length of time. With her beside me, I was therefore able to pin the pattern onto the fabric within the hour.

We were just about to begin cutting the fabric when Eleanor hurried into the room, her color high, her breath hurried. "Lady Periwinkle says they are to fumigate the dormitory this afternoon, and we will be allowed to go out."

I stuck myself with a needle, and even Jane's capable hands turned momentarily clumsy. The sooner the quarantine was lifted, the sooner I would have to face my test, not to mention the countess—and Lord Seagrave. Given her intimacy with Agnes, Eleanor inevitably knew this—explanation enough for her confident smile.

"But how can that be when Beatrice has not yet recovered?" Jane asked.

"The duchess has been asked to remove Beatrice to a set of private apartments," Eleanor said, her smug tone proof she had not forgiven Beatrice's grandaunt for scolding her after she'd dipped her fingers into last night's raisin pudding.

"How do you know all of this?" I asked.

"Cook told me," she replied in an officious voice.

So that explained the hours the reed-thin Eleanor had been spending in the kitchen lately, growing no fatter despite her fast friendship with Cook.

"But Cook is under quarantine, too," Jane added.

"She wouldn't want it publicly known, but she has been sneaking out at night to meet one of the butlers. It is he who told her the news. Apparently," Eleanor continued, adopting a sly tone, "the queen is determined to meet with Lady Sherringham and Agnes."

Isn't it the other way around? I almost said, but what would be the point now that Eleanor had become Agnes's dearest friend.

"Be sure not to forget the curtains," the duchess called to her attendants, fanning herself with a bejeweled fan made entirely of long white plumes as Buttercup surveyed all from his silken cushion nearby. "After all, it's impossible to know what sort of rooms the queen has assigned us, and you know I cannot abide a room without a view."

"You're really going, then," I said to Beatrice, who stood folding her gowns, all signs of fever gone, though the troublesome rash persisted.

"Don't look so glum," she said. "The sooner I depart, the sooner you'll be able to meet with the queen's ladies."

"Precisely." I slouched against Beatrice's trunk.

"Come now, Miranda. Having presided over the sewing of so many of the tournament gowns, your skills must be up to any challenge the queen's ladies might propose."

"What if Charlotte asks me to attempt something impossible?" I said, reminded of the intricate pleats on one of my grandmother's gowns, but reminded, too, of the way Charlotte had smirked at me behind her peacock feather fan. "Or worse, what if she sabotages my efforts?"

"Perhaps Charlotte will have a change of heart and recognize in you a kindred spirit."

"You do not honestly believe that, do you?" I said, as

Beatrice examined the dress that had rescued me during my meeting with the queen.

"No, though it sounds nice, doesn't it?" She grinned. "Gives one something unrealistic to wish for—"

"How can you?" I said, finding this hint of glee unforgivable.

"Really, Miranda, don't you remember what I said about humor? What else do you think is seeing me through this crisis?" She held out her arms. Above the line of her gloves the red bumps lingered.

"If you must know, I almost envy you this opportunity," she continued as I helped her latch her trunk, which naturally refused to close, given the quantity of clothes. "My grandaunt tells me that Charlotte has an annuity of some fifty pounds a year, enough to keep her in silks and pearls, and then she saves a great deal in living expenses, seeing as she always goes on progress with the queen."

"You do not sound like someone determined to become Henry Raleigh's bride."

"You forget, I may admire your needlework, but I am against manual labor in all its forms."

"Perhaps you should leave something behind," I said as we continued our struggle with the trunk.

"You may have a point," she said, frowning over her wardrobe.

"Hurry, Beatrice!" the duchess called from afar.

"Coming!" she said, then lifted the newly restored black velvet gown.

Before I could refuse, she placed it in my arms. "But you said this was special," I protested.

"Hurry, darling!" the duchess called again.

"Just take it. Besides," Beatrice said almost kindly, "it suits you."

⌐※⌐

Once Beatrice, the duchess, and their entourage had departed, the queen's workmen arrived to lay down the bundles of sage and other herbs for the purifying fire.

"Come along now!" Lady Periwinkle called, gathering the maidens to her as the workmen moved between the rows of beds, shifting cupboards and wardrobes in an effort to create space.

"I was beginning to think we would never be allowed to leave," Bridget said, her enthusiasm for running up and down the dormitory steps having at last worn thin.

We were only going so far as the smallest and most neglected of the palace's rose gardens, an overgrown spot with strong associations to Henry VIII's first wife, Catherine of Aragon, the reason this garden, which had once bloomed from April until October—or so the old-timers said—now went untended.

Still, I had no need to ask why Jane was dressed in a particularly lovely gray gown with just a hint of blue in the weave. Nor would I have found it surprising were we to stumble upon George Mountjoy seated beneath a flowering pear tree, or strolling along the grounds.

Only Agnes, dressed in a gorgeous gown of black satin with slashed sleeves and ebony beading, gave me pause. As she practiced smiles and curtsies before the looking glass, the reality of her meeting with the queen sank into me with the heaviness of yeastless bread. How soon would it take place? And what an advantage she now had, given the polka dots decorating Beatrice's skin.

"Oh, Miranda," Lady Periwinkle called, once we were halfway down the steps, "with all of the commotion, I almost forgot. I have a message for you—from the queen's ladies."

The way Agnes pretended to busy herself with a snag along the hem of her petticoat proved she was eavesdropping. Thankfully, Lady Periwinkle was discreet enough to hand me the note without revealing its contents.

Dear Miranda,

Now that the quarantine has been lifted, it is at last time for you to meet with us in the seamstresses' workshop. We have devised a marvelous project for you, one we believe will please you as much as it does us.

Anticipating your company with pleasure, I remain,
Margaret Stanley, the Duchess of Dewberry

"Quite an honor, my dear," Lady Periwinkle said. "You will have a favored glimpse of many of Her Majesty's clothes long before anyone else has a chance to view them."

"When am I expected?"

"The day after tomorrow. And this time I do hope there will be no more trouble about your clothes disappearing."

"No chance of that," I said, leveling my gaze at Agnes.

⟞✳⟝

"I did not expect to be summoned so soon," I told Jane as we walked together toward the rose garden, and I fretted the finishing of my gown.

"Well," Jane said practically, "perhaps you had best modify the design."

I was reluctant to relinquish a single detail, so eager was I to dazzle the ladies with my skill. Even so, I understood it would be impossible to include the white lawn in the sleeves. The embroidery, too, would have to be forsaken—unless I salvaged work from another gown, of which I had few.

That night as the moon rose higher in the sky, I sewed by candlelight, little by little realizing the bodice alone would take me until morning. As for the waist, I planned to stiffen the pleats with buckram, a fabric that proved as temperamental as its effect was dramatic. How would I possibly finish the gown in time?

As if she had intuited my distress, Jane appeared, a single luminary guiding her way. "How is it coming?" she asked.

"Slowly."

"Why don't I help?" she said. "I couldn't sleep anyway."

The light may have been faint, but it could not hide her blush. "Thinking of George?" I said, recollecting the pollen staining her nose after he sent yet another bouquet.

"I am." She gave a blissful sigh.

With Jane's assistance, I managed to complete the bodice by morning. We finished both sleeves by midafternoon.

"Would you help me with the skirts later tonight?" I asked, just as Lady Periwinkle called us to supper.

"I'm sorry, Miranda, I cannot," she said, yawning. "I've barely been able to keep my eyes open all day."

"But I meet with the queen's ladies on the morrow," I insisted.

"Perhaps you ought to curb your expectations," Agnes said, startling me as she came up from behind.

"Perhaps you ought to keep your distance."

"Very well," Agnes said, a malevolent glint to her smile,

"but don't say I didn't warn you. Neither the queen nor her ladies think kindly of those who try to overstep their bounds."

"In that case, you ought to watch your own footing."

Agnes seemed to pirouette on her slippered toes before turning away.

"Well?" I said to Jane, once Agnes had gone.

"Honestly, Miranda, I've been dreaming about my goose-down pillow and quilt all day. Perhaps, in this case, Agnes has a point."

⤙⋇⤚

Jane's words returned to me that midnight as I struggled to stay awake while pinning the pleats into place. What good is a new bodice without its skirts? I asked myself, longing for one of Eliza's remedies—surely, just as she knew a cure for sleeplessness, she could help me to stay awake.

I picked up my work and resumed the pinning, only to feel something tickle my ear. I swatted at the air, expecting to shoo away a fly. Instead, something fine and gauzy adhered to my fingertips.

A spider! The industrious creature was spinning its web in the corner behind me. "And I thought I was the only one awake at this hour," I said aloud.

Entranced by its nimble movements, I recalled the

spider embroidery on the queen's forepart. What if this image—one I originally found so threatening—could now provide the solution to my problem? Instead of an entirely new skirt, I could sew a forepart from the Russells wool and sew it onto the velvet skirt of the gown Beatrice had given me. There could be nothing amiss in pairing black with charcoal, I told myself before hurrying over to the wardrobe secreting Beatrice's dress.

CHAPTER EIGHTEEN
May 23, 1580

The seamstresses' workshop was housed in a high-ceilinged, many-windowed room on the top floor of a building; the queen had recently built it to replace the former workshop, which, according to Lady Periwinkle, had been overrun with mice, pets of the late Queen Mary, who, after their mistress's death, tunneled deep into the cracked walls and sloping floorboards, establishing a colony as populous and determined as the court itself.

As soon as I stepped inside and the ushers closed the doors behind me—so quiet I could almost hear fragments of conversation from the courtyard below—I became even more aware of the smallness of my person in this grand space with its quartet of French windows and its floor of polished wood. As in so many other rooms at Whitehall, here, too, the ceilings had been ornately painted, and the rafters gilded with gold. The walls were adorned with portraits of the queen, her ladies, and other members of the Tudor and Boleyn families.

Among them I found more than one by Sabine Eggilsworth, the miniaturist the Duchess of Suffolk had praised. The intricacy and delicacy of Miss Eggilsworth's portrait of the late Jane Grey was particularly fine—the paint incandescent, the brushstrokes invisible—and I trembled a little at the standard against which I would be measured.

Not surprisingly, Henry VIII's other wives were absent from this visual history, with two exceptions, the first being Jane Seymour. Though the painter was the revered Hans Holbein, Henry VIII's third wife looked more peevish than pretty. This came as little surprise, given her motto, *Bound to obey and serve.* (The appetites and the unreason of her husband would give any wife reason for such a dour face.)

There was also a somber image of the revered Katherine Parr, the only woman Elizabeth could really have called mother. Ensconced in a gown of loose purple velvet that made her look far older than her thirty-five years, Katherine Parr's portrait hung in a place of honor beside Anne Boleyn's.

I stepped away from the paintings, aware of the soft

tread of my slippered feet on the polished wood, and of the eyes of the portraits' sitters, which seemed to follow me as I moved. Nerves, I told myself, troubled more than a little by Jane Seymour's discontented gaze.

Reminded of the satisfaction I'd felt in creating the design, I began to examine the tools, which, unlike the workshop, were reassuringly familiar. In the largest cupboard I located shears, scissors, measuring sticks, rotary cutters, and a variety of more specialized tools used for pinking and stamping, as well as one for embossing leather—the queen being the only woman in the kingdom to own a pair of leather riding breeches, or so Bridget, whose brothers often accompanied the queen on the hunt, claimed.

Nearby, a narrower set of cupboards contained nearly half a dozen drawers filled with needles, threads of varying weights and materials, and thimbles, including several with curious messages such as "A stitch a day keeps the doctor away" and "Seamstresses make industrious wives." On an opposite wall, shelves held stiffening materials such as steel boning, millinery wire, and cane. Tucked into a corner I found freestanding boxes containing sundry-colored lace, all variety of buttons and tassels, spangles, and loops.

When I considered that these tools had been used to create clothing for the queen—the proof of which lay in the petite dimensions of the canvas and buckram toiles that mocked out her measurements for various styles of clothing—my hands turned unsteady, and my mind raced so that I feared I would not be able to concentrate on the task so soon to be set before me.

Until I remembered something my mother had said a few too many times. "Now that she's become queen, it would do Elizabeth well to remember that she, too, wears a petticoat. And even *her* slippers need to be sweetened with marjoram and essence of lavender."

"Phoebe is to be commended for the choice of fabric," the Duchess of Dewberry said, entering so silkily it was as if she were borne on water. That day she wore a gown of the lightest dove gray satin that brought out the blue in her eyes, and her golden hair was crimped into the fashionable puffed halo. "I must compliment you on your skill, as well as on your good taste," she said, examining my dress.

"Thank you," I said as a pair of attendants, dressed like the others in the vibrant Tudor green, wheeled in a gleaming silver tea service accompanied by peaches and plums and a variety of cakes, their powdered sugar toppings as enticing as snow on Christmas morning.

"Your backstitch looks flawless," she said, stepping closer. "And I do admire your decision to integrate a forepart into the fabric. So inventive! It always impresses me the way a rule governing dress often yields the most marvelous creativity. However did you have time?"

"I managed," I said as nonchalantly as possible.

The attendants poured our tea, and we talked for a while about life at Whitehall in general and about the quarantine and illness in the Maidens' Chamber in particular. I told the duchess about Beatrice and the arrival of her grandaunt, then narrated the details of their departure.

She listened and smiled and even managed to hint at the Duchess of Suffolk's overbearing nature without in the least making her words sound like a criticism. So soothing was her voice, and so gentle were her eyes, I would have felt almost comfortable, had it not been for the anticipation of Charlotte Raleigh's arrival.

"When will Lady Raleigh be joining us?" I asked, trying to sound calm.

"Shortly, I hope. Her Majesty has a toothache, and then there is the lingering presence of those troublesome French ambassadors. At such a time, only Inez's jests or Charlotte's poetry can soothe her.

"Now then," the duchess said, once we'd finished a second slice of the moist cake and two more cups of the fragrant tea, "until Lady Raleigh arrives, would you like to see a sampling of Her Majesty's gowns? Most are here for repair, or a thorough cleaning, and yet they remain exquisite creations."

I was on my feet at once. "I would like that very much."

She opened the first of many wardrobe doors, then

drew forth a cobweb lawn cloak of semitransparent silver silk with a large, heart-shaped collar that had been stiffened with cane; its one flaw, the hem, had grown ragged.

"It's lovely," I said, admiring the fine needlework.

"And it's nearly impossible to clean despite the linen shifts our queen is so scrupulous about wearing underneath. Of course," the duchess said, "Her Majesty only wears the cloak during the warmest of days, and then only to play a game of cards or to meet with a few of her ladies in private.

"And here is the ensemble from the Duchess of Cavendish," she said, displaying a gown of blue velvet and a matching cloak embroidered with carnations. "I do not like to take pleasure in misfortune, but this giver is so vain, I could not help but smile when the gown was torn during one of the season's first court dances."

I touched the elegant fabric. "How did it happen?"

"Dancing a galliard. The queen is always so lively, nearly all of the courtiers—even the very young ones—must struggle to keep up with her. This time she found a kindred spirit in her partner." The duchess's smile vanished, and I knew at once who the queen's partner had been.

"Do you think the queen will forgive him—and my mother?"

"I do, Miranda. Such men are not so plentiful these days."

I swallowed hard. "You are fond of Lord Grey, then?"

"I am. He is intelligent and reliable and enviably free of the machinations of so many of the others here at court. If only the queen had not convinced herself that he, like Christopher Hatton, would continue on in perpetuity as knight to her unattainable lady. . . ."

"Ah," I said, recalling Hatton's elaborate declaration during the tournament. Had Lord Grey, too, vowed such undying loyalty and love? And even if he had, the queen knew, far better than anyone, that courtly love, despite its elaborate display, was an art form, like dancing or painting.

"Now then"—the duchess touched my cheek—"you mustn't brood. It will only sap the strength and creativity you will require. Besides, I have only shown you a fraction of the clothing. What would you like to see next?"

I pointed to a gown of primrose satin lined with cream sarcenet, one very unlike its elaborate, bejeweled companions, especially since its neckline was rather high and the others, low-cut.

With real tenderness, the duchess lifted the gown into the light. "This is one of the gowns the queen wore before she inherited the throne. It possesses great sentimental value."

"I admire the style of the sleeves," I said sincerely.

"They are as practical as they are lovely," the duchess agreed, her gaze lingering on the dress. "She wore it during her final weeks with the late Queen Dowager Katherine Parr."

"Ah," I said, instantly understanding the catch in her voice, my mother having told me of the role Henry VIII's last wife played in Elizabeth's life, granting her sanctuary at her home and caring for Elizabeth as if she were her own daughter.

And then, as if afraid to give way to memory, the duchess said in a brighter voice, "Perhaps you know that it is our queen who is credited with the disappearance of those impractical bell-shaped sleeves so popular with her half sister."

"My mother, too, disliked wearing them," I said, sensing her need to keep our tone light.

"Of course she would. With what difficulty I remember dining in public while outfitted in such a costume. Impossible to keep one's sleeves out of the soup!"

"What of this one?" I said, pointing to a fantastic jacket of white satin embroidered in varicolored silks with a lion, trees, birds, cherubs, a castle, spiders, and other insects.

"Ah yes, the work is amazing, is it not?" the duchess said, placing the fanciful creation in my arms.

"Whose embroidery is it?" I asked, never having seen anything quite like it, and not imagining anyone would have time to fill the entire surface of the jacket with such intricate stitches.

"The Scottish queen's," the duchess said. "The poor

creature made it for the queen during her captivity."

"From the looks of the buttons, it would seem the jacket has never been worn," I said, unable to find anything in need of repair.

The duchess's cheeks flushed the very shade of rose as the cherubs' wings. "Have a close look here." She pointed to the ovals at the front of the bodice. "Her Majesty believes her Scottish cousin sewed the jacket from one of her petticoats."

"Ah," I said, understanding at once why the queen would not wear it, and even more impressed by the curious forms of revenge a woman—especially a woman who was also Elizabeth's prisoner—might resort to.

In addition to the gowns, the duchess showed me a collection of farthingales designed by the royal farthingale-maker, John Bates. "The queen always chooses this one when it's important her listener be kept at a distance," the duchess said, gesturing to the widest of the group, a daunting creation consisting of buckram, the stiffening ropes covered with white kersey.

"The French ambassadors?" I said, unable to resist.

"But of course." Her eyes sparkled a little. "The French, loving fashion as they do, did not make the connection."

There were several wardrobes devoted to accessories: handkerchiefs edged with lace or silver thread, long-fingered gloves of buttery leather and other fabrics, starched ruffs, stiff gauze collars; petticoats in all weights and textures, including one that had been embroidered with monsters, and another with pomegranates; a hat of beaver fur ideal for winter travel, another of black silk with a high crown trimmed with a jeweled spray of flowers, and nearly a dozen of wide-brimmed straw, with which she protected her complexion during the summer months.

"And then there is the queen's collection of French hoods," the duchess said, leading me over to the seventh wardrobe.

I was immediately drawn to a hood of Venice silver and gold wrought with chain stitches and adorned with what must have been a thousands teardrop pearls.

"The work of Blanche Markham," the duchess said with obvious admiration.

"Is she still in the queen's employ?" I asked, having heard of her gifts from my mother.

"I'm afraid she was dismissed from the queen's service last October."

Although I sensed I shouldn't press further, curiosity had the advantage. "Why?" I asked.

"My dear Miranda," the duchess said, for the first time assuming a distant tone, "it is impolite to be so direct. But if you must know, poor Miss Markham is now with child. Although the queen settled a generous living on her, the woman will never again be welcome here at court."

A long and most awkward silence followed in which I imagined the possible fate of an unwed mother, which was inevitably grim even now with a woman on the throne.

"But let us not dwell on such difficult subjects when we have the marvels of the queen's wardrobe before us," the duchess said at last, then pointed to a bejeweled hood. "This one has always been my favorite."

Together we examined it as she cradled the headpiece in her hands. "The sapphire billaments are so finely placed, and the workmanship as fine as anything of its kind. One day, when the queen is in a particularly generous mood, I will ask her to make a gift of it for my granddaughter, Sara."

"And what of these boxes here?" I asked, pointing to a high shelf.

The duchess flushed, and in a very soft voice whispered, "Wigs."

I bit my lip to keep from smiling, reminded of what my mother had said when she'd learned her royal cousin could be counted among the women who wore hair that was not their own.

As if she had read my thoughts, the duchess quickly produced two small pouches. The first held a pair of intricately detailed white satin gloves trimmed with sage green velvet. At first I thought the pink and green birds outlined in black had been embroidered onto the fabric, but in reality they were painted on.

"Thomasina presented these gloves to the queen for Christmas during her first year of service."

"Exquisite," I said, only now appreciating the dexterity of the dwarf's tiny hands.

"Yes," the duchess said, obviously pleased by my appreciation. "In Florence, where Thomasina was born, her father belonged to the first guild of painters.

"And here, the queen's very first pair of silk stockings," the duchess said, opening the second pouch, then laying the gloves in my hands. "They were knitted by Sylvia Robbins, one of her dearest ladies, during a particularly hot August. Of course, once the queen wore silk," the duchess said, pointing out a dozen more pairs, all awaiting mending, "cotton would no longer do."

"Of course," I said, though I could not possibly imagine such a luxury. "How many of the queen's gowns are housed here at Whitehall?"

"Only seven or eight hundred. Even so," the duchess considered, "it's quite a sight on Lady Day when the gowns undergo a general airing—last year, more than three cartloads of coal were required."

"Not wood?" I asked, for such was our practice at home.

"No, the Master of the Robes swears coal provides a cleaner fuel, the wood smoke leaving an ashy dust behind."

"Where are the other gowns kept?"

"Most are kept at Richmond Palace, though there is

also a small collection at Hampton Court and one at Hatfield. Haven't you visited there with your mother?"

"I'm afraid not," I said.

"I see." The duchess laid a finger to her lips. "I did not realize the rift between them to be so great or so long-standing. For a time, they were close."

"Did you know my mother then?" I ventured quietly.

"Just a little. I had small children of my own to look after when she was here, and so I came infrequently to court."

"But you did know her," I said, almost embarrassed by the pleading note in my voice.

"I did." The duchess stroked my hair and regarded me gently. "Your mother had just become engaged to your father. What love and mutual admiration there was between them then. From all I understand, they maintained these qualities throughout the years."

"Yes," I said, "though my father's absences preyed upon her."

"As they would any loving wife. . . ."

Talking about my parents felt so natural with the duchess, I would have liked to continue, especially with the sunlight slanting in through the curtains, the familiar smell of well-cared-for clothing, and the soft chiming of bells in the distance.

But then Charlotte Raleigh strode into the room. "I'm

sorry to keep you waiting, Margaret—"

"How is the queen?" the duchess asked, the intimacy we had shared vanishing with the closing of the last wardrobe door. "Better, I hope?"

"The doctors want her to have the tooth out," Charlotte said with uncharacteristic weariness. "But she will not hear of it."

"If only our queen would give way to the doctors on this point," the duchess said. "My mother has had four teeth pulled in the last few years, and although she was reluctant to part with them, it is far better to be free of such pain."

"But don't you see, Margaret"—Charlotte began tapping her fingers along the tabletop—"this is precisely the problem. It is your mother who had her teeth pulled, not you."

"As always you are right, Charlotte," the duchess said, sighing a little. "Now, what of your friend Lady Sherringham? Is the queen's tooth too painful, or will she be able to meet with her and her granddaughter?"

"Really, Margaret, given the circumstances, I think it best to progress directly to the task for Miranda."

I waited, but neither woman spoke.

"Have the doctors prescribed apple cider into which has been poured the fermented root of spurge?" I said, recalling the cure I'd helped Eliza memorize.

"Certainly not," Charlotte said, as if I'd suggested a diet of spiders and crows.

"Wait a moment," the duchess said. "Perhaps we should not dismiss such a possible remedy so quickly." When Charlotte shrugged, the duchess said, "It's worth a try."

"Although I believe such a beverage will only revolt our queen, at your insistence I will mention it to her doctors."

"Very well," Charlotte said, once she'd finished copying out the remedy. "I assume the duchess has told you of our project."

"Actually, I thought you, being so much cleverer, would present our reasoning more clearly," the duchess said.

"You flatter me," Charlotte said, helping herself to tea. "Remember, Margaret, it was your idea."

"Was it?" The duchess frowned.

"But of course. Now"—Charlotte's voice turned a shade more cordial—"do let us begin."

"Our aim is to boost Her Majesty's spirits," the duchess said, and stepped across the workshop, the floors so highly polished they held her reflection as she moved. "We thought it fitting to propose a sewing project that would bring a cheering memory of her mother back in time to celebrate the anniversary of Anne Boleyn's coronation month."

"A wonderful idea," I said, hoping I sounded confident.

Charlotte smiled at me behind her teacup. "We're glad you think so."

"Come and have a look at this portrait of the queen's mother." The duchess motioned to a large painting on the far wall—one I had not noticed earlier.

I studied the striking figure garbed all in white, her litter carried by two palfreys outfitted in white damask; and above her head, a canopy of cloth of gold with gilt staves, borne by four knights in equally magnificent clothing.

"A depiction of the coronation procession of the queen's mother," the duchess explained. "I was but a girl at the time. Yet I'll never forget how beautiful Anne Boleyn was on that day, a scepter of gold in her right hand, a rod of ivory in her left."

"Your task will be to re-create the costume Anne Boleyn wears in this portrait," Charlotte said, joining us just as tears pooled at the corners of the duchess's eyes.

With the queen's ladies flanking me, I stared at the figure of Anne Boleyn, understanding such a project would take at least two weeks to finish, and only if I worked from early morning until nightfall, the gown being of an intricate Henrician design made from the fragile white cloth of tissue, and trimmed at the scalloped bodice and wrists with lace. The equally detailed mantle was of the same temperamental and costly fabric, and had been edged with the fur of the white ermine, adding yet another layer of difficulty.

Unable to imagine the queen sparing the time to stand

before me for a fitting, especially when she was suffering from a toothache and the French ambassadors, I said, "How will I calculate the measurements?"

"We have recorded all of the queen's measurements in the log over there, and then there are the toile pieces to be used as you refer to specific dimensions for sleeves and other parts," Charlotte said, her clipped reply proof it had been she and not the Duchess of Dewberry who had come up with this test.

"I think it only fair Miranda have an assistant," the duchess said.

"One of the maidens, then," Charlotte said reluctantly. "I will not hear of the professional seamstresses being engaged."

Not Agnes, I prayed, a thousand ways for her to sabotage my efforts swirling before me.

"A person of Miranda's own choice," the duchess said at last.

"Hmm." Charlotte ruminated for a little too long. "If you think Miranda capable of choosing wisely."

"But of course!" the duchess said with so much spirit I could have kissed her.

"I think a week's time sufficient to complete the project," Charlotte said.

"Ten days," the duchess said, surprisingly firm.

"Really, Margaret, that's a bit indulgent, don't you think?"

"Your work may be with words, Charlotte dear," the duchess said, "but I have spent many hours with the needle. I therefore know whereof I speak."

⟨※⟩

"Ten days," I repeated as I strode across Whitehall's grounds. Ten days in which to prove myself worthy of a life independent of Lord Seagrave.

"Miranda," someone called out. "Yes, surely, it is you!"

My heart started. The familiarity of that voice—

I turned to see Henry Raleigh on the verge of leaving the queen's apartments. In his Venetian cloak of umber broadcloth, and fawn leggings, he looked almost too fine. At least I was wearing my new gown, the cut and detailing of which flattered my figure. And then, though I would have been loath to admit it, the knowledge that I was wearing Beatrice's altered skirt gave me a little thrill of power.

"It's good to see you again, and especially looking so well," he said with what seemed true sincerity, before he bowed to kiss my hand. "I was most concerned to learn there was illness among the queen's maidens."

"Yes."

"And Miss Cunnington," he said, "has she recovered?"

"Not entirely," I replied, recollecting the spots along

307

Beatrice's arms, as well as her certain fury if I so much as hinted at her rash.

Ashamed as I was to admit it, the worried look that entered Henry's eyes troubled me more than a little. If Beatrice really was nothing more to him than a tournament partner, would he have spoken so warmly?

"Is her grandaunt nursing her?" he asked.

"She is."

"She is in capable hands, then. The duchess nursed three husbands and a dozen stepchildren besides."

"Not many men remember facts such as these," I said, my voice wobbling a little.

"I am both blessed and cursed with a tenacious mind," Henry said. "Once I learn something, especially something of import, I never forget it."

How could it not impress me that he considered a woman's domestic arts—specifically her gift of nurture during illness or difficulty—to be of so much value?

"Now tell me," he said, "where are you coming from?"

"From the seamstresses' workshop, and you?" I said as we stood in the central courtyard, a few courtiers pausing to bow or nod at us, several of the queen's ladies glancing our way as they took the air or hurried about an errand. Such casualness startled me, for they behaved as if our presence together was the most natural thing in the world.

"I had an appointment with the queen," he told me.

"And did it go well?" I managed, as a particularly distinguished-looking gentleman, his aubergine doublet attesting to his extremely high standing, tipped his hat in our direction just before he sauntered into the building housing the queen.

"Given that I have managed to accomplish precisely what the queen asked—giving the French continued reason to hope while promising nothing—I was sure she would see me. Unfortunately," he confided, "I arrived to discover that the meeting had been delayed. I spent the better part of the last hour listening to Lady Marlborough. An interminable lover of France and all things from that country, she quizzed me on their current fashions, of which I know painfully little."

"I'm sorry," I heard myself say, though I would have enjoyed such a conversation.

"Yes, well"—his voice and manner turning a shade less formal—"it is no matter, now I see the advantage of my liberty." He offered his arm. "Join me?"

Reminded of the tension of our last conversation on the barge, I hesitated, especially given the look that now returned to his eyes—one I still could not define, though it beckoned as much as it held me back.

"Please, Miranda," he said with unexpected warmth.

I looped my arm through his, and he drew me just a bit closer. My heart beat too quickly at first, but after a while the rhythm of walking soothed me, and I found myself almost able to relax into our stroll across the palace grounds.

And what harm was there in such a walk, I told myself as our footsteps fell into pace. What harm when it was such a fine day, the sky a dreamer's shade of blue, the sun warm without being over-hot, the roses in bloom or in bud, as well as the deliriously sweet lilacs. And then there were the early wildflowers—pussytoes, maiden pinks, and oxeye daisies among my favorites—which the queen insisted on cultivating. Why, even the air was fresh and clean-smelling thanks to a gentle wind. I did not want to consider if Henry Raleigh's company added to my growing and, given the circumstances, most unexpected ease.

"Every time I return, I am reminded of how splendid a palace Whitehall is," Henry said, breathing deeply as we passed beneath a canopy overrun with rambling roses of the most intoxicating scent.

"It pleases you to be back at court, then?" I said, reminded of what so many, including Agnes and her grandmother, were saying about his destiny as a great courtier.

"For now." He paused to smell a golden rose, its petals beginning to unfurl.

"Your pleasure is only temporary?"

He laughed, and the crescent moon along his left cheek seemed to laugh with him. "I wouldn't put it exactly that way. I always value the company of men like George Mountjoy and a few of the queen's councilors, in particular Lord Burghley. That said," he continued in a graver tone, "I always prefer not to stay too long."

"No," I said. "Why not?"

What seemed a sad smile traced his lips. "You truly wish to know?"

"I do," I said, the sincerity I heard in my voice troubling me a little.

"There are the endless rules, for one thing. Sumptuary laws and codes of conduct and decorum. And then I find it difficult to have any privacy here. One never knows who to trust, what to believe."

"My father felt so as well."

"Yes, he told me several stories that saved me from many a scrape. Unfortunately, not even your father's lessons proved safeguard enough. When I arrived last autumn, one of the older courtiers seemed to take a genuine interest in me," he said, his voice quieting a little. "I was hungry for such care. Only much later, and much to my own misfortune, did I discover the courtier's interest was of the kind that is ultimately focused on his own preferment."

His fingertips strayed to the scar on his cheek, and I wondered if this self-interested courtier had been the cause of it—a duel perhaps? An embattled confrontation?

"Even so," he said, as if realizing he'd said too much, "I am resolved to profit by the opportunities at court—and there are many."

"Ah." Despite the tenderness in his allusion to my father, I felt my doubts about him returning.

We walked beneath a second canopy of roses and found ourselves engulfed in the heady fragrance, the glow of the blossoms caressing our faces. Soon we reached a courtyard containing an elaborate fountain, this one adorned with marble mermaids and tritons and a dozen golden fish. In the pool below, innumerable coins, the evidence of as many wishes, sparkled.

"Shall we?" he asked.

Before I had a chance to reply, he handed me a coin.

Custom required me to close my eyes as I tossed the money into the pool—why then did I suspect Henry was watching me? And why, when there was so much to wish for—the chance to return home, the chance to escape Lord Seagrave and the countess—why, given all I lacked, was it Henry's image that presented itself to my mind's eye?

"I want to apologize for the curtness of my sister the other night," he said, brushing aside the fallen blossoms as we sat down on a bench in the shade of an old apple tree, its gnarled branches lit up with white flowers that opened to reveal delicate pink hearts.

"Charlotte bears you no ill will personally. It's just that it matters to her, terribly, to see our family rise to the importance we once had. And then Charlotte has as many enemies as friends. Sometimes it is difficult for even my clever sister to distinguish between the two. Something you have no doubt discovered?"

"The plain truth is your sister does not like me," I said, determined not to reveal anything related to my experience—and especially nothing involving Agnes.

"You are your father's daughter," he said, his tone momentarily recollecting those other words.

You are a spirited girl!

"As for my sister, do not put too much stake in her distance."

"No?"

"No. She is ambitious, a trait she inherited from her mother."

"Lady Mooreland?" I said, recalling Agnes's overblown praise.

"Yes," he said neutrally. "Despite her lineage, my father's first wife grew up exceedingly poor. Such a combination can be extremely potent in a person of strong will and constitution. When Lady Mooreland married my father, she believed he would rise at court and make them both very rich. After he failed to do so, she invested her hopes in Charlotte."

"And your mother?" I said, realizing only now how little I knew about her, the link between Henry and myself having been created by our fathers. "What is she like?"

A gentler smile curved around the edges of his mouth, one that changed his expression entirely, and I felt myself growing more comfortable with him. "Nothing like Charlotte's. My mother came to court only once, and when Charlotte or I ask her to return—they are great friends despite their many differences—my mother always replies that one visit was enough for her, though she has expressed a desire to see Ireland at least once in her lifetime."

"And will that be possible?"

"I do not think so. The wildness of the country suits me, but my mother's constitution is no longer so strong.

"What about your own mother?" he asked when I made no reply. "You must miss her a great deal."

I recalled my mother's enthusiastic description of Wingfield Park, pictured her sitting beside the lake, walking through the arbor of scented trees. Did he resent her? Nothing in his voice suggested as much.

The breeze wound its gentle way through the apple tree.

"She is focused on restoring the gardens at Wingfield Park," I said at last.

"A worthy undertaking," he said sincerely. "In their heyday, those gardens were spoken of throughout England. The collection of rare birds there is extraordinary."

"You've been there, then?" I asked, instantly regretting the naiveté of my words.

After all, he was heir to Lord Grey's title and his estate.

"As a boy I often spent a part of the summer there— the air being so fine, and my own lungs so delicate, they feared for a time I would not survive."

"Your constitution must be much improved, given your ability to make several journeys to Ireland."

"Yes." A new lightness stole into his face and voice. "By the age of ten I was climbing fences and stealing apples from the trees."

"A habit I once shared with my brother," I heard myself say, then held back from adding that Caroline—now the bride of someone else—had been our companion on these jaunts.

Henry turned to me and said in a voice almost too intimate, given our changed relation, "Is it possible you have not heard the news yet?"

"About her move to Wingfield Park?"

"Ah, then they really have not told you—"

I stood. "Told me what?"

He took hold of my hand, and once more I sat down beside him. "Lord Grey wrote to me—"

"To you? I do not understand. Why did Lord Grey write to you about my mother?"

"He is family and my godfather. But you mustn't take offense. His was an efficient letter only." He hurried on to say, "One meant to convey important news. He tells me your mother is in good health."

"Well, of course she is," I said, though already I'd begun to doubt it.

His hold on my hand tightened. "Miranda, they are expecting a child in the winter."

So courteous was his manner, he said nothing when I began to cry, only reached for a handkerchief so I could wipe my eyes.

"It would be so much easier if you were angry," I said at last. And how could he not be when we both knew a male child would supplant him as Lord Grey's heir?

"A useless emotion," Henry said as a chorus of robins began their cheerful song. "At best, it must occupy a temporary place in any man's—or woman's—heart."

"Am I correct in assuming this news cannot be spoken of at court?" I said, the ease I'd felt on our walk dissolving.

"You are."

I dared not ask if he thought it possible they were keeping silent only because of the queen's potential wrath. Perhaps the real reason for their silence was that they feared some complication. So many women lost their babies; a woman might even lose her life.

⟷✳⟷

"Miranda!" Jane called when I returned to the dormitory courtyard. "Is something wrong? I hope you are not falling ill."

"It must be the heat and the exercise—too much exertion after the quarantine."

I suspected Jane did not believe this. Yet how could I risk telling anyone, even someone as quiet and faithful as Jane, what I had learned from Henry, when I had no idea how the queen, when she finally discovered the news, would react?

"Tell me all about your afternoon with George," I said instead, once I assured her again I was perfectly all right.

"I'm afraid there isn't a great deal to tell." Jane blushed the color of the apple blossoms' pink hearts.

"Except that you are more in love than ever and on the verge of becoming engaged," I said, trying to banish Henry Raleigh's smile when he and I parted at the garden gate just beyond the apple tree. Had it been my imagination, or had he kept hold of my hand just a moment longer than necessary before bidding me good-bye?

"I *am*, Miranda," Jane said, and squeezed my hand.

317

"Well then, *tell* me."

She spoke to me of their ride past a stone church on a hill, past dark yew trees and majestic oaks, to a clearing filled with the scents of honeysuckle and sweet broom. "There, in a grassy knoll, we picnicked in the open air—"

"And talked only of your future."

"Yes." Jane's features turned dreamy.

If only our conversation could have remained on Jane's and George's impending happiness.

Instead, Jane told me she had further news of my unpleasant suitor. "It's about Lord Seagrave's tenants in Essex."

Eleanor strolled by alongside Cook, the two of them followed by the swift-footed Bridget, her kirtle dirtied by the courtyard grounds, her cheeks flushed with exercise for which Lady Periwinkle would inevitably scold her, to no avail, of course.

"George made some inquiries," Jane said, once they had passed. "His brother is on the Privy Council, you see— and he learned that back in Essex, Lord Seagrave is known for his bullying."

"Please, Jane," I said. "You must tell me. I do not care how bad it is."

"Very well. Lord Seagrave tried to evict the old park keeper and his family even though his grandfather had given the man and his family the right to occupy the house until all of the old man's children were married and settled elsewhere."

"And?" I said, pressing on, though I dreaded what more she might say.

"He tried to starve the family out. It was winter, and Lord Seagrave prevented firewood from being delivered to the keeper's house."

Agnes approached, her grandmother accompanying her, both of them looking as smug as two cats slinking away from a pigeon coop.

Only after they'd proceeded beyond the dormitory with affected smiles and a hello to Jane and me, did Jane reveal that Lord Seagrave recently had himself appointed the local magistrate in Essex.

"Don't tell me," I said, my stomach churning as I compared the truth of Lord Seagrave's position with the delusion clouding my brother's letter, "he bent the law to serve his own purposes."

"It's very likely he would have."

"What prevented him?"

"George's brother doesn't think Lord Seagrave is as smart as he would have everyone believe. It wasn't criminal behavior that finally brought on a heavy fine from the Privy Council—"

"What then?" I said.

"Incompetence."

"Oh, Jane, the earth will begin revolving around the moon before I marry him," I said, then proceeded to tell her about my meeting with the Duchess of Suffolk and Henry Raleigh's half sister, explaining all about the painting and the type of gown they wanted me to reproduce, and why.

"I'm allowed one assistant—someone from among the maidens," I said, looking hopefully in her direction.

"Well, thank goodness for that," Jane said. "On your own it would be impossible to complete such an elaborate project in so little time."

"It would indeed. That's why I'm asking you."

Jane looked as if she would sneeze.

"You're an excellent seamstress." I stood and turned all the way around, showing off my dress. "Without you, I would never have completed this gown so quickly. Please," I said, for she seemed to hesitate, "will you help me? Don't say no."

"No, of course not." Jane's freckles shimmered in the sun. "I mean—yes, I would be honored. I'm simply amazed that of all the maidens, it's me you thought to ask."

CHAPTER NINETEEN
May 24, 1580

"This is the costume the duchess and Lady Raleigh would like you to copy?" Jane asked as we stood together in the workshop, studying the coronation portrait of Anne Boleyn.

"Yes," I said, unnerved by Jane's tone coupled with her creased brow. "Remember, I showed you the design this morning."

"And it is so fine we are sure to succeed." Jane clasped my hand. "As I said, I am entirely at your service. Not even the Duchess of Suffolk could have asked for such a faithful assistant."

Recalling the way Beatrice's grandaunt continually ordered her attendants, her maid, and poor Lady Periwinkle about, while Buttercup barked his assent, both of us began to laugh.

"Good morning, Miranda," Charlotte Raleigh said, entering just as I was in the midst of imitating Lilabet straining under the weight of the duchess's possessions on the day of their departure.

"I suppose," Charlotte scowled, "I should be pleased to find you in such high spirits."

"Yes, well——" I stammered, unable to look away from her doublet of white silk embroidered with caterpillars and sprigs of columbine.

"A birthday present from the queen," Charlotte said, aware of my attention. "She wore it only once. How fortunate I am that Her Grace made the doublet as fashionable for women as it is for men."

Charlotte turned to Jane. "And you are?" she said, almost critically.

"Jane Radcliffe," she said, and curtsied.

"Ah, I should have recognized you at once." Instantly, Charlotte's tone became more cordial. "Such a pity your grandmother could not have accompanied you and Lady Cloudberry to Whitehall. Such an extraordinary woman. Such a facility at languages. And a patron to some of our finest poets." She seemed to smile sincerely. "A true exemplar to our sex."

"I am honored," Jane said politely.

While Charlotte asked Jane about her grandmother's health—with such friendliness I felt sure it was only a matter of days before the queen consented to George and Jane's engagement—I spread my drawings along the largest of the worktables.

As if on cue, the Duchess of Dewberry entered, the sun lighting her from behind, her frizzed halo of hair piled even higher today and flecked with opals, endowing her with the look of a good angel, an impression furthered by her silvery gown edged with white lace and tiny seed pearls.

"Good morning," Jane and I said as we dipped into curtsies.

"I won't have you standing on formality with me, Jane Radcliffe." The duchess reached for Jane's hands, and kissed her on both cheeks.

Only after they reminisced about their shared history—one which included a love of gentle horses, clotted cream with scones, cottages with thatched roofs, and meadows—did the duchess turn to my patterns for the coronation gown and mantle, patterns I had spent most of the night and much of the early morning perfecting.

As the duchess reviewed my work, she alternately sighed and frowned, and the opals in her hair changed from milky blue to white. After her fourth sigh, I worried that despite her initial reaction she would ultimately not find my attempts up to the royal standard.

"Although the style was well before your time," she said as the butterflies wove in and out of my rib cage, "you seem to understand the dimensions of the Henrician silhouette perfectly.

"Why"—she traced the low, square-cut neckline of the kirtle as well as the gown's bodice—"you have even managed to re-create the effect of the forepart perfectly. Even the train is of the precise length, and how beautifully you've reimagined the pleats at the waist. I do admire your accuracy here.

"Now, Charlotte"—her tone was both warm and chiding—"you really must have a closer look!"

"I rely on your expertise here, Margaret." Charlotte raised her eyes only briefly before returning to a thick manuscript. "As you reminded us yesterday, your skill is with the needle, mine is with words. Besides, the queen requires my attendance in a quarter of an hour."

"You are leaving us, then?" Jane asked with a sincerity that jarred me a little, given my own eagerness for Henry's sister to be gone.

"Our queen is suffering from the toothache," Charlotte told Jane, as if that statement explained all.

I wanted to ask again about Eliza's remedy—if she had suggested it to the queen or her doctors—when the duchess said, "The queen summoned Charlotte because of her soothing verse."

"While I recite my words, Malvolio will make jests at my and Lady Bornwell's expense."

"Malvolio? But what of Inez?" I asked, recalling her motley attire at the tournament.

"Inez may be the wittiest fool at court," Charlotte said, "but at present she is a bit out of favor with our queen."

For a moment no one spoke. Although her loyalty to the queen was nonpareil, Inez was Spanish and Catholic, a background that could still prove troublesome, as Kyd had implied.

"What will you recite?" Jane asked, smoothing out the silence.

For the first time, Charlotte seemed to actually smile. "A new poem based on the myth of Artemis."

"Didn't she turn a man into a stag when he spied her bathing?" Jane asked.

"And if I remember correctly," I added, "the man was devoured by his own dogs?"

"According to Ovid's version, but I have revised the myth." Something in my face must have betrayed my interest, for Charlotte soon began telling us all about it, her face flushed with an enthusiasm I had not seen before. "My Artemis is a figure for our queen. It therefore stands to reason that she would set him free in a wood instead of seeing him killed."

"I hope you are not being too idealistic, Charlotte," the duchess said. "Your wood is not to be an arcadia free of wolves and foxes—"

"I would have thought you of all people would have approved, Margaret. But do not worry. I have not idealized the woods surrounding Whitehall. Now," she said as she began gathering up her papers, "I have lingered long enough. If I do not proceed to the queen's rooms at once, I will be the one transformed, and my fate will be far worse than that stag's."

After Charlotte had gone, the duchess proceeded to point out which cupboard held thimbles and needles, and which the tools for the more specialized work to come later.

"And we're to use the smaller hearth to build a fire for the water?" I said, careful to act as if everything she said was absolutely new to me, for I dared not let on that I'd already examined the room on my own.

"Exactly. And you'll find the steam iron in the far cupboard with the lead block to be placed underneath.

"And remember," the duchess said as Jane and I stood together at one of the worktables, "if you need anything, one of the apprentices is always downstairs and will know where to find me. Tea will be brought to you at eleven a.m. sharp, and you are free to finish here with enough time to prepare for supper. Is there anything more you require?"

"Everything is perfect except for the damask that we're to use for the kirtle," I said, once we had matched the fabrics up with each pattern.

326

The duchess looked at me quizzically, "Yes?"

"The fabric seems a bit too heavy to capture the delicacy—the flowing movement—of the costume Anne Boleyn wears in the painting."

"I see your point. There is the taffeta, but it would be too informal for an occasion such as this," the duchess said, folding up the damask. "I will write to Phoebe Buckingham promptly."

"Shall we sew the calico first?" Jane said after the duchess left us.

"Yes." I was pleased Jane did not suggest that we immediately cut into the costly fabrics. The design may have been for the queen, but such precious stuff as silk could not be wasted.

We opened the windows, and the May breeze—heady with the fragrance of flowers and blossoming trees—flowed in and out of the workshop, lilting through the curtains and occasionally sending a piece of paper or a gauzy bit of fabric sailing into the air.

After I prepared the hot water for the press iron, and Jane fetched the scissors and chalk, we stood side by side, she holding the fabric, I pressing the wrinkles out of it. So the hours of this first morning passed in companionable silence; the familiarity of the iron's weight, the solidity of the lead block underneath, and the clean smell of the fabric soothing me.

Once we began to sew, the softness of the calico seemed to bring my mother close. I recalled the morning she first sat me on her lap and placed the needle between my fingers, then guided my hand through the fabric, teaching me the movement and rhythm of making something that would charm the beholder's eye while serving the wearer's purpose.

By the time I was ten, my mother had taught me the running stitch, the backstitch, and the slip stitch. Later, she and I practiced and ultimately perfected the knife pleats that so beautifully brought out the texture of winter's wools and velvets, as well as the more delicate cartridge pleats we used to gather fabrics of lighter weight. And while we sewed, my mother spoke to me of her girlhood and marriage; spoke, too, of her hopes and dreams for my sister, Laura, and for me.

As my fingers worked the needle, in and out, over and over again, I discovered anew that calico was a yielding, almost forgiving fabric. It was then that my history with my mother rose before me, so that it felt as if the recent troubles were not so very great, not when compared to the whole. Absorbed in this way, as one absorbs a picture or the effect of a beautiful gown, my anger began to unravel. In its place, concern took hold, and a deep wish to see her again.

But when? And how? She was so far away.

"I came early today because I must organize a luncheon between the queen and a prominent but rather taxing countryman," the duchess explained shortly after we arrived in the workshop the next morning.

"Surely the queen can postpone such a meeting, the tournament having only just ended," I said.

The duchess shook her head. "Given that the man has been put off three times already, each time with a promise that this will be the last delay, the queen believes she must at last meet with him."

"I imagine it must be very difficult to settle on a menu when Her Majesty's tooth gives her pain," Jane said.

"It would be impossible," the duchess said. "Fortunately, the queen's tooth is much improved."

I longed to know if my suggestion had had anything to do with the queen's return to health, but understood enough not to put myself forward just then, especially not when the duchess had proved such an ally.

"Unfortunately, this gentleman is fussy when it comes to food," the duchess said. "Do you remember, Jane, the week your grandmother had that German baroness to stay?"

"I do." A small smile stole across her lips.

"The quantity of eggs she could eat for breakfast."

"The chickens could not lay them fast enough." Jane giggled.

"And then there was her penchant for pettitoes. I could barely look at her plate during meals."

The two of them began to laugh.

"How do you find the work we have done thus far?" I asked. With my future resting on the outcome, I was eager to speak not of chickens, pigs' feet, and difficult people, but of our calico models of the coronation costume.

The duchess lay an affirming hand on my shoulder. "Perfect. This reminds me: I'm afraid Phoebe Buckingham has not yet been able to meet our request for another fabric."

"Is there a problem?" I knew the damask would never fall properly and would therefore give the coronation gown a bulky look, at odds with the lighter cloth of tissue.

"Only that the featherweight satin she recommends will not be available until the day after tomorrow."

"That should be enough time."

"I should think so," the duchess said. "Skilled seamstresses such as yourselves require the finest materials."

"Please," I said, "we are not so good as that."

By eleven o'clock, sunlight poured into the workshop, endowing every object in the room with the clarity of a perspective glass. In another few hours, the heat would become a bit oppressive, but for now the sun offered reassuring warmth.

"Tea, ladies," the attendant said, breaking the easeful quiet in which we had worked for so long, as he carried in the tray.

As soon as the tea was poured and the attendant closed the doors behind him, Jane began telling me of her morning meeting with George, lingering over her description of his gift basket of fresh honey cake along with a spray of flowers.

"That explains your good spirits despite the slightly charred ham," I said, a part of me longing all the while to be blessed with a future half as happy as hers.

"We did not speak of only ourselves, but of you also." She smiled at me over her teacup. "George has asked his brother Algernon, the one who sits on the Privy Council, to send for the keeper's son."

"In truth?" I said, a little amazed that George Mountjoy, even though I was Jane's friend, would go to such lengths on my behalf.

"Yes." Jane spoke with new pride.

"Still, the council already knows of Lord Seagrave's abuses, and here he is an invited guest at court."

"For the moment," Jane said with remarkable authority. "Remember, the keeper's son is living proof that Henry VIII confiscated the monasteries' land, the keeper's father having been originally employed by the monastery that is now Lord Seagrave's great Essex residence. George believes the presence of the keeper's son here at court will remind the queen of her father's abuses."

"And the queen would do anything to keep her own reign free of shame," I said. After all, it wasn't just Elizabeth's vanity that was at stake in the connection; it was the authority and the purity of her very reign.

⊰✳⊱

That evening when we returned to the Maidens' Chamber, we found Lady Sherringham and our matron drinking Madeira wine in the sitting room. Agnes's grandmother was dressed as usual in an expensive gown, this one of oxblood satin trimmed with Spanish lace, her throat and wrists and several of her fingers adorned with garnets and a single large and rather sharp-looking tiger's eye.

"Why Jane, dear," Lady Sherringham said, as we tried to slip past unobserved, "I was just telling Lady Periwinkle how lovely you looked as May Queen. Very few young women could have carried off a crown of white roses with such sincerity."

"Thank you," Jane said, and curtsied, her graceful movements accompanied by a fit of sneezing.

"You aren't catching cold again, Jane?" Lady Periwinkle said. "So good of you to help Miranda. But the combination of long hours and your delicate constitution worry me. And then, the royal workshop can be drafty."

"Tell me, Jane." Agnes's grandmother produced her toothiest smile. "How are you helping Miranda?"

"A sewing project," Jane said, with just the proper note of mystery.

"Ah, I do love clothes." Lady Sherringham covered Jane's hand with her own. "You simply must tell me all about it."

"Nothing would please me more, but I'm afraid I cannot." Jane spoke with a court lady's finesse. "It's a surprise, you see."

"Well then," Lady Sherringham said, slightly piqued, "I suppose I will have to keep silent when I see the queen. Yes, Agnes and I are on the way to her apartments now." Her gaze sought mine, though she seemed to make it a point not to address me directly. "I do not like to see my granddaughter missing chapel. But what can I do when the queen has invited us for a game of cards? And as I was telling Lady Periwinkle, there is a matter of great importance we wish to discuss, a matter concerning my Agnes's future."

And Henry Raleigh's, I knew she would have liked to add.

"That reminds me," Lady Sherringham said, laying down her teacup, "it is growing late, and the queen does not like to be kept waiting. Lady Periwinkle, would you be so kind as to summon—?"

"No need, Grandmother," Agnes said, stepping into the room in a stunning black gown, the one with the ebony beading, a single strand of pearls around her neck and another around her waist. She was the very picture of a demure maiden, with the exception of the glint in her eyes as sharp as her grandmother's jewels.

How long had she been listening?

⬥

"It will all turn out well," Jane assured me after we returned from chapel, only to find Agnes seated before the mirror, her usually pale cheeks abloom, her eyes so bright it was as if they had been lit by tiny flames.

Instantly the other maidens flocked to her, Eleanor leading the way.

"Of course my grandmother and the queen being old friends, we met in the Privy Chamber," Agnes said as the others gathered even more closely around her.

"That is high favor indeed," one of them said.

"Was Charlotte Raleigh there too?" another asked.

"Certainly," said Eleanor. "She and Lady Sherringham

334

are intimate friends, are they not, Agnes?"

"Well"—Agnes played with her pearl choker—"if you must know, yes."

"You're too modest," Eleanor continued. "The queen's ladies know Charlotte already thinks of Agnes as a sister. From all that I've heard, it is only a matter of weeks until she becomes exactly that."

CHAPTER TWENTY

June 2, 1580

Despite her mock discretion, I had no doubt that Agnes had encouraged Eleanor's talk. It surprised me, then, when several days passed, and still there was no firm announcement about an engagement. I dared not scrutinize it, but my own relief at the postponement of something that seemed inevitable troubled me more than a little.

Nor was there any word from the keeper's son.

I dared not tell Jane, but every day that came and went without any news seemed to give Lord Seagrave a bit more sway, despite the promise of freedom that accompanied our progress on the coronation gown. Thankfully, it was taking shape with enviable authenticity and would be finished by day's end or early on the morrow, a probability confirmed when the duchess joined us in the workshop on the sixth day, carrying with her the much-awaited fabric from Phoebe Buckingham.

"At last!" Jane jumped up from the worktable.

"Yes, the satin for the kirtle has arrived." The duchess spoke without her accustomed mirth.

"Has something happened?" I asked.

"Yes," Jane added. "Is it the queen? Her tooth?"

"No, no, fortunately the queen no longer suffers from that problem."

When we continued to press her—politely, of course—the duchess's fingers strayed to the hairstyle that today seemed for the first time less tidy, less artfully arranged. "If I breathe a word of this to you," she said with a gravity that defied her inherently airy demeanor, "you must promise to keep this news between us alone."

"Yes, of course, depend upon it," we replied in unison, instinctively reaching for each other's hand.

"We don't speak of it openly at court," she said, still reluctant, "but the queen's coffers are less than bountiful now that the tournament has ended."

"Ah," I said, realizing the duchess was, in the politest terms, telling us that the treasury needed funds.

"What with the lavishness of the festivities," she continued, "and the entertainment of the French, who stayed far too long, though they have at long last departed, and not a day too soon . . . Unfortunately"—again she

337

fretted her hair—"there remains that troubling but wealthy gentleman."

"The fussy eater? The one who would not be put off?" Jane asked.

The duchess seemed to hesitate, and her hands still trembled.

I ran my fingers across the folds in the satin again and again, reminding myself that *he* could not possibly be influential enough to press an audience with the queen.

But when I looked up, the duchess's pale face told all.

"It's Lord Seagrave, isn't it?" I said, feeling as if I were sinking.

"Would that I could help you," the duchess said, her hairstyle wilting a little as she crumpled into the chair. "When money matters are pressing, the queen is—I am forced to say—a bit too vulnerable." A defeated smile traced her lips. "He has agreed to help in the interim."

⚜

Though my stitches no longer gave either one of us the power we believed, as the sun rose higher in the sky, Jane and I continued to work diligently, completing the sleeves with their slashed cuffs, and both panels for the skirt, before midafternoon, as if this furious sewing could some-how keep my future at bay; as if a perfectly sewn bodice and elegant cuffs were a fortress, each buttonhole and bit of lace a soldier or a mounted guard who would protect me from Lord Seagrave.

By four o'clock we were ready to reinforce the hem. In the late afternoon light, the cloth of tissue actually glowed—the fact that we could not discern our stitches through the luminous fabric a testament to their fineness.

"It will be a perfect replica," Jane said, comparing the gown to the one in the portrait.

"Yes," I said. But now the gown seemed proof of how high a woman could rise, only to fall further than her worst nightmares.

The door opened. I expected the duchess.

But it was one of the ushers. "The queen has requested your presence, Miss Molyneux."

I reached for Jane's hand. "Will the duchess not accompany me?"

"The Duchess of Dewberry is already with the queen."

"Oh," I said, wondering how I would bear the long walk between here and Elizabeth's apartments, a distance comparable to a prisoner's journey from the Tower to the scaffold.

This time when I entered the queen's residence, I turned away from the high columns adorned with heraldic beasts, and the paintings of the queen. Not just the guise of the older queen, but even the features of the young

Elizabeth framed in the accession portrait seemed to stare back, as if waiting to do me harm.

"Miss Molyneux, Your Grace," the usher said, bowing so deeply to the queen that he seemed to kiss the ground.

Afterward I proceeded alone through the heavy gilded doors, conscious of my every step. The sunlight slashed a path for me to follow along the polished floor, my feet heavy despite the lightness of my slippers.

Just before I curtsied to the queen and bowed my head, I met the compassionate eyes of the duchess and almost felt reassured, but then I saw *his* angular figure.

On this day, as on so many others, Lord Seagrave was dressed in a severe black doublet and cloak that brought out the censorious quality of his eyes and the hawkish arch of his nose. "As I was saying, Your Grace, patience is a virtue I have always cultivated. The one virtue."

"Is it, my lord?" The queen's tone was neither complimentary nor critical.

I remained bowed before her, wishing she would not ask me to rise, so reluctant was I to meet my unsavory suitor's eyes.

"You may stand, Miranda," the queen said at last.

Elizabeth's person had surrendered none of its awe. Her gown was of flamboyant pink satin, the skirt adorned with rainbows, suns, and other wondrous natural emblems intended to suggest her power over the elements. And around her throat circled countless ropes of pearls, both creamy white and the rarer smoky gray bordering on black.

"Dear Margaret has kept me informed of your progress," the queen said after giving me her bejeweled hand to kiss. "Though neither she nor Charlotte will tell me of the costume itself, insisting—whenever I ask—it is a secret to commemorate my mother's coronation month."

As the queen spoke almost playfully of the clothes I was making, as if some trifle and not my future were at stake, I believed I understood at last why my mother, dangerous though such a feeling was, did not like her all-powerful cousin. . . .

"And you and Jane Radcliffe, such a wise choice for a helpmate, are so close to finishing the costume," the queen said. Instantly she began counting off the remaining time—once so precious, and now of so little import, given Fortune's fickleness—on her long fingers.

"Yes," I said, my voice spiritless.

"Very good." The queen smiled. "It pleases me immensely to know this surprise project will not be delayed."

As Lord Seagrave feigned a smile meant for me alone, I stammered, "We have Your Grace's permission to continue, then?"

"Why, Miranda, my permission has been there all along. I told you as much the first day. I told you, too, as

I recall, your desire to do *anything* might very well prove to be a dangerous thing."

So it has, I thought, though I was smart enough not to speak the words aloud.

She turned away, and I followed the lavish swish of her satin skirts, as with certain calculation Elizabeth stepped over to the portrait of herself as the sun goddess by the Italian artist—a portrait, I realized, accurately captured her mercurial as well as fiery temperament.

"I wonder if your mother would approve of the sewing you are doing here," the queen said, turning toward us once more.

"What do you think, Margaret? Do you think the new Lady Grey would approve of her daughter's labors, or am I selfishly keeping Miranda from being of assistance to her mother in these months before her own *labor* begins?"

"I do not know, Your Grace." The duchess spoke without emotion.

I must have flinched or made some other sign. "Yes," the queen said, "I learned of the pregnancy only this morning. Quite a time for news. Now that the French have gone, I thought I would at last have a bit of tranquility!

"I did not scold Charlotte. Although at times out-spoken, she is also loyal, and then there is her solicitude for my health. Yet it seems my dear lady-in-waiting has known of the pregnancy for several days now.

"Of course, I do not know if I would be so generous toward her were it not for the remedy Charlotte found somewhere." The queen chuckled, revealing the yellowish cast to her teeth. "Perhaps I should dismiss these expensive doctors with their fancy cures and send my ladies searching through the healers' ancient books. I might save a good deal in medical fees."

I dared not say anything immediately for fear I might be wrong—or worse, that Charlotte might have twisted the story. Still, I had the nagging suspicion that it was Eliza's remedy that had cured the queen's toothache.

I tried to think of a way to broach the subject, but then Lord Seagrave cleared his throat and took a step toward me, his bad leg hindering his already graceless movements. It took everything within me to keep from crying out.

"Now then, Miranda, you must be wondering why I called you here today," the queen continued, her eyes as sharp as those of her father, who I could imagine sitting in a room very like this one, a room with a ceiling so high and vast, all sound echoed before being swallowed up.

Henry VIII would have sat just where his daughter now stood, beside the long window, the wolves and lions and other predatory animals watching from their perches atop the pillars; and he would have spoken merrily as he signed the warrant for some poor soul's death.

"It's premature to speak of the news just yet," said the

queen, "but I trust your discretion, Miranda, and yours, Reginald."

"My discretion goes without saying, Your Grace," he said, his lips curling a little as he smiled.

"Very good," the queen said, though I remained silent. "You will not be alone in your happiness."

I closed my eyes and steeled myself in preparation for her announcement of the engagement of Agnes and Henry Raleigh.

"This morning, young George Mountjoy requested permission for Jane Radcliffe's hand in marriage," the queen said instead. "Permission I gladly gave. I am generous insofar as I am able, thinking always of the welfare of my England." The queen paused and began to play with her pearls. "Is that not true, Margaret?"

"It is, Your Grace," the duchess said, and although her voice was brighter now, she remained pale.

"Now, how delightful if we were to have two, perhaps even three engagements here at Whitehall," said the queen.

"Have you nothing to say, Miranda?" the queen asked, her voice soft as a fox moving through deep snow.

"Only that it is my deepest wish not to be forced into marrying him, Your Grace."

The Duchess of Dewberry inhaled deeply, and again Lord Seagrave cleared his throat.

The queen simply said, "Forced? That is a strong word,

Miranda, though I understand, indeed I sympathize with, your reluctance. Truly I do, being disposed to the unmarried state myself.

"That being the case, it remains God's law that a woman's highest duty is marriage. A woman"—she paused—"who is not an anointed queen and married first and foremost to her kingdom."

"But Your Grace, there is my test to consider. There is your promise."

"Promise?" Again the swish of her rainbow skirts, again the calculated hesitation of a master procrastinator. "What I offered you was an opportunity. And now," she said, and smiled, "opportunity, at least our view of it, has changed.

"You see, my dear, I have come to recognize the value in seeing you safely and most comfortably situated as Lady Seagrave. Surely no man in England would be so certain of your many virtues as the one who stands before us now. Given the losses of your father—losses I did my best to help your family overcome—very few men would still wish to have you as a bride."

Lord Seagrave stepped toward me, the look in his hawkish eyes proof he was determined to secure some sign of my favor, or at least my consent, while the queen watched, as if ours were a court play designed for her alone.

He stretched out those spidery hands and smiled, and I

feared he intended to embrace me. How to escape?

"Miranda—"

I felt myself on the verge of panic.

It was then I recalled Anne's tactics at Turbury, the way her body conveniently slipped to the floor under moments of duress. Although my own constitution was far too hardy to allow for such a loss of consciousness even under circumstances as appalling as these, none of the people gathered here knew this about me.

I raised my hand to my mouth and made a sighing sound as Anne had done, then collapsed, keeping my eyes tightly closed. As my head hit the hardwood floor, I bit my tongue to keep from crying out.

I opened my eyes just as the sun was about to slip beneath the lilac-and-rose-colored horizon.

"I'm sorry, sir. I'm afraid it's absolutely impossible for a gentleman to enter the Maidens' Chamber at any time, under any circumstances."

Lady Periwinkle's voice.

"Yes, yes, I will certainly deliver your message to Miranda, and the flowers also. Such a pretty bouquet, though you mustn't pluck posies from the queen's garden again, unless you have the royal gardener's permission."

The hallway muffled the other person's voice.

So I was the subject of this conversation—but with whom was Lady Periwinkle speaking? Given his growing intimacy with Agnes, Henry Raleigh could not possibly be the visitor. The very idea was unthinkable. As for Lord Seagrave, he would never bring me a bouquet of flowers. Besides, the thought of him here filled me with queasiness and dread.

"The doctor's diagnosis?" Lady Periwinkle said as I strained, in vain, to catch the other speaker's voice. "No, it is nothing so grave as that," she continued. "Who told you? . . . Emotional strain . . . She must have plenty of rest."

Though I had already been asleep for several hours, I closed my eyes once more just as Lady Periwinkle reached my bedside. Only after she turned away did I open them to find a grand vase filled with purple irises and the brightest yellow daffodils.

Perhaps it was the sweet wine in the tisane the doctor had prescribed, or the balm of myrrh coupled with the soporific valerian, or perhaps it was my desperate need for rest, not to mention a foreboding as cloying as molasses or tar. Whatever the reason, it was only later I learned I had slept for a full day and a half, waking at last on the day the copy of the coronation costume was supposed to be finished and made ready for presentation to the queen.

"You mustn't worry about the costume," Jane said, when sunshine forced my eyes awake, and I found her keeping watch at my bedside.

"But there's still the kirtle to be sewn, and what of the mantle? I need to finish it. I want to prove—"

"I know." Jane stroked my hand tenderly. "Under the circumstances, the duchess has managed to convince the queen to allow you—to allow us—a reprieve of another three days. Time enough for the costume to be finished for the queen's celebration."

"But why would she do that?" I said, recalling the queen's coldness, proof enough, it seemed, she had no intention of being generous with me.

"The duchess stressed the queen's charity," Jane said; "though the practical truth is most likely the queen's eagerness to enjoy her new clothes."

"Jane! I have never known you to be so canny."

Jane only shrugged. "You've heard some of the lords talk about the cost of the queen's wardrobe—and her ladies' defenses on the subject. Her love of fashion is no secret."

"But I never realized how well you will do as one of them," I said with real admiration.

"Thank you." She blushed. "It's a bit of a struggle, but I have my future to think of—my responsibilities to George."

My gaze strayed to Jane's hand—on her ring finger, a single perfect ruby set in a simple but solid band of gold. "Oh, Jane. I have not congratulated you."

The rising spots of color in her cheeks were proof of her happiness. "But how do you know?"

"I had only to listen to you talk just now, but truthfully, the queen announced the engagement to me the day I was summoned to her presence." Announced it to me along with Lord Seagrave's intentions, I almost added, then thought better than to link my calamitous situation with Jane's joy. "When is the marriage to be?"

"In mid-June, once my stay here has ended and the court travels to Windsor for the summer months. Before George joins his brother on the Privy Council."

"And will you have a house?" I asked, realizing I must allow her the pleasure of speaking of her happiness.

"Oh yes; though we'll be obliged to keep a small place in town, we're to have a lovely house about an hour's ride from London." Instantly, her voice brightened. "There will be gardens and an orchard, and land enough for horses."

Her words brought to mind my own parents, who, when Ireland had not divided them, had managed to make a satisfying life together. I felt a door closing behind me, a door to a dark room where Lord Seagrave's voice echoed in the distance.

"What of the keeper's son?" I asked. "Has there been any word?"

"George thinks we could try to present someone who could testify on his behalf."

I bit my lip. "But we don't have much time to find someone willing."

There was no way our queen would delay my marriage to Lord Seagrave now that she'd found a way to replenish the treasuries.

Until I realized I might just know someone who could not only present the keeper's son's testimony, but one who, if he were willing, would be able to act the part. . . .

⁂

"You seem especially nervous today, Miranda," Agnes said, appearing beside me once Jane had left to fetch pen and paper. "Surely Lord Seagrave will ask the doctors to prescribe something. As I was telling Henry during our stroll in the most private of our queen's rose gardens earlier, a gentleman's wife"—she toyed with the white rose on her bodice—"no matter how that gentleman came by his fortune, cannot be of a excitable nature."

Understanding she wished only to taunt me, I did my utmost to stare back at her, clear-eyed, all the while saying nothing.

"Has your future husband managed to silence you so quickly?" she said. "Well, Miranda?" Her tone and expression grew more taunting. "Is it because you are practicing to be a model of obedience that you make no reply?"

"It is your dishonor and lack of scruples that force me to hold my tongue lest I unleash words not fit for Whitehall," I said, wishing I could shake her.

Agnes laughed. "I should pity you. At the very least, this is certainly an occasion for me to practice that ultimate virtue, forgiveness, though you slander me."

She plucked the rose from her bodice and inhaled deeply. Her calm infuriated me, and I would have said more, but then I caught sight of Jane returning, and did not think the retort worthy of my effort.

***

"And you'll be sure the courier delivers the message to Marlborough Street today," I told Jane, once I'd drafted my letter.

"Yes, of course."

"The courier must deliver it into the hands of the addressed party himself. No one else must receive it on his behalf, and do urge the person to give the messenger his answer immediately."

"But, Miranda," she said, leaning over me as I impressed

the seal on the cooling wax, "you must tell me to whom you've written. Remember, we are joined in this—"

"I cannot risk it. What if we're found out? The queen may be more willing to forgive you than me, but there's no telling. You remember what happened to her favorite, Sir Philip Carew, don't you?"

"The young lord banished for life?"

"Yes. And his only crime was his refusal to come to Whitehall when the queen summoned him during his wife's illness."

Jane sneezed.

"And even when the Earl of Leicester's first wife, Amy, died of mysterious circumstances—"

"Miranda." Her face filled with panic. "Such words border on treason!"

"Yes, which is why the less you know, the better.

"Think of George," I said when she continued to hesitate. "There's no need to jeopardize his future."

"Perhaps you are right," Jane said at last.

"Any news from Beatrice?" I asked, once Jane returned and assured me the message would be delivered today.

"I went to see her yesterday," she said, sitting down beside me.

"And? How did you find her?"

"In mixed spirits."

"I do not understand," I said, wondering if I had forgotten something when I fell. Dr. Snead did say I hit my head hard.

"Lilabet tells me that the last three mornings Beatrice has stood in front of the looking glass and screamed. The duchess's little Buttercup has taken to hiding under the bed"—the shadow of a smile traced Jane's lips—"as has one of her attendants."

"The rash still hasn't improved, then?" I said, picturing poor Dr. Snead banished to that rainy northern village, his years under Henry VIII no match for the duchess and her grandniece's wrath.

"On the contrary, the rash is nearly gone. It's Beatrice's pallor that distresses her—and her grandaunt. To help restore her peachy glow, they have Lilabet shuttling back and forth between the duchess's apartment, the herb garden, and the apothecary for oil of primrose sweetened with honey and a few drops of frankincense."

"A most costly remedy."

"Well, given the circumstances," Jane said in a more confidential voice, "you can well understand."

"Circumstances?" The word called up the image of Henry Raleigh visiting Beatrice in her convalescence, an impossibility since the queen herself had practically sanctioned his suit for Agnes.

"Oh dear," said Jane. "Don't tell me you don't know?"

"I'm sorry, Jane," I said, my heartbeat quickening, "but I feel as if you have stepped through a door to which I do not have the key."

"Your brother is here at court."

I collapsed against the pillows. "My brother? Here?"

Jane flushed crimson. "I'm sorry, I thought you knew." She pointed to the purple and yellow posies at my bedside. "Didn't your brother bring the bouquet?"

"I never asked." I said, reminded of that unidentified visitor in the hall. "I was afraid the bouquet had come from Lord Seagrave."

"Surely they are from your brother. He brought a similar bouquet—though much grander with its inclusion of scarlet roses—to Beatrice yesterday."

※

Two hours later, I found myself seated in the dormitory courtyard beside Robert. Before meeting him, I twined my hair into two neat but unadorned plaits and donned my humble calico, resisting any form of adornment, if only to impress upon him the desperateness of my situation.

Robert was dressed in a newly fashionable mandilion, the umber sleeves split to reveal an equally elegant and new

354

evergreen doublet beneath—clothes he could only have paid for with money from Lord Seagrave, unless his luck at the card tables had changed, or he had managed to convince the tailor to give them to him on credit.

"But when did you arrive?" I asked, once he'd told me about his room overlooking the tennis courts, his sumptuous breakfast, the kindness of several of the queen's men.

"The night before last."

"Did Jane Radcliffe contact you?"

"No. It was your friend Agnes Somerset who wrote to tell me you were ill."

"Agnes?" I bit my tongue, tasted blood. "You had a letter from Agnes?"

"A most concerned letter—"

I searched the garden for those sly eyes, but with the exception of a few of the younger maidens, their rosy cheeks and giggles proof of their interest in my handsome and very well-dressed brother, there was no one there. "Robert, she is not and never was my friend."

A stunned look came into his eyes, and he smiled nervously. "But her words were all concern. When she wrote of her own impending engagement to Henry Raleigh"—he took my hands in his—"I knew you must be distressed, even though she took pains to make me understand how sorry she was that her happiness coincided with your disappointment—"

355

"She wrote to you of this?" I said, brushing his hands away, unsure if I was more furious or distraught.

"Yes." His voice was grave. "She said you would take it badly. This is why she begged me not to hold her responsible. So sympathetic were her words that when I arrived at Whitehall, I feared you were gravely ill."

Recalling my last terrible exchange with Agnes in the dormitory, the laughter that escaped me was far more desperate than Beatrice's as she'd held out her spotty arms that last day in the Maidens' Chamber.

"Miranda"—Robert laid a hand on my arm—"yours was a nasty fall. Perhaps you should rest."

"I am perfectly well, thank you." Again I brushed his hand away. "It is only the thought of marrying Lord Seagrave that makes me ill," I said, though in truth the image of Agnes and Henry unsettled me nearly as much.

"But, Miranda—"

"But nothing! You do know Lord Seagrave occupies a former monastery—confiscated lands, Robert! How could you possibly think I would marry such a man? Unless you saw some benefit, some mutual benefit?" I stared pointedly at his new clothes.

I expected Robert to fight me.

Instead his expression became that of the chastened little boy caught stealing coins from Father's money box, the expression of the older brother who'd cut up my sewing once in a fit of anger, only to repent and ride into town to buy me enough fabric for a new kirtle, though the cost required he sacrifice his much beloved belt of Spanish leather.

"What do you expect me to do?" he said at last. "Mother has gone to live in a distant country, Caroline has married another, and Father's debts remain such a burden."

"Father's debts are my inheritance also," I said sharply. "Nevertheless, I remain resolved not to have my future determined by them."

Robert's face grew pale, and for a moment I thought he would cry.

Poorest earl. Reckless earl. Heartbroken earl.

"What of Beatrice?" I said. "She is my friend, and already there is talk of a courtship between you. I must therefore ask: do you truly care for her?"

Robert stared at his boots. They were scuffed and in need of new heels, and after so much confusion and deceit, I was extremely grateful to see them. "Well?"

"I could come to," he said at last. "Truly."

⟞✳⟝

"You're absolutely certain no one has brought me a message?" I asked Lady Periwinkle once I returned to the dormitory.

357

"My dear, I really do not know what it is you're expecting—or from whom." Lady Periwinkle spoke as if I were still in the throes of illness. "But for the second time, I tell you no."

"Who would have thought that Miranda would be so nervous, especially now she has a suitor of her own," Agnes said, her eyes wide, as she used her most innocent voice.

"Yes, well, I wish you could share some of your calm with her." Lady Periwinkle's face was all concern as she fidgeted with the laces on her gown. "You two were such good friends when Miranda first arrived. What, my dears, has happened?"

"I cannot imagine," Agnes said. "As you know, Lady Periwinkle, were it up to me, we'd be just as intimate as ever." Agnes looped her arm through our matron's. "Just this morning I told my grandmother I would like nothing better than to have Miranda stand beside me as matron of honor. Her marriage will surely take place before my own."

"You see, then, Miranda, it's up to you," Lady Periwinkle said, the naturalness in her tone further proof that the engagement of Agnes Somerset and Henry Raleigh would soon be a reality.

"It's just as I told my Amelia and my Jillian after I lost my dear Walter." Lady Periwinkle's hand sought the miniature of her late husband pinned to her breast. "Whenever they quarreled, I sat them down and said, 'Should anything happen to me, you will have only each other.'"

Although such well-intentioned advice, if advice it was, meant nothing to two people who were unrelated, I smiled and tried to look sympathetic. This seemed to satisfy Lady Periwinkle, who soon bustled away, proving herself as blind to emotional complexities as she was to color.

"Dear Lady Periwinkle, how rosy the world must appear through her eyes. I do believe I will ask Grandmother to send her a deep pink gown to wear to my wedding. After all," she said smugly, "I couldn't bear to disenchant her, could you?"

And before I had a chance to reply—when what I most wanted was to throttle her—Agnes turned and walked away. Of course she lifted her skirts just high enough for me to be sure to see the stockings—silk—she'd received from the queen. Or so she and Eleanor would have everyone believe.

CHAPTER TWENTY-ONE

June 3, 1580

STANDING BESIDE JANE IN THE SEAMSTRESSES'
workshop the next morning, I beheld not just the
finished gown, the cloth of tissue made more luminous beside the perfectly sewn cuffs and neckline of
gossamer lace, but the kirtle also, the satin light as a
moth's wings and as incandescent.

"Never would I have dreamed that you would
choose to spend the first days of your engagement on
the coronation costume," I said, imagining the
honeyed mist with which the betrothal usually began
when the two people were eager to marry, or so my
mother had always said.

"What sort of friend would I be otherwise?" Jane
asked.

Despite what the future might bring, at that

moment an inner sun seemed to warm me from within, and I resolved to hold to my promise and make Jane a wedding gown fit for a queen.

❖

Just as Jane finished threading a wide-eyed needle with the silk thread she would use to finish sewing on the ermine fur, her delicate hands being more suited to such work than my own, someone knocked at the door.

"I'm sorry to disturb you," one of the attendants said. "It's just that there's a gentleman downstairs to see you, Miss Molyneux."

Jane and I exchanged glances. "He came in the rain?" I asked.

"Yes, miss," the attendant said. "If there is a problem, I can tell him you are unable to meet—"

"No," I said, and stood. "I will go right down."

"Good luck," Jane said, and squeezed my hand.

Outside, I found my visitor sheltering beneath the building's archway. He was dressed in very fine traveling clothes, his back turned as he stroked his horse's muzzle. I was about to call out to him, but something was not quite right—where was the shock of mercurial hair? And that horse—?

"Miranda." It was Henry Raleigh who turned to face me.

361

At first I could not speak, so great was my confusion. "Why have you come? Are you leaving Whitehall?"

"I am." He came closer, the rain intensifying in the courtyard beyond.

"In such weather? Don't tell me you have already had your fill of court life," I said, determined to reveal nothing of what I had learned. On his own, would he have the courage to tell me of his intended engagement to Agnes? Could I bear to hear it from his lips?

"Not exactly. I have a pressing errand." He looked down and toed the ground with his boot as his horse whinnied softly behind us.

Was he leaving to seek Burton Raleigh's blessing? Surely this was just a formality. The man Lady Sherringham had referred to as her "darling ogre" would undoubtedly support the match.

He looked up, the moon-shaped scar luminous on his wet cheek.

For a while we just stood there staring at each other, the horse watching us both through mild brown eyes that put me strangely in mind of those other horses, the Exmoor ponies on the moors—only this one was mateless.

At last he said, "I wanted to be assured of your recovery. I heard about your fall, you see. There is no lasting injury?"

"I am perfectly well, thank you."

It was a struggle to maintain my composure as the questions vying for answers were coming faster now: What was he doing here, especially outfitted for a journey? Was he feeling guilty about my circumstances? Did he know of the alliance the queen seemed to have made with Lord Seagrave?

"If you require anything . . ." he said.

"Really, my situation no longer—is not—your concern. And perhaps you know my brother is here," I said, wondering if Agnes had dared even hint to him of the letter she had written. Very soon they would recite the vows of marriage. "Besides," I said, "I can always depend upon the friendship of Chidiock Kyd."

"Ah yes, your partner from the tournament." Sadness seemed to trace his words, or did I only imagine it?

"Shouldn't you be on your way?" I said, disconcerted by the way he lingered there, as if he expected something from me—but what? "The weather is bad," I told him. "If yours is a long journey, you had best get started."

"I have seen worse weather. Besides"—he clicked his tongue and his horse trotted over, obviously intimate with this gesture—"Innisfree is a faithful, sturdy horse."

She seemed to whinny her assent as Henry retrieved an apple from his pocket and let her eat from the palm of his hand.

"Innisfree?" I said, my voice tight in my throat. "You gave her that name?"

"Yes." Did he know Innisfree was the village in Ireland my father often spoke of, a green village beside the sea he'd hoped to show me one day? Given the time he'd spent with my father, Henry must have known. And yet, under the circumstances, the question was impossible to ask.

"Allow me to say at least one thing more," he said when it came my turn to stand there staring, my own feet suddenly heavy, rooted.

"Very well."

"You asked why I came."

"Yes?" I said, thankful for the everlasting rain, if only because it drowned out the pounding of my heart.

"To say good-bye, and to encourage you to hold fast to your beliefs."

There was tenderness in his voice, but I could not embrace it. Despite the confidences of our last conversation— the news of my mother's pregnancy, his own confessions beneath the apple tree—he no longer had the right to speak to me thus. Besides, what value did such advice have from one whose actions proved that he had abandoned those beliefs my father believed one must always hold dear?

Henry Raleigh continued to linger there, the look on

his face and everything in his manner implying he wanted to say more.

But for me the time was only agony. How could it have been otherwise when our futures had once been linked? When I now believed I could care for him? Besides, shouldn't he have known better than to expose me to any further risk when he would soon be engaged to Agnes, if he was not already engaged to her?

"For these words, I thank you," I said at last. "And now, as you must know, I am needed upstairs."

"Of course. Take care, Miranda," he said, and bowed.

"I wish you a safe journey." My words came out stiffly. Still, I yielded my hand for him to kiss.

Despite the cool weather, his lips were warm. As I turned away, I found myself wishing I had worn gloves.

"You're drenched," Jane said, hurrying to the workshop door. "Now tell me, was he downstairs? The person you wrote to?"

"No," I said, trying to keep my voice and expression neutral.

"Who was it, then?" she asked, then hurried to fetch a warm blanket from one of the cupboards. "Your brother?"

"Robert? The queen herself couldn't compel him to rise before nine."

"Who then, Miranda?" Jane asked, wrapping the blanket around me.

"Henry Raleigh."

"How strange." Jane looked toward the windows as if expecting to find some answer there. "Well, what did he say? Did he come from the queen? Has there been some change? The keeper's son?"

"He came to say good-bye."

"Good-bye? I don't understand. He's among the most highly favored young courtiers. George believes it is only a matter of time before the queen gifts him with property in the west country, as well as with a house along the Thames—close enough to Whitehall that she can visit him by barge. Why would he possibly leave now?"

Despite the fact that she, too, knew of Henry's impending engagement to Agnes, my good-as-gold friend did not say, *And why would he say good-bye to you when he is practically affianced to Agnes?*

Even so, I felt sure the question lurked behind her mild eyes, and how could it not when Agnes talked as if she were ready to begin ordering her trousseau, while her Machiavellian grandmother had no doubt already composed a guest list for the wedding to be held at her Devonshire estate. Why, the queen herself had taken much care to hint at its coming reality with needling accuracy.

"All he said was that I should hold fast to my beliefs,"
I replied, stumbling a little over the words.

"How extraordinary."

"Yes it is, extraordinary." I turned toward the window. Although I searched, I did not find Henry Raleigh's retreating figure along the road. How quickly he must have ridden away, despite the rain. But of course, if Innisfree was the horse's name, she must have been comfortable or at least experienced with such changeable weather.

"Whatever could he mean by such a cryptic message?" Jane's nose began to twitch, and she seemed on the verge of sneezing.

To Jane, who continued to stand by me, I would have liked to reveal the truth, but I had told her nothing of my history with Henry Raleigh. She therefore had no reason to believe him a traitor to those beliefs to which he'd urged me to hold fast.

⤝✳⤞

By noon, the rain had given way to sun. At precisely two o'clock, Jane reinforced the eyelets around the mantle's sleeves for a second time while I misted the coronation costume with lavender water. What else, other than sit in idleness, could we do until the queen's ladies arrived to inspect our finished work and prepare us for our meeting with the queen?

"So the costume is complete at last," the Duchess of Dewberry said, entering in a gown of silver silk edged with black bone lace. With her she brought the scent of the pink and yellow tea roses she carried in her arms. "The poor flowers were nearly beaten down by the rain. Though the gardener is lamenting the plunder of the gardens, I had no choice but to cut them."

"Let him complain," Charlotte said, following in a similar gown. "There are enough flowers at Whitehall to gift every woman in London with a bouquet—and every man with a nosegay.

"Besides," she said in a less pleasant tone, "it would seem one of the less-seasoned visitors has been plundering the beds with a vigor permissible only because of his naiveté."

Of course Charlotte knew about my brother. How could she not, given her affiliation with Agnes and Lady Sherringham? Who knows? Perhaps Charlotte had been the one to suggest to Agnes the letter to Robert.

Charlotte was about to say something further, but then the duchess took hold of her hand. "Look, Charlotte!" She gave a blissful sigh. "Such exquisite work. Were I to close my eyes, I could almost conjure the queen's late mother as she was then, a beautiful young woman, her hair flowing loose, a circlet of diamonds adorning her white brow, the king himself so pleased with her, one would never have imagined the horror that came later."

Following such a dramatic introduction, Charlotte had no choice but to turn to the coronation costume, framed by the workshop windows, the light endowing the shimmering cloth of tissue with an enchanted look worthy of some fairy-tale romance—though the story of Anne Boleyn was anything but that.

The way the duchess smiled and said something further about "the fineness of the work," and especially Charlotte's partial smile, seemed proof that the gown met with their approval.

The mantle they seemed less sure about, or so the duchess's frown as she stepped closer to examine it, and Charlotte's exaggerated sigh, suggested.

"Is there something faulty about the work?" I asked, the butterflies within me metamorphosing into a group of fat sparrows trying to find their way out of a cathedral, as the two ladies began to whisper between themselves.

"Only now do we realize you have taken a bit too much liberty with the collar," Charlotte pointed out.

"Yes, it's higher and more close-fitting than the original," the duchess said, a bit more gently.

"We did ask for a faithful replica." Charlotte's voice, despite her smile, was accusatory.

I stared at Jane. How had that happened when I'd taken so much care to be exact?

"Well?" Charlotte said, sounding a little too pleased with my mistake.

The sparrows swept up into the eaves, battering themselves against the stone as they tried to escape.

"It was Miranda's idea," Jane said finally.

I stared at Jane. Why would she possibly say such a thing?

"Really?" Again, Charlotte.

"Yes," Jane began. "The queen's throat no longer being as youthful—"

"It is unwise to point such a thing out," Charlotte said to me, her voice clear and cold.

"You misunderstand," Jane continued. "Miranda's inventiveness conceals it. That is the purpose of the design."

"Ah," the duchess said, examining the collar more closely. "What a brilliant strategy!"

The sparrows flew lower. Even so, they beat their wings swiftly.

I clasped Jane's hand. Against mine, hers felt remarkably cool. How had she managed to come up with such a swift response? Truly, she would be a court lady yet.

In the courtyard below, a horse approached, the creature's hoofbeats keeping pace with my heart as the two ladies stood close together conferring in hushed tones. Was it possible, after so much effort, they would not find the costume up to the royal standard?

"It seems as if congratulations are in order," the duchess said at last.

"So it seems," added Charlotte, less pleasantly.

The windows of the cathedral opened, and the sparrows escaped.

"What an honor, then, to present the costume to the queen," I said, believing that, in spite of everything, I might still have a chance once the queen saw my work.

But neither woman replied.

Instead, while Charlotte busied herself with folding up the kirtle, the duchess remained before us, her fingers steepled, her brow furrowed in thought.

"I'm afraid Her Majesty is indisposed," the duchess said when I managed to catch her eyes at last.

My legs felt newly unsteady. "But you said the costume pleased you."

"We will, of course, show the queen your work as soon as we are able." The duchess's voice, like her gaze, was kind but without hope.

"But you must let us see the queen," I insisted, my boldness compelled by my desperation.

"*Must?*" Charlotte said. "Is it possible you, Miranda, the younger daughter of a woman on shaky footing with the queen, a woman who has made a secret marriage to one of the queen's favorite courtiers, dare to dictate terms to the duchess and to me?"

"I am only insisting on what was promised me," I said, concealing my trembling hands behind my back.

Tears of sympathy pearled in the corners of the duchess's eyes.

Charlotte's arctic gaze remained unchanging. "Such insolence does not merit an answer. Besides, the duchess and Jane worked on the costume after you were taken so suddenly *ill*, aid that was never part of your test. Come, Margaret," Charlotte said, looking back at the duchess just once, her ermine skin flaring scarlet.

After Charlotte left, the study door clicking shut with peaked finality, the duchess did everything but apologize for her peer's behavior and promised she would do what she could. Despite her abundant empathy, her grave tone gave us little hope.

The next thing we knew, the ushers were escorting us downstairs and out into the fresh air, where we stood dumbly looking up at the high windows as if we'd never been inside.

"It's not fair," Jane said in a forlorn voice. "Such hard work—how could it end like this?"

"It hasn't ended yet," I told her, though I felt drained of spirit now that my fury at Charlotte was spent.

"Shall we go back, then?" Jane asked.

Not far from where we stood, Henry Raleigh and I had said good-bye, I realized. If I listened closely, I almost believed I could hear Innisfree whinny.

Would I see him again? Did it matter?

"Miranda." Jane touched my arm. "Shall we go back to the dormitory?"

"You go ahead. I couldn't bear the questions or the looks of the others right now." To Jane I did not have to mention that Agnes was already privy to my disappointment, and all too ready to profess it in the most distorted terms.

"Perhaps I should come with you." Just then, Jane's amber eyes were as mild and full of understanding as those of Henry's horse.

"That's very kind, Jane," I said, forcing a smile, "but I think it best if I'm alone for a while."

Jane took hold of my hand. "It's not too late, you know. The person you asked to help—he could still arrive."

"I hope so," I said. But even though it was Chidiock Kyd I had called, it was Henry Raleigh I thought of at that moment.

Once I passed out of the farthest courtyard, I unpinned my hair, which still held the moisture from the rain, and let the breeze have its way with it. There was no reason to hurry—no one seemed to expect me—and so I continued leisurely on toward the tournament grounds, pausing when I reached the vegetable garden where I'd sought refuge after my first encounter with the garnet-encrusted Lady Sherringham and the spiteful Lady Mariah.

Walking, memories of the tournament once again arose before me, as did my hopes—which now seemed so fool-hardy and naive—at the idea of coming to the benevolent attention of the queen through any talent of my own. As for my continued attraction to Henry Raleigh, it could only shame me.

By the time I reached the Thames, a wan sun had begun to disperse the clouds, and the landscape wore a misty look worthy of some fantastic theatrical. Had it been any other day, the river sounds would have soothed me. But today an image of Lord Seagrave sneering down at me on our wedding night seemed to take shape in the river. The watery visage reached for me, grinning all the while, a terrible gargoyle grin.

I stepped back.

What would happen if I walked on and exchanged my court clothes for simpler things? Could I assume another name and offer my services as a seamstress at a tailor's shop? Begin again as someone else?

The prospect tantalized, especially after this last confrontation with Charlotte Raleigh. I was not afraid to work hard. My months at Turbury had prepared me well for hardship—self-discipline, the countess called it. Surely it was worth a try.

Until I realized the queen might send people to find and fetch me. People had been locked away for lesser crimes than this fantasy of mine, I knew.

And even if I were not found out, would I not be haunted daily by the possibility of recognition and probable arrest? And of course, if I did not return to court, I would not be able to communicate with Jane or Beatrice or the duchess. As for Henry Raleigh . . . I banished the thought, scolding myself once more for being so foolish. Nor would I be able to contact my mother, or my sister, or Robert, not to mention the coming child. Were I to leave now, I would have to keep away from anyone who cared for me so as not to jeopardize their lives as well as my own.

And what sort of life was one in which I never returned to my beloved tower room at Plowden Hall, never wandered again among the rolling greenery of Cumberland? Was I not Miranda Molyneux, the late Earl of Plowden's daughter, above all else?

This time when I looked down, the Thames sent forth a continuum of ripples that recollected the silky fabrics with which I loved to work. The patterned movement soothed me until, in the rippling rhythm, I began to hear a voice that beckoned me to forget both the anonymous risks of London and life as wife to a man I could never come to love or respect. Lingering there, the occasional duck or goose alighting on the water and troubling the pattern just a little, I thought of those lost souls who sought an escape in its cold depths. Dizzied by the movement, I stepped closer to the river and looked down, the water whispering to me all the while.

A tiny wren alighted on a nearby tree branch and began its reedy song.

Perhaps it was the bird's music mingling with the movements of the tall grass that eventually shook me out of my reverie. I recalled something my father had said about perspective—that necessary ability to stand outside oneself. It was that ability, he told my mother and me just before he'd left that last time, that enabled him to return to Ireland. Yes, it was his duty to go—but it gave him a great deal in return. Despite the separation, the rough living, the financial strain, my father had known a kind of freedom there.

Only now did I understand it must have been that ability that had given my father the courage to journey to court, where he'd held his head high and spoke not in the broken voice of a man who had lost a great deal, but with the surety found only in a person of vision.

Was perspective not my father's greatest gift? I asked,

as the wind streamed through my hair, and the wren continued its song. Was perspective not the one thing he'd never surrendered, even when he lay dying far from home, understanding he would see neither my mother nor any one of us again?

At least not in this life.

Hold fast to your beliefs.

How could I have failed to see that Henry Raleigh's words echoed those spoken by my father so long ago?

CHAPTER TWENTY-TWO

June 3 & 4, 1580

IT WAS TWILIGHT BEFORE I FOUND MY WAY back to the palace, a crescent moon and a few lonely stars my only guides as I navigated the elaborately sculpted shrubberies and paths lined with flowering trees, the moist air sweet with their fragrance.

Although I dared not trust my eyesight, after I stepped into the dormitory courtyard and neared the fountain, something seemed to move. Was it Agnes? The countess? My brother?

"Who is it?" I called out.

"Miranda?"

I stepped closer, glimpsed her gingery hair. "Jane!"

"Thank God!" Gathering her skirts, she rushed toward me.

"What are you doing out here?" I said, catching

hold of her chilled hands. "It's late, and the air is damp—you'll catch cold."

"Never mind me," Jane said. "After that meeting with the queen's ladies, when you didn't return . . . I was terribly worried about you. When supper ended and there was still no sign, I imagined all sorts of horrors. I should never have left you alone."

Banishing the watery visage of Lord Seagrave, but also the river's call, I said, "I never meant to scare you. I found a path through some trees. The walk helped me to regain my perspective."

"Then you have not heard?"

I shook my head, my mind drifting back to the silence of the wood, the discovery I'd made there.

Jane glanced around the courtyard, but the nymphs and tridents seemed our only onlookers.

"What is it?" I asked.

"Wait." She guided me over to a more secluded area of the shrubbery, where we sat down, the only other sound the growing music of crickets and the distant rush of a fountain.

"Henry Raleigh has been arrested. And"—a sob escaped her throat—"so has George."

"I'm sorry, Jane, but I don't understand," I said. "Henry Raleigh left court—I told you."

Jane shook her head and held my hands more tightly.

"You only thought he left. It seems George—independent of me—convinced Henry Raleigh to disguise himself as the keeper's son and appear before the Privy Council to testify."

"What? When did this happen?"

Jane breathed deeply. "Today."

"Go on," I said, trembling as I recalled Henry Raleigh's manner when he said good-bye to me in the rain, the meaning of our meeting—and his parting words— suddenly taking on a different aspect. Had he been trying to communicate something to me then—a message— cloaked in words that echoed my father's?

"No sooner had the council meeting begun, the queen prominently in attendance, when the real keeper's son arrived."

"So we were wrong. Lord Seagrave did not get word of the plan and have him apprehended?"

"Apparently not. The young man, who came all this way on a horse far too old for such a journey, said he'd been delayed not by a menacing landlord, but by the poor roads. When the council found itself confronted with two keeper's sons, the members asked the pretender to step forward. It was then Henry Raleigh confessed, and George, my George, revealed he had been the one to encourage him."

"Where are they now?" I asked, the hurried rhythm of my heart intensifying.

"Under armed guard in one of the most remote rooms at Whitehall. Some are even talking about their removal to the Tower."

"But that's preposterous. They are hardly dangerous!"

Jane's upper lip quivered, and she was overcome by a fit of sneezing so severe she could not speak for a moment. "If they are lucky," she managed, her sneezes replaced by tears, "the queen will dismiss them with a heavy fine. If not . . ."

"The queen wouldn't actually send them to the Tower?"

Jane's continued to cry, and for a moment even the crickets ceased their chittering, as if they, too, were moved by her distress.

"But the queen adores George—and Henry Raleigh." Once more I pictured him standing in the rain, felt the kiss on my hand, before he bid me good-bye. "They are two of the most promising courtiers of our generation. Their performances during the tournament proved as much."

"The queen may have felt that way about them once," Jane stammered, "but the arrival of the real keeper's son has stirred up a great deal of bad memories."

One's fortune could change in a moment. My own experience had taught me as much.

"Didn't the council try to prevent this? Wasn't it in their best interest to hush such talk?" I said.

"They were in error, many of the members knowing far too little about the rising Catholic sympathies here at court—feelings the Catholic French reawakened."

"Slow down," I said. "You've set my mind racing."

"The arrival of the keeper's son seems to have brought the tensions between the Protestants and the Catholics here at Whitehall into the open, especially since two well-born Catholic lords sit on the council. In the past, both have been suspected of entering into secret discussions with the Scottish queen. The elder, Lord Strondehouse, has even been linked with an earlier rebellion, and he is close friends with one of the French ambassadors."

Instantly I recalled the jacket embroidered by Mary Queen of Scots, the one the queen never wore, an item refashioned from her Scottish cousin's petticoat. Until now I had given little thought to the fact that Mary had been Elizabeth's prisoner since she'd sought refuge from her warring countrymen here, her imprisonment compelled by her claim to the throne of England and especially by her Catholic faith.

"But why would the queen blame Henry Raleigh and George for religious tensions?" I asked. "They are fervent Protestants."

"Because it seems there is some new plot afoot. I haven't all the details, but the duchess tells me there was a gown sent from France, a gift from the Scottish queen's Guise relatives. Once examined, the gown, although of the latest fashion, was revealed to house a noxious substance secreted among the lace. The material is being tested to see if it's poisonous."

"Poisonous!" France was a Catholic country. And Mary was once married to the French king's son and heir. And Henry had so recently been sent there as our queen's emissary. Slowly I began to understand how his desire to help me—but why would Henry Raleigh help?—had been transformed into something far more sinister, given this conspiracy of circumstance.

Despite my vow of perspective, despite the possible punishments George and Henry might face, I could not help but feel something akin to ecstasy at the very idea that Henry, who had so recently spoken of the necessity of adhering to his family's will, had risked so much on my behalf. *Hold fast to your beliefs.* Even if it was the honorable thing, would he have done so were he on the verge of becoming engaged to Agnes? Had I been wrong in believing Henry a traitor to those beliefs to which he told me to hold fast?

"I understand George's motives," Jane said, blowing her nose. "He admires you, his admiration trebled by my own high praise. But why, Miranda, why would Henry Raleigh jeopardize his future for you? I can see no reason."

A thrill coursed through me, akin to the way I felt when an intricate pattern in my own embroidery began to emerge, as I began to understand at last what it was Henry had tried to tell me the day before. "I can," I said.

"Well then"—Jane clasped my hands—"tell me."

Soon we were traveling all the way back to my father's experience with Henry Raleigh in Ireland, the starting point for his hope to one day see the two of us married.

"This is like one of those old tales my grandmother used to tell to me before bed," Jane said, once I had finished.

"Let us hope that it ends as all such tales are meant to," I said. This time it was my turn to hold tightly to her hand.

⌘

"Yes, theirs is one of the oldest names in England. Nevertheless, my grandmother always said the Raleighs were a family of dark horses," Agnes said over breakfast the next morning, helping herself grandly to the abundance of sweet cakes. "Charlotte Raleigh is the exception, of course."

"Of course," Eleanor said, her own appetite rivaling Agnes's, as she spread marmalade onto her cake. "But then, Charlotte is only his half sister, is she not?"

"She is, and then she so much more closely resembles her dear late mother, a descendant of John of Gaunt and cousin to the present Earl of Southampton, you know."

384

"I do indeed," Eleanor said, as if she herself had sat down to tea with the earl many times before.

"Henry Raleigh's mother is a person of much more common birth," Agnes said.

"She isn't a lady, then?" one of the younger girls asked.

"By marriage only," Agnes said. "And then there is the fact that she never comes to court, preferring her horses and dogs to the elegant people here. Why, someone actually told my grandmother the woman allows her hounds to sleep on the bed."

"Shocking!" Eleanor agreed.

"But the Duchess of Suffolk's Buttercup——"

"Is a spaniel," Agnes said, as if that explained everything, and pushed away her pottage.

"Besides," Eleanor added, "the Duchess of Suffolk began life as a farmer's daughter."

"Did she?" Bridget leaned forward almost eagerly. "That must have been an energetic sort of life."

"How fortunate the queen realized her error before it was too late," Eleanor said, ignoring Bridget. "And you too, Agnes. Imagine the horrors were you to have become formally engaged to such a person as Henry Raleigh."

"My heart would cease beating if I thought too much on the subject," said Agnes, batting her long lashes.

"Let Agnes's experience be a lesson to all of us," Eleanor said, gesturing with a candied violet. "We maidens are so innocent, so dependent upon our elders' guidance, provided their intentions are clearheaded."

"Too true," another maiden seconded.

"Fortunately, my grandmother is one of the clearest-thinking people I know," Agnes continued with feigned innocence. "She soon came to see the danger of such a choice in the nick of time."

"Do you think Henry Raleigh was after your fortune?" one of the youngest maidens asked.

"I do," Agnes said, narrowing her eyes; "though Grandmother believes he fell under the spell of my beauty. Again, how fortunate I am to have her as a guardian. Bighearted as I am, I pitied his poverty. How close I came to disaster." She gave a theatrical shudder.

"Now, according to my grandmother"—Agnes poured herself more ale—"a person of far greater potential is Edgar Darlington. No coincidence he will soon be the queen's favorite, with looks and manners as fine as his name."

"But he did not compete in the tournament," Bridget said.

"Because he was in the West Country," Agnes said; "his family being great landowners there, as well as the most devout Protestants—people who always deplored the influence of the Catholic cousin of our queen. . . ."

"Are the Darlingtons related to the Lancasters?"

Eleanor asked, refusing to be outdone despite her friendship with Agnes.

"They are, dear," Agnes cooed; "though the Darlingtons are much more closely related to Charlemagne."

While some of the younger maidens sat entranced by Agnes's sketch of the Darlington family tree, each branch detailed further by Eleanor, I fought the urge to counter her words with some of my own. As the gossip slogged on, I wrapped two sweet cakes in a napkin, then stood and left the dining hall.

What a relief to abandon the confines of the building for the breeze of the courtyard. There I loosened my stays and breathed in the honeysuckle scent of the blossoming shrubs.

"Miranda!"

It was Jane returning, in close conversation with the Duchess of Dewberry. So preoccupied had I been at breakfast, I did not realize that Jane had been missing. What sort of friend was I when I had heard Jane weeping throughout much of the night, falling asleep at last only after Lady Periwinkle administered a special tonic?

"Good news, Miranda," the duchess said, once I hurried over to them.

"George and Henry Raleigh—have they been released?" I asked.

"Their futures have not yet been decided," the duchess

said, her airily upswept hair looking immaculate for the first time in days. "Still, the queen said just this morning she would never send two such young men to the Tower."

"Truly?" I asked.

"Cross my heart," the duchess said, proving herself to be as benevolent as she initially appeared.

"But what of the Catholic plot?" I asked. "The poisonous gown from France?"

"The substance turned out to be a sweetening powder instead of poison. Apparently the fragrant odor of pulverized orrisroot, citrus, and violets raised some of the more nervous—or just fervently Protestant—councilors' suspicions. The combination, although pleasing to the French, seems unsuited to our olfactory tastes. At the very least, the preservative seems to have turned during the crossing."

"So the Queen of Scots is not vying for England's throne?"

"Not effectively, anyway," the duchess said. "She does continue to correspond with her troubling Guise relatives, and her correspondence continues to be intercepted by the queen's allies."

"And that's not all," Jane said, seizing my hands. "All talk of your marriage to Lord Seagrave has at last been forgotten."

My eyes swept upward in a worshipful gaze, and

I almost knelt before the duchess as if she were my queen.

"Do not thank me," the duchess said, looking, for a moment, like a woman half her age.

"Surely you spoke to the queen on my behalf," I said.

"Yes, of course, but the queen was in no mood for my pretty words. No, the credit belongs to yet another one of your admirers," the duchess said, her kind face taking on an extraordinary look of mystery.

"Another?" I stepped away from them. "What do you mean?"

"It seems you have more than one, Miranda," the duchess said, in such a way I sensed she somehow knew my real feelings for Henry Raleigh.

"A third person arrived very early this morning," Jane said, her freckles realigning themselves as she smiled. "He, too, claimed to be the keeper's son."

"The Privy Council has not officially released the man's identity," the duchess said, "but when he was forced to disrobe—"

"They noticed his red hair." Jane began to laugh.

"Kyd?" I said, amazed.

"I should have known he was the one you'd written to," Jane said, seizing my hands.

"But why did he not respond to my message?" I looked from Jane to the duchess. "And why the delay? He could not blame it on the roads when he lives in London. He could have been here within the day."

"The verdict is not yet official," the duchess said with reassuring composure, "but it seems some rather suspect men, employees of the armory who are now under orders to leave the country at once, under penalty of immediate arrest, delayed this second pretender as he made his way to court."

"Where is Kyd? Not hurt?" I said, fearing he, too, was now under arrest.

"He is not injured." The duchess patted my arm.

"He defended himself admirably," Jane added.

"But where is he?" I pressed.

"With the queen," the duchess said.

"Is he in danger? Is the queen thinking of imprisoning him? If so, I am the one who should be held responsible."

"I think he will be safe, Miranda," the duchess said with an enigmatic smile I longed to decipher. "Once the queen learned a third keeper's son had arrived, she summoned Dr. Snead to treat the onslaught of a severe headache, and then she ordered this third man to meet with her in private, thinking it best not to draw further attention to the situation."

"But why do you think the queen will deal any more kindly with him than with Henry Raleigh or George Mountjoy?" I said, then stopped myself from mentioning the fact that Kyd was of much more common birth, something I had faulted Henry Raleigh for dwelling on. How could I be so hypocritical?

"Listen, and I will tell you," the duchess said.

We began to walk, three across, along one of the paths through the shrubbery still glistening with dew at this hour, the robins and chaffinches continuing their song in the environing trees. Several of the courtiers and ladies nodded at us with real interest as we passed, and more than a few whispered my name.

"You've excited a lot of talk, Miranda. You've burned the ears of the court," Jane said with girlish eagerness, as Lady Claribel Wynard, who had kindled the ardor and heroism of many a courtier, graced us with a smile.

"Understandably," the duchess said, "when your knights-in-arms are willing to go to such risks. It seems your red-haired pretender managed to imprison his attackers in the very room within the armory, where they'd hoped to leave him."

"Valiant," I said, reminded of how quickly Kyd had learned the art of jousting.

"Indeed," Jane observed.

"The queen's own athleticism and spirit compel her to recognize and reward those traits in others. And then"—a sly look crept into the duchess's eyes—"there is the matter of fashion. Intuition tells me the queen and your friend will soon come to an agreement on the subject of hair."

"Is that so?" I said, picturing Elizabeth gazing covetously at Kyd's fiery locks.

Reminded of the queen's ample collection of wigs, I wondered how she had convinced him to part with his hair.

"That's not all, Miranda," Jane said. "Ask the duchess to tell you about Lord Seagrave."

"Oh yes, if he is gone for good, I long to hear all about it," I said.

"Simply this: he left Whitehall in disgrace early this morning, his connection with the armory severed."

I dared not smile for fear of mocking Fortune. "What of the keeper's son?"

"After he bathed and dined, the poor man was given one of Whitehall's finest beds, and the queen willed the contested house and its surrounding land to his family in perpetuity."

I breathed deeply, relieved that justice had at least been done on this point; and even more relieved I would never see that contested Essex property, or those spidery hands again, unless of course he were to try to press my family for the money he so obviously gave or lent to Robert.

"You needn't worry about Lord Seagrave troubling you or your family at some dark hour of the night," the duchess said, as if reading my thoughts.

"But my brother, Robert—"

"Never mind Robert's folly," she continued, as several

more ladies strolled by, nodding or waving their fans in curious acknowledgement. "The Duchess of Suffolk, concerned for her grandniece's reputation, sent your former suitor packing with a tidy sum and a pledge to keep his distance."

"But the word of such a man is worth so little," I could not resist saying.

"Not to worry. The Duchess of Suffolk's third husband was a lawyer. She therefore understands the value of documentation—and a binding signature."

While Jane and the duchess lingered in the courtyard, I returned to the dormitory, taking the stairs as Bridget did—two at a time—and found Lady Periwinkle stuttering about the hallway. "Is there a problem?" I asked, holding fast to the duchess's words.

"Only that the countess has been waiting for you this past half hour," Lady Periwinkle said, her farthingale, despite its breadth, no barrier to protect me.

Instantly my hopes turned to sand between my fingers.

Unlike Lord Seagrave, there was no cause for the queen to banish the countess.

"She is waiting for you in the conservatory," Lady Periwinkle said, so somberly I knew she would not sing the countess's praises again anytime soon. What had taken place between them?

Although I walked at a tortoise's pace as I rounded the corner, someone came careening around the other side. I reached out a hand and braced myself against the wall just in time to avoid a collision. "You should watch where you are going!"

"Miranda!" The voice was feminine—and familiar.

"Beatrice?" I said, utterly surprised by her return.

"Just the person I was looking for." Her violet eyes were as luminous as jewels.

"What are you doing here?" I asked, almost sorry she had not knocked me down. Unconscious, at least I would have been able to evade the countess. "Do you plan to rejoin the maidens?"

"Those days are long behind me," she said, as if she had just been promoted to a Lady of the Bedchamber. "No, I've come to collect the rest of my belongings. I did, however, leave you my favorite pair of gloves—I took no chances of them getting mislaid. You'll find them beneath your pillow."

Newly dizzy, I reached for the wall. "You're leaving, then?"

"Yes, later today. Thankfully, my grandaunt, like me, is not an early riser."

It was the first time I'd seen Beatrice since she'd been moved out of the dormitory. Not only was her beauty restored, it seemed possible she was even more ravishing. Was it Dr. Snead's treatment? Or my brother's attentions?

"I cannot talk now," I said. "The countess is—"

"Waiting. Yes, I know. Grim woman. When I encountered her on the stairs, she couldn't even manage a 'good day,' much less a smile. Instead, the woman looked at me as if I were a barmaid at some disreputable tavern.

"By the way, I congratulate you. Such sweet disorder! The news only broke this morning, and already everyone is talking about it: *three keeper's sons*. Even my grandaunt is impressed, and this is no small compliment coming from a woman once courted, ardently, by dozens of men, many from the highest ranks. Really, my dear"—she pressed my hand—"I did not think you had it in you!"

A familiar ring glimmered on her finger—a ruby surrounded by diamonds, and an object of great worth that had been in our family for generations. "Grandmother's ring," I said, the lustrous stone erasing any doubt about our future relation.

Beatrice smiled. "Who'd have thought? We're to be sisters. Given your recent behavior, I must say, I am almost proud."

"I don't know what Robert told you, but he is as penniless as I am," I blurted out.

"I know." She covered my hand with her own. "I came here to ask you to be my maid of honor, circumstances permitting, of course. I mean"—she bit her lip to stop a malevolent grin—"so long as the queen does not lock you up or anything."

"You truly want to marry Robert?"

"I do," she said, admiring both the ring and her white hand.

For the first time, I felt as if I might actually faint. Was it possible she truly loved my brother when there was neither money nor influence to recommend him—only a title and the unfortunate nickname of the poorest earl in England?

"And you're not troubled by a residence as remote as Plowden Hall?" I said.

"It will do, though only for occasional respites. We'll live close by my grandaunt most of the time—she owns a most suitable house adjacent to her property. The house-keeper there sent word that a family of swallows is nesting in the eaves; a prophetic sign!"

Amazed at this domestic turn in my friend, I stood there speechless, until I recalled the commanding presence of the duchess glowering over Dr. Snead and ordering everyone about. "And your grandaunt agreed to the marriage?"

"She did. Your recent coup certainly helped." And then more slyly, "Though I dare not speak of it often, Auntie's never been able to refuse me, believing me to be just like she was at sixteen. It's why we are leaving: our removal was the chief condition of the queen's blessing. That"—she hesitated—"and a tidy deposit to the queen's treasury."

"And Robert?" I said.

"My grandaunt and I are not among the more sentimental members of our sex. Nevertheless, we were nearly on the verge of tears when he described his plight, and yours. I did not know how you had suffered! I cannot imagine dining on porridge for a week, much less a fortnight.

"Fortunately, suffering has not ruined him, for his was a most romantic proposal. He quoted a sonnet and . . . Perhaps," she said, suddenly coy, "I'd better leave it at that."

I shook my head, unsure if I was more eager or mortified to hear any more of the story Robert had concocted. Besides, I anticipated the countess at any moment. "*No*, I meant, where is he?"

"Where? In his rooms. I saw him just before I came here. He was occupied in writing a letter to your mother. Who would ever have guessed I'd be traveling to Wingfield Park as a daughter-in-law? Well"—Beatrice laughed—"at least I will now have a chance to see it. And your mother is having a baby at her age! Really, Miranda, your family is full of surprises. I do believe she and my mother will become famous friends."

"Miranda!" The countess's straight, black figure appeared in silhouette in the doorway. Although it didn't seem possible, her stance seemed to have grown even more severe since I saw her last.

"Good luck," Beatrice said, kissing my cheek before we parted.

Once the door closed behind the countess, I noticed how pale she remained despite the return of sun.

"Good morning," I managed, wishing I could hide behind the framed harp that graced one corner of the room.

"What makes it good?" she said, her white hands nervously twitching the pomander. "It could not be the departure of Lord Seagrave."

I could not stop my smile.

"Ah." She stepped toward me, the troublesome scent of oranges and spices engulfing us both. "So that is the reason for your high spirits. What you don't yet understand is that there are few men as wealthy or as benevolent as he. She paused beside the harp, where she plucked the strings so that the instrument made a hissing sound. "Especially when it comes to marrying a wellborn young woman with only her family lineage to recommend her."

Instinctively, I took a step back.

"If you think Beatrice's family will come to your aid," she said, as if she could read my thoughts, "you are very much mistaken. The Duchess of Suffolk is interested only in her grandniece, which is why she is determined to get the creature married as quickly as possible. Robert proved a cheaper son-in-law than most."

I closed my eyes, felt for the ground beneath my feet as a rumbling fury burned through my belly. "Why did you wish to see me?"

"Life at Whitehall is becoming a strain," the countess said. "I am planning on leaving within the week. You will, of course, accompany me." Again she plucked the harp. "I am still your guardian. Do not forget that."

Calm, I told myself. *Remain calm.*

The countess fixed me with her gold-flecked eyes. Were she a cat, she would have twitched her tail. "We both know the queen has decided to have it both ways; you have completed your sewing project, and yet she has not liberated you as you hoped, has she?"

How I wished I could have made the countess vanish.

She spoke more confidently now. "From one woman to another, I tell you I would far prefer to sew for my husband, who would care for me properly, rather than be subject to the will, and perhaps also to the whim, of another woman, regardless of how highly born. For where are you now, Miranda?"

She drew even closer, and I breathed again that sickly sweet fragrance that had forever robbed me of a taste for oranges and cloves.

"You cannot think I will return with you," I said.

"Oh no? If you think you will seek your living elsewhere, I urge you to seriously consider who, in a vast place like London, will shelter or employ a young woman who cannot deliver a single reference.

"And if that doesn't dissuade you, perhaps I should

remind you of Emily. The poor woman has been so ill of late," the countess said. "Given how hard she has been working, forced to lose herself in her responsibilities now that her daughter has so thoughtlessly abandoned her, under your influence it would seem. No one would think twice were she to succumb to depression and further illness—"

I backed away from her. "You wouldn't."

"It is you who have allowed the thought to take root." She laughed, the sound akin to a rusty lock. "But you mustn't let those thoughts run away with you. Remember, Miranda, you are proving to be a person of great persuasive powers, as the current situation—three keeper's sons—attests. With such a mother as a precedent, I'm surprised the queen tolerated so much."

I shuddered, reminded again of what Eliza had said about her mother still being at Turbury. Such a silent place. So many days went by before I'd even known of Anne's existence.

The countess touched the cloth of my gown. "Your abilities as a seamstress have improved in your time here. I will have to remember this. It is a point to recommend you. We will leave court within the week. Do be sure to be prepared for the journey."

I raised my chin and met her gaze straight on.

"Such spirit," she said, and smiled so that her long, narrow teeth showed. "Perhaps I will teach you to hunt after all."

CHAPTER TWENTY-THREE

June 5, 1580

THE FOLLOWING MORNING FOUND JANE AND me seated beside the courtyard fountain, the marble faces of the nymphs intent on ours, as if they too were intrigued by what Jane had just told me.

"And you're absolutely certain George said the queen is sending Henry Raleigh to Ireland?" I pressed her yet a third time.

"I am. She may have pardoned him, but the incident has shaken her. She swore she would never keep a man capable of creating such disorder here at court."

"But what of George?" I asked, worried he, and therefore Jane, would share Henry's banishment.

"George can no longer accept a post on the Privy Council," Jane said.

I covered her hand with my own. "Oh, Jane, I am sorry. After the great lengths you went to on my behalf. This is my fault."

"No, Miranda," Jane said, "it is all to your credit."

I startled. "But you won't be a great court lady—"

"Thank goodness." Her amber eyes shone with tears. "Yes, for George's sake, I could have grown used to it. The truth is, I would like nothing better than a country life where my greatest concerns are my husband and the management of a household that includes horses, dogs, and many, many children. My elder sisters must be godmothers to the first two babies," she said, coloring, "but I would be so honored if you would agree to fill the role to my third."

"I would be honored."

"Oh good, you are here, Miranda," Lady Periwinkle said, coming into the courtyard, her current farthingale even larger than the one she'd worn the day before, as if she needed to appear more imposing in this time of instability among her maidens. "There's been a message."

"The countess?"

"No, my dear," she said. "It is the queen who has requested to see you. Now hurry and wash, and do fix your hair, for you look a bit of a shambles."

"You may look up, Miranda," the queen said, once the attendants admitted me into a long room that had been painted a soft shade of blue, the trim done all in white. In the corner, right beside a sunny window, a small monkey with a wizened face and coal black eyes perched on a branch inside a high-ceilinged cage, its green sarcenet cover pulled back to admit the day.

I would have been unable to look away from the quizzical creature had it not been for the queen's costume. She was wearing the coronation gown and mantle Jane and I had stitched, and it fit her perfectly. With the sunlight shielding her face, I could almost have believed it was Anne Boleyn standing there, triumphant and happy after the bishop had crowned her with the sacred diadem and pronounced her queen.

"With so much upheaval at Whitehall of late, I spent all of yesterday in bed and was only able to try the costume on last night." She ran a much-bejeweled hand along the mantle's ermine trim. "Such a thoughtful idea of the duchess's and Lady Raleigh's. Better than anyone else, these two devoted ladies know the anniversary of my mother's coronation has always been very difficult for me, bathed as it is in such a flux of contradictory emotion."

"I am so honored that my work—and Jane Radcliffe's—gives you such pleasure," I said.

"So you should be." The queen turned on her heel,

affording me a privileged look at the cartridge pleats of the mantle, which cascaded perfectly from their appointed place beneath her shoulder blades. Even the hem, cut exactly the right length, caressed the floor in a fluid movement that recollected running water.

She stepped over to the monkey cage, opened the latch, and allowed the monkey to scurry onto her arm. "Once I tried on the gown," she said, turning to face me, "I found myself reconsidering my decision regarding your future."

"Yes, Your Grace?" I said as the monkey watched me from her shoulder.

"I see now I may have been a degree too eager to see you settled as most women would wish to be settled," the queen said.

At that moment, the cloth of tissue endowed her face with an ephemeral, almost angelic expression. I vowed not to allow myself to be deceived. If I did not tread carefully, I could easily falter.

"I thought you desired most to become a wife."

It took all my self-control not to cry out in protest.

"And how could I not?" the queen continued, averting her gaze from mine. "Such was your mother's wish when she married your father. And then there was her rush toward Lord Grey.

"Besides," the queen continued, "in your case, the opportunity seemed a good one, given the circumstances."

I noted the calculated savvy of a sovereign queen in her decision to leave out the dishonored Lord Seagrave's name.

"Of course I was suffering from a dreadful toothache at the time, and pain has always clouded my judgment, at least temporarily." She plucked a rose from a vase and raised it to her nose, breathed its scent, but then the monkey snatched it away and set about nibbling at the petals.

The queen began to laugh. "It seems I have overlooked the fact that you suggested the remedy to Charlotte. At the very least, you pointed her toward the proper book."

"I did, Your Grace," I said as the monkey began to chatter, though *I* knew well enough to hold my tongue.

"And so I am grateful to you," she said. "The toothache is one of the great plagues of these last years of my youth. It is my gratitude that prompts me to grant you one wish."

"I ask to be freed from the Countess of Turbury's care," I said at once.

The queen snapped her fingers, and the monkey leaped from her shoulder onto one of the tables, dropping the rose. "It is done."

Remarkably, the countess's moon-wide face and gold-flecked eyes, along with our last conversation, the hissing sound of the harp, the sickly sweet pomander—vanished like smoke after a fire.

All was still, until at last the queen said, "Your request

for freedom has put me in mind of your future. You have no dowry to speak of. How will you earn your bread?"

"I hadn't considered—"

"You must consider, my dear. Although you are a most distant relation, I am concerned for your welfare." The queen's long-fingered hands stroked the ermine edging the mantle. "What of sewing? You are a talented seamstress. Your work here at Whitehall has proved as much."

Would the queen ask me to join the seamstresses employed within her royal workshop? Reminded of Jane's gratitude at being freed from a future as a courtier's wife, not to mention Henry Raleigh's own confession, I felt newly unsure of how I would answer. And then . . .

"Unfortunately, I cannot possibly offer you a position here at Whitehall at the moment," the queen said, interrupting my thoughts as she smiled, pleased, it would seem, by my continued attitude of humility.

"No?" The word fell from my lips before I could retract it.

"No." Her smile broadened, revealing the yellowish cast of her teeth. "Not at the moment, I'm afraid, and especially not when you have been the cause or at least the occasion around which there has been so much unfortunate disorder—and just a hint of scandal. How I wish you maidens would remember you are ambassadors of your country and your queen."

The calculated, indeed, the teasing ambiguity of Elizabeth's words raised the hairs on the back of my neck. Did she want me to humble myself further until she convinced me of her generosity in letting me work for her for a pittance, if not for free?

The queen raised her white hand to her forehead. "Circumstances such as these give me the headache, you see," she said.

"And then there is my funny friend Olivier." She beckoned to the creature, who now seemed reluctant to return to her shoulder. "Olivier was a gift from an earlier suitor, also French, though far less pleasant than the recent duke. He does manage to keep me amused, laughter being a marvelous antidote for the headache.

"Of course, his real purpose," she said as the monkey leaped to the floor, scurried away on his hind legs, then hid behind the drapes, "is as a tester of poisons.

"Is it only my suspicion," the queen went on as I managed to hide my astonishment, "or am I correct in supposing you hope now for something else?"

I could not possibly say as much to Elizabeth, but I knew if I was honest, I would have to admit the practice of my art was not what I exclusively thought of. In spite of everything, what Jane had told me about Henry Raleigh's dismissal—and his impending return to Ireland—sparked my own courage to follow as independent a path. For just a moment I dwelled on our parting, heard again the rain falling all around us, the tenderness in his voice.

"Well, Miranda?" The impatience in the queen's voice suggested I had been silent too long.

"I'm sorry—"

"Ah." There was no pleasure in her smile. "I thought you might be closer in character to your dear late father, but it seems now you are indeed your mother's daughter," the queen said, the lace at her mantle collar parting as she leaned toward me so I discerned the wrinkles at her throat. To think my camouflage had been an accident. "I bid you good-bye, then," she said, "and good luck."

⟵◈⟶

Once outside, a feeling of lightness buoyed me as I left the gilded rooms and stepped onto the path. There I breathed again the fragrant honeysuckle, and turned my face to the sun, believing myself, as much as it were possible, a free woman.

Penniless, yes.

Yet I had my talent. And was this not something I could build upon?

"Miranda!" Kyd's voice!

I turned to find my friend looking as mercurial as ever, if not more so without his exuberant red hair, exchanged, as the Duchess of Dewberry implied, for his freedom.

"I did not think you would come—"

"And miss the opportunity to blacken Lord Seagrave's already black name?" he said, nibbling a carrot. In his right ear a single diamond now glinted. "He's left at last, I hear?"

"Yes." I heard the relief in my voice. "And in consummate dishonor."

I told him about my meeting with the queen.

"Now that the queen has given you your freedom," Kyd said, "what will you do with it?"

"Do?" I looked up just as a skylark lifted into flight, ascending higher and higher until it disappeared into the blue. "I'm afraid I don't have any definite plans," I said truthfully.

"Well then"—he clasped my hands—"I would be only too honored to escort you into the working Londoner's world. With talent such as yours, and my energy and wit"—his smile grew bolder—"I've no doubt we can revive my family's haberdashery. This diamond, a gift from the queen, could do a great deal toward a fresh start," he said, touching his ear.

"Oh, Kyd," I said kindly, realizing how little encouragement from me it would take for him to propose.

"I did not think you would accept," he said, running his palm across his shorn head.

I leaned close to kiss his cheek. "You're a true friend."

"Well," he said, "at least I've had the honor of accompanying a real lady in one of the queen's tournaments—"

"You will find someone," I assured him.

He let go of my hand and bowed.

And I curtsied.

"Remember," he said, just before we parted, "my offer stands."

After we parted, I walked on, wondering what my mother would think were she to see me now. Though she must approve my decision to leave the countess, would she—despite her conflicts with the queen—have been so quick to refuse the chance to court Elizabeth's favor? As Beatrice said, the women close to the queen lived very well. Many, such as Charlotte, held places of real importance.

Why then did my thought return to what Henry Raleigh had said to me about holding fast to my beliefs? Could I have misjudged him? Had he, too, remained true?

And now it turned out the queen was sending him back to Ireland.

A backwater, Beatrice—and the world—called it.

I was very near the river now.

In the sky before me, more than half a dozen swallows seemed to be testing the span of their wings.

By the time I reached the Thames, someone else—a

410

man—was standing there. He, too, seemed to be watching the swallows.

Hearing my footsteps on the path, he turned. Indigo eyes. Chestnut hair. The scar shaped like a crescent moon. Only his clothes seemed plainer.

"Henry." Blushing, I looked down, feeling as if he could sense the transparency of my thoughts.

His look of preoccupation gave way to what could only be real happiness as he stepped toward me. "How did you know where to find me?"

"I didn't," I said. "I simply—I like this place."

"As do I." He seemed as amazed as I was. "But how foolish—" he said, recollecting himself as he offered me his arm.

As on that afternoon so many weeks ago, we walked together, silently though companionably at first, our footsteps falling naturally into a common rhythm, our breath synchronized. I thought fleetingly of the ponies on the moors, the amity in their shared solitude—until at last he told me about the trial, his exposure before the Privy Council, the queen's shocked fury, his and George's arrest.

"I find myself in your debt," I said, once we stopped to rest beneath some shade trees, and I watched a pair of wrens alight upon a branch. Instantly, they began their reedy song.

"No," he said. "Helping to ensure the dismissal

411

of a man like Lord Seagrave was honest work."

I could not resist a smile.

"It's true, howsoever contradictory dissembling might appear. If our queen is to remain respected, not just within England but throughout the continent, she must distance herself and her reign as much as possible from the less-honorable actions of her father. That means keeping far afield from men like Reginald Seagrave."

"Spoken like a true courtier," I said, and this time I made sure to summon the proper note of admiration.

When he did not answer, I said, "It's accurate, then, what I heard? The queen is sending you to Ireland when very few men, or women, will ever be so loyal—or so valuable?"

"Yes, but you needn't look so solemn. As I told you, the court, although I find myself able to adapt to it, is not where I wish to spend all of my time."

"Actually," I said, "those were not your exact words."

"My exact words?" He actually seemed to blush. "You remember them?"

I nodded. "You told me you had your reputation to make, and named court as the place you must be if you were to be a success."

"I am certain I said nothing about making my reputation, having already made and"—he hesitated, a smile playing about the corners of his lips—"lost it. Still, your

412

memory is undoubtedly better than my own. I stand corrected, then," he said, and bowed.

"And then——" I stopped myself, all that Agnes had said about her impending engagement to Henry Raleigh returning.

"Yes?" He stepped closer, the breeze teasing the hair around his face, the crescent moon beckoning—how I longed to touch it.

"There was some talk of you becoming engaged." I looked down at the ground.

"Ah." He raised my chin, very gently.

Though I remained silent, my color betrayed me.

"Need I remind you that my engagement, were it to have taken place, would not have been so very different from that between your brother and Miss Cunnington?"

"They genuinely care for each other," I said, relishing his defensiveness as if it proved something more.

"Are you asking me if I cared for Miss Somerset?"

"Yes," I said, holding his eyes, "I suppose I am."

"Very well. Speaking truthfully, I tried to. She has beauty, wealth, and respectability, despite the drawbacks of such an irritating grandmother. So, to speak with complete candor, yes, I tried." The indigo of his eyes turned a deeper purple as he looked at me in that troubling way I first recalled from the queen's barge.

"You were not successful, then?" I said, aware of how

close we stood to each other, the hem of my gown brushing against his boot.

"No. I liked her well enough, for she possesses the essentials for a court lady. But I understood marriage to her would have forever kept me—kept our relationship—on the surface. In other words, we would have been like so many of the married couples here at court. We would have been like my father and Charlotte's mother."

"An alliance," I said, realizing only now he was implying that his father and his own mother had married for love—as my parents had.

"At first I believed I could be satisfied with such an arrangement."

"What changed?"

He did not answer at first, though I sensed the reason in his gaze. "Ultimately, I realized I wanted more from my life."

"I understand," I said, my gaze flickering upward to follow the ascension of a pair of swallows.

"And what of your Chidiock Kyd? He courageously came to your rescue, I hear."

"He is a friend," I said. "A true friend."

"He is only this?" I felt sure I heard earnestness in his voice.

I looked at him directly. "Yes."

"That is good news—your friendship, I mean, for it

seems I misjudged him," Henry said, a lighter note entering his voice.

"You did?" I said, recalling the hauteur of his words on the barge, what he'd said about Kyd.

"You chastised me then, do you not remember?"

"Yes."

"You were correct in doing so. His courage is equal to any noble's. Only"—he frowned—"I cannot imagine why he parted with his hair."

I did not answer, unsure if I was more amazed or pleased by this ignorance about fashion and the queen from one so intimately acquainted with life at court.

The wind tousled my hair, and for just a moment Henry hesitated, but then I smiled, and he lifted his hand to tuck a lock behind my ear. He took my hand, and we stood close together watching a pair of swallows chasing each other just above the surface of the water.

"You met with the queen this morning, did you not?" he asked.

"I did. She was wearing the coronation gown that Jane and I stitched."

"And what transpired at that meeting?"

"The queen granted me my freedom, though I simultaneously sensed her eagerness to be rid of me," I said, seeing no point in relating to him the vexing chess-game manner in which our conversation proceeded.

"You proved a bit too unruly to handle," Henry said.

"Is such a word, 'unruly,' not improper?" I asked, though the word—the sound of it—pleased me.

"I mean it as a compliment." He spoke in a jesting tone. "And perhaps as a point of comparison."

"How so?" I said, matching his tone.

"*Unruly* is a term the queen used to define me."

"We are in the same position, then?" I said.

"You know it to be true," he said with real satisfaction.

"Well then," I said, "we can at last meet each other as equals."

"I prefer, kindred spirits." His hand moved to my waist; I lay my own on top of his, and yielded so he could turn me toward him.

Intuitively, my other hand reached for his face, lingering on the scar. "How did you come by this?" I asked. "I'm certain you did not have it three years ago."

"You do possess a fine memory."

"Tell me—"

"Perhaps some stories are best kept secret until after we are married," he said with tantalizing obliqueness.

Married. My heart already knew this to be our fortune. Still, my body, slower to learn, startled.

Henry laughed. Then in a gentler voice, he said, "Though your father is not present, he granted me his permission once in the past. Now I ask you. And perhaps, given your independence and your spirit, this is the proper way."

The next thing I knew, Henry was kneeling before me. Sun caressed our shoulders, swallows soared above us, and with a courtesy that revealed far more than it masked, Henry Raleigh asked me to be his wife.

"Your family will not be pleased by such a marriage," I told him as tears, light as the first rain in spring, caressed my cheeks; "especially not your sister."

"Like the court that changes its mind as often as it changes its fashions, my sister and the other members of my family will come around. My mother's consent, I do not doubt."

A warmth kindled within me. "It will be a great honor to meet her," I said. "Do you believe she will like me?"

When he shook his head, I felt as if I might begin falling.

"A jest." He touched my cheek. "My mother will adore you. Now, what of your family? Your brother, on the verge of marrying, will undoubtedly be too preoccupied to pay us much attention. But your mother—" His voice turned momentarily grave. "How will she take such news?"

I considered telling him about my long silence, but would there not be plenty of time for such stories during the long journey to Ireland, not to mention during all the days—the years—that lay ahead?

"She will be happy for us," I said, understanding I would write to her this very afternoon.

With a gentleness that beckoned me near, he kissed me,

lightly at first, but then he twined both his arms around my waist, we drew each other closer, and our kisses deepened, so that it felt now that we had come together, we must never be apart.

"Are you sure you will not think your talents wasted if you find yourself sewing clothes for hard weather and a rough sort of living?" he whispered, his breath soft and warm against my ear. "Remember, we will often travel on horseback, and the roads are very poor."

"On the contrary," I said, breathing in the clean, fresh smell of him, a smell I believe held the green fragrance of Ireland. "To put my talents to such good use would be honor enough for an entire lifetime."

Henry kissed me again and again, and each of his kisses I returned, until at last I opened my eyes, noticing for the first time the hint of gold threading each of his irises, delicate as a pattern in the most exquisite of tapestries.

When I next looked around me, despite the proximity of London, the landscape seemed as lush and wild as it was green, and my future felt full of possibility. The swallows soared overhead, and with Henry beside me, and the wind in my hair, at that moment, I, too, felt I had grown wings.